A whirlwind of intrigue, lies, politics, and adventure swirls around one woman—and the prize she's been sent to reclaim . . .

It was her talent for tracking magic that got Anna Zhdanov sent to catch a thief. A scholar's daughter sold as a bond servant, she has no desire to recover the Emperor's jewel for herself. But a chance to earn her freedom has driven her to the untamed Eddalyon province, awash with warm breezes, lapping waves, and more danger than she could possibly guess.

Within days her cover as an indolent noblewoman is in question, and it's clear there's more to Anna's task than she knows. Soon she's the captive of the unpredictable pirate captain Andreas Koszenmarc, hunted by the Emperor's guard, besieged by a brigand queen, and at odds with her only friend. She must trust someone if she is to survive. But when all that's certain is that everyone is hiding something, it's no simple thing to choose. . .

Novels by Claire O'Dell

The Mage and Empire Series
A Jewel Bright Sea

The River of Souls Series
Passion Play
Queen's Hunt
Allegiance

The Janet Watson Chronicles
A Study in Honor
The Hound of Justice

Writing as Beth Bernobich
The Time Roads
Fox & Phoenix
A Handful of Pearls & Other Stories

A JEWEL BRIGHT SEA

Claire O'Dell

REBEL BASE BOOKS
Kensington Publishing Corp.
www.kensingtonbooks.com

REBEL BASE BOOKS are published by

Kensington Publishing Corp.
119 West 40th Street
New York, NY 10018

All Kensington titles, imprints, and distributed lines are available at special quantity discounts for bulk purchases for sales promotion, premiums, fund-raising, educational, or institutional use.

Special book excerpts or customized printings can also be created to fit specific needs. For details, write or phone the office of the Kensington Sales Manager: Kensington Publishing Corp., 119 West 40th Street, New York, NY 10018. Attn. Sales Department. Phone: 1-800-221-2647.

Rebel Base and Rebel Base logo Reg. US Pat. & TM Off.

First Electronic Edition: September 2019
eISBN-13: 978-1-63573-079-1
eISBN-10: 1-63573-079-1

First Print Edition: September 2019
ISBN-13: 978-1-63573-081-4
ISBN-10: 1-63573-081-3

Printed in the United States of America

CHAPTER 1

The innkeeper at Iglazi had promised her ruins—magnificent, ancient ruins, which surely dated from an age before the Empire conquered these islands. He had not uttered the word *romantic*, but that was implicit in his description of the tumbledown walls covered with vines, the courtyard and its statues, and his breathless mention of an underground passageway.

Anna Zhdanov surveyed the expanse of broken stone before her. There were walls, yes, if you counted that knee-high mound of rubble as a wall. Here and there she spotted the remains of statues as well, though these were more dust than stone. The man had not exaggerated about the vines, at least. These ruins stood in the midst of a tropical forest, after all, with vines growing in profusion over everything except this desolate square.

A breeze sifted over the stones, carrying with it the scent of overripe flowers and the fainter tang of salt. Anna shivered, in spite of the heat.

Magic vibrated in the air. She felt its echo in her bones; she could almost hear the chants of priests from a civilization long dead.

What had brought Lord Aldo Sarrész to this strange and lonely place?

Her horse shifted underneath her, as if sensing her uneasiness.

It was just a case of nerves, she told herself. Over the past three months, the search for Aldo Sarrész had led her from the city of Duenne, the heart of the Empire, through half the western provinces, and across the ocean, to this island called Vyros in the midst of the Eddalyon archipelago. Everything here felt alien, from the dense jungles and the overbright sky to the sense of ancient magic permeating the stones. She reminded herself that once they completed their mission, she could leave the islands behind and go home to Duenne. Besides, as the supposed Lady Vrou Iljana, she had a reputation to uphold. Folly. Extravagance. A taste for excitement.

Anything to explain why she had insisted on this most improper and possibly dangerous outing.

Her two companions in this adventure drew their horses next to hers. Both were men skilled with sword and knife. Both of an age between forty and fifty and, by accident or planning, they had the same sharp-cut features and ruddy brown complexion of the northeast provinces as she did.

At Lukas Raab's signal, the six young men who served as their guards obediently arranged themselves in a loose circle. Raab had hired these men from Iglazi's local market, where the free swords often gathered, and he'd spent the past three days drilling them in proper military discipline. With little success, apparently, because Maté Kovács regarded the men with a faint air of exasperation.

With a sigh, Maté turned away from the guards and indicated the ruins. "Well, Lady Vrou. Does this please you?"

"I don't know." She sighed in return. "Perhaps. It is a ruin, to be sure. And it is ancient."

The hired guards exchanged amused glances. Anna could tell what they thought: here was yet another eccentric noblewoman seeking adventure. Even though that was precisely what she intended them to believe, she still wanted to box their ears, the hypocrites. According to Raab, these young men were all the sons of minor nobles, who had come to Eddalyon with a small allowance and large taste for gambling. Having squandered their money, they hired themselves out as common guards to avoid bonded servitude.

They had no way of knowing their Lady Vrou Iljana Klos was really Anna Zhdanov, a bonded servant herself, ordered by Hêr Lord Brun to recover the valuable artifact Sarrész had stolen from the Imperial court— and not just any artifact, but a rare magical jewel said to be a gift from the goddess Lir herself. One the Emperor depended upon for his endless wars to expand the Empire's territory.

Maté knew her identity, as did Raab, but then, they served the same master.

"Raab," she said. "What do you think?"

Raab shrugged. "I think you are hungry, Lady Vrou."

Maté scowled. Anna tried to calculate the best response. The Lady Iljana would reprimand a servant, but Anna Zhdanov knew who actually commanded this mission. "I *am* hungry," she said. "But I would like to know if I am safe as well. That is why my father hired you."

One of the guards choked down a laugh. Raab shot a glare at the man but managed to tamp down his irritation. Perhaps he too considered the roles they had to play.

"I have not forgotten," he said stiffly. "If my lady will excuse me, I should inspect the grounds. Kovács, come with me. You three"—he pointed to the three closest guards—"take the outer watch. The rest of you stay with our Lady Vrou."

He and Maté dismounted and tethered their horses. The three guards he indicated dismounted as well and moved to the perimeter of the square. The others settled into their saddles. They were not bad young men, Anna thought, merely foolish. She wished she could have set out on today's expedition with only Maté and Raab, but no one jaunted about in the wilderness without half a dozen guards, especially not a member of the nobility. And though she was only pretending to be a noble, the risk was very real, here on the edge of the Empire.

A risk she had agreed to, in spite of all the dangers. Hêr Lord Brun knew Anna all too well, damn him. Deliver Sarrész and the jewel by autumn, he'd said, and she would not only receive a generous sum of money, but he would sign all the papers, pay every Imperial clerk, to cancel her bond. She might travel wherever she liked, live however she wished, instead of depending on his goodwill. She would be free.

I could buy a pair of rooms for myself. One for my books. One for my bed and a fireplace to cook my breakfast. And a lock on the door...

She swung down from her horse and tossed the reins to the nearest guard. Thoughts of doors and locks and the absence thereof made her restless. She set off across the empty square, ignoring the ripple of magic beneath her boots. Walking wasn't enough to drive away those memories, but it was all she had.

I told him yes. But what does yes mean when no means less than nothing? I had no home, nowhere else to go.

She fetched up against the opposite boundary of the square. For a moment, the stones did not register, nor the forest beyond. She still saw Brun's face, that assessing gaze of his, as he calculated whether to use seduction or the age-old rights of nobles over slaves and bonded servants. In the end, he had not forced her—at least by the ordinary use of the word.

She blinked, and Brun's face dissolved, replaced by the impenetrable mass of green a few yards away. Sunlight beat down upon the open square, but the forest was dark even at this late morning hour. Off to one side, the hired guards were muttering among themselves, no longer sounding amused or bored. No doubt they had heard tales of brigands and pirates along Vyros's coast. So had Maté, who disliked this expedition and had expressed that dislike, in spite of all the clues that led them here.

"My lady. Lady Vrou."

Maté burst from the forest at a jog, with Raab close behind. Both were breathless, as though they had galloped a mile up the mountainside. With great effort, she pretended to yawn. "What is the matter? Did you discover a ferocious mouse?"

Neither man laughed, and Raab glanced around at the guards, as though to reassess their worth. Maté's expression was much harder to read. Excited? Anxious? She could not tell.

"Nothing so terrible, my lady," Raab said. "But we've discovered a far better prospect for your picnic."

"Ah, interesting." Anna looked toward Maté. "And you, what do you say?"

He shrugged with a fair show of indifference. "Our friend is correct for once. We've come across the perfect site for you—an exquisite patch of shore, with an equally exquisite expanse of ocean." His voice dropped low, in an imitation of their innkeeper's breathless tone. "Indeed, it cannot be matched elsewhere."

Sarrész, she thought. *He's found a clue.*

"Excellent," she said. "Let us mount up and you shall lead me to this nonpareil view."

* * * *

A narrow trail, little more than a gap in the forest, brought them down from the summit to a wider path. Anna noted the carefully tended road with growing unease. This was not another work of priests from centuries past. Someone had cleared away the tangle of trees and vines, someone else had paved sections with bricks and stones against the late-summer rains, and those *someones* were most likely bandits smuggling goods over the mountain. She wiped the sweat from her face and wished the air wasn't as close or as humid.

Raab had placed himself directly behind Anna, while Maté took the lead. Neither of her companions had spoken for the past hour. Their guards, those young and feckless creatures, rode silently at the rear. Perhaps they understood both men considered them expendable, a mere barrier in case brigands did appear.

As soon as the path widened enough for two to ride abreast, Anna urged her horse forward next to Maté. "*Was* he there?" she asked quietly.

Maté glanced back toward Raab, then to the guards.

"I believe so," he said just as softly. "We found evidence of a large company, ten at least. They built a fire and buried their garbage, all very neat, which tells me our friend Sarrész hired professionals."

The bondsmaid Iouliana, back at the inn, had mentioned a company of expensive guards, but Anna had not believed her. Sarrész was the younger son of a minor lord, with only a small allowance from his father. She remembered seeing him once or twice in Lord Brun's household. A man of middle years, his manner smooth, his smile much too easy. He must have borrowed the money for the ship's passage to Eddalyon. He had definitely borrowed more from Iglazi's moneylenders, but gossip said he had spent as much as he received.

Maté's voice sank lower. "They shifted six or seven stone tiles outside the temple walls and dug a hole at least three feet deep. One of the tiles had been marked with an X in grey paint, nearly invisible against the stone. The hole was empty, of course."

Oh. That was significant.

Their theory said Lord Sarrész would seek a buyer for the jewel as soon as possible. Clearly, he had not found one on the mainland. Just as clearly, the matter had proved more doable in Eddalyon. Anna had heard the rumors about the trade in legitimate and not-so-legitimate goods throughout the islands. Even so, anyone who dared to buy the Emperor's jewel would have to do more than produce enough gold. They would have to know a second market, one where they could dispose of the jewel before the Imperial forces caught up with them.

"He found a buyer," she said flatly. "The trade did not take place."

"No," Maté agreed. "My first guess is Sarrész cheated his buyer. He took the money, kept the jewel, and fled back to the mainland, where he will repeat the game as many times as he can. He's a greedy man, Lord Sarrész."

She nodded slowly. "That fits his character. What about the guards?"

"The guards are the flaw in my theory," he admitted. "If Sarrész meant to run off with the jewel and the money, he'd never take them along. At the same time, we didn't find any sign of an ambush by the temple. This trail we're following shows tracks from a large mounted company. I suspect a third party was involved."

Anna wanted to ask more about this supposed third party, but they had already talked longer than usual for a lady and her servant, even if that lady did have a reputation for flouting rules.

It was such a delicate balance, this disguise Brun had insisted upon. Lady Vrou Iljana had access to the same nobles Lord Sarrész would, and no one questioned Anna when she inquired about her old friend, under whatever name he used. But there were boundaries even the most eccentric noble dared not cross, and Anna was certain she had violated them more than once.

And then there was the secrecy Lord Brun had imposed...

With a sigh, she drew rein to let Maté resume the lead, while she turned over the implication of his words.

Sarrész had arrived on Vyros twelve days before them, showering silver and gold on the servants at the inn. The girl Iouliana had chattered on about his charm, his habit of bedding the servants, his odd comings and goings around the city, and his curiosity about the trade between the islands. Though he called himself Hêr Lord Gerhart Toth, it was obvious he was the man they were hunting.

And he came this way not three days ago.

Patience, she told herself. They had nearly caught up with Sarrész on several occasions, and each time, the interval between their arrival and his escape had grown shorter. Certainly this time they would succeed.

Two more hours passed. They rested the horses frequently, but Anna could tell the beasts were weary from the long, long descent. She was about to ask Maté if they ought to pause again when they rounded another bend and the silent green forest broke open into sunlight and the roar of surf.

Maté had already reined his horse to a stop. He tilted his head back and sniffed. Now he glanced over his shoulder. "Vrou?"

She caught the uptick in his voice. "Yes? What is it?"

"The shore lies ahead, as you can see, but I've sighted an object that might interest you. An item from before the Empire days..."

Sarrész. He *had* come this way. The hired guards were listening, however, so she kept her voice bored. "*Tscha.* You've promised me exotic memorabilia before, Kovács. Is this thing any different?"

"I make no guarantee, Lady Vrou. If you would prefer to ride on—"

"No, no. Let us examine this curiosity of yours."

She dismounted with an air of impatience. Maté took charge of her reins and tethered both their horses to a nearby tangle of roots. Anna had not missed how her mare flicked her ears back and forth, while Maté's normally placid gelding trembled under his touch. Anna sniffed, just as Maté had done, but the air was too close, too thick with scents from flowers and trees and the nearby ocean.

Raab ordered two of the guards to take up positions ahead. The others remained to the rear, while Raab himself dismounted. All of them had their weapons drawn and ready.

Maté too had a blade in hand as he crept into the undergrowth to their left. Once, twice, he stopped and sniffed. Then suddenly he plucked up an object from the ground. He beckoned to Anna.

"What is it?" she said softly, once she had reached his side.

"Our first tangible clue."

He said the word *tangible* as though it were a magical word.

Anna crouched amongst the vines and bushes and examined the clue. In his palm lay a short length of wire. Maté's eyes were not upon the wire, however. She followed the direction of his gaze down and to the right.

Vines and bushes grew thickly here, but they could not hide the signs of battle. All those leaves crushed, the branches trampled, the dirt churned up…. She sniffed again and caught the unmistakable scent of rotting flesh.

Theory number three. The buyer—or that possible third party—had lured Sarrész and his guards away from the temple and its open square into the forest, where they were forced into a single file. And here, within sight of the shore, the ambush had taken place.

"Where are the bodies?" she whispered. "Or did they take prisoners?"

"I doubt they bothered with prisoners," he said. "No, they dumped the bodies in the ocean, though they missed one or two, which accounts for the stink. Sloppy work," he muttered. "Though truth be told, I don't see why they bothered. Our friend was here, however."

Was. Silently she uttered a curse on Aldo Sarrész's soul. Three months chasing after the man, only to find him murdered at someone else's hands. Lord Brun would not be pleased. *Not pleased—dear gods, what an inadequate phrase.* Anna shuddered at the thought of how Brun might express his displeasure.

Meanwhile, Maté continued to examine the ground. The attackers had strung metal wire across the path to dismount their quarry, he told her. They had attacked using crossbows to take down the rest. The guards had fought hard, but all signs pointed to the party being overwhelmed and everyone slaughtered. Even three days later, splashes of blood marked the leaves and brush.

"Someone dragged a body here," he murmured. "We might get a clue…"

Before she could ask which body, or what kind of clue, Maté plunged into the thicket of bushes, hacking at the vines with his sword. The guards were muttering openly now. A sharp comment from Raab silenced them, but Anna could sense their nervousness. She could hardly blame them.

She checked the knife in her boot, the other at her wrist. Not that that made any difference. When Brun had first announced their mission, Maté had insisted she learn the rudiments of what he called practical defense. How to hold a blade. How to throw a knife. Anna had spent her afternoons with a newly hired set of tutors for magic, and her early mornings with Maté in the stable yard. All very good, but she was a scholar and the daughter of a scholar, not a warrior. A shudder passed through her, despite the close, hot day.

After a long interval, Maté returned. His eyes were bright, and he had that same odd air of anticipation she had noted before, back at the temple. "I found only the one body," he said softly. "Not our friend. But there are other signs I want you to see before our horses and guards trample over them."

He headed back into the underbrush, beckoning her to follow. Anna hurried after him, swearing under her breath. A short distance ahead, the trees stopped abruptly.

They stood at the edge of a lonely inlet, little more than a notch in the coast, with a few dozen yards between them and the rushing surf. A wind blew steadily from the ocean, lifting the sweat from her face. Then a flicker of movement caught her eye—tiny crabs popped up to the surface, only to disappear as soon as she spotted them.

"Look," Maté said quietly.

He pointed at the ground. Deep prints dug into the dirt and sand, heading straight for the ocean. Other footprints overlaid the first pair. They had converged from all different directions, and though wind and rain had smoothed the open shore, the sands closest to the trees still showed traces of a struggle. She glanced around quickly. No sign of blood here.

"They took him prisoner, then," she murmured.

"Nothing quite so simple. Come with me. I have something to show you."

With rising excitement, Anna followed Maté onto the open shore. He took a path that angled away from the confusion of footprints, then circled around cautiously until they came to a point where the sands were still damp from the tide.

More footprints.

A single line of footprints that arrowed directly toward the sea, remarkably clear even after three days and several tides in between.

"What happened?" she whispered.

"Our luck," he answered with satisfaction. "We had a lovely high spring tide four, five days past. That means wet sand that takes a good set of tracks, and no more tides since to wash them away."

The daily rains had softened the tracks, but she could guess what had happened. At the edge of the high-tide mark, their quarry had swiveled about, leaving a muddle of prints. Something—a momentary loss of breath? The sight of his pursuers?—had caused him to take a step back, leaving a deep, clear print. Then he had taken off again, straight for the ocean.

Where the tide had washed away all traces of what happened next.

Damn you, damn you, Aldo Sarrész.

She let her breath escape in a hiss that matched the soughing of the waves. Cursing a dead man would do her little good. Besides, Sarrész himself didn't matter, not really—only the jewel.

So let's find out what did happen to the jewel.

She knelt and let her hand hover over the sands. Oh, that was strange. Traces of strong magic itched at her fingertips, and the signature—the magical signature—reminded her of sunlight refracted by diamonds, bright and blinding and filled with all the colors of the universe. Except... According to all the reports Brun had supplied, Sarrész was a mere dabbler in magic.

She growled in frustration.

"What is it?" Maté asked.

"Magic," Anna said. "Not Sarrész's, however. I need to investigate."

"First let me call Raab and the guards. We don't want any surprises. Pretend you are enraptured with the beauty of the prospect, Lady Iljana."

She wanted to argue—all her instincts yammered at her to investigate now, this moment, before the traces of that magical signature vanished—but Maté was right. They could not discard their roles yet. Not until they had recovered the jewel and bought their passage back to the mainland.

Anna fluttered her hand to one side in agreement and, with some effort, arranged her expression into one she hoped passed for *enraptured*.

She did not have to wait long. Maté returned with Raab close behind. They both surveyed the shore, then conducted a brief, tense conversation about logistics and the possible necessity of spending the night away from Iglazi. Then came the guards themselves, with the horses. Raab ordered three to stand watch while the others dug a firepit and set to work preparing a meal for the lady. Within a short time, Maté appeared with a plate of toasted bread and hot tea.

"For my lady's relief," he murmured.

She ate and drank mechanically, only half hearing what he said about the ride back to Iglazi and the possibility of visiting this inlet another day. Her attention veered back to those mysterious footprints just a few yards to the left. Once she finished her bread and tea, she set her cup and plate aside and knelt beside them.

Ei rûf ane gôtter, she whispered. *Ane Lir unde Toc. Komen mir de strôm.* An invocation to the gods. To Lir and her brother Toc. To the magical current. Words spoken in the ancient language of Erythandra, the language of magic, of the Empire's ancestors, who rode from the far north to conquer the mainland.

A soft green scent mixed with the ever-present salt tang. The air thickened before her eyes, then wavered, as her vision narrowed to the footprint, then to the individual grains of sand that glittered in the brilliant sunlight.

Lâzen mir älliu sihen. Lâzen mir älliu hoeren.

She recalled those hours in her father's study as they practiced the invocation to magic, the simplest spells, to light a candle or seal a letter. Then later, as they explored far more complicated spells, to lift one's soul from the body and wander free throughout time and place. It was her skill in magic, after all, that had inspired Lord Brun to send her on this mission.

Lâzen mir älliu sihen. Lâzen mir älliu der gëste sihen.

The crash and gurgle from the surf doubled, reverberating from past and present. A tiny bird wheeled past—just a black dot spinning across the skies. She turned in time to see it vanish into the forest. Down and deeper down into the past. Slow and slower still, until the moments stretched out, and she could examine each one as she would a physical object.

...the skies a dark blue, smudged with rain clouds. A wind blew steadily from offshore, clean and cool, buzzing with the residue of lightning. Then, a flock of birds exploded from the trees. She heard a garbled shout, the high-pitched squeals of panicked horses. Next came a series of thuds and metallic crashes. A man burst into view, running straight toward her. She recognized Sarrész at once—a slim man of middle height, thick dark hair tied back loosely. But unlike her memories of the man, this Sarrész was splattered with gore and his mouth was twisted in horror.

He passed directly through her. She gagged on the stink of blood and sweat....

Sarrész *had* escaped the first onslaught. But then what? There was a heaviness in the air that felt wrong. And the man was gabbling to himself. Prayers to the god. A plea for deliverance. Words of magic mixed with curses against the gods. What was he doing?

Her gaze flickered back to the jungle. Five men and a woman were hurtling toward her. All six armed with short swords stained with blood. The five men howling like savage beasts. The woman silent, her cold dark eyes fixed directly upon Sarrész.

Even though she knew she watched events from three days past, Anna flinched. Her vision wavered, then resolved to show the same six standing much closer, their sweat-soaked faces stiff with shock. She spun back to face the ocean.

Nothing except sand and bright blue skies and the empty seas.

Startled, she lost her grip upon the past. The magic current vanished and she tumbled back into the present. Maté caught her as she pitched forward.

"Softly, Lady Vrou," he whispered in her ear. "You've taken ill. Too much sun, I believe."

She blinked and her vision cleared. Hours had slipped away while she delved into the past. All that remained of the sun was a golden thread running along the horizon. Raab stood over them, one hand on the hilt of his sword.

"Our men were unsettled by your magic," he murmured. "However, I gave them a tale of how your father indulged you with tutors. Did you discover any sign of our friend?"

"Oh yes," she said, her voice like a croak. Maté set a flask of water to her lips. Anna drank it dry. "He was here three days ago, just as we suspected. Not captured. Vanished. With magic. Very strong magic."

Maté's dark eyes narrowed. "Lord Brun's reports about the man were wrong, then."

"I don't know." Anna struggled to sit up, in spite of the ache that gripped her skull. "I could make out two different signatures. One very weak, almost useless. *That* would match the Sarrész I expected. But another signature that overlaid his. The signature *intertwined* with his. It's not like anything I've come across before."

"Could it belong to the jewel itself? Or another mage?"

Anna shook her head. "Magical objects don't have a signature. They reflect or amplify the signature of whoever used it. As for another mage...I don't know."

She didn't, and it frustrated her. She had thought herself talented in dissecting magical signatures—those fingerprints left by every magic worker, whether a skilled mage or a dabbler like Aldo Sarrész. That was another reason Brun had chosen her for this assignment.

She pushed Maté away and bent close to the tracks once more, frowning. Her head throbbed from magic and sun, but she forced herself to focus on those elusive signatures—Sarrész's weak and imperfect, that other so vivid, even after so many days. But whose? There was no second set of footprints, and if she could trust her magic, no sign of any other human mage on this shore. So where had Sarrész gone? And how?

Another crab popped up beside her, then scuttled over the sands toward the foamy edge of the tide. Her gaze flicked toward it and she caught a whiff of a sharp, green scent—so faint she almost missed it—drifting toward the ocean.

Her skin prickled. She recognized that other signature. The not-Sarrész. Curiosity tugged her forward, to follow that elusive...scent? Texture? Whisper? Anna could never decide how to classify the layers that made up a magical signature. Half-blind to her surroundings, she scrambled to her feet and took a step forward, cast about, and took another.

"Lady Iljana. Please."

Maté, his voice uncharacteristically anxious, intruded. Anna waved him away. She nearly had the scent again and she already knew what Maté wanted to say. That it was too late. That the location was too lonely, too dangerous. But if they left now, these faint traces might vanish altogether. A short distance away, Maté and Raab argued about what kind of watch to set and who had precedence. Raab gave orders to their guards, something about fetching the lanterns and setting up the Lady Vrou's tent. She hardly cared. Here were stronger, clearer traces, high above the sands, rising upward...

A sharp neigh broke her concentration.

Anna stumbled, lost her hold on the magical current, and dropped to her knees.

The sun had vanished completely. The air was thick and grey, while overhead a sprinkling of stars had appeared. Maté stood next to her, a lantern in one hand, his sword in the other. Raab was a few steps away. He too had his sword drawn. The horses were restless and stamping.

"Visitors," Raab said shortly. "Those bandits we've heard about."

No sooner had he spoken than dozens of masked men swarmed out from the forest. With a curse, Maté flung the lantern to the ground. Oil scattered, illuminating the shore in a burst of flame and blinding their attackers.

"Run!" he called out. "Make for the trees. Both of you."

"No! I can't leave—"

"You can, and you will."

The next moment, Maté and the guards had joined with the brigands.

Raab took hold of Anna by the arm and dragged her toward the sea. "On your knees," he growled. "We'll circle around the fighting and—"

"But what about Maté?"

"Shut up. We have no time for a university debate. Go!"

He dropped into a crouch and glided swiftly along the waterline. Anna scrambled after him. Raab had already vanished into the trees before she reached the far edge of the shore. The commotion behind her was louder than before. Sword striking sword, the metal ringing over the sands. A strangled cry, cut short.

She stopped, her pulse hammering against her skull.

You won't survive this mission unless you learn how to kill, Brun had told her. Over her protests that she was no murderer, he'd hired tutors who specialized in battle and assassination. They had stuffed her head full of spells, only now she was afraid to use them.

A shadow loomed up beside her. "Hah. Found her. Andreas!"

The man grabbed her arm. Panic blanked her mind. Without thinking, she snatched her dagger from its sheath and slashed out wildly.

He screamed. A gout of blood splashed Anna's face. She doubled over, retching. Before she could recover, another seized her arm and threw her to the ground, so hard her dagger went skittering over the sands. In less than a moment, he'd captured both her wrists and was dragging her over to the other bandits.

"We have our prize," the man announced. "At a cost."

"I hope she's worth it," someone else said.

"I hope so too. What do you think, Lady Vrou?"

He swung her onto her feet. Anna gulped down a breath as she took in the scene. At least four dozen brigands gathered in a loose circle. Several of them held up torches, so bright that the sands blazed silver and gold. Four men, gagged and bound, huddled in the center of that bright expanse. Three bodies lay stretched out on the ground and the sand around them glistened darkly. One lay on his back, his arm flung over his face.

It was Maté.

"No," she whispered. Then louder, "No! *Ei rûf ane gôtter. Ei rûf—*"

Her captor clapped a hand over her mouth. Anna bit down hard. The man grunted and loosed his hold. She spat out the blood and salt, drew a lungful of air, ready to summon the magic current, when a fist struck her skull and all went black.

CHAPTER 2

She woke to the pitch-black of midnight and a vicious throbbing in her skull. Without thinking, she lunged upward, only to be caught by a pair of hands. Anna struggled, but those hands held her steady while someone else inserted a glass vial between her lips. A cold liquid, viscous and bitter, poured into her mouth. She spat it out and twisted away.

"Drink, you idiot child," said a woman's voice, low and rough. "Unless you like that headache of yours."

She gripped Anna's chin in one hand and forced the vial between her lips a second time. Against her will, Anna gulped down one mouthful, then another. Her vision cleared momentarily and she could make out a collection of shadows off to one side. She wanted to demand where she was, what had happened, but that proved too much of an effort. With a sigh, she dropped into sleep.

* * * *

She dreamed—a dream so vivid, she knew at once this was a memory of a past life.

She stood on the deck of a ship, one arm wrapped around the forward mast, her face lifted into the stiff breeze. Nothing but ocean around them, the waves rolling toward the horizon, great vast swells of indigo that glittered with sunlight and the foam of the ship's passage. Six more ships followed, each with two masts, two prows, and a great deck in the center. West and west they sailed, the season growing colder, the stars shifting and changing with their passage, and if the gods were generous, if their prayers and visions held true, they would discover new lands over the horizon.

Anna knew this dream, this life. Knew this ship and this crew. Everyone dreamed such things, her father had explained when she woke in terror as a child. Like Blind Toc, who died and was reborn, so did all souls pass over the river of souls from one life to another.

And with each new life, her father said, we are free to make new choices. But remember, we are bound by those choices, life after life.

* * * *

The second time she woke, she saw patches of moonlight that seemed to roll and pitch along with the rest of her world. Her head ached, but not as much as before. Her gut felt sore and pinched. She groaned and tried to lever herself upright. Once again, hands firmly caught her by the shoulders and another vial was placed at her lips. She drank more of that soothing potion, which tasted of the familiar and the strange. She tried to thank the person, but they merely hushed her and laid a hand over her forehead, murmuring words of magic.

The aches unraveled from her bones and muscles. She sighed in relief.

"She'll do, I think," said a voice, the same one as before. "But you might want to take precautions."

CHAPTER 3

She woke the third time to find herself blindfolded, her wrists and ankles tightly bound. The air was hot and close, and vibrated like a plucked string. She could taste the thick salt tang of the ocean on her tongue, the old, metallic flavor of blood, and a sourness at the back of her throat.

What happened?

Fragments of memory drifted back. Sarrész and the jewel. Riding with Raab and Maté along a winding trail toward the coast. Maté anxious. Something about brigands and smugglers—

Oh. Gods. Maté.

The entire episode flooded her memory in sharp, unwanted detail. The splash of fire when Maté threw the lantern. The shadows swarming toward them. Raab vanishing into the dark. Her capture. Maté's blood-soaked body lying on the sands. She gasped and struggled against her bonds. Mistake. Her stomach heaved against her rib cage. Just in time she flung herself to one side and spewed.

"Steady," a man said.

He took hold of her by the shoulders and swung her around onto her back. She rocked to and fro in a nest of cords, her stomach still fluttering and her skin drenched with cold despite the heat.

"Huh," the man said. "I know you had a bad knock on the head, but Thea said you would do. Unless you have a touch of seasickness..."

He rested a hand on her forehead. Anna managed not to flinch, but only barely.

Ei rûf ane gôtter. Ei rûf ane strôm.

The cool green scent of magic washed through the air, erasing the stink of sweat and vomit. For a moment, Anna imagined herself standing in a pine forest, in the hills above faraway Duenne. Her stomach untangled, and she could breathe more easily.

"Better?"

Yes. For some definition of *yes* that included raw terror.

"Who are you?" she whispered. "And where am I?"

"Never mind who I am. As for where... You are aboard my ship."

He had a nobleman's accent, the vowels all rounded and soft, the rhythm languid, but with the occasional clipped tone that could be a remnant of a military life. A trace of the southern provinces, as well. Clearly not an islander.

Water splashed nearby. The man smoothed back her hair, which had come undone from its braids, then wiped the vomit from her face and neck with a damp cloth. He worked thoroughly and without any fuss, as though he'd performed this task before. He wasn't a servant, however, not with that accent. And he had said *my ship*.

When he had finished, her mysterious caretaker dried her face with a clean rag. Anna heard the clatter of a bucket, then the sounds of scrubbing as he cleaned up her mess on the floor. Her head still ached, in spite of the magic, and her skull seemed to vibrate in time with the hum that filled the air.

The hum rose higher and higher, until it became a groan that set her teeth on edge. Abruptly, a whistle sounded, then dozens of feet thumped past overhead.

The man stood. His fingers brushed against her forehead.

She shrank back. Immediately, he withdrew his hand.

"Feeling better now?" he asked.

She licked her lips and shivered.

"Right. You need water. After that, some broth."

He raised her head with one hand and set a flask to her lips. Cold, clean water spilled over her lips. She drank until the flask ran dry.

"More," she croaked.

"Not yet. You'll have another accident if you drink too much, too fast."

He eased her back into her swinging cot. He was humming a melody, one that seemed to run in counterpoint to the humming from above. She recognized the tune, a popular song she recalled from her childhood back in Duenne, in the days when men and women from the Court and the University called upon her father to discuss logic and philosophy. They also brought gossip, stories about theatre and musical performances—an influx of the wider world.

The man lifted her head and brought a second flask to her lips. This one contained a mild broth, mixed with an infusion of greens. "Just a few sips," he said.

The rich smell made her stomach lurch. She twisted away from the flask and her cheek grazed against a cloth. A bandage? Then another memory dropped into her brain. Oh gods, yes. Him. She could almost taste his blood on her tongue.

"You," she breathed. "You're *that* one."

He gave a soft and almost soundless laugh. "Who else should I be?"

She could almost hear the shrug in the man's voice. "You think yourself clever and strong," she said in a low voice. "All you are is a murdering bully. Your father must be so proud—"

"Do *not* speak to me about my father."

His voice was short and sharp, all trace of amusement gone. Anna flinched from the expected blow. A long moment passed, with nothing more than the hiss and hush of the ship's passage.

At last the man sighed. "Enough games, my lady. We need to talk, you and I."

"We have nothing to discuss," she said breathlessly. They had killed Maté and maybe Raab as well. They had only saved her for their amusement. Once they had finished with her, she would die too.

"But we do," he replied. "Your father, for one thing."

Her stomach gave another lurch. "What do you mean?"

"I mean you've had the bad luck to fall in with pirates, but the good luck to fall in with my particular company. Those others would mistreat you, just as you obviously fear. Me, I do a brisk trade in runaways. Your father will likely pay a high price to see his daughter safely home."

So that is why he had kidnapped her. She'd evidently played her part too well with the innkeeper and everyone else on Vyros. *Well, then, let us continue the charade.*

Anna lifted her chin and stared in the direction of his voice. "You shall have your money, you miserable piece of scum," she said coldly. "And after that, my father will have you whipped."

At that he laughed out loud. "Oh, you are magnificent. They must miss your sparkling conversation at Court."

She lunged at him, teeth snapping. He only laughed louder. All at once Anna's fury deserted her. Maté was dead. So were the others, lying like bloody rags on the sands. All the arrogance in the world could not recall them. She choked back a sob, glad the blindfold hid her tears.

It was my fault. I insisted we follow that signature. I lost myself in magic. If only I had listened to Maté...

"Would it help if I promised my people will not harm you?" he asked quietly.

"You've already harmed me," she whispered. "You murdered my—my people."

"I have my own dead from that encounter. But I see your point." There was a brief pause, then he said, "Was that man your lover?"

If the ropes were not bound so tightly, she would have savaged him. Maté was her friend. Her companion. Her ally. The one person in Lord Brun's household she trusted. Had trusted. It was her fault he was dead, and there was nothing, nothing she could do to bring him back.

Her eyes burned with tears. All those lessons from her tutors—how to kill with a single word, how to shape the magical current into a weapon—tumbled through her mind.

But there were too many unknowns for such an attempt, even if she could bring herself to kill. The size of the crew. The other magic-worker who had tended her during the night. In spite of her grief and rage about Maté, she was not yet done with caution.

"I have no lover," she muttered. "They are not worth the trouble."

The man said nothing. Anna wished she could see his face, to guess what he might be thinking. From far away, a sailor called out. Another echoed his words, then the floor beneath her leaned to one side. How many hours or days had passed since they had taken her prisoner?

"Where are you taking me?" she said reluctantly.

"Have you decided to cooperate?"

"Do I have a choice?"

"No. But if you do, you'll find it makes your time aboard easier." When she did not answer, he sighed. "Very well. Let us take these matters in smaller steps. Will you consent to eat, Lady Vrou? Then we can talk about terms and parole. I've already sent word to your father, but we have a month or more before he replies."

And those months would be spent as this man's prisoner. What then? Barône Klos would deny her, of course. Meanwhile Sarrész would escape with the Emperor's jewel. He might even find a buyer this time. Any number of rebel provinces might wish to turn the Emperor's chief weapon against him to regain their freedom.

She frowned and pretended to consider. "Very well. But I want to see your face before I promise anything. You won't untie me, I know, but please take off the blindfold."

"Fair enough," he said. "Hold still now. My people tied these knots very tight."

He took hold of her chin with one hand and slid the blade underneath her blindfold, just behind her ear. With a quick jerk, he cut through the cloth and it fell away.

He knelt beside her, the knife in one hand, the other holding her hammock steady. His face was so close it filled her vision. Lean and angular, nearly as dark as her own, with a nose like a hawk's and eyes the color of new straw, so pale they appeared ghostlike. A dusting of beard covered his jaw and his thick black hair was cropped short. For a moment he studied Anna with narrowed eyes. Could he see the tears on her face? Or was he calculating the size of the ransom?

"Happier now?" he said. "Or is that a foolish question?"

Her lips curled back, but before she could make a reply—or bite him—a rap at the door interrupted.

"Captain!" a boy called out. "Daria's back. She's got news."

The man's attention veered from Anna to the door. She caught a flicker of—anticipation? triumph?—in his expression, but just as quickly it vanished.

"Of course she does," he called back. "Tell her to report to my cabin. Pass the word for the rest of my officers. Oh, and we better have Thea as well." To Anna, he said, "As for you, you have a temporary reprieve from our discussion. Expect me back before the glass turns."

He exited the cabin and shut the door firmly. Anna sank back into the swinging cot. Her stomach felt hollow, her bones felt weak. She whispered her own invocation to the magical current, which eased the remaining aches in her skull, but she could do nothing about the panic that fluttered just beneath her ribs.

Before the glass turned. Did that mean an hour? Or less?

For the first time, she took stock of her surroundings. Her prison was a stark box of a room, everything scrubbed clean and polished smooth. Bright sunlight poured through the small porthole, and a faint whiff of magic, like freshly crushed herbs, overlaid the sour smell of sweat and vomit. Off to one side was a stack of crates. One held a tray with biscuits. Another had a pitcher of water and a mug. On the floor she spied a few crumpled sheets of paper. *Letters to my supposed father.*

She twisted her hands, trying to loosen the ropes, until her wrists were raw. No luck. She spent a useless moment wishing the captain had cut the cords, but the man was no idiot. A murderer, yes. A kidnapper. Brutal and devious. He would pretend kindness even as he planned how to extort money from her supposed situation.

She had to get away, but how?

Think, Anna, said a cool, dispassionate voice from her memory. *Identify the obstacles, then consider how to overcome them.* Her father's voice had led her through intractable problems of logic and magic so many times. He had never foreseen his death, or her capture by pirates, but his lessons had taken on a new usefulness over the years.

How many did she face? One captain, who would preserve her only as long as he believed Anna to be Barône Klos's daughter. An unknown number of crew, some of them vicious, violent men. All of them vicious and violent, she corrected herself. This Daria had returned with important news, which might occupy the officers, but that left the regular watch, not to mention any special guard posted.

I have to take the chance. They won't kill me if I'm caught. Not until they find out I'm worth nothing to them.

Another whistle sounded overhead, followed by more thumping. Anna closed her eyes and pinned her thoughts upon magic. There was a thin divide between the worlds of magic and mundane, her father always said. The tipping point, he called it. A skilled mage could cross that divide into the magical plane called Anderswar, could stand upon the edge of all the worlds and lives, but for now, Anna would be satisfied if she could unravel the ropes.

Ei rûf ane gôtter. Ei rûf ane Lir unde Toc. Komen mir de strôm...

It took only a moment to reach the balance point. Magic spiraled around her, like the breeze from Duenne's northern hills, edged with snow and frost and the tang of pine fires. Like the sharp wind from her life dream. She reached into the rope with her magical self...

She had the barest of warnings—a spark, a sudden flare of heat. No time to counteract that spell. The ropes exploded into fire and seared her wrists. Anna bit down hard on her lip to keep from crying out. *Damn, damn, damn.*

The magic vanished almost at once. Anna let out a gasp, then another. Her eyes blurred with tears of pain. Gods, it hurt. She didn't need to look to know what had happened. Her wrists were burned raw and bleeding. Her boots had disintegrated into charred bits. Nothing remained of the ropes that bound her except a cloud of ashes drifting through the air.

So much for being discreet. She had to act quickly now, and never mind the rest. Gritting her teeth, Anna eased herself from the hammock. Her treacherous legs folded underneath her and she sat down with a loud thump.

She cursed again, breathless and terrified, fully expecting the captain to reappear, but there was no sign anyone had heard.

No time for panicking. She had to keep moving. Teeth gritted against the pain in her throbbing wrists, Anna crawled over to the nearest porthole and hauled herself to her feet.

Finally. One small bit of luck in an ocean of disaster.

Anna had half expected to find herself on the open seas, but there, not so very far away, a thin strip of land showed above the waves. It was not the same cove she and Maté had searched, but one very like it—a small round inlet, bordered by pale sands and tall trees.

She crept toward the door and tried the latch. Her heart jumped when it gave way. Unlocked? Truly? Either this pirate captain was stupid, or he believed her safe enough aboard his ship. Still, she could not believe he had not posted a guard.

Hardly daring to breathe, she eased the door open and peered through the opening. Nothing. No shouts or challenge. Anna slid into the narrow corridor and glanced in both directions.

One end was dark. At the other end, a ladder extended from the lower decks upward into the sunlight. She took a wary step toward the ladder. And another. She was about to take a third step when a woman's voice sounded from the nearest hatch.

"Dammit, Andreas. I know what you think of Druss. But she *is* the key to our puzzle."

"Maybe." That was the captain's voice. "But I can't trust her."

"No one asked you to," another voice said. This one was a man's voice, slow and cautious. "But Druss loves a good bribe, you know. If we offer enough gold, she might share a few details about that idiot. Besides..."

The conversation dropped into a murmur, but Anna had already guessed they were talking about Aldo Sarrész. She didn't recognize the name Druss, but if—*when*—she reached safety, she could send word back to Brun.

Though she was tempted to linger to overhear more of that fascinating conversation, Anna forced herself to continue along the corridor to the ladder. Below, the rungs dropped into a thick darkness that stank of grease and fish and oil. Above her was the sky and open deck. She set both hands on the rails and climbed the ladder, teeth gritted against the pain from her burns. A step below the deck she paused and listened. No alarm had been sounded, but for all she knew, ten pirates stood about waiting for her to show herself.

She poked her head above decks.

Her luck was holding true, she thought as she scanned the ship. Fifty yards of the narrow deck, if that, stretched out from bow to stern. Perhaps ten yards from side to side. She counted four men in view, all of them facing the opposite direction, plus half a dozen boys and girls racing up and down the rigging, hallooing to each other.

Anna scrambled onto the deck, ran to the closest railing, and swung a leg over. For one heart-stopping moment, she paused. All her earlier confidence vanished as she gauged the distance from ship to shore, a distance that seemed to grow with every moment.

Before she could lose her nerve, she dove into the milk-warm water. Felt the shock of salt in the wounds around her wrists. Almost at once, the ship's roll dragged her back. She kicked hard, again and again. On the fourth try, she broke free of its pull.

Anna sucked down a lungful of air and arrowed through the water as long as she could hold her breath. When she broke the surface again, she had put several dozen yards between herself and the ship. Ahead, the jagged silhouette of trees rose above the watery horizon. Her wrists stung from the burns and the salt water, but she felt a bubbling exhilaration at her escape.

Shouts echoed over the water behind her.

"...over there..."

"...get the captain..."

In a panic, Anna dove beneath the surface and kicked hard toward the shore. Her lungs were burning when she came up for air again. The shore lay much closer, a shallow arc of white sands edged by a thick, dark forest. Beyond, the land rose in a series of hills toward a low, round summit.

More shouts came from the ship.

"...goddamned stupid son of a..."

"...wasn't anyone keeping watch..."

The captain's voice cut through the chatter with an order to lower the boats.

Anna didn't wait to hear more. She struck out for the sandbar, which reached out like a welcoming arm. A wave rolled under her and carried her along toward the shore. The next moment she was in among the breakers. Her hand smacked against the bottom. She grabbed at silt and stone, only to have the waves drag her backwards. Anna sputtered and fought against them, until at last the surf flung her onto the wet sands.

She lay there motionless, hardly able to do more than gasp for air, while the waters surged about her. Then, came the ripple of voices across the water.

"...over there..."

Anna jerked herself onto her feet, coughing and spitting up salt water. Her riding costume tangled about her legs and she tripped, clutching at the nearest tree, only to scrape her hands on the rough bark. She dropped to her knees and cradled her bleeding hands against her chest.

Damn, damn, damn.

She could hear Maté's lectures even now. Footprints in the sand. Blood on the tree trunks. Threads dangling from every bush and thorn. She'd left a blazing trail for the pirates to follow. How could they miss all the signs?

She took a precious few moments to roll up her trousers before she staggered on through the tangled underbrush. The going became difficult. Rough stones that tripped her. Thorn bushes that snagged her bare arms. The thick vines hanging from the trees.

Once she reached the crest of the hill, she had a clear view of the ocean. She paused, one hand on the tree next to her, one pressed against the stitch in her side. The pirate ship had remained well away from the shore—good. She also spotted two smaller boats sailing toward it. Had they truly given up on her that easily?

The boats pulled alongside the ship. Small figures clambered up rope ladders and a sharp whistle cut through the air. As the crew hauled up the boats, more sails unfurled, filled by an invisible wind. Slowly the ship turned and headed out toward the open sea. The impossible, the improbable had happened. They *had* given up on her.

Anna sank to the ground. *Safe, I'm safe.*

Her head felt unnaturally light, as though a fever were coming on, and the burns around her wrists stung. She cradled her head in her hands and breathed slowly. *Ei rûf ane gôtter. Komen mir de strôm. Komen mir de kreft.*

The cramps in her side eased. The burns on her wrists and ankles stopped bleeding. It would be enough to keep her until she could make it back to Iglazi. She released the magic current and its presence ebbed away, like the tide running out to sea. Another spell whispered erased all its traces. A habit of discipline, which both her father and her tutors had insisted upon.

Anna levered herself to her feet. Her legs felt shaky and unreliable, despite the magic, and with her first few steps, she stumbled and had to catch hold of the nearest tree. She hoped it wasn't too many miles to the nearest village or town.

"You need help, Lady?"

Anna whirled around and snatched up a rock.

A boy stared back at her, a thin, dark shadow in the midst of the trees. He was no more than twelve or thirteen, skinny and barefoot, wearing only a pair of dark blue trousers tied with a sash. An ugly scar covered one cheek, like a pale spider that had attached itself to his face. Except for the scar, he looked like any of the other children she had seen in Iglazi's markets, the same hawk nose, the same thick black hair braided in intricate patterns close to his skull. A child, but children could be dangerous too, she reminded herself.

"You want help?" he repeated, in a thick islander accent. Then he offered a grin, easy and cheerful.

Slowly she lowered her hand. "Why should you want to help me?"

He rolled his eyes. "You was running from those pirates," he said slowly, as if he doubted her ability to comprehend words of more than one syllable. "Maybe I know sommat about them. They like to let you starve here on this spit of sand, then come fetch you after dark. Unless you can magick yourself across the water, just like you magicked yourself better. Can you?"

It took her a few moments to parse his meaning. Oh. Yes. There were a hundred or more known islands in Eddalyon, and a hundred more that had never been mapped. Those pirates had no reason to remain within sight of Vyros and its garrison.

She needed another moment before she could speak calmly, however.

"Where are we?" she asked. "I want—I need to get back to Vyros. To Iglazi. Do you know where that is?"

He gave an indifferent shrug. "It's not that far, and I gots me a canoe that's fit for the seas. Five, six hours, across the channel. I can take you there, Lady Vrou. Not for nothing, of course."

Oddly, her hope, which had faded, revived at this demand for money. "How much do you want?"

"Twenty denariie. Gold ones."

An outrageous sum, and the boy knew it. "I'll give you twenty silver ones," she countered. "Thirty, if we make the gates of Iglazi before nightfall. But you'll have to trust me for the sum. I don't have any money with me."

The boy hesitated. "Fair enough," he muttered. Then louder, "We best hurry. Come on." He held out a hand.

He did not precisely drag her, but he did hurry her down a winding path that led them around to the opposite side of the small island, to a shallow cove where a stream emptied into the ocean.

The boy pointed to a canoe fitted with long poles on either side and tied to a tangle of tree roots. "That's mine. Hurry, in case those pirates change their minds."

Anna clambered in awkwardly. The canoe had no real seats, just a plank across one end and two paddles stowed underneath. Lines with hooks were coiled loosely on the floor, along with a folded net, some canvas, and a tub of raw bait. She wedged herself between two rounds of rope.

The boy was observing her with a frown. "You look hungry. Didn't those stupidos feed you? I guess not. Here, drink this." He fetched a stoppered flask from underneath the canvas.

The flask contained a mild fish broth, thickened with powdered biscuit. She drank it down in small gulps, with pauses in between. The boy nodded with approval. "Thought you might need sommat. I'll fetch us sweet water from the stream, then get us launched. If you wants more, there's biscuits in that tin over there."

He vanished upstream and came back with a canteen brimming with water and two wet scarves. One he handed to Anna; the other he wrapped around his head. Then he untied the canoe and pushed off from the bank, using the paddle to guide it into the calm water of the cove.

"Did you eat a biscuit?" he called over his shoulder.

"No," she called back.

He spat into the water. "Stupid Vrou. Eat one. It keeps you from tossing your stomach into the sea."

Anna hunkered into the bottom of the canoe. "It's never helped before. And if you don't hurry, we won't make Iglazi before nightfall and you won't earn your thirty denariie." She glanced nervously toward the open sea.

The boy laughed. "Don't you worry. They won't see us, those pirates."

"You said they might come back."

"Not now," he said with obvious disgust. "I said they *might* come later, once they know you're too tired and hungry to run. Besides, they don't like a long chase. Not on land anyways. I know that from my cousin, who works a ship to Hanídos—that's our main port on the mainland. He knows more about pirates than I'd ever want to."

As he steered the canoe along the shore, he continued to chatter about his cousin, about ships, about the fish you might find swimming close to shore, and the ones far out to sea, which the bigger fishing fleets chased after. There was good money in swordfish, hiring out as fisherfolk and captains for the rich folks who came to Eddalyon. The rest came because they liked an adventure and they'd heard too many songs and stories.

"Is that why you came here, Lady?" he asked. "You wanted some fun?"

She groaned to herself, thinking that fun was the opposite of how she would describe her reasons. "Never mind why I came to the islands," she said. "Do you want me to help paddle?"

The boy snorted. "Not unless you like swimming."

Anna suppressed a smile. Cheeky boy. Maté would have called him a water rat.

Her breath caught at the sudden recollection of Maté lying dead on the sands, and her eyes blurred. She swiped away her useless tears. Later she could weep for Maté, she could curse herself for dismissing his very real concerns about pirates and brigands. If she let herself grieve now, she might never stop.

Luckily the boy appeared wholly absorbed in his task. He guided the canoe around the curve of the coastline, to a point where the coast turned abruptly eastward. Above, small, brightly colored birds swarmed through the air, their high-pitched cries ringing over the water. The boy angled the canoe around and pointed across the open water. "That way. Can you see it?"

A dark, rumpled outline showed above the horizon. Clouds smudged the highest peaks, and a band of mist obscured the island's base, so that it appeared to float above the sea.

"Is that Vyros?" she asked.

He nodded.

"That doesn't look so very far."

He made an impatient noise. "It's not, if you know what you're doing. But then we've got—we *gots* weather and current and such. A bit o' cloud would be nice, though, what with the sun and all. Wrap that scarf around your head. Good. Now hold tight."

The canoe pitched down. Anna grabbed for the side, thinking they would go under. The canoe shuddered, then rose over the next swell. Anna's stomach rose and fell. Frowning, the boy applied his paddle to change the canoe's angle. They took the next wave more smoothly, and soon they were sliding down its back and up to the next.

Anna held tight to the canoe's sides and the conviction she would not throw up. When she was Lady Iljana, crossing from the mainland to the islands, the steward himself had attended to her with potions and possets. Nothing could compare to this dreadful passage, as the hours rolled by, their goal rising and falling from view. She could ease the worst of the cramps with magic, but she always felt on the verge of spewing.

Was it her imagination, or did Vyros's coastline look closer than before?

"Did you eat that biscuit?" the boy shouted.

By now she could only clamp her lips shut.

Muttering to himself, the boy left off paddling and rummaged through the seemingly random collection of bags. He came up with a tin of biscuits and another canteen. Anna nibbled at one biscuit, if only to convince him to leave off attending her and to keep paddling. She choked down the mouthful, then took a swallow from the flask.

Ale. Watered down, but it still burned her throat.

The boy muffled a laugh. He evidently found her predicament funny.

Miserable rat, she thought. She forced down a second biscuit, in between swallows of water and ale. Her stomach stopped leaping against her ribs and she wiped a hand over her clammy forehead.

I will never go aboard another ship again. Not even for passage back home. If I can't pay a mage to magick me across the water, I'll just stay on Vyros the rest of my life.

By the time they came within hailing distance of the shore, the sun was dipping toward the horizon. Ahead lay a smooth expanse of pale brown sands, littered by rocks and tree trunks whitened by salt water. Beyond stood a dense forest that reminded her of the forest around the ancient temple. But there were no houses or any sign they were close to Iglazi's well-populated harbor. "Where are we?" Anna demanded.

"Not far."

His answer came too quick for her liking. "Where are we?" she repeated. "You promised to take me to Iglazi."

"I am," he insisted. "We're not but a few turns from where you want to be."

She growled. "Why not take me directly there?"

"Oh, that." He spat into the water. "Those harbor crows're always wanting money. Money for taxes and fees. Money for spitting the gods-be-damned wrong way. Just tying this boat to a dock costs fifty denariie, and they won't take your promises the way I did. Don't worry, Vrou. I said I'd bring you back safe, and I will. Now sit back and let me make land."

Reluctantly she sank back among the ropes and bait. The boy turned the canoe's prow toward land, and sent it shooting in with the next wave. Up and up they slid along the wet sands. Just as the canoe shuddered to a stop, the boy jumped onto shore. "Out!" he cried. "Now!"

Anna tumbled from the canoe into the surf. The boy waved her farther onto land. "Come on," he said.

He dragged the canoe into the underbrush at the edge of the forest. With only a glance behind, he set off down a faint path that wound between bushes and trees. Anna stumbled after him. When she fell behind, he stopped to let her catch up, but she could tell he was nervous. Robbers or brigands lurked in these parts, she suspected. The same who had kidnapped her, or ones just like them. She walked faster.

Soon they came to the coastal road, which was deserted at this late hour. The hard-packed surface meant they were close to the city, but the boy seemed even more nervous than before and urged Anna to hurry, hurry, unless she wanted to fight off the island's wild dogs. Still, it was another hour before they reached the thatched cottages that surrounded Iglazi's outer walls.

Twilight had fallen and the first faint stars appeared overhead. They were on the westward side of the city, opposite where the garrison stood. It was this same gate she and Maté had taken on their ill-fated expedition to find Aldo Sarrész just a day before.

Anna stepped forward and pounded on the gates. A guard peered through a spy hole, scowling. But when Lady Vrou Iljana Klos gave her full name and demanded entrance, others swung the gates open at once.

"Lady Vrou," said one guard, his voice filled with amazement. "They told us— We thought you lost to the brigands. How did you escape?"

Anna turned to find her guide, but he was gone. How strange. Then she recalled his comments about harbor crows. "Never mind how. Call a chair to take me back to my inn. Send word for them to expect me. At once, do you hear?"

Her assumed role could do that much, at least. The guards left off their questions and shouted an order for a sedan chair, which arrived quickly, then helped her inside. Anna collapsed into the cushions. Now that she had escaped, all the aches and bruises returned with force. Her palms were scabbed, her wrists still tender from the burns. And her clothes had dried into stiff, uncomfortable folds.

I want a bath. I want food. I want...

What she really wanted was Maté's sensible, familiar presence. At the thought, her throat squeezed shut. She wiped away tears with the back of her hand. Tomorrow she would find the garrison commander and demand that he take action against the pirates. It was what Vrou Iljana would do. It was not quite enough for what Anna Zhdanov wanted, but it was a start.

The bearers carried her into the inn's courtyard. Bondsmaids hurried forward to help her from the sedan chair, while farther along, slaves opened the doors and knelt on the stones in silent welcome. The innkeeper himself came forward and exclaimed over her terrible misfortune. "We thought you lost forever, Lady Vrou. Your man Raab came to us with the report about bandits. We notified the garrison at once, of course. The commander promised to launch a search the next day. Not soon enough, your man Kovács said—"

Anna cut him off with an abrupt gesture. "What—*What* did you say?"

"That your man, Kovács—Ah, here he is."

Anna spun around. Not a dozen steps away, Maté had paused on the threshold, looking tall and mountainous and more than a little overset. His clothes looked rumpled, as though he'd slept in them, and his face was creased with lines that made him seem suddenly much older.

"You," she whispered. "You're alive."

"My lady." He covered the dozen steps between them and clasped her hands. For a moment they were Anna and Maté, good friends and equals. Then Maté took a step back and Anna remembered that ladies, even those of questionable character, did not treat their servants as friends.

Maté had remembered as well, because he swept into a bow. "My lady. We are amazed and relieved by your appearance. How did you escape?"

"They were careless," she said. "I escaped and swam to shore. We can discuss the particulars later. And you, you escaped as well, I see."

Only now did Maté take in the condition of Anna's clothes and her injuries. "My escape does not matter. We must call a surgeon for those burns. Come. You've had a terrible ordeal, my lady. Let me support you to your chambers."

He offered an arm, which Anna gladly took. Only when they had passed from the entry hall and mounted the stairs did he quietly say, "What did happen? How did you get those burns?"

"Magic gone astray," she said in a low voice. "But Maté, they let you go. They told me—"

"They knocked me over the head," Maté said with a scowl. "Their captain was a man called Koszenmarc. He bundled us all into his ship. Dropped me and the boys on shore near Vyros. Told me to wait for instructions about your ransom."

Ah. Yes. The ransom for the mythical Lady Vrou Iljana.

"What about the guards?" she asked.

All the joy vanished from his face. "Those gods-be-damned pirates murdered two of our boys. The other four…" He drew a deep breath, and for a moment it was as though he still saw those guards as soldiers under his command. "They've cracked skulls and some nasty gashes, but nothing worse. The surgeon promises they should recover soon enough. I filed a complaint with the garrison commander, of course, but he seems curiously reluctant to chase after our new friends. I suspect he takes bribes. But as you said, we shall discuss the particulars later."

They had arrived at her suite of rooms. Maté gave orders to Lady Iljana's personal maids for a warm bath and a meal. "And quiet," he said with a worried glance in her direction. "She's had a wearisome adventure." To Anna, he said, "Vrou, let me call a surgeon to attend you."

Anna had no desire to argue. Her maids led her to her private bedchamber, where they soon prepared a warm, scented bath. They offered her soft sponges, perfumed soaps, and fragrant oils, while others laid out a fresh dressing gown and slippers. When she was clean once more, they helped her to dress and brushed out her hair, winding it into damp, dark coils tied with ribbons. Her meal waited for her pleasure, they told her with an obeisance. Her man Kovács had sent a slave to fetch the surgeon, who would attend her within the hour.

For once she was grateful for her assumed identity. She could dismiss the servants and eat alone, and they would only think her eccentric. As for the surgeon, she would see him to please Maté.

She ate slowly, relishing the flavors. Cool broth spiced and thickened with unfamiliar greens. Slices of flatbread smothered in honey. With every spoonful and mouthful, her strength trickled back.

Home. Home and safe. Neither was exactly true, but at least she was alive, and so were Maté and Raab. She rubbed her head, gently exploring the knot beside her temple. It no longer hurt, but it was still tender. A trace of the captain's signature remained, faint and unfocused, along with stronger traces from the healer named Thea.

Why had he let her go?

She was fairly certain he had. He could have sent any number of boats after her once she escaped. He might have done exactly as that cheeky boy had said—waited until dark, waited until she was exhausted and starved, then captured her once more. She sighed and poured herself a cup of hot, strong tea. As she went to replace the teapot, a square of paper tumbled from the table onto the floor. Anna paused, suddenly wary, before she bent down to pick up this mysterious paper.

The paper was a simple square, folded over once. The outside was blank, with no address, nor any wax to seal it. Her heart beat faster as she unfolded it.

I'm glad you found my boy a useful guide. —Andreas Koszenmarc

CHAPTER 4

Anna flung the paper away and scrambled to the nearest door, shouting for Raab and Maté. Her maids took up the panic, calling out in terror, until Maté arrived at a gallop, sword and dagger drawn, with Raab only a few steps behind. Her two companions searched every room and closet and finally declared them safe from marauding pirates. Another hour passed while they interrogated the innkeeper and his servants. The results were… less terrifying than expected. One of the kitchen boys had accepted a bribe to tuck the note on Lady Iljana's tray. The innkeeper dismissed the boy without a reference and begged Lady Iljana to forgive the lapse. Anna wasn't certain which infuriated her more—Koszenmarc's trickery, or the innkeeper's groveling.

In the meantime, the surgeon had arrived. He *tsk*ed over Anna's badly burned wrists and ankles, murmuring that she ought to have summoned him at once. A quick invocation of magic eased the worst of her injuries. After that, he mixed up a salve that she was to apply twice each day, then prescribed an infusion of herbs, which would allow her to sleep, he said.

At last Anna dismissed her attendants. Only Raab and Maté remained behind. Their presence would lead to new rumors about the Lady Iljana's unseemly behavior. They would have to complete their mission soon, before she lost her reputation entirely and lost whatever advantages her role allowed.

The innkeeper had sent up a veritable feast of island delicacies and several bottles of fine wine—his unspoken apology for failing to protect his noble guest. Maté set to work arranging the platters and dishes. Raab made his own circuit of the room, inspecting every door and window, while Anna set spells to ensure their privacy.

Ei rûf ane gôtter. Ei rûf ane strôm. Stille. Stille.

Magic whispered over her skin as she spoke, like the breath of a ghost that had lost its way between lives. Though nothing within the room itself had changed, those sounds from beyond—footsteps from the courtyard below, the trill of insects, the small, secret conversations of night—took on a faraway quality. Whoever attempted to eavesdrop on their conference would hear a faint murmur and nothing more.

Maté poured cups of water and wine with a practiced air. Strange how he seemed equally comfortable playing the attendant as he was with knife and sword, or crouched in the mud as they followed their quarry. More than once she had wondered at his history. He spoke freely about his childhood on that farm in distant Károví, and just as freely about his service in the army, but over the past six years she had noticed gaps in those apparently artless stories. He never did talk about why he had sold his bond, for one thing, nor the early years with Lord Brun.

We both have our secrets, after all.

A single bell from the garrison tolled the hour. Midnight.

Raab finished his rounds and dropped into the nearest chair. He and Maté had scarcely acknowledged each other since her return, except for the occasional sharp-edged glance. She had the impression of a quarrel that had broken off only in her presence, and even then was barely suppressed.

"Sit," Maté told her. "You've had a long day."

"So have you. Both of you," she added.

Raab's mouth twitched, as if amused. *Do not pretend to be my friend* was the message. Anna remembered the day Lord Brun had introduced the man and announced his part in their mission. Handy with a sword and a knife, was how Brun had phrased it. Our own personal guard dog, Maté had muttered.

Yes and no, Anna thought. If Raab was a dog, he was Lord Brun's dog, sent to watch over the man's interests. It would not do, after all, if Anna and Maté decided to abscond with the jewel themselves.

As if they were stupid enough to risk the Emperor's fury, never mind Lord Brun's.

Maté offered a cup of wine to Anna. "Better a miserable day than none at all. Sit," he repeated. "We need to discuss what to do about our new friends."

Anna sat and accepted the cup but did not drink. "If you mean those pirates, I don't see that they matter. We'll have to hire more guards, of course, and make another search of the shore where Sarrész disappeared, but—"

"We need to leave Iglazi," Maté said. "Tomorrow, if possible."

Anna drew a sharp breath. "What? Why? All the clues to our mission lie *here*."

"Because of those same damned pirates. They know too much."

He sank into the remaining chair and picked up a wine cup, but set it aside with a dissatisfied air. Two days with little sleep and inadequate food had exacted a toll. His eyes were like hollows, the folds around his mouth seemed deeper than before, and the lamplight picked out a glittering of silver in his hair.

All the while, Raab watched them both with cold and assessing eyes. Anna finally took a sip of her wine to cover her own uneasiness.

"I've made a few discoveries," Maté went on. "Our friend Koszenmarc is more than your ordinary pirate captain. He also happens to be the second son of Hêr Duke Vitus Koszenmarc of Valentain. According to my sources, Andreas Koszenmarc spent three years at the Imperial Court in Duenne, serving as his father's representative. He vanished from Court without a word eight years ago—there was a scandal when his father disowned him. No one is certain what happened, though everyone likes to speculate. However, Koszenmarc likely *did* meet Hêr Barône Klos at Court. It follows he will soon guess you are not Vrou Iljana."

His words echoed her own fears, ever since she'd heard Koszenmarc's voice and recognized the lilt of a noble-born accent. But she could not give up, not yet.

"Then we remove to another island," she said. "We take up new identities and renew the search from afar. But if we do, we must act deliberately. If we simply disappear, that will only start new rumors and—"

"And you think no one will notice? Lady Iljana and her attendants depart from Vyros. Another young woman makes her appearance a few days later, on another island, perhaps with the same attendants, or perhaps with an entirely new set. Both lead to questions."

She opened her mouth to argue, but he slammed a fist onto the table. "Anna, don't be stupid. Sarrész has vanished. We can't even say if he survived the ambush. I say we let Lord Brun hire a Court mage to track the man down. Better, hand the matter over to the local authorities. Commander Maszny knows these islands far better, and he's the Emperor's man—"

Raab set his wine cup onto the table, hard. "No. We stay here."

Maté drew his lips back in a snarl. "And I say we go."

They were like two rough and battered dogs, facing off against each other.

"We must go," Maté repeated. "We've uncovered every single clue we could, in spite of our lord insisting on this idiotic game of secrecy. Let *him* handle the problem from now on."

Raab's mouth flickered into a smile. "He already handles it. Through me. You know that."

Maté scowled at the man. Before he could say anything unforgiveable, Anna laid a hand on his shoulder. "Maté, he's right. Lord Brun gave him the final word. Besides…I agree. We cannot give up now."

His gaze swung up to hers. "You aren't afraid of Koszenmarc? You seemed terrified before."

"I was," she admitted. "But I doubt the man will make a second attempt. We'll take extra care the next time we visit that cove. And I will lodge a formal complaint. It would look strange if we did nothing."

She glanced at Raab, who nodded. Permission given.

Maté, however, studied her with an oddly intent expression. "If you insist."

"I do."

"Ah," he breathed. "Well, then, that is a different matter. Very well. Raab and I shall hire more guards in the morning."

"And I'll have another word with our innkeeper," Raab said. "He ought to hire guards of his own, after this last episode."

He tossed off a second cup of that expensive wine before he departed. Maté, however, lingered over their feast, untouched except for the wine. He broke off pieces of the loaves and crumbled them into bits. He dumped spoonfuls of each dish onto the plates and stirred them into a mess. Soon their untouched feast no longer appeared quite so untouched.

"You are a thorough man," Anna said softly.

He shrugged. "They tell me it's a valuable skill. Do you have further requirements of me this evening, Lady Vrou?"

He was unhappy. She could read that plainly from his tone and the way he avoided her gaze.

She sighed. "No. Thank you."

Maté bowed and moved toward the door. Before he turned the latch, however, he stopped, his face turned away into the shadows. "Tell me," he said softly. "Why did you agree to this mission?"

Anna started at the unexpected question, and the implication that she had a choice. "Because…our lord and master ordered me to."

"And you did not wish to cross him."

He made it a statement, not a question.

She nodded. "It seemed wiser not to."

Maté smiled faintly. "True. He can be a hasty man, our Hêr Lord Brun. So you believe we can track down this Sarrész? In spite of everything?"

For a moment, she wanted to confess everything, but that would mean confessing that Brun had offered to cancel her bond but not Maté's.

"I do," she said.

"Then I should go. Shall I send in your attendants?"

She shook her head. He bowed and took his leave, as lightly and silently as always. Outside, he spoke to the waiting servants, his words still muffled by the secrecy spells Anna had laid over the doors and windows.

She turned back to the table and poured a full cup of wine, but before she had done more than taste it, she set it aside.

I lied to my friend. My best and only friend.

* * * *

She slept at last, aided by the surgeon's herbs and several glasses of that most excellent wine, but her sleep was restless and plagued by dreams so intense she might have called them dreams of past lives, except that all the images were from the day before. Maté's strangely intent expression, mirrored by Raab's cold one. The boy's hesitation when he negotiated the price of her rescue. The moment when Koszenmarc cut her blindfold and she saw his face just inches from hers.

Eventually she dropped into a deeper sleep and did not wake until late morning, long after the rains had ended and a fresh breeze sifted through the half-shuttered windows. There were no bells in Iglazi, nor anywhere in the islands outside the Emperor's own garrisons. She missed them, the various melodies that marked the different quarters in Duenne. Once more she had the distinct sense that she had arrived in a different world, one stranger and more alien than if she had leaped through the magical plane into another existence entirely.

Anna rubbed a hand over her eyes. Her head felt clear. Her aches had all vanished overnight. Her wrists were still tender, however, and she felt a lingering regret that had nothing to do with pirates and everything to do with her friendship with Maté.

The moment she stirred, her maids glided into her chamber with fresh pitchers of water. That had been her first chore in Lord Brun's household, fetching the water—a simple task that would not only accustom her to the house itself, but to her duties and her new status as a bondsmaid. That status had changed over the years, from maidservant to apprentice scribe to trusted assistant to the lord's own personal secretary, and with each finely judged advancement, she found herself with more privilege. Tutors in magic and history. More freedom within the house. And then that final change of status…

She pushed away those memories. She would talk to Maté again. She would tell him…not everything. But she owed him some sort of explanation.

You see, Lord Brun wants a wife. A wife who can offer rank and influence and money. If that happens, he'll want me gone. Sold, unless I give him good reason to set me free.

Three of the inn's bondsmaids entered with pots of tea and a tray piled high with those light, flaky pastries she had come to adore.

"Where are Raab and Kovács?" Anna asked them.

"Maester Raab is instructing the new guards in their duties, my lady," said the senior maid. "Maester Kovács said he had errands to run."

Ah yes. Maté would be searching out clues about those pirates, no doubt. In between all his other duties, he had befriended a number of "interesting people" throughout Iglazi, people who had provided him with the local gossip. Which reminded her, she too had errands to perform, including a visit to Hêr Commander Maszny at the garrison.

Anna made a careless gesture, as if the matter of guards or errands were not important. "Very well. I suppose they know their business, those two. Please bring me my letters."

The maids obeyed at once, and soon Anna had a stack of cards and letters next to her breakfast dishes. Vrou Analiese expressed a desire to further their acquaintance. Vrou Antonia invited her to the spas for her health. Barône Sellen's eldest son, a well-known flirt and a gambler, wished to call upon her later in the day. Luckily, none of them appeared to know Barône Klos or his daughter.

The last one had familiar handwriting on the cover.

Lord Brun.

"Fetch me my writing case," she said to the maid who awaited any orders. "And tell Innkeeper Huoron I want a chair within the hour. Send for Raab and tell him to have those guards ready."

As soon as the maids scattered to their errands, she opened the letter from Brun. Or rather, the letter from her supposed man of business, who corresponded regularly with the Lady Iljana.

On the surface, the letter appeared to be a tally of her expenses and income for the previous quarter. She could decode the references as she scanned the pages. This was a reply to her second-to-last report, which relayed their intention to pursue Sarrész to Eddalyon. Raab had already examined the letter and had underlined certain phrases that spoke of bills exceeding income and the need to balance her expenses before the end of the quarter.

Brun was not happy with their progress, she deciphered. He wanted Sarrész either captured or killed and the jewel recovered within the month. Once they had accomplished that, they were to send word and he would meet them in Hanídos. Underneath the signature, Brun had added a postscript about steering clear of local moneylenders as the fees were too high—a reminder for her to avoid mages and the authorities.

Anna remembered Brun's clipped tones when he first told her that restriction. *The Emperor,* he'd said, *would strongly dislike it if his personal concerns became publicly known.*

Translation: Brun did not wish his own concerns to become known.

She wrote back a detailed reply, using the agreed-upon story of a missing letter of credit to relate the progress of their investigation, Sarrész's mysterious disappearance, and their hopes of recovering the trail. Her pen hovered over the paper as she considered how much else to report. Not Maté's astonishing demand that they simply give up, of course. Could she even find the right phrases to imply that with their code? And what about Koszenmarc?

I'll tell him later, if I must.

Or Raab would, in this same reply. Neither Maté's suggestion, nor the business with the pirates, would please Brun. She only hoped he did not punish Maté. She set her reply to Brun aside and started on her letter to Commander Maszny.

By the time she had finished, her maids returned. Anna blew the ink dry and handed it over, unwaxed and unsealed, with orders to have it carried at once to Maszny. The second one, to Lord Brun, she tossed onto her desk, saying that Raab would see to its delivery. Then she sauntered off to her bath with an indifference she did not feel.

Commander Maszny's reply arrived just as she finished bathing. Anna hurried her maids through the task of dressing her in her newest costume, a confection of linen and lace, which had arrived from the seamstress the day before their ill-fated expedition to find Aldo Sarrész. She allowed them to brush out her hair, then ordered them from the room so that she might read the reply in private.

A very odd, unexpected reply.

The answer itself was simple enough. Lady Vrou Iljana would be received whenever she wished. It was everything else that made her eyes go wide. Expensive, scented parchment, covered with line after line of ornate phrases, written in the flowing script of a courtier.

...delighted...astonished...my heartfelt service...a jewel of society...

She set the letter aside with dismay. Maszny was the younger son of an exceedingly wealthy prince, whose title and holdings dated from long before the Empire existed. And Maszny himself had received numerous decorations for his service in the military. There was even talk the Emperor would appoint him as the first Imperial governor of Eddalyon. This letter was more like those she'd seen from parasites of the Imperial Court, the ones who sent pleading letters to Hêr Lord Brun from time to time, asking for his patronage.

Her maids returned with the news that the two senior guards awaited her in the entry hall. Anna followed them, still occupied with the seeming contradictions between Maszny's letter and what she knew of his background.

The two men stood at attention in the hall. One was an older man of middle height, with pale grey eyes that looked even paler in his dusky brown face. His companion was younger, with the flat cheekbones and arched nose of an islander.

The older man bowed to Anna. "Lady Vrou. We are yours to command."

She handed them a silver denariie each. "Very good. I wish you to accompany me to the garrison. You have ordered a chair?"

He bowed again. "Of course, Lady Vrou. It awaits you even now."

* * * *

By this hour, the morning breezes had died away, leaving the city breathless and close, the sedan chair closer still. Anna closed her eyes and wet her throat with sips of lemon water from the flask a serving girl had handed her before she left the inn. From time to time, she flicked open the curtain to judge their progress. The part of her that was Lady Iljana was indifferent to the passing streets. The other part, the part that was her father's daughter, could not help taking note of the city.

According to the histories, the first people had arrived in Eddalyon a thousand years before. Very little of those settlements remained, just a few pockets of stone structures, and most of that buried under layers of dirt and stone. A second wave of settlers from four or five centuries ago had built walled cities and grand palaces for their kings. The other islands still possessed remnants of those palaces, but the ones on Vyros had been destroyed by the Empire's invading troops.

The garrison was the largest of the newer structures. It lay on the eastern side of the city, on a shoulder of land overlooking the harbor. As she stepped down from the sedan chair, Anna took in its high, thick walls, the towers at every corner, the numerous soldiers patrolling the walkways and standing before the gates. These were all signs of a steady, competent hand in charge.

How, then, to explain the style of the letter she had received?

She could only hope her interview would explain these contradictions.

Inside the garrison, her guards and her chairmen were directed to a room to await their lady. A young woman in uniform escorted Anna through the compound, past numerous sentries and gates, and up a flight of stairs to the commander's office, where she exchanged passwords with more guards.

The door opened and her escort motioned for Anna to proceed.

"My Lady Vrou."

Anna entered the room and paused.

Commander Maszny's office was cool and shaded. Its floor was tiled in dark blue, its walls the same pale brown as the rest of the garrison and hung with large maps of the region. At the far end of the room, two men stood over a table. One was a much older man, black-skinned and with features cut in sharp lines, his springy white hair cropped close to his skull—clearly a mainlander from the southeast provinces. The other was a younger man, dressed in the same uniform, but with more badges affixed to his collar.

The younger man stepped around the desk and bowed. "Vrou Iljana. I am Hêr Lord Prince Dimarius Maszny, commander of this most desolate province. I am delighted to receive such a lovely ornament of Duenne's Court."

It took all her control to keep from staring at this welcome. "Commander Maszny. Hêr Prince. I am *not* delighted. As I wrote, my reason for this interview is anything but pleasant."

"Oh, ah, yes. Those brigands."

Anna bit back an angry reply. "Those were pirates, not brigands, my lord," she said evenly. "And however delighted I am that you have received me so quickly, I am also angry and distressed. My people tell me you were strangely indifferent to my plight yesterday."

Maszny waved a hand. "And I am distressed by your distress, my lady. Let us partake of refreshments while we discuss the matter." He gestured toward a table set with elegant cups and decanters. "As for you, Captain Rouphos, I must banish you to oversee the garrison, while I attend to Vrou Iljana's needs."

Captain Rouphos coughed, but said nothing. He bowed to Anna and saluted Maszny before he withdrew. Maszny appeared not to notice. He swept his hand around to guide Anna toward the table. "Would you care for some wine? Or anything stronger?"

"Tea," Anna said. She managed to disengage herself from the man and sat down. The tone of his letter ought to have warned her. Even so, she could not picture anyone like Maszny taking command of such an important post as Eddalyon.

Maszny himself appeared amused. "My dear Lady Vrou. Please don't abandon all good opinion so quickly. You have a complaint to lodge, and I must perform my duty." He inspected the various decanters, made a face.

"My unreliable servants have provided us no tea, but we do have strong coffee, brewed in the Eddalyon fashion. Will that suffice?"

He poured a cup. She accepted it from his hands, noting the calluses on his palms. A swordsman, then. That fit with the reports she'd had about the man. It did not fit with his manner today.

She glanced up in time to see him studying her. At once, he smiled and offered her a plate of biscuits powdered with cinnamon. Anna accepted one and sipped at her coffee, which was chilled and spiced even more heavily than the biscuits. Maszny, she noticed, had poured himself a generous cupful of wine. He leaned back and took a long swig.

"So you have crossed paths with our local brigands—pirates, I mean."

"Yes, Hêr Commander. Or rather, they have crossed me."

"Ah, a terrible thing. Tell me everything, if you please, my Lady Vrou."

So he was amused, she thought. She let her annoyance leak through as she told him, in blunt phrases, about the attack and subsequent events. She wanted to speak about the dead and wounded guards, but Vrou Iljana would not, no matter how Anna Zhdanov wished it, and so she dwelt upon the outrage to her person and her position. Her father the Barône would not take the matter lightly, she said. He had connections in Duenne's Court. He would not suffer the insult to his family.

Throughout her speech, Maszny listened with eyes half-lidded, his mouth relaxed into a faint smile. She could almost believe he'd fallen asleep, except that he occasionally took a sip from his wine cup. Once, when she mentioned leaping from the ship to escape, his eyes widened, but he offered no other reaction.

"And not one hour after I returned to my rooms, he bribed a kitchen boy to smuggle a letter into my private chambers," Anna said, her voice catching on a deliberate sob. "He dares too much."

"You are not so very wrong about that," Maszny murmured. Then in a louder voice, "So. What are your exact wishes in this matter?"

"That you hunt down these pirates, Hêr Commander. That you guard Vyros and its citizens, as your Imperial orders no doubt require." Remembering the pirates' attack, the glitter of steel sweeping toward her, it was not hard to sound angry and frightened.

"You are overset," Maszny said. "Quite understandable."

He poured a cup of wine for her, but she waved it away. "You have my official complaint, lodged by my man Kovács, and now you have mine. You know my wishes in this matter. Let me only add that I believe this attack was not entirely random."

"Indeed?" He drank from his cup, now seemingly bored. "How so?"

Anna dropped her gaze and hesitated. "This is difficult for me to say, but… You know I came to Eddalyon to, to seek an old friend from Court."

Maszny lifted an eyebrow. "An old friend?"

His tone was offensive, but Anna decided to ignore it. Best if she pretended embarrassment. "I hardly dare speak more plainly, Hêr Commander, but surely you understand me."

A glance through her eyelashes showed Maszny smiling. "I believe I know your friend," he said.

"Then you know that he, too, vanished suddenly, not far from the place those pirates attacked me and my guards. I believe they took him hostage."

Maszny was silent a moment before he replied. "I understand your concern, but I see a few contradictions. Unlike your father, Lord Gerhart has no money, nor any family of high standing."

Anna gave a careless shrug, as if these contradictions meant nothing to her. "Then he is a stupid man. Or perhaps this Koszenmarc believes all nobles to be as rich as my father." She paused. "You are investigating Lord Gerhart's disappearance?"

"Oh, we investigate everything, Lady Vrou. Do not trouble yourself about the matter."

"I cannot help it, Hêr Commander. You understand why. If you would be so kind—"

"—to let you know the details of our findings?" Maszny laughed softly. "Would that comfort you, Lady Vrou? What if we discover your lordling did not survive his capture? What comfort might I offer you then?"

His voice was soft and husking. Anna abruptly stood at the insult. "None at all. I believe we are done here, Hêr Commander."

Maszny unfolded himself and held out a hand. "The Lady Vrou is cruel."

She ignored his hand. "Do your duty, Hêr Commander—"

"That I can easily promise, Lady Vrou. In spite of my disappointment."

"—and you *will* let me know your findings, or I shall write to my father, and my father to the Emperor, to express our dissatisfaction."

She stalked out the door before he could reply. Outside, the same young officer waited to escort Anna back to the gates. She hardly noticed. Maszny had proved useless. Surely he had obtained his rank and his position through intrigue or favors, if not by outright bribes.

Outside the garrison, her new guards gingerly handed her into the waiting sedan chair. Anna closed her eyes and rubbed her aching temples. *I used to be a calm woman. My father always complimented me on my manners.*

It was Eddalyon that had changed her. That and Lord Brun's mission. She ought to have argued with him. He sometimes listened if she approached him the right way. But no, she knew his ambitions. He simply would have bought or hired another in her place, then handed Anna off to another household. She could picture the conversation: *She's young enough, pretty enough. She doesn't make a fuss in bed.*

A hard bump yanked her from her bitter thoughts. The sedan had stopped in the middle of the street. More chairs jostled around hers, and from not far ahead came the noise of others trapped in the chaos. Anna opened the shade and rapped on the door. "What is wrong?"

"A blockage in traffic, Lady Vrou," said the leader for her chair. "May I suggest we take a different route?"

"Whatever you think best." She rattled the shade closed and collapsed in a puddle of irritation. Gods-be-damned traffic. Gods-be-damned fops that bought their rank as officers in the Imperial Army. She wished, not for the first time, that she could vanish into some anonymous name and position, in a city far away from Duenne and its intrigues.

But it was Duenne and those same intrigues that guaranteed her freedom.

With some awkward maneuvering, the carriers threaded their way back and around to a side street. Anna drew the shade back a few inches. She could see little except the blank facades of several tall buildings. A few laborers passed by with baskets perched on their heads. Then no one. It was quiet here, and the streets were shadowed by overhanging buildings. She didn't even see a member of the watch.

Without warning, the sedan chair tilted to one side. Anna yelped and flung her arms out. Before she could catch hold of anything, the chair tilted wildly in the opposite direction, then crashed to the ground.

Anna lay bruised and breathless in the wreckage. "Guards?" she croaked. She sucked down a breath and tried to remember their names. Then she recalled they had not mentioned their names, nor had she asked. "Guards?" she repeated.

No one answered.

Truly frightened now, she disentangled herself and climbed from the wreckage.

She was alone. Tall windowless buildings lined the shadowed street. Far below, down a series of steps, lay the avenue they had left behind. A scuff of boots against the pavement gave her scant warning. She pivoted about and found herself facing Andreas Koszenmarc.

"Vrou Iljana," he said. "Good day."

Anna resisted the urge to lick her dry lips. A dozen men poured from the alleys and doorways ahead. More footsteps sounded behind her. He had trapped her neatly.

"Don't worry," Koszenmarc said. "I shan't kidnap you again. Even I can see there's no profit in it."

He's guessing. He can't know anything, Anna told herself.

But when Koszenmarc circled around her, she flinched.

"Ah, the lady breathes," he said softly. "I had begun to think you were made of stone, like the statues of sea monsters that line the harbor. Have you seen them?"

"I have no interest in statues."

Koszenmarc continued pacing around to face her once more. Though she kept her gaze upon him, Anna felt the presence of all the other pirates. It was precisely for accidents such as today that Lord Brun had insisted on those lessons in battle magic. *Think,* she told herself. There must be one spell that could drive them all away.

His mouth curled into a smile that did nothing to reassure her. "So. No statues. I wonder what does interest you. Lord Gerhart, for one. Magic, for another." He waited a moment. When she didn't answer, he shrugged. "They say those who come to the Eddalyon Islands are dissolute nobles, or the runaway sons and daughters of the same. You, you fit none of these categories, despite your efforts to pretend otherwise. Why are you here?"

He spoke softly, but she had not missed the sword at his belt, nor the dagger that suddenly appeared in his hand. Here was no foppish courtier. He would not hesitate to kill her. It made the choice to attack easier.

"I am here for my health," she said evenly.

His teeth flashed bright against his dark brown skin. "Such bravado. Not that I would expect less from a vrou of the first rank."

Now, she thought. *While he believes he holds the advantage.*

Swiftly she turned her focus inward, to the point between magic and the world, and called upon the gods. *Ei rûf ane gôtter. Ei rûf ane viur. Lâzen alle liehten.*

A wall of bright fire leapt up between her and Koszenmarc. He jerked backwards. Anna caught a glimpse of his face through the translucent flames, his golden eyes wide with astonishment. With another phrase and a sweep of her hand, she sent the fire billowing outward, forcing him and his men beyond the next intersection—a narrow lane between the two nearest storehouses.

Anna darted down that lane. A shout sounded behind her—Koszenmarc calling out orders. The fire would die out within a few moments. Once that happened, the pirates could overtake her. She veered left at the first cross street. When she came to an alleyway slanting down toward the harbor, she turned again. If she could reach the main avenue, she could dodge into any one of the shops that lined the street and send someone for the city watch. Her pursuers were gaining on her, she could tell. She gulped down a breath and rounded a corner—

—and ran straight into Maté.

"You," she gasped.

He grabbed her by the arm. "Come with me. Hurry."

Before she could ask how he knew where to find her, Maté pulled her into a narrow passage between two houses. They fled down a series of steps to the next ring of streets. Above the thrumming in her ears, Anna heard the clatter of boots on stones. Maté drew her close. "Quick and silent now," he murmured in her ear. "Can you do it?"

She nodded.

They hurried through a maze of passageways, through an even narrower tunnel that opened into a square crowded with chickens and goats. Opposite them was a wooden gate—locked, of course. Maté pried loose several slats, and they squeezed into another, larger courtyard.

High walls surrounded them, an expanse of pale brown brick darkened by moss. Several windows opened onto the courtyard, all shuttered against the sunlight, except for one high overhead. The ground here was dark and hard-packed. Matted grass and a few stubborn flowers grew in the corners. A spicy scent filled the air, mixed with the faint smell of rotting garbage from an unseen heap.

Maté made a quick circuit, pausing at each door and gate. At length he nodded, as though satisfied. Anna leaned against the closest wall, trembling. "What next?" she said softly. "Can you find our way home from here?"

"Not yet."

His voice sounded odd to her ear—strained and unhappy. She was about to ask if something was wrong—something more than pirates and kidnapping and a heart-stopping flight through Iglazi's back alleys—when Maté turned around. His eyes were flat, his expression so closed it frightened her.

"It's time," he said, "that you told me the truth."

CHAPTER 5

From far away came the rumble of street traffic, the hum of voices drifting upward from the marketplace, but here in this secluded courtyard, Anna had the impression that a veil of silence had fallen over them, much like the spells she had used the night before. "I don't know what you're talking about," she whispered.

"Don't lie to me, Anna. You know what I mean."

Like a soldier delivering a report, Maté listed all the times Anna had met with Brun over the three months before their mission began. He noted that half those private conferences had taken place late at night, and though most of the staff believed Brun had merely summoned Anna for the usual reasons, he doubted the man would suddenly take to using rooms sealed against spies. He had not bothered before, after all.

"You used that same spell last night," Maté said. "Curious, or not so curious a coincidence. You've spent so many hours closeted with those new tutors Lord Brun hired. And let us not forget the couriers."

What couriers?

Maté grinned at her expression, but it wasn't a happy grin. "I confess I hadn't noticed them at first. Hêr Lord Brun has so many friends throughout the Empire, after all, and everyone knows he likes to collect any and all news about Court and politics. It wasn't until I heard the stable hands gossiping about those midnight visitors, the ones escorted directly to our lord's private chambers, that I wondered."

"But Lord Brun—"

"—is a secretive man. I know. I served him ten years before you ever did, Anna. But too many things strike me as peculiar. Why did he insist on this idiotic game, with you pretending to be Vrou Iljana? And why aren't we allowed to approach the Emperor's own people in Eddalyon? He claims the Emperor doesn't want his affairs to become public, but if our lord acts in Marius's name, why don't we have proper documents in case of any misunderstanding? Why his secrecy, Anna? Why *yours*?"

For a moment she couldn't answer. Lord Brun had given such a reasonable explanation for the secrecy. Or so she thought at the time.

"We must talk," she said softly. "We'll go back to our rooms and—"

"No. We talk here. Now."

She flinched at his tone. "It's not safe here, Maté."

Not with Koszenmarc and his gang hunting them. Maté must have understood because he nodded. "Very well. I know a decent wine shop. We can sit quietly until things calm down."

She took his offered hand and hoped this wine shop was not very far away. All her panic had evaporated, leaving her weak-kneed. To her relief, Maté set a much slower pace as they retraced their steps to the public streets. A few more turns brought them into a small sunny square on the edge of the hill. There was a weaver's shop, a candlemaker, and in the far corner, marked by a wooden placard, the wine shop. All of the signs in this neighborhood were written in Eddalyon's native script. Once more she had the sense of entering a secret, alien world, hidden within the larger one she knew.

"Do you come here often?" Anna murmured.

"Once or twice. Stavros serves me the occasional bit of news along with a good meal."

The wine shop owner leaned against his doorway and watched them approach. Like most men in the islands, he wore dark blue trousers tied with a bright sash and an undyed cotton shirt. His grease-spotted apron did not inspire Anna's confidence, but his hands looked scrubbed, and he wore a patterned rag over his braided hair.

"We want soup, wine, and bread," Maté said. "We're hungry, my friend."

Stavros heaved himself upright with a grunt. If he wondered about a noblewoman coming here with one of her minions, he made no comment. "I've new cheese," he said. "The bread isn't so fresh at this time of day, but the soup makes up for it. My Phaidre's best."

"I believe you," Maté said. "Tell your Phaidre to make the portions big ones. My lady is starved and I'm not far behind."

He led Anna into the shop, to a large table next to the windows. Anna glanced around, taking in the dusty floors, the windows smudged with grease and smoke. Two old men occupied a table near the door, smoking pipes. Off in one corner, several men and women crouched over a game with cards and markers. For the most part, they spoke the island language—Kybris, it was called—with a few Veraenen words here and there. None of them acknowledged her presence.

The wine shop's owner vanished down the passageway and soon returned with mugs, plates, and a jug of wine. Off he shuffled again, this time coming back with the promised bread and soup, along with a jug of plain water. Maté tossed him several coins. The man caught them in one meaty hand and retreated to his post by the door.

Maté poured wine into their mugs, then cut several slices of bread and cheese. "Eat first. You look as though you might faint otherwise, my lady."

Anna nibbled at the bread, then tasted the soup, which was chilled and peppery, thickened with bits of a red, fleshy fruit. Both soup and bread were far better than she had expected, given the appearance of the shop's floors and windows. She had become too particular over the years, apparently. Or perhaps she had taken on too much of her role in this game that she and Maté played.

She ate slowly, finishing off the soup, then nibbling slices of bread and cheese, interspersed with sips of the wine, which turned out to be excellent. Once the shopkeeper had cleared away their dishes, Maté refilled their mugs, then leaned over the table. "Now we talk."

She glanced around the room, uncertain.

"Are you afraid of breaking a trust?" he said.

"I'm not certain Lord Brun *trusts* anyone, but yes."

"Hmmm. Interesting. Which brings me to my next question. Did he order you to keep secrets from me? No, never mind. He did. But did *you* never question why he's kept so many secrets? From me. From you, as well."

Anna bit her lip. She could not say anything without saying too much.

Maté let a laugh escape. "Confused about how to begin? Let me start, then. Our Lord Brun is an ambitious man. He's taken it upon himself to recover the Emperor's jewel, because that will lead him to...to whatever he values most. Am I right?"

Irritation pricked at her. "Why should I say anything if you can guess yourself?"

She spoke more sharply than she intended. The shop owner came alert at once, but at Maté's gesture, he subsided back into indifference. Maté himself had gone utterly still, as though he waited for prey. For a moment, she had the unsettling thought that *she* was the prey.

She drew a deep breath. This was her friend, her best and only friend, the man who had explained the factions among the servants in Brun's household when she first arrived, the friend who had hugged her while she wept after each time Brun took her to bed. He was the brother she'd never had. And he was right about keeping so many secrets. In a low voice, she said, "Lord Brun told me nothing, so I can only guess. I believe he heard about the theft—"

"How? I hardly think the Emperor—"

"I hardly think that too. There must have been rumors."

"Perhaps." Maté appeared unconvinced. "Wherever he heard this news, I cannot believe our lord would send off three bonded servants, spending money like water, for just a scrap more influence at Court. He must have some specific reward in mind."

Anna dropped her gaze to the tabletop. "I wouldn't know about that."

"No?" Maté said softly.

She released a long sigh and curled her fingers around her mug. "He didn't share his plans with me, but I can guess. He wants to marry well, as the saying goes. Recovering the Emperor's jewel would—how shall I put it—further those plans."

Maté's eyes widened. "The princess?" he breathed. "He wants to marry *her?*"

He did not need to specify which princess. There was but one royal princess these days, after the recent arrests and executions. Her Royal Highness, Karin Emerita, the youngest granddaughter of the Emperor Marius. She was just nineteen. Thus far, however, she had proved adept at keeping her grandfather's trust while she navigated the shifting alliances and factions at Court.

"That's only my guess," Anna said. "Whatever his goal, he won't keep me in his household. Of that I'm certain."

Maté was shaking his head in wonderment. "He aims high, our Lord Brun."

"He was always ambitious," Anna murmured.

Ambitious, clever, and charming. Qualities that he could summon up in a moment to gain what he wished. Anna remembered his manner when he invited her into his household. Very proper, even as he handed her over to the housekeeper and her new duties. Very different from that night, four years later. She had been twenty, older than the princess, but younger in the ways of Court and society. Remembering that night, Anna reached for her mug and wet her lips with wine. *He didn't force me,* she told herself. *At least I can say that much.*

A phrase she had repeated to herself often over the past two years.

"I'm sorry," Maté said softly.

She shook her head. "It might have been worse. But thank you."

She took another drink of wine, then added water. All around them the wine shop's other customers continued their endless games, their quiet conversations. In the kitchen, a woman started singing. Phaidre, perhaps.

"Where would you go?" Maté said at last. "Or could you go?"

She knew what he meant. Did she have the price of her bond, or would Brun sell her to another household?

It was time to admit the rest.

"He promised…" This next part was more difficult to confess. "Lord Brun promised me a reward," she said. "If I deliver the jewel by autumn, I get my bond returned and a sum of money above that. I could go into free service with another Hêr Lord. I might even obtain a position with the University, as a clerk or scribe. My father was friend to dozens of scholars and tutors. It's possible one might remember his name and offer me a chance."

"And Hêr Lord Brun?" Maté said. "Will he mind having you in the city?"

Anna smothered a painful laugh. "I doubt it. I'll be invisible, living in another world entirely from the Imperial Court."

"Your father was not so very invisible, as I recall."

Her laughter faded at once. It was because her father had known both Court and University that Lord Brun had visited their small house to inquire about obscure points of law or magic. And because he knew the scholar, he had offered to pay Michal Zhdanov's debts after he died, and to provide the daughter employment in his household. For a price, of course.

"No," she said sadly. "He wasn't."

She glanced up to see Maté regarding her with a strange expression. "I remember when you came to us," he said softly. "A skinny child with unkempt hair and eyes the size of twin moons. You've changed a great deal—except for the eyes."

She had been sixteen. Still grieving for her father, still terrified by that interview with the moneylenders, who had described in great detail how much her father had owed them, and how those debts were now hers. And grateful, so very grateful to be rescued by Lord Brun.

She was not certain she had changed much in the past six years.

"I'm sorry I lied," she said.

He shrugged. "Eh. We have Lord Brun to thank for that. No doubt he wished to keep us uncertain of each other. He does that with his friends, you know, as well as his enemies."

Anna let her breath trickle out. A mountain of dread and anxiety seemed to have vanished, now that she and Maté had been honest with each other. "I missed you," she said simply.

He smiled. "And here I was thinking I was right by your side these past three months. No, I know what you mean. We shall find that jewel, Anna. And you shall have your freedom. Though," he added, "I cannot promise not to argue with you from time to time."

She smiled back. "I like it better when you argue."

"Liar." But he was laughing softly. "Come. Speaking of troubles, we must return to the inn. Lukas and I discovered our new guards tied up and snoring behind the stables. We didn't stop to question them, we only knew we had to find you as quickly as possible. Lukas took one direction. I took another. If he returns before we do, he might execute them in a fit of rage."

Anna shook her head at the thought of Maté and Raab charging through the streets of Iglazi. Then her mood sobered. Maszny had not disagreed when Anna had called Koszenmarc a dangerous man. She gave a shudder, in spite of the heat.

"What's wrong?" Maté asked.

She hesitated a moment. "Nothing definite. Something Maszny said about the pirates, Koszenmarc in particular. He's a very odd man—Maszny, I mean. Not what I expected."

"And I've news about our friend Sarrész. The three of us need to hold a conference this afternoon."

Back to their mission, in other words. Maté left to order a sedan chair for Anna and a horse for himself. Anna waited with a bored air, sipping her wine. He was never at a loss, she thought, whether it came to fighting brigands, or tracking down a thief, or playing the part of escort and guard.

She was glad she had finally told him the truth.

* * * *

Raab had not executed their newly hired guards, but Anna and Maté found him standing over them with a grim expression on his face, his hand set on the hilt of his sword. Several of the stable boys and girls loitered nearby, clearly fascinated by this new spectacle.

"My lady," he said shortly. "I am glad Kovács found you in time."

Mindful of their roles, Anna said, "Not exactly *in time*. I had to extricate myself from a most uncomfortable situation. However, he did prove very useful in keeping me extricated. I shall have to commend both you and him to my father."

"That's good to know." Raab glanced at the half dozen men lying in a heap on the stable floor. "My apologies for neglecting you, Lady Vrou. I thought it best to question these idiots. Perhaps I did wrong."

"No, you showed good sense," Anna said. "Koszenmarc might've murdered these men to keep them quiet."

Maté was frowning. "They look drunk."

"Drugged is more likely." Raab prodded one of the men with his boot.

Anna wrinkled her nose at the smell. "Disgusting. But I suppose we must summon a healer for them. Which one of you volunteers for this errand?"

"Neither," Maté said. "My Lady Vrou, let me send one of the stable hands. We can question the men ourselves before the healer doses them. First impressions are often important in matters such as this one."

Meaning, Anna needed to examine the men for any magical clues before a healer erased those traces with their own magic.

"Very well," she murmured in a dissatisfied voice.

She settled herself on a bale of hay. Raab ordered one of the stable boys to fetch a neighborhood healer or surgeon, whichever one proved the least expensive. The rest he dismissed back to their duties. Once that was accomplished, he and Maté searched through the guards' clothes.

"No extra cash," Raab said. "They weren't bribed, which is as much as we expected. Lady Iljana, if you wish to make your own inspection, this one might prove useful. He's the man I put in charge of the others, to my everlasting regret. Kovács and I will question him afterwards."

Anna knelt by the man Raab had indicated. He was older than the rest by a few years, but still young to her eyes. His hair was matted and greasy, and the stink of sweat and sour wine wafted up from his clothes.

She placed her fingertips over the man's eyes and lips.

Ei rûf ane gôtter. Ei rûf ane strôm. Lâzen mir sihen der gëste.

As her perception drifted down and away from the present, a queasy sensation washed over her and her mouth filled with the harsh taste of cheap wine, which barely disguised the tang of raw herbs. Were they fools, not to recognize the wine had been drugged? Or no, the taste changed within a moment to something sweeter, softer. That was the work of magic.

She thought she recognized Koszenmarc's own signature—it reminded her of gemstones catching sunlight, bright flashes with darkness in between. Another signature lay underneath his, a sharper, stronger one that reminded her of the healer Thea, the one aboard Koszenmarc's ship.

Her own thoughts faded, subsumed by the guard's memories and emotions.

...the glimpse of a dark brown man offering him a flask. She recognized Koszenmarc's face, his pale eyes narrowed with humor. A sense of trust and camaraderie washed over her, as the stranger tipped back his own flask and drank. "To us," Koszenmarc said. "To a fine day and bright futures."

There was an argument about who deserved the next swallow, but Koszenmarc immediately produced a second flask. The leather was warm from the sun, the wine sweet and cool. It wasn't until she took a second, longer drink that a sudden chill exploded in her stomach and dizziness gripped her. She knew, the guard knew, the wine had been drugged. Someone caught him, dragged him into the alley behind the stables. He struggled but his arms and legs wouldn't obey.

As the guard's consciousness faded, Anna undid the bonds between them, like cutting stitches from a seam. One last glimpse of the past carried over, not of sight but sound. Koszenmarc's laughter.

She released a long, slow breath and murmured another spell to erase her signature. When she opened her eyes, she found both men watching her intently.

"What did you see?" Raab demanded.

"Exactly what we guessed. Koszenmarc drugged them, and those fools let him."

Raab grunted. "We ought to question them anyway. Maybe we can pick out a few details. Find out what Koszenmarc planned for us."

For me, Anna thought. But she did not correct him.

The results were more depressing than surprising. These were more of the young men who frequented Iglazi's markets, hiring themselves out as guards, laborers, anything to avoid bonded service. They'd heard about Lady Iljana's adventure with the pirates and hoped for a bit of excitement. They hadn't expected two hours of sword drill and another hour of Raab lecturing them about discipline. Raab had left them with orders to clean their gear and practice those drills until the lady required their service. But half the morning passed, and the lady still hadn't sent for them. When a stranger offered to show them a few tricks with the sword, they were happy to agree, and when he suggested a drink—

"You trusted him," Maté interrupted. "A stranger who offers you drink while you're on duty?"

The oldest of the guards mumbled, "I didn't think he'd—"

"You didn't think at all." Maté made an exasperated noise. "Lady Vrou, we must hire new guards. Experienced ones. As for these young fools— We shall do our duty and pay for their healing, but we cannot keep them in your employ."

Anna pretended an attack of compassion. "Oh, but they are so young..."

"Old enough to know better," Raab said. One of the guards had rolled over and was gagging. The others groaned softly.

She sighed. "Very well. I trust your judgment in these matters. But please, do take more care next time. I am weary of these constant interruptions." She rose and yawned. "I believe I shall retire to my rooms. It has been a most exhausting day. Raab, please deal with our guards and the healer. I want Kovács to escort me."

Maté stood at once and offered his arm. Raab did not argue. Perhaps he had further questions he didn't wish Anna or Maté to overhear. Good enough. She had observations she didn't want to share with Raab.

They wound their way through the stables into the shaded courtyard between the stables and the inn's main building. There, she and Maté paused under a tree while Anna made a show of admiring the rows of pots with orchids and other flowers.

"Their account matches what I saw in their past," she said softly. "But that tells us nothing about Koszenmarc's intentions. A pity he didn't confess his plans in all their glorious detail."

Maté snorted. "If he had, I would mistrust it. What puzzles me is that he did the deed himself. He ought to know any skilled mage could do what you did and discover his part."

"Or he sees himself as beyond the law. But there's more…"

Anna went on to describe her encounter with Koszenmarc. "He said there was no profit in taking me hostage again," she said. "He must guess I'm not Klos's daughter. Do you think he might have sent those useless guards himself?"

"As a double ruse?" Maté asked. "No, that seems a needless complication. Those young idiots are honest ones. We ought to thank Lir and Toc that Koszenmarc simply drugged them. He might have slit their throats to stop them from talking. No, he's playing a complicated game—"

He broke off and laid a hand on Anna's arm. "Did you hear that?"

Anna listened. "No. What is it?"

If anyone had overheard them…

Maté darted into a mass of bushes next to the orchid pots. There was a scuffle—noisy but brief—that ended with him dragging a boy into the courtyard. One of the inn's stable boys, judging by his clothes and the scent of horse. "Who are you?" Maté demanded. "Why're you following the Lady Vrou?"

He gave the boy a shake that must have rattled his bones, because the boy stopped struggling. "I'm not—Vrou Iljana, I only wanted—it's about Hêr Lord Toth."

Anna sucked in her breath. "What did you say?"

The boy glanced from Anna to Maté. He was as nervous as a sparrow, she thought, a small brown sparrow with bright black eyes. "You were asking questions about Lord Toth. Iouliana told all of us how much money your men offered for any news. You gave her a silver denariie because she knew all the gossip and—"

"And you thought you wanted a silver denariie yourself," Maté said.

He shook his head. "No. I mean, yes, I want the money. But I know a few somethings Iouliana doesn't."

"Do you now?" Maté glanced at Anna, who nodded. "Well, then, would you like to come with us to the vrou's parlor? We could talk more comfortably there."

But that only made the boy shake his head harder. "I've been gone from my post too long already." He jerked his chin in the direction of the stables. He might have overheard Sarrész and the guards before they departed on that last fateful day. Anna felt a prickle of excitement.

"Go back to your post with my man Kovács," she told him. "He'll make things right with the stable master." To Maté, she said, "Ask him a few questions. Pay him, no matter what, but we might want to have that quiet chat later. I'll go directly to my rooms. I should be safe enough inside the inn."

Her maids had already poured water for a bath. Anna dismissed them with orders to lay out a fresh costume while she indulged herself in an unhurried soak. Maté would tease out the boy's story, she was certain of that. Raab would hire a fresh round of guards, ones who knew their trade. Anna herself would demand yet another interview with Hêr Commander Maszny to report this latest outrage to her person. Even Lord Brun, with his obsession for secrecy, would agree that a Lady Vrou could not overlook such insult.

And perhaps with this interview, the commander would take her complaints seriously.

She emerged from the bath and gave herself over to her maids' attention. They dried her hair and dressed her. They applied scent to her skin, jewels and ribbons to her hair. Though her nerves hummed with excitement, she forced herself to play her role as the privileged and not very clever daughter of a wealthy noble.

Maté had not yet returned, nor Raab, which puzzled her. Perhaps they had decided the matter of new guards trumped any secrets the stable boy had. She demanded writing paper and ink and applied herself to creating a suitable letter for Maszny.

"Lady Vrou!"

Maté burst through the door and fell to his knees.

"Lady Vrou," he said, "my apologies, but you must understand—"

Anna rose to her feet. "There's nothing I *must* do," she replied sharply. "If you wish to speak with me, you may do so—respectfully. But first, I have a few words to share with you."

She gestured for her maids to withdraw. Their eyes were wide, their looks openly curious as they fled to the outer rooms. Anna hardly waited for the door to shut before she rounded on Maté. "You were too precipitate, no matter what your concerns."

Her harangue continued for as long as Anna could invent new insults and scolds. Then she dropped to her knees as well and whispered, "What happened?"

"The boy," he said. "That gods-be-damned stable master said the boy played truant and he dared not encourage him, not without good reason. The hint was heavy enough. I paid him for the boy's time and offered him a commission. That is what took me so long. Giannis will meet us by the front gates with horses for you, me, and Raab. And oh, yes, he has some very interesting news indeed."

Anna could hardly breathe. "He knows who kidnapped Sarrész, then."

"No, we're not so lucky. But he was on duty two days before Sarrész vanished, when Lord Gerhart insisted on a ride through the city. He had a particular destination in mind, Giannis remembers. He asked the boy for directions and paid him three silver denariie for the favor."

"He paid far too much," Anna murmured. "He made himself memorable."

"Agreed," Maté said. "Our thief's been cautious until now. I can only guess the city moneylenders expressed their impatience, and he needed to find a buyer quickly. Back to the boy. Like any worthy child, he was curious. He tracked our man to a tavern near the docks, one of the more reputable places. Two men and a woman waited for him outside. Sarrész went inside with the woman. Giannis didn't wait to see what happened. He ran back to the inn and gave the stable master some excuse for his absence. But he does remember that Lord Gerhart did not return for several hours."

"Did he recognize the woman?"

Maté shook his head. "No. But he might recognize her again. He was frightened of her, though."

A new clue, but what could it mean?

"Can he guide us back to that tavern?" Anna asked.

"Already arranged," Maté said. "I told the stable master we wanted the boy as a guide in the city. Raab and I will be your escort. You can use your magic and see what happened yourself."

Good enough. Anna paused to inform her maids that she meant to go riding along the city walls, and they should not expect her back before supper. Then she hurried along the corridors toward the stables, with Maté trailing behind.

A scowling Raab met them in the courtyard outside the stables. "The boy's run off."

"What do you mean, run off?" Maté demanded.

"He's gone. I don't know where or why. I was arranging for our horses with the stable master. There was also the matter of the healer, who wanted his payment for seeing to our idiot guards. I told him he could apply tomorrow but he wouldn't take that for an answer. Kovács, you should have sent a messenger to our Lady Vrou—"

"Enough," Anna said. "When did you last see him?"

"Not long after Kovács went to find you. Quarter of an hour. Maybe a bit more. There aren't any bells in this gods-be-damned city."

"He can't have gone far," Maté said. "I'll talk to the other servants."

"Good. I'll make a circuit around the inn. He might have slipped out for a lark. You stay with our lady."

"That makes no sense," Anna said quietly, once Raab had left them. "Lukas must have frightened him."

"Lukas frightens most people. Let's see what the stable master has to say."

The stable master had nothing but apologies. "Lady Vrou, the boy is a flitter-wit. He'll catch a whipping for playing the truant. I'll find you another guide for your expedition today, if you like."

"Are you talking about Giannis?" One of the older girls approached. "He went to the back gates. He said the Lady Vrou sent a message to meet him there."

Anna and Maté exchanged glances.

"He must have misunderstood," Anna said. "Have the horses brought around to the front of the inn, please. You," she said to the girl. "Which direction did Giannis go? That way? Thank you. Kovács, come with me and let us find our wayward guide."

She and Maté hurried through the passageway the girl had indicated. It brought them along the inn's stables, through another passageway, clearly meant for servants, then finally to a paved courtyard.

"This doesn't seem right," Anna said.

"No, it doesn't," Maté replied.

High walls surrounded them, covered in vines, with blooms the color of a new moon. Insects buzzed in the air, unnaturally loud in the glaring sun. To their left stood a pair of wooden doors, which undoubtedly led into the kitchens. The gate itself was very plain—nothing more than black iron bars. This would be where the kitchen took its deliveries. Right now the yard was empty.

"Let's see what's outside," Maté said.

The gates opened onto a shaded lane that bordered the inn. It too was empty.

"Strange," Anna murmured. "Where did the boy go?"

"Perhaps Lukas came across him. We'll go back to the stables." Maté ushered Anna back through the gate. "If he's not there, we should—"

He stopped short, and his hand tightened over Anna's arm.

"We must go to your rooms," he whispered. "Now."

"Why? What did you—?"

Then she too saw the bright splash of blood over the stones, off in a corner of the yard. Then the body, with more blood pooling underneath. A small body, like that of a small brown sparrow, forever stilled.

CHAPTER 6

Anna swallowed against the uprush of bile. "Dear gods. Giannis. Who—who did this?"

She started toward the boy, but Maté's fingers dug into her arm. "He's dead, Anna." And when she continued to struggle, he said, "I'm sorry. There's nothing we can do for him. Not when he's lost that much blood."

"But who—"

Maté glanced around the courtyard, his gaze strangely remote, as if he didn't see their surroundings, only a stream of clues flickering past his mind's eye. "I would say that someone has tracked our doings in the islands. Sarrész's enemies, or possibly we've acquired enemies of our own. Let's get back to your rooms before someone discovers us here."

He hurried her toward the passageway—too late. The outer gates swung open and a squadron of soldiers poured into the courtyard. More soldiers blocked the passageway into the inn, and the kitchen doors banged open to reveal another squad. Maté whipped his sword from its scabbard but checked himself with a muttered curse. Moving very deliberately, he laid his weapon on the ground and stood with his arms held loose at his sides. Anna had uttered the first few syllables of the magical invocation, but she swallowed the rest as Maszny shouldered his way past the soldiers to stand before them.

"Vrou Iljana," he said. "How unfortunate to find you here."

"What do you mean?" she asked faintly. "I had nothing to do with—"

Oh, but she had. Someone had spied on her and her companions. They must have murdered Giannis while Raab was distracted and when Maté came to fetch her. He would be alive right now if not for her.

But how did they get word to Maszny so quickly?

Maszny was studying her coolly, all traces of the courtier gone from his manner. "We have witnesses who swear that you and your man spoke with the boy Giannis not two hours ago. You were quite agitated, they said, to discover the boy spying upon a private conversation. Now the boy is dead, and your other man's fled. That leaves you and Kovács to answer my questions."

At his gesture, four soldiers seized Maté. Maté resisted only a moment before he surrendered with a sigh of resignation. Within moments, they had shackled him with irons hand and foot.

Maszny nodded in approval. "My thanks for not making trouble. But in case you forget yourself..."

He murmured a phrase in Erythandran, a call to the gods and to magic. A sharp green scent exploded in the air. Maté slumped to the ground. Before Anna could take a step toward him, Maszny caught her by the wrist. "No rescues, my Lady Vrou. You two are hostage for each other. You understand?"

His voice was cool and precise, implacable. Much like his magic signature. She nodded.

The soldiers half dragged, half carried Maté through the gates. Another squad poured into the inn, while others swarmed around the boy Giannis's body, taking great care as they eased him onto a blanket.

As if any of them gave a gods-be-damned about that poor boy, Anna thought.

Her eyes stung with tears.

Maszny shifted his grip from her arm to her elbow. "We go now, Lady Vrou."

His fingers dug into her arm. She winced, in spite of herself. "No magic?"

"Only if I must," he said. "But I don't believe it will be necessary. I've had you watched since you landed on Vyros. I know you won't betray your friends."

Her throat went dry at the implications, and all her protests died away. "I'll make no trouble. I promise."

"Thank you. I accept your parole."

Still holding fast to her elbow, he steered her through the gates and into the lane, where dozens of soldiers waited. Maté had been draped over a mule, bound and limp, with a dozen guards around him. More soldiers arrived in the meantime, equipped with pallets, blankets, and bottles stinking of magic. So many soldiers, such detailed preparations, unnerved her. There was much more than just a murder accusation at stake here.

"I must frighten you," she said harshly. "I and my friends."

Maszny shrugged. "I prefer caution over regrets. And I would know who did such an infamous deed."

At least he did not gloat. At least he pretended to care about the dead boy.

A young man emerged from the crowd with two horses in tow. One was a tall grey gelding, the other a small dun-colored mare. Maszny swung onto his mount, his weapons rattling into place around him.

"You ride, of course," he said.

"Of course," Anna snapped.

"Good. Then we shall take a longer route. I want to avoid the main squares."

He spoke so matter-of-factly. Anna wanted to strike him.

"Ashamed?" she asked.

"No. You might be, however."

Oh. Damn him. How dare he believe...

"I did not kill that poor boy," she said in a low voice.

His gaze flicked toward her, back to the gates. "Perhaps not. We shall find out, however, who did."

"But I tell you—"

She choked back her protests. If Maszny had trained mages under his command, they could extract the truth as easily as they wished. She would have to confess everything—Lord Brun's orders, his demand for secrecy, her suspicions about his ambitions. She was innocent of murder, but if the Emperor could execute his own children so easily, why should he spare a minor lord and his underlings?

The thought made her faint. She leaned against the mare, taking comfort in its warmth, the steady rise and fall of its sides. Noise around her recalled her to her surroundings. Maszny had swung his grey around. Belatedly, she mounted her horse. She was trembling, despite the heat.

"Frightened?" Maszny said.

"No," she lied.

"What then?"

"Nothing that concerns you."

"Everything about you concerns me," he said. "We shall discuss how much at the garrison."

He spoke quietly, but the threat was obvious.

I only wanted a pair of rooms. A lock on the door.

Perhaps the execution would be swift. Perhaps her next life would be different.

They set off down the lane at a slow walk. Anna rode in the center with Maszny at her side, the other mounted soldiers forming a barricade around them. Maszny rode easily, his hands lightly holding the reins, as though he did not need them. Was there any accomplishment he lacked? Commander. Mage. A skilled swordsman, judging from his callused hands. Clearly a sharp instrument the Emperor wielded in these parts.

At the main boulevard, ten riders split off toward the harbor district, along with the mule carrying Maté.

"Where are you taking him?" Anna asked.

Maszny ignored her. With a hand signal, he ordered the rest of his soldiers—two dozen at least—into a smaller formation. They crossed the boulevard to another side street angling toward the north and east through a district of small shops, many of them shuttered against the late afternoon sun. The man was taking excessive precautions, Anna thought. Did he honestly expect her to break free, in spite of this troop of soldiers, in spite of Maszny himself?

It was then she understood the situation.

He's not afraid of me. He's afraid of Koszenmarc.

She almost laughed, which caught Maszny's attention at once.

"You're pleased?" he said dryly.

"No. I simply realized that you are afraid too, my lord."

"I am not afraid. Intrigued is a better word."

She shot him a sharp glance, but his expression was grave. "Why?"

"Because you are the key to a very strange puzzle. Or so I believe."

That, she had no answer to. She rode on in uneasy silence, thankful he did not press his point. They had come to a wider section of the street where the shops gave way to apartment buildings, each of these divided by iron gates. Behind them lay kitchen gardens, just visible through the bars, and poultry yards, with chickens and geese and the cries of other birds she could not identify.

Maszny had just ordered his soldiers into a smaller square when a herd of wild pigs—huge black-bristled monsters—charged through a nearby open gate into the lane. Two riders went down, their horses entangled with the pigs. The next moment, six masked riders galloped into their midst, brandishing clubs. Maszny shouted orders and the soldiers closed ranks against their attackers. Anna fought to keep her own mare under control.

A dozen more masked riders appeared, brandishing sticks and swords. One of the men flung a small, dark object into the midst of the churning crowd of soldiers. A cold green scent rolled over the square. A bright light exploded. Anna's mare jerked up in panic, so fast she threw Anna to the ground.

Anna hit the pavement with a loud smack. For a moment, she could not breathe. Hooves stamped inches from her face. She tucked herself into a ball and squirmed closer to the nearest wall. Her ribs ached with every breath. *Oh, how splendid,* she thought, trying not to throw up. With one hand pressed against her side, she lurched to her feet.

"Vrou Iljana."

A man, mounted on a rangy horse of indeterminate color, reached down to her. Her vision swam, but she could make out a dull grey tunic. One of the soldiers?

"Come," said the man. "Take my hand."

She staggered toward him. He grabbed her arm with both hands and hauled her into the saddle before him. A sharp pang shot through her ribs and she choked back a cry. "Ah, you took a heavy fall, Lady Vrou," the man said. "My apologies. We'll have you tended to as soon as may be."

"Koszenmarc!" Maszny's shout cut through the din. "What are you thinking?"

Koszenmarc?

Anna tried to twist around, but her bruised ribs protested. "You," she gasped.

She struggled to break free. The horse danced in protest. Koszenmarc tightened his grip around her waist. "Stop that, Lady Vrou. Unless you want to fall flat on your stubborn face." He shouted across the square. "My apologies, Hêr Commander! But I cannot stay to explain."

He wheeled the horse about, so fast that Anna had to grab the pommel to keep from falling off. The horse leaped between a knot of pigs and another of battling soldiers and masked riders. Then they were free of the confusion, galloping headlong down the lane. Anna had to choke back a scream. It was like her flight with Maté through Iglazi's back alleys, only atop a monstrous horse. Why, oh why, had she taken his hand?

The horse soared over a pile of lumber and trash and landed with a bone-rattling thump. Before she could catch her breath, Koszenmarc leaned left and the horse responded, taking the next corner so close, Anna could see the cracks between the stones. The street dropped away, pitching downward in a series of steps.

Koszenmarc leaned back and the horse slowed, barely. She was certain they would go sprawling and break their heads.

"You. Won't. Make. It," she gasped, hardly able to speak.

He laughed, but she could hear the breathlessness, and she knew that he wasn't certain either. "Trust me," he whispered, his breath tickling her ear.

"Why should I?"

They charged directly into a crowded market square at the bottom. Shrieking children scattered. Goats bawled as they dodged Koszenmarc's horse. Somehow, they avoided them all. They veered around a fountain and then into a narrow street slanting up the hillside.

The street emptied out, with no more than a few men and women carrying market baskets. One girl, scrubbing the doorsteps in front of a shop, glanced up curiously as Koszenmarc brought the horse from a gallop to a walk, but no one else seemed to notice them. When they reached a deserted courtyard, Koszenmarc dismounted and dug through a pair of saddlebags.

Anna swung a leg over the saddle, ready to jump and run, but he took hold of her ankle and yanked her back into the saddle. "None of that, Lady Vrou," he said. "I need you to cooperate. If you ever want to see your friend Kovács, that is."

She hissed. "You are scum."

He seemed amused at the insult. "So they tell me."

As he spoke, he pulled off his tunic and boots. The sword slid into a sheath over his back, hidden under the shirt that now billowed around him. Face-to-face he would never deceive anyone, but from a distance, he no longer resembled the pirate captain that had ambushed Maszny and stolen his prisoner.

"Now for you," he said. From the same saddlebags, he produced a loose gown and matching scarf. "Put these on and take off your sandals."

Anna thrust them back at Koszenmarc. "What about Maté?"

"Him? Don't worry."

Still she balked. He muttered a curse and seized one foot. Anna kicked at him, causing the horse to jerk its head and sidle away. Koszenmarc was laughing and swearing as he regained control of the reins and brought the horse under control. "Stop arguing. We haven't much time. And don't worry about your man. It's you Maszny wants."

"Why? I did not kill that boy."

"You idiot. He knows that. Someone wants you and your people dead and dishonored. My money's on Druss, and I would wager double that Maszny thinks the same. But he wanted an excuse—"

He glanced over his shoulder. "They're coming. Tell me now. Will you trust me, or shall I leave you to Hêr Commander?"

She hesitated just a moment, then kicked off her sandals. Koszenmarc thrust the gown into her hands. It slipped over her head and arms, falling almost to her knees and covering her fine dress better than any cloak. With a few twists, she fastened the scarf over her jeweled and beribboned hair.

She felt a pang of dismay at how thoroughly Koszenmarc had planned this rescue. Or kidnapping. From her point of view, there didn't seem to be much difference.

I should blind him with magic. Take the horse and gallop far away. But where could she hide? And what about Maté?

Meanwhile, Koszenmarc had stuffed her sandals and his boots into the saddlebags. He swung onto the horse behind Anna and urged the horse into a walk. *Slow and easy,* she thought. Nothing to attract attention. Leaving the courtyard behind, they entered a narrow street that wound up the hillside. There wasn't much traffic about. One freight wagon piled high with goods under a canvas sheet. A few scruffy boys and girls playing a fierce game of stick and rag-ball. At one point, Koszenmarc had to dismount and lead the horse up a set of stairs, but no one appeared to notice them.

"Where are we going?" she demanded.

"Away," Koszenmarc said shortly. "Well away."

To his ship, she realized. "You won't make it past the gates."

"Possibly."

They entered a lane bordered by crooked houses, and behind that the mountainside jutting upward into the thick forest. Below them, the city of Iglazi spread down toward the ocean in steps and terraces and sudden steep slopes, like a multicolored cloth flung upon the mountainside. Beyond lay the limitless ocean.

Koszenmarc brought the horse to an even slower walk. The streets were empty here, packed dirt trails with the dust rising in the midday heat, with only the occasional dog lying in the shade, or a flicker of motion that could be a cat, or a monkey. Anna did not mistake this slow pace for confidence, however. Koszenmarc held her tight around the waist, and she had not missed how often he glanced from side to side.

Just as the street angled downhill once more, they came upon a small gate, flanked by half a dozen sentries, most of them lounging around a card game. Anna tensed at once. Koszenmarc said nothing, but he pressed her closer in a gesture that could be reassurance, or a warning.

One of the sentries scrambled to his feet at their approach, then visibly relaxed. "Oh, heh. Andreas. What news?"

Koszenmarc grinned and tossed the man a coin. "Nothing much. I found a new friend, though."

"She doesn't look friendly," said a second soldier. He flung down his cards and ambled toward the gates to open them.

"That's why I like her," Koszenmarc said. "I want a good challenge."

The guards laughed. Anna tried to drive her elbow into Koszenmarc's stomach, but he caught her arm. "No fighting," he said easily. "Not until we're in bed."

He whistled to the horse and they proceeded forward to the gates. Then Anna heard a shout from the lane behind them. The first guard came alert and peered down the street, past Koszenmarc, while the guard at the gate paused with his hand on the latch. The rest rose to their feet.

"It's the commander," the first one said. "What's he up to? Andreas, you should know—"

Koszenmarc whipped a cloth ball from one pocket and threw it to the ground. A stinking cloud exploded between them and the guards, followed by a burst of flames. The horse skittered to one side, but Koszenmarc had a firm hand on the reins. He gave a sharp whistle, and the horse surged toward the gates. The nearest guard tried to pull it closed, but he was too late. The next moment, Anna and Koszenmarc were galloping over a narrow track that snaked between the cliffs and steep mountains above Iglazi.

Koszenmarc tossed a second rag-ball over his shoulder. Anna did not dare to twist around to see what had happened, but she heard the howls and curses from the soldiers. He threw one last ball, then leaned forward, almost crushing Anna between him and the horse's neck as they pounded along the trail. She caught glimpses of the city below—the garrison on its point, the harbor speckled with ships, the jewel-bright sea. The rest was a confused blur of mist and trees and the rise and fall of the horse's neck.

The thunder of many, many horses sounded behind them. Anna closed her eyes and gripped the horse's mane. Magic buzzed over her, like the rush of salt water over fire-scorched skin. Koszenmarc was humming a wordless chant. The horse was flying now—or so it seemed—its hooves pounding faster than any horse's could. Or was it that she had never ridden like this before, heart thumping, not knowing if the next step brought her freedom or death?

Without warning, they burst into the golden light of the late afternoon sun. A high rock cliff leapt up beside them. On the other side, the forest dropped away, so steep and far, she pressed back against Koszenmarc in sudden fear. He was shaking with laughter and babbling to himself. *Almost. Almost. Almost. Almost.*

They rounded the hillside. Below them, the coast curved around from Iglazi's harbor. Two ships stood close to shore beside a fat arm of sand, little more than small black smudges against the brilliant blue waters.

"Ready?" he said.

Anna had time for one glimpse before the ground dropped away. She gulped back a scream.

Ei rûf ane gôtter. Ei rûf ane strôm. Ei rûf ane...

They were sliding through loose dirt, catching on roots and vines, then breaking free. Tiny bright birds exploded from the trees before them, screeching. Koszenmarc's horse scrabbled to keep its footing. It crashed into a thicket of vines, sending a mob of small red monkeys leaping high into tree branches. All around the noise and confusion rippled outward.

Koszenmarc worked to keep them both in the saddle until the horse regained its footing. Then a deep hooting from the cliffs above caught his attention and his chin jerked up. "Damnation."

Anna followed his gaze upward, squinting against the sunlight. Soldiers lined those cliffs. One figure had dismounted to peer over the side. She knew at once the man had to be Maszny.

Her gaze met his, and his teeth flashed white against his dark face. He turned and spoke to someone behind him.

"He's guessing faster than I thought," Koszenmarc murmured. "You might want to close your eyes again."

He shifted his weight. The horse skittered and spun around.

If the first abrupt descent had frightened her, she had no words for this second one, jolting and tumbling through a dense green ocean of leaves, branches whipping at their faces. With a thump, they landed on another goat track. The horse stumbled, shook its head, then started off at a canter that soon turned into a gallop, but not the impossible headlong rush of before. Anna heard the soldiers calling to one another, but their voices were fainter, and she could almost believe they would escape.

Almost. Almost. Almost, she chanted, and heard Koszenmarc's voice a beat behind hers.

Still galloping, they came to the shore. Ahead lay the two ships. The smaller one had raised its sails and edged toward the open waters. The second one lay close to shore, beneath a low rise. Gulls and terns veered away, keening angrily. A strong wind blew in from the sea, and she could see the white disc of the sun, streaked and smeared by pale clouds. There was a sharp metallic scent in the air, as though lightning were about to strike.

The ship wavered by the shore, lurched forward, then began to glide away. More swearing from Koszenmarc. A tremendous commotion off to one side, and a shout that told her Maszny had sent even more soldiers to the shore to cut them off. They would never make it in time.

But Koszenmarc had not given up. All magic cast aside, he was pleading with his horse. The horse had faltered in the last few moments, but at

Koszenmarc's voice, it gathered itself for one last run, a hard gallop straight for the ship. A bright blue width of water had opened up between the ship and land. Surely Koszenmarc could not expect it to actually—

The horse reached the cliff well before Maszny's riders. Without a pause, it leaped.

CHAPTER 7

The horse cleared the railing with only inches to spare and continued its charge the length of the deck, the crew scattering to either side and that gods-be-damned Koszenmarc yammering like a daemon from beyond the void. It was the mountainside all over again, except with masts and ropes, and beyond the railing, a ten-foot drop into the sea.

They rounded the bow, the horse slithering dangerously. Anna was certain they would tumble over the side, but at the last moment, it kicked against the railing. They covered half the length of the ship again before the canter slowed to a lope, then a stumbling walk, then the horse dropped its head and stopped, its sides heaving.

Anna nearly slid onto the deck. Koszenmarc caught her in time. She choked back a cry when his grip pressed against her sore ribs.

"My apologies," he murmured in her ear.

Her bones were rattled, her nerves undone. Her throat felt raw, as though she had been screaming. She wanted to pummel someone—preferably Koszenmarc—but she did not have the strength to do it.

By now half a dozen sailors gathered around them. A boy took hold of the horse's bridle and spoke in a soft wheedling voice, telling the beast how great and wonderful a horse she was. An older girl appeared with a bucket of water and a blanket. She directed a look at Koszenmarc that was one part admiration and two parts impatience.

Koszenmarc swung one leg around and slid onto the deck. "Don't fight me," he said to Anna. "Otherwise I can't guarantee I won't hurt your ribs again."

He was laughing again, his spirits at a too-high pitch. She sucked in a breath, braced against another stab of pain, but he caught her underneath her arms and eased her down from the horse with only a twinge. The moment she had both feet on the deck, she stumbled. Koszenmarc held her steady as the ship rolled under their feet, all the while calling out orders to his crew—something about sheets and sails and stays.

"And where the hells is Joszua?" he finished up.

"Here, Captain." A wiry young man with thick black hair dropped into view. "You wanted me?"

"So glad you had the leisure to join us," Koszenmarc said. "Take our friend below. She can share the cabin with our other guest."

He handed over Anna and vanished into the confusion.

Anna had time to spit in Koszenmarc's direction before the ship lurched and her stomach heaved against her ribs. She swallowed. When the ship gave another lurch, she stumbled over to the railing. Dimly she was aware of a whine close to her ear, then Joszua urging her to go belowdecks. She shook her head and gave another heave.

"Come along, Lady Vrou…"

Another thin whine passed close by, followed by a *thunk*. Joszua yanked her away from the railing. "Come with me," he repeated. "You'll be more comfortable below."

He shoved his way down the deck between his crewmates, tossing off insults and orders as he went. "Watch your feet, Karl. This is a lady, not a cow. Uwe, get a hand on that rope, or aren't you done with your nap yet? Here we are, Vrou. Down that hatch."

He propelled Anna along, not roughly, but clearly in a hurry. Anna twisted free and braced herself against the frame of the hatch. "Stop pushing me, damn you."

An arrow *thunked* into the deck next to her feet. Anna gave a yelp and scrambled down the ladder. She lost her footing and landed on her hands and knees on the deck below. Joszua swung down beside her. "Hush, my Lady Vrou. No need to cry. We likely won't die tonight."

"I am not crying," Anna shouted.

She wasn't, but she was very close to something like it. She took refuge in snarling at this unknown young man, who seemed to find everything so amusing. Joszua merely smiled and took her firmly by the arm as he steered her down the passageway. "Just as you say, Lady Vrou. The captain wants you here."

He paused before a small hatch and with a practiced twist had the latch undone and the door open.

Anna made a pretense of testing him, but she already knew she could not fight him. With a sigh, she walked through the door.

The door clicked shut behind her. An iron bar dropped into place.

Anna sucked down a breath and felt the seas roll beneath her feet.

Just like a mouse in a trap, she thought bitterly.

Her newest prison was a dark box of a room. No convenient porthole. No lantern hanging from the ceiling. The air smelled of sweat and terror, with no sweet herbs to leaven sourness.

A faint snorting breath sounded close by.

Anna jumped. Only then did she remember Koszenmarc's final words. *She can share the cabin with our other guest.*

What other guest? Another idiot nobleman who got himself kidnapped? A breath of silence followed. Then the groan of someone in pain.

Her stomach fluttering in terror, Anna called up the magical current. She curled her fingers and felt the current collect inside her palm, then whispered the rest of the invocation for light.

Ei rûf ane gôtter. Komen mir de leiht.

The light flared bright and warm. She held it a moment before letting it drift upward to illuminate the room.

Her first impressions had not been so very wrong. The cabin measured just a half dozen paces in each direction. Two hammocks were slung in each corner, and an unlit lantern hung from the ceiling. She caught sight of several shadowy objects off to one side, heaps of blankets, two buckets, and what appeared to be a chamber pot.

Another groan sounded, almost unintelligible, except for the trailing curse words at the end. She knew that voice at once.

"Maté!"

Anna dropped to her knees next to the hammock.

He was not dead, not even close, and someone had kindly tucked his left arm under his head to make a pillow. But his other arm hung limp over the edge of the hammock and his face was utterly slack.

Maszny did this to him, she thought. *Maszny and his gods-be-damned soldiers.*

"Can you hear me?" she asked.

His lips moved, but only a garbled noise came from his throat.

Anna took his right hand in hers and pressed her palm against his callused one.

...a lethargy consumed her. Muscles and flesh melting into a thick liquid. Maté tried to speak, but his throat could do nothing but spasm. All that

was left to him were the essentials. He could breathe. He could swallow. His heart beat on...

Permeating everything was Maszny's signature, a vivid imprint that called to mind sunlight upon mountains. *The work of a master mage,* she thought, remembering how he had executed this complex spell with just a flick of his fingers. Where had he learned such control?

An odd wriggling in the magic caught her attention. A loose thread in the spell's pattern. Her breath came faster as she recognized the implications. This...this had to be Maszny's key to undoing his own spell.

She reached out with her mind's eye and plucked at the thread...

...the magic unraveled, a cascade of living threads tumbling away...

Maté's fingers curled around hers. "Anna?" His breath came short and uncertain. "No...gods...I know it's you. No one...else...so damned stubborn."

She gripped his hands in hers and kissed them. "You're alive."

"Of course I am, miserable child. I hurt too much otherwise. Help me out of these ropes."

He tried to roll out of the hammock. Anna pressed both hands against his chest. "Stop. Take a few moments before you try to conquer the world."

"As though I ever could. Where are we?"

"Captured by pirates and heading out to sea. Our friend Maszny was chasing us, last I saw."

Maté uttered a few choice words about Maszny and Koszenmarc and pirates in general. Anna wanted to laugh, except it described her own feelings so exactly.

"At least we're alive," she said.

"For now," he replied. "Help me up, if you can."

Between the two of them, Maté finally rolled himself upright. He sank back, balanced in that uncertain nest of ropes, but when she reached out to steady him, he shrugged away. "Leave me. I'm well enough."

She ignored his rough tone and wrapped her arms around him. *My mountain,* she thought. She had no idea what she would have done if Koszenmarc had left Maté behind.

"What happened to you?" she whispered.

His voice came out in gasps. "What you see. Soldiers took me through the wharf district. Like a sack of wheat. Could hear and see. Couldn't talk." Then his gaze sharpened and he looked more like himself. "You? Are you—"

"I'm fine. Bruised ribs, but nothing worse." She shook her head, thinking over the chaos in the streets. "Maszny expected an attack. He insisted we take back streets and alleys, and he never once stopped watching. It wasn't enough. Then Koszenmarc attacked. I fell off my horse and let myself get taken. Again," she added bitterly. She leaned into Maté, who shifted around to drape his arm around her. Her ribs protested, but she wanted the hug too much to care. The chase was over. Maté found and restored. She started to shake from terror delayed. She pressed her face against his chest and held him tight.

"No need to fret," Maté whispered. "We were both taken. He's a clever man, that Koszenmarc."

"Pigs and brigands and galloping horses," she muttered.

"What?"

"Never mind. Oh, Maté, I was so worried. I thought Maszny—"

"He expected an ambush," Maté said. "He got two, instead. A group of hoodlums came charging through the middle of the docks. Before anyone could do anything, they'd knocked the soldiers over the head and carried me away to this ship."

Anna couldn't help herself. She laughed into his shirt. "Kidnapped. Both of us."

She went on to give him a more coherent account of her own so-called rescue, including the business with the clothes, and how Koszenmarc seemed to have planned for every eventuality. "It's as though he knew everything about our arrest," she said. "When and where, and what routes the commander would choose."

"Or he was lucky."

She shook her head. "He's lucky *and* clever. And he knows too much."

It was Maté's turn to laugh. "Before, it was you telling me he's no danger."

"I was wrong. I'm sorry."

The door swung open. Joszua paused and blinked at the magical light. His mouth quirked into a smile. "I see you won't be wanting any lanterns," he said. "But you might be wanting this." He dropped a covered basket on the floor of their cabin. "We're a ways from home. The captain thinks you'll want a bite in the meantime."

"But what about—"

The door slammed shut. She flung herself at the door and rattled the latch. Locked. She growled. "Pestilent young man."

Maté appeared unconcerned. "Let's see what the captain sent us."

They dug out the contents of the basket—metal bowls and spoons, a kettle of fish stew, several rolls of flatbread, and two leather flasks. Maté laid out the dishes on the floor of their cabin for a picnic meal. "Eat," he told her when she demurred. "We both need our strength, for whatever comes next."

It was more likely she would eat, then spew her dinner. Now that she was no longer distracted by terror or worried for Maté, Anna felt her stomach rolling along with the ship. She murmured the spell she had learned from the ship's surgeon during their passage from the mainland—was it only a few weeks ago?—and felt the chaos subside. At Maté's prodding, she accepted a bowl of the stew and a fragment of bread.

One of the flasks contained wine, the other fresh water. Maté poured them each a mug of the water, then dug into his portion as though this was one more task in a very long day. Anna tasted the stew. Her stomach decided to cooperate, apparently, because moments later she had finished off the stew and the flatbread. The fluttering inside eased and she no longer felt as though she would collapse into a limp and sweaty heap.

She filled her mug from the wine flask and took a sip. "They didn't take Raab," she said quietly.

"So I guessed. I'm not sure it matters."

"It has to matter. He might—"

Maté shook his head. "Forget Lukas. At least for now." In a softer voice, he added, "Be careful what you say. A ship doesn't have much privacy."

The thought of Koszenmarc eavesdropping sent a shudder through her. But she could not leave the topic alone. She leaned close to Maté and whispered, "Do you think Raab might send word to our friend back home?"

Maté did not reply at first. He turned his mug around and around in his hands, his gaze far distant from this tiny cabin. Then he sighed. "Perhaps. But I'm not sure what our friend could do, with him so far away. He might decide we aren't worth the trouble, not with the commander suspicious. I'm more worried about our pirate friends. They won't kill us right away," he said in a musing tone. "They want something from us."

Such a comfort, Anna thought. She took another sip of wine, which did nothing to stop the trembling inside her.

"Drink the rest of your wine," Maté said. His voice dropped into a whisper. "I want to see if our pestilent young man accidentally gifted us with something useful."

His search turned up very little. The spoons for the soup could be hammered into weapons, Maté said, if only they had the tools. They did not, alas. The bowls were useless, though in another situation they might make a small shield. If they had sand, they could transform the flasks into bludgeons.

"If only I had a great big rock," Anna grumbled.

"You do," Maté said. "You have a great big rock called magic. But I suspect our captain has others with rocks of their own." He glanced around the cabin, as though searching for more weapons, then sighed. "Our chief problem is that we are two, and they are many. And we are miles away from shore. Let's get some sleep. Tomorrow might bring us a better chance."

He sank into his hammock and seemed to fall asleep within moments. Anna poured herself another mug of wine and sat with her back against the wall of the cabin. The light she had summoned was fading, as if the magic were leaking from this world back into the void between worlds.

Where were they going? she wondered. Why had Koszenmarc rescued them? What did he mean by, *Our commander wanted an excuse*? And what about Raab?

When the light had vanished completely, she finished off her wine and climbed into her own hammock. *Why* and *how* kept tumbling through her brain, until the ship's steady rise and fall over the swells, its strange song of creaking planks and ropes humming in the wind, detached her from her useless speculations and she fell into sleep.

* * * *

A day or more passed with no sunlight or any means to track the hours. Joszua appeared four more times at irregular intervals. He brought them more baskets stocked with pots of that same fish stew, and once, a thick soup of dried beef and beans. He exchanged their full chamber pots for empty ones with that same cheerfulness. They were not in want of water, but they never had so much that Anna dared use their supply to wash her face. At least her ribs no longer felt sore.

Maté asked for a pack of cards and was refused. Two hours later, both cards and a bag of dice arrived with their next meal, and Maté taught Anna the rudiments of a game he called Complication, which involved the giving and taking of points based on a formula involving the worth of the card, the current score of each player, and the results of the previous throw. There were more rules, he assured her, but these were enough for a beginner.

He was trying to distract her, she knew. It worked. She spent a furious two or three hours attempting to rob her friend of all his cards. She had no thought for the ship's motion or what lay at the end of this journey. Eventually, however, her patience ran out and she admitted it was time to sleep. This time, she kept her magical light burning because she could not bear the darkness.

* * * *

She woke to a sudden blinding light in her eyes. She bolted upright, the first words of the magical invocation on her lips, only to be checked by a strong grip on her arm. "Not so fast, Lady Vrou."

Two grim-faced pirates stood over her. One held a lantern and a dagger, while the other hauled her to her feet. Her own magic had been extinguished, and she detected faint traces of another signature that overlaid hers. *Someone else with a great big rock,* she thought.

Maté had already been roused from his hammock. He stood in the opposite corner, hands bound behind his back, with a third man standing guard. At her questioning glance, he shook his head.

No chance, said his expression.

Not yet. Perhaps never.

The three pirates hustled them out of the cabin and up the ladder onto the deck. Night had fallen. Stars speckled the skies and the moon loomed bright and full overhead. Ahead was a brilliant constellation of lights that outlined a high peak, much taller than any ship. An island?

Their ship glided around the peak and into a narrow bay. Walls of stone rose up on either side, an endless black expanse that seemed to ripple in the passing lamplight. By accident or design, the pirates had permitted her to stand next to Maté. He leaned closer, just enough to brush his arm against hers. She glanced up to see him smiling at her.

"Courage," he murmured.

But his voice was not as steady as usual. Was there, after all, a limit to his seemingly endless spirit?

She pressed her forehead against his shoulder. Well, and if they died tonight, at least they were together.

Now they entered a circle of water ringed by stone cliffs. A burst of shouts echoed from the walls, with more answering from the ship. Anna heard a squeal, then a splash. The ship jerked, glided on, jerked again, and came to a halt. A second, smaller ship navigated around them to drop anchor only a dozen yards away.

One of the crew flung down a rope ladder. Moments later, more pirates clambered over the side and onto the deck, among them several boys and girls. One of them paused and stared at Anna.

Brown-skinned, his hair braided close to his skull... Anna blinked in recognition. This was the same boy who had rowed her to Vyros.

The boy grinned and made a sweeping bow. "Lady Vrou. I'm glad to see you again."

Anna growled, but the boy only laughed. "The captain told me to row you to shore. He said you might want a friend and not some stinking toad like Uwe here."

Uwe aimed an open-handed smack at him, which the boy dodged.

"Enough, Nikolas." A woman swung over the ship's side and onto the deck. "Don't act like a wild goat." She turned her attention to Anna and Maté. "Can you climb down a rope ladder? Both of you?"

Anna nodded. Maté grunted in agreement.

"Good," she said. "Karl, you and Isaak see them safely over the side. No dunking, no tricks, or I'll set you both to the most miserable chores I can find. That goes for you as well, Nikolas."

The boy Nikolas grinned again. "Yes, Ma. I'm not a goat."

Before Anna could sort out all the details, she was hurried over the side and guided down the ropes by strong, capable hands. Nikolas was already in the boat, along with several large men. Maté was not with her—she felt a spurt of panic—then the woman's voice called out from a short distance away, something about taking her boat in first.

Their boat shot forward toward the shore lit by moonlight. The sailors jumped out and hauled the boat onto a gravelly expanse. One picked up Anna and deposited her on the narrow beach. She caught a few words here and there, enough to understand the crew was excited about their success.

"Lady Vrou." Nikolas appeared in front of her. "Come with me, please."

She'd lost track of Maté in the confusion of landing. "Where is…"

"Don't worry about your man," the boy said. "The captain said he'll take care of him."

Which was no comfort at all. But she allowed Nikolas to lead her away from the landing to a rope ladder that climbed the face of the cliff. Nikolas motioned for her to go first. "Grab the ropes, just like on a ship. One hand to reach, one to keep you steady. There you go."

Up and up they climbed, what seemed a height greater than any ship. At last Nikolas called out that theirs was the next landing. "Wait for me," he said.

He swung off the ladder and scrambled up the wall itself, using handholds that she swore were invisible, and took her hand. "Easy, lady. The ledge is a bit narrow. Don't stumble over those rocks. Here we go."

He led her through a narrow gap in the wall, around to a point that overlooked the ocean. The lamplight had died away, but Anna could make out the opening Nikolas pointed to. She ducked under the low arch and found herself in a small grotto, little more than a hole in the side of the cliff. Three fat white candles were set on a stone ledge, and their light threw the rough walls into sharp relief.

"Would you like water?" Nikolas asked. "Or another dish of stew? Oh, and there's a pot in the back, if that's what you need."

"Does it matter what I want?" Anna murmured.

The boy hesitated. "Someone will come for you soon." Then he was gone.

Anna let out a long, unsteady breath. Someone, meaning Koszenmarc.

She glanced back to the cave's entrance. A fresh breeze carried in the scent of the ocean, of mud, and the unexpected scent of wildflowers and newly sprouted grass. Only air and water lay in that direction.

The rest of the grotto did not leave much to be uncovered. One hammock, slung from iron hooks set into the rock. Two dusty cushions. A makeshift table made from planks set over bricks. The pot the boy had mentioned.

Beyond the hammock, the grotto narrowed to a point. Cracks and fissures led deeper into the cliff. When she leaned close, a puff of stale air grazed her face and she caught the scent of cold ashes. A small black spider popped from one crevice and skimmed over the wall into another.

"Lady Vrou."

Anna started and turned to see a silhouette in the entrance, blocking the stars. "Yes?" Then she recognized the voice. "You're Nikolas's mother?"

"I am Eleni Farakos, second-in-command to Captain Koszenmarc," the other woman replied crisply. "Follow me. The captain wishes to speak with you."

She turned to one side and gestured. Metal flashed in the lamplight from a knife in her hand.

Two more pirates waited outside, both of them armed. They took the lead, while Eleni indicated for Anna to follow. Back through the narrow gap, up a rope ladder, then around again toward the ocean side of the island. If a man's household reflected his character, then this Lord Koszenmarc was a complicated soul.

At the halfway point between sky and sea, her two guards swung off the ladder. Anna glanced down to Eleni, who offered her a most unreassuring grin.

Very well. We play this game to the end.

All too aware of the emptiness below her, Anna cautiously left the safety of the ladder for the ledge. Her legs swayed, and she nearly pitched over the side, but one of the guards caught her by the arm. "Through there," he said, pointing to a narrow opening in the stone flanked by torches.

The tunnel bent and twisted back upon itself before it opened onto a sizable cave lit by oil lamps. Dozens of men and women—all of them armed with knives or swords—stood along the walls, two and three deep. Islanders, most of them, though a few had the pale eyes she associated with Ysterien or the Empire's southwest provinces.

A long low table occupied the center of the chamber. All the benches were empty except one in the middle, occupied by a broad-shouldered man, his hair tied in a serviceable knot. Even though he had his back to Anna, she recognized him immediately.

"Maté." She hurried forward.

Maté swung around, but before they could do more than clasp hands, Eleni stepped between them and laid a hand on Anna's shoulder. "You, sit over there. And no talking."

Reluctantly, Anna let go of Maté's hands and took a seat at the far end of the table. Maté seemed subdued and had a dark bruise over one eye. Not a good sign.

Eleni took a seat opposite Maté. She had the same dusky brown coloring as her son, the same hawk nose and thick black hair tied in braids close to her skull. Like him, a pale white scar stretched over her left cheek. More scars mottled her arms.

She laid her knife on the table. Maté scowled. She smiled back in a way that made Anna think they had exchanged a few words, and none of them friendly.

Koszenmarc entered the cave from yet another passageway. He and his second-in-command exchanged a glance that seemed to convey an entire conversation of questions and replies.

They've known each other for years, Anna thought. *Perhaps since he first came to the islands.*

Friends, just as she and Maté were friends.

Koszenmarc took the seat at the other end of the table. He had changed into clean clothes. His hair was damp and slicked back, but a rough beard shadowed his jaw and there were smudges under his eyes, as though he had not slept in quite a while. Faint lines beside his mouth and eyes deepened as he returned her glance. She noticed he no longer wore a bandage where she had bitten him.

"So," he said. "Let me be plain. We know you aren't Barône Klos's daughter. You came to these islands chasing after the same thief as me. Now the man has vanished, together with the object he stole. I have a client who will pay a great deal of money for that object. I want you to join my company and help me find the man and whatever he stole."

Anna stared at him. "Why?"

Koszenmarc shrugged. "Profit. Yours and mine. And your friend's," he said with a nod to Maté. "Or does he work for other wages?"

Maté slammed his hands on the table. "I am not—"

Three things followed swiftly. Eleni Farakos swept up her knife and threw. The blade flashed as it whirled between Maté and Anna, to be caught one-handed by another pirate. The rest of the pirates surged forward, stopped by a gesture from Koszenmarc.

Maté blew out a breath and subsided. Anna swallowed against a very dry throat. "I am no pirate," she said. "I cannot help you."

"Then what are you? Why did you come to Eddalyon?"

"I..." All the reasons Lord Brun had impressed upon her flooded her memory. Reasons that she no longer trusted, but even so, she had no reason to trust Koszenmarc either. She shook her head. "I'm sorry. I cannot say."

"I'm sorry as well," Koszenmarc said. "Since you refuse to cooperate, we must hand you and your friend over to Commander Maszny. It's not much of a reward, but better than nothing. You have tonight and tomorrow to reconsider."

At his signal, five pirates hauled Anna to her feet. Six more took hold of Maté. Anna struggled to break free. She would not go back to that miserable hole in the rock. She would not wait and wait for some perfect moment to escape. If she died, at least she would die cleanly.

She drew a breath, spiraling her focus down as quickly as she could. *Ei rûf ane gôtter. Ei rûf—*

"No!"

Koszenmarc leaped over the table. At the same time, Eleni Farakos grabbed Maté by the hair and yanked his head back. She had yet another knife in her hand and pressed it against Maté's throat.

"No," Koszenmarc repeated. "Do not fight my people. You are both hostage to each other."

Anna swallowed and glanced at Maté. His eyes were closed to slits, and he was breathing quickly. A trickle of blood leaked from the knife at his throat.

"I promise," she answered.

"Good," Koszenmarc said. "We understand each other now."

Eleni released Maté and snapped out a series of orders. Two guards hustled Maté out another exit, while Anna's own guards bundled her out a different direction to the rope ladder, then down to the grotto, where they dropped her just inside the entrance. She fell to her knees, gulping down breath after breath. It had all seemed so simple, godsdammit. Find Sarrész. Recover the jewel. Win her freedom and live quietly.

She could almost laugh at her naivete. There was nothing about politics that could be simple.

Tomorrow, Koszenmarc would transport her and Maté back to Vyros and Commander Maszny. A man who had his own reasons for taking them prisoner. Questioning would come first. After that, the execution. Outside her prison cell, far below, the surf crashed against the shore. A woman's voice called out, answered by the higher piping of a boy's from another point, then a louder halloo from directly outside the cave—guards and lookouts calling to one another. A reminder that Koszenmarc was taking every precaution.

Damn him. Damn them all, Anna cursed.

The other candles had guttered. One more remained. Anna reached to extinguish it, when she noticed a trunk that had not been there before.

It did not take long to explore its contents. One pair of trousers and a sash. One shirt. No shoes. Two flasks of water and another of ale.

Enough for one night and one day.

Anna sat down heavily. Was it possible to get word to Raab? He had escaped both sets of enemies, she was certain of that. And though he might be indifferent to her and Maté's fate, he was Hêr Lord Brun's loyal man. He would hunt them down and free them, if only to make sure their mission did not fail.

But only if she could get him word.

She drained one flask of water, then exchanged her filthy clothes for clean ones and climbed into the hammock, which swung gently back and forth between the hooks.

They said a person minded the dying only as long as it lasted. Once the soul took flight into the void, there came a period of blankness, of blessed forgetfulness, before the next life. Even then, even with memories and dreams of times that came before, no one had ever claimed to remember exactly the point when breath fled the body and the heart ceased beating. It was all conjecture, the subject of poetry and endless speculation by philosophers.

Would it matter if I knew?

Outside, a bell tolled from some distant point, and on its heels, the guards called to one another. She thought she recognized Nikolas's high cheery call, and she wondered how he and his mother had come to serve Koszenmarc. Were they happy as killers and thieves, or had the life overtaken them by a series of unfortunate choices?

As though I have the right to judge them. Me, with my own bad choices.

Her thoughts drifted back and back and back. To Lord Brun. To that night, when he had summoned her to his rooms to take a letter for the couriers. How his glance had fallen upon her, nearly sliding away as it might slide over a passing dog or a chair. How that glance caught and held. His eyes had darkened, his expression changing from remote to intent and warm. How he had plucked the letter from her hands and let it drop to the floor before his fingers caressed her cheek. How her stomach had twisted into a knot and it had taken all her self-control not to struggle.

Back and back, to her father, the memory of his face already blurred by the years. Of her mother, none at all.

Outside, another bell, a whistle, another series of call to call to call from the guards.

CHAPTER 8

The dream began as an ordinary nightmare. She and Maté were aboard Koszenmarc's ship once more, fleeing Vyros and the Imperial Navy. But this time, their pursuers overtook them. This time, Maszny and hundreds of his followers swarmed aboard. Just as Anna turned to face her enemy, the nightmare vanished...

She stood on the deck of the double-hulled boat, braced against the swell. For ten days, the wind had failed them, and they pulled oars in shifts, from captain down to the youngest boys and girls. Now storm clouds bubbled on the horizon; the seas had turned dark, flecked with foam and ice, and the salt-stung air cut through her jacket. They'd come so far, had not lost a single ship, but their stores had sunk to almost nothing. Over the roar of the seas, she heard the chant of the crew, calling out to the gods, to Lir and Blind Toc, to bring them safe to shore.

Her beloved wrapped an arm around her waist. He murmured the invocation to magic and the gods, and a pale yellow light rose into the air to light their way.

* * * *

Anna woke to the dawn's grey light and the sensation of rocking to and fro.

Her first thought was that she was back on the ship, locked in that dreadful cabin with no light except her magic, no air but what leaked through the ship's sides. But then memory blinked and stuttered to life. The whisper of the ship's passage became the crash of surf on the shore. The motion she felt was her hammock swinging in response to her own restless sleep.

I am alive.

That first burst of relief vanished in her next thought.

Until tomorrow. Oh. Oh gods.

She rolled over and tucked herself into a ball. She and Maté both were doomed. She wanted to curse Lord Brun for his ambition. Or herself for daring to dream of freedom.

You have two choices when you face an opponent, her father once said. *You can refuse to engage them in debate. Or you can fight them with all the logic and reason and passion you possess. Neither choice is automatically correct. Neither is automatically safe.*

Safe or not, death was a powerful motivation to do *something.*

So get up and think, Anna.

Anna levered herself from the hammock. Most of the cave lay in shadows, with only a faint grey light from the grotto's entrance. She found the candle she had left by her hammock, but it had melted into a shapeless lump, with not even enough wick left for her to light it by magic. Just as well. Magic would only attract attention, and she wasn't ready for that yet.

She groped her way to the trunk with its provisions. One flask of water remained. She rinsed her mouth and swallowed. Her bones still ached from that long rattling gallop over the mountain, the even longer hours spent in that tiny cabin while the ship sped away from Vyros and the Imperial ships.

A breeze sifted into the grotto, stirring up the thick air and cleansing away the scents of smoke and tallow. The sky outside had brightened, and a pale grey light spilled over the threshold. Anna crossed to the entrance and drank in the fresh cool air of dawn.

All was still. All was quiet except for the endless surf. Above the stars had faded, each one blinking out as night retreated, but a scattering remained. This far south, she recognized none of the constellations except Lir's Necklace, a string of bright points directly overhead that arced from the northeast. All the rest, the Crone, the Hunter, had shifted north and north since her long journey south from Duenne, until they had vanished altogether.

A ripple broke the shadows off to her right. Anna flicked her gaze to the right, then the left. Just as she expected, she caught a glimpse of light reflected off metal, the familiar gesture of a hand reaching for its weapon.

Guards. One on either side. Both alert and watching.

That decided her.

Anna cleared her throat. "I want an interview with your captain," she announced. "I want Maté Kovács brought to that interview as well. Send word to your captain and tell him we must talk. Now."

Both shadows jerked to attention, but neither spoke. She waited.

"He won't like your tricks," a woman off to her right said at last.

Anna huffed. "In case you had not noticed, I have no tricks. If I did, I'd be a hundred miles away from this gods-be-damned island."

"A hundred miles would drop you in the open seas, or nearabout," the other guard murmured. Her voice was low and amused. "But I see your point." She gave a sharp whistle. Moments later a girl swung down the rope ladder and dropped onto the ledge. "Tell our captain our Lady Vrou wants a talk with him," the guard told her. "Oh, and she says to bring the other one too."

The girl sent a curious glance in Anna's direction. It was hard to tell in the dim light, but she looked about fourteen or so, long-limbed and sturdy, with springy dark hair braided close to her skull and a sprinkling of freckles over her pale brown face. She said something in the island language to the guard, then sprang up on the ladder and was out of sight.

Anna expelled a breath. Step one of a very long march.

The guard who had whistled for the girl shook her head. "He might refuse you, you know."

"I know," Anna said.

Abruptly, she stalked back into her prison. She could not bear to look in their eyes and see pity. Pity might undo her.

The days aboard the ship, the restless night in the grotto, had left her red-eyed and grimy. Anna scrubbed her face and hands with her precious store of water. She worked her fingers through the worst of the knots in her hair and rediscovered the ribbons and jewels set there by her maids, only a few days and a hundred years ago. She pocketed the jewels—they might make useful bribes—then gathered her hair in a loose plait. She had just finished when a thump sounded outside the entrance.

"Lady Vrou," one of the guards called. "You've got your wish. The captain says he has a few moments to spare."

Yes. Anna forced herself to take a breath, pass a hand over her impossible hair. Then she crossed over to the grotto's exit. "Thank you. Will you show me the way, please?"

One guard snorted. The other shook her head, but with a faint smile. "Follow me."

They brought her around a fold in the mountain to a rope ladder. Anna tried not to glance down. It had been far easier the night before, when darkness hid the shore below, the waves crashing and seething among the rocks.

"Up you go," the first guard said. She swung around Anna and clambered up a few feet. The other guard prodded her gently until Anna mounted the ladder. She found it easier to stare directly at the cliff face, moving her gaze only a few inches when she reached for the next handhold.

Heights. It joined ships and oceans as another thing to avoid. She had a list of those by now. She ticked through them—doors without locks, a man's unrelenting gaze that reduced her from a person to a thing, the argument that security was worth the price of freedom—and really, when you considered the whole dispassionately, the heights and the ocean were the least objectionable of them all. Before she realized it, they had climbed yards and yards past the landing from the previous night. Beyond that came a blank stone wall that stretched up at least a hundred more feet. By the time they reached their destination at the island's peak, Anna was short of breath and the ability to fear.

The guard in the lead held out a hand to Anna. "Step quick and you won't notice the drop."

"I am quite sure I would," Anna muttered, but she did not refuse the help. The other woman hauled Anna up and onto the ledge, next to a round entryway dug into the rock.

"One hand for the ship, one for yourself," her guard said. "Catch hold here. Steady now. The wind is sommat fierce today. Go through there, my brave. Captain is waiting for you on t'other side."

Anna ducked into the passageway. Her heart beat hard and fast from the long climb, and the sudden relief from the wind left her breathless. She needed a moment to recover her composure. But this was only a momentary respite. She sensed the presence of both guards behind her, watching and waiting. And Koszenmarc, ahead.

Courage, said a voice very much like Maté's.

She expelled a breath and went on.

The passageway was short and ended in a square doorway. Several steps led down to an open, airy room, with two great windows facing south and east. Lamps hung from hooks set into the walls, their light fading with the rising sun, and overhead the ceiling arced and twisted to a narrow cleft, almost like a chimney. She noticed more cracks and fissures around the edge of the floor. The air was filled with the scent of salt tang, and a faint whispering drifted up from below.

What caught her attention, however, were the books—hundreds of them, set upon shelves carved into the rock. Great thick volumes with leather spines and metal hinges. Scrolls in leather tubes, arranged in ironwork racks. Rows and rows of smaller books, some of them little more than a few dozen pages, bound in thick paper. More books were stacked neatly to either side of a flat rock that reminded her of a nobleman's grand desk, and behind the desk itself hung several enormous maps. Most were of the islands—detailed charts marked with shoals and depths and currents—but one showed the sprawling continent to the north, each nation named and the borders marked, from the Empire, which occupied the entire center of the mainland, to the various smaller ones in the north and west.

Off to one side was a smaller map, obviously older, showing the duchy of Valentain.

She recalled Maté's original report about Koszenmarc—that he was the second son of Valentain's duke. How his father had disowned him after he abruptly left Court.

And yet, he has not entirely forgotten his family.

Koszenmarc himself stood next to the desk. He was dressed simply, in loose trousers and a plain white shirt, the trousers tied with a blue sash, and his cropped hair was slicked back with water, but she was pleased to note that he too had the look of someone who had slept badly and not long enough.

He indicated a low table, surrounded by cushions, in the center of the room. "Please, sit. You've reconsidered your decision, they tell me."

No sign of Maté. No acknowledgment of her request for his presence. Very well.

She sat. A few plates of flatbread and a bowl of yellow fruit, cut into squares, occupied the center of the table. There was also a jug of coffee, blessed coffee. Koszenmarc poured out two mugs. He set one in front of Anna, then took a seat opposite her. His expression was impossible to read.

Anna drank her coffee as slowly as she could. Her thoughts cleared with every sip, even if her nerves still buzzed with anxiety. When Koszenmarc offered to fill her mug again, she waved him away with as much nonchalance as she could muster. Her role was no longer that of Lady Vrou Iljana, daughter of Barône Klos. She would be a thief, a smuggler, someone who dared to make demands of a pirate and live.

"I have reconsidered," she said. "But I want better terms."

Koszenmarc nodded, but said nothing. He wanted to hear more.

"First, I want you to release Maté."

"No."

She smacked the table with the flat of her hand. "He cannot help you, *Captain*. He knows nothing about Gerhart. Nothing about magic—"

"And I refuse to negotiate. Do you have other terms?"

Anna let her breath trickle out. She had not expected him to agree, certainly not right away, but there was an edge of barely contained anger in the man's voice. No, not anger. Contempt. Ah, strangely enough, that she could deal with.

She met his blank expression with one of her own. "I do. Once we find the man and the object he carries, I want a share of the money your client promised—one third, delivered the same week Gerhart is taken, plus safe passage to the mainland for me and my friend. Note, please, I shall have to trust your word about the amount."

His expression eased somewhat. "A fair request. Agreed."

She eyed him with obvious doubt. The man had said yes far too easily.

Koszenmarc tilted his hand to one side, as if to dismiss her doubt with a gesture. "Do you have any other terms to negotiate? Other than the release of your friend, of course."

She still did not trust this easy victory, even if the victory was hedged and barred by all manner of difficulties. This man—this noble—might decide her cooperation was worth a lie or two. Once he discovered exactly what the *stolen goods* were, he might decide to discard her as easily as Lord Brun would. And far more permanently.

He watched her steadily with those pale eyes. "You have no reason to trust me," he said. "But if it makes a difference, I swear on my name that I will honor my promise to you and your friend."

All trace of contempt had vanished from his voice. *A noble's promise,* she thought bitterly. Her own experience with the class told her to distrust anything they said. But she had the strong impression this particular noble told the truth. As if he had lost and regained his honor at a high price and would not risk it again.

"I…I have no other requests."

"Good." That strange intensity ebbed and he was once more the pirate captain bargaining with a potential ally. "Then let us bring my officers and your friend to this discussion."

Koszenmarc gave a sharp whistle. At once a girl appeared—the same one as before. "Pass the word for my officers," he said. "Send for our other guest, and have the kitchen send up coffee and tea."

After that, he seemed to forget Anna's presence entirely, because he returned to his desk, where he sorted through various papers. Anna watched as he picked up one, glanced at it briefly, then compared its contents with one of the maps. The impression came back to her, stronger than before, of a nobleman occupied with the affairs of his estate.

What had driven him away from Court and Valentain to come here? She remembered that flare of temper when he had first taken her prisoner and she asked if his father was proud of him. Had he left Court because of his father? Or had the trouble been Duenne's Court, that poisonous collection of enemies who called themselves friends? She had heard enough about the Court from her own father that she could believe it.

One by one, the senior officers arrived. Koszenmarc introduced them. Old Hahn, a rangy, elderly man, with grizzled braids and keen eyes. Joszua, who greeted Anna cheerfully. A woman named Daria Ioannou, who bore a writing kit as well as several knives in a belt slung over one shoulder. Last of all came Eleni Farakos, followed by her son Nikolas. Nikolas set a basket packed with more mugs and more stoppered jugs on the table. He left at once, but not without a long curious stare at Anna.

Eleni sent a glance in her direction. "You wanted Kovács here?" she said to Koszenmarc. "Is that wise?"

He shrugged. "Our friend here has offered her services. I want to make sure he agrees with her conditions."

Eleni muttered something in the island language. Hahn choked down a laugh. Anna kept her expression carefully bland, but vowed she would learn the Kybris language as soon as possible.

Mugs were handed out, coffee and tea poured, and several of the officers helped themselves to the fruit and flatbread. None of them acknowledged Anna. She poured herself a second mug of coffee and pretended to herself that this was another ordinary day for an ordinary thief. Very soon, she would have to find a moment with Maté so they could arrange their stories.

Not long after, Maté himself arrived. Or rather, two guards dragged him through the passageway and dumped him onto the floor. Maté staggered to his feet. His clothes were rumpled, his hair was spiked with sweat, and a fresh cut over his forehead bled sluggishly.

Anna rounded on Koszenmarc. "What have you done to him?"

He raised both hands, palms out. "Nothing. I promise. He's a clumsy man, your friend."

Eleni muttered something about *enormous feet*. Maté snarled, but the two guards seized him by the arms again. He swung his gaze to Anna, still snarling. For a moment, she didn't recognize him, this bloodied and furious dog of a soldier, and she flinched away.

But only for a moment. Maté gave a sigh and the rage visibly leaked out of him. "I won't make trouble."

"Good," Koszenmarc said mildly. "Because you would not make trouble for very long." He pointed to the remaining seat at the table. "Sit. Your friend has agreed to my demands, and I have agreed to hers, or most of them. I want your reassurance that you will hold to our bargain."

"Which is?"

"You and she will join my company—temporarily—to search for our thief and the stolen object he carries. In return, you two will get one third the sum I expect to receive from my own client, plus safe passage back to the mainland."

Maté nodded slowly. "I can agree to that."

He had not offered a single glance to Anna since that first snarling glare. Anna wanted to believe he played the same game as her, that they were two thieves easily bought into service, but it was so strange to see him this way.

She covered her confusion by filling a small plate with a helping of the yellow fruit. It was sweet and sticky, with a tart edge to its flavor. Her hands were shaking—from hunger and weariness, she told herself.

Koszenmarc watched her with an expression she could not quite decipher. Not quite the contempt from earlier, but something far more unsettling. "Very well," he said. "Now that we understand each other, let me tell you what we already know. Three weeks ago, a man who called himself Hêr Lord Gerhart Toth arrived on Vyros with a great many debts, which he increased further by visits to the moneylenders."

We knew that, Anna thought. What puzzled her was how Koszenmarc had come to suspect Sarrész as well.

Her expression must have betrayed her thoughts, because Koszenmarc smiled briefly. "Lord Gerhart has attracted attention from many quarters, yes. Even so, debts are nothing remarkable for a nobleman, certainly not here in Eddalyon. But within a day, he sent out word that he had an extremely valuable item for sale. That is what brought him to the notice of a woman named Isana Druss. And what interests Druss, interests me."

Druss. Anna could not suppress a start at the name. Druss was the name she'd overheard Koszenmarc discuss with his officers, the first time he'd taken her prisoner. The one whom Maszny suspected of murdering the boy Giannis.

Koszenmarc had not missed that reaction, damn him. "You know her?" he said.

"I've heard the name before," she admitted.

"Then you know she runs a gang of pirates. She showed up in Eddalyon twenty years ago with a handful of denariie, a dagger, and an attitude. A month after she joined a mercenary crew, she murdered the captain and convinced the crew to swear allegiance to her. Druss...Druss has made a career of murder, robbing ships, trafficking in stolen goods, whatever makes a profit. Without any checks, she and her crew might soon call themselves the true kings and queens of Eddalyon."

Anna shivered, remembering the sight of Giannis's body and the pool of blood. Killed because his path had crossed Druss's.

Now Koszenmarc was studying her closely. "I see you *have* heard the name," he said. "To continue... Three days before you and your friends arrived on Iglazi, Lord Gerhart left on an expedition with twelve hired guards. He never returned. Curiously enough, you took rooms at the same inn where he did, and you went on a very similar expedition."

Anna suppressed a start at how precisely he'd tracked her movements, and forced herself to meet his gaze directly. "You and I both did, my lord."

His eyes narrowed. "That we did. So. I've shared what I know—at least in part. Time for you to answer a few questions. We know you are not Barône Klos's daughter. Who are you?"

Anna had expected that question. "Call me Elise. Elise Fischer."

Now he smirked. "A fisher of lies."

"Of course, it's a lie," she said sharply. "But if we're talking about *the truth*, my lord, you've told a few lies yourself. Unless you expect me to believe the second son of Duke Vitus Koszenmarc had a good reason to take up piracy."

Silence dropped over the room. Daria and Old Hahn went still. Eleni curled her fingers around the hilt of her knife. Maté bowed his head, as though praying to the gods to deliver him from such fools and allies.

Koszenmarc, however, gazed at her with that same expression of... curiosity? A look far different from his earlier contempt, at least. "Elise it is," he said. He turned to Maté. "And what about you? Do you wish to use a different name, Kovács?"

By now, Maté had helped himself to coffee and bread, and though he was still bloodied, he no longer resembled an angry dog. "Kovács will do. I've used the name thirty years at least. It fits me now."

Koszenmarc's lips twitched. "Understood. But I've shared a few secrets with you both. It's your turn. Tell me what *you* know about the man who called himself Lord Gerhart Toth."

Anna let her breath trickle out. Now came the delicate task of admitting enough to win the man's trust without giving away the whole of Lord Brun's secrets.

"His name is Aldo Sarrész," she said. "Six months ago, he stole a valuable object from our client. My two partners and I tracked Sarrész from Duenne to Vyros, where we discovered he had vanished once again. However, we had word that he took a company of guards and set off for the ruins of an ancient temple. We followed his trail from the temple to the shore. We had just discovered an important clue when you and your people interrupted us."

Koszenmarc nodded, as though he compared her account with other details he already knew. *And which he did not tell us,* she thought. Fair enough. They were both dancing a cautious dance.

"What clue did you find?" he asked.

"A very strange one," she said. She described the scene of the ambush, the confusion of footprints at the edge of the forest. "We know he survived the attack. His footprints clearly showed him running toward the shore. They vanished before the waterline—"

"Then the tide washed them clear," Hahn said.

"No," Maté said. "It was a spring tide that day."

There was a moment of silence at his words. Not disbelief, Anna thought. More like dismay.

"Sarrész vanished," she said. "Exactly that. And no, I cannot explain how or why. I can only say I found traces of very strong, very complex magic. A specific kind of magic that suggests he made what the scholars call a leap into Anderswar—"

"The void between lives?" Koszenmarc asked. "Is he dead, then?"

"I don't know. I believe not. There are texts that describe how one might transport oneself to the magical plane and return to this world—or even another. It's possible Sarrész acquired such a spell before he arrived on Vyros."

"Interesting," he said. "The object belongs to your client?"

Anna hesitated. The urge to glance toward Maté was strong, but she knew that would be a mistake. "It does not," she said. "He's acting as an agent for the true owner. More I cannot tell you."

Again he nodded, as though her words had confirmed other details on that unknown list. "Your client won't be pleased if you simply hand over that object. But perhaps my client will make arrangements with yours."

Perhaps. Or perhaps Lord Brun would simply point the Emperor's people to this other client.

But Koszenmarc had continued to speak—something about the spell Sarrész might have used. "What else do you know about it?" he asked.

No time to wonder about Lord Brun and her possible future after Eddalyon. First, she had to ensure she had a future at all. "I had so little time to examine it that day." She added in a drier tone, "As I mentioned, we were interrupted."

That provoked a laugh from two of the officers, and another brief smile from Koszenmarc. "So you were. Then our first task is to return to that inlet so you might continue that examination. Hahn, Daria, we'll take the

Mathilde. Kovács, you come along as well. We might find a few extra clues at the site of the ambush."

"What about that temple?" Daria said.

"Too dangerous," Hahn said. "Druss might've set spies."

"More likely, the commander has," Koszenmarc replied. "He was none too happy with our last adventure. But you have a point," he said to Daria. "If we don't find anything useful, we'll return later and investigate those ruins. But for now... Daria, Hahn, report back with any shortfalls in supplies for the *Mathilde.* We might need to stop to take on more water along the way, but I want to sail with the noon tide. Eleni, our new friends will need temporary quarters until then. We can decide later where they bunk."

The officers dispersed to carry out their orders. Eleni took her charges back through the passageway to the rope ladder. "You might as well spend the morning together," she said. "Elise's quarters from last night will do. You'll be out of the way there."

Where they could not make trouble. But she noted that Eleni did not call for any guards to accompany them as they descended the ladder, nor were there any guards waiting by the entrance to the grotto. A sign of trust? Or they simply realized Anna could not deliver herself with a word of magic.

"I'll have the kitchens send up a proper meal," Eleni told them once they reached their destination. "And a set of clean slops for you." She eyed Maté doubtfully. "Let us hope you earn your keep."

"I hope so too," Maté said. "But then, I'm a hopeful soul."

Eleni gave a huff of laughter. "Are you now? Is that why you took a new name, when you were all of twelve or so?"

"More like fifteen," he said mildly. "It seemed like a good idea at the time."

Eleni drew a quick breath. Taken aback, Anna thought, as though Maté had touched a raw memory with those words. But all she said was, "Yes, I know how that is." Another pause. "I'll send word when you're wanted."

Anna waited until the other woman had left, then released a long breath. "She reminds me of a dangerous wildcat."

"Eh, she's a pirate. Soft and gentle pirates do not survive." Maté glanced around the grotto. "Very nice. Almost luxurious, compared to the dank dark pit where I spent my night. Every time I stood up too fast, I cracked my head against a rock." He ran his fingers over his scalp and winced. "Could be worse."

His knuckles were bruised and scraped, which made her frown. "You *were* fighting."

"A bit. I don't like dark, cramped holes. Reminds me too much of... Never mind that. Anna, we need to talk."

Even though Eleni hadn't posted guards, Anna didn't want to take any chances. She motioned for Maté to follow her to the back of the chamber. The air was still here, except for a faint breeze with the familiar scent of cold ashes. "One moment," she murmured.

Ei rûf ane gôtter. Komen mir de strôm. Lâzen mir sihen ob anderes uns hoeren...

The sharp green scent of magic sparked in the air. Oh so faint, as faint as she could manage it. A breeze curled around them, making the spiderwebs flutter, and washing away the scent of ashes. Anna carefully tested all about them for any spells laid upon this chamber, or upon Maté himself. It would be like Koszenmarc to leave them alone so he might eavesdrop on their secrets—she would have done the same—but she sensed nothing.

She recited the spells to erase her magic, then released the magic current. "No listening spells," she whispered.

"Good. Now explain what madness you've agreed to, Anna Zhdanov." She smiled pensively. "I tried to convince Koszenmarc to release you. He refused."

"Of course. Always keep a hostage."

"You say that as though it's reasonable," she replied tartly. "Oh, very well. I suppose from a pirate's point of view, it is reasonable. But, Maté, he did agree to the rest of my demands—and I asked a great deal. One third of whatever sum he expects for delivering Sarrész and the jewel. Safe passage for us both to the mainland. And we leave as soon as we capture Sarrész—he promised."

Maté looked thoughtful. "I don't trust him. He agreed too easily, and he gave up too much. Even if Koszenmarc does keep his promise, *Lord Brun* won't be happy. He's a man who likes his secrets to remain secrets."

"Then I was wrong?"

"Of course not. You had no other choice. But he's played a clever game, this Lord and Captain Koszenmarc. He takes you hostage. When you dive off his ship, he doesn't give chase. He leaves notes in your bedroom, ambushes you in the street, then rescues you at the last moment. He plays rough then gentle, like a cat with a mouse, so you don't know what to expect."

Anna blew out a breath. "I know. What happens when he decides he's hungry?"

"We don't wait for that. We work for this man, gain his trust. And at the first chance, we escape."

CHAPTER 9

Not long after, their promised meal arrived, along with two water casks and a fresh set of clothes, obviously drawn from spare stores. The shirt and trousers were patched and threadbare, but clean. Once he washed his face, Maté no longer appeared so battered, and with a plentiful breakfast and more coffee inside her, Anna no longer felt quite so desperate. By the time Joszua came to fetch them, she thought she and Maté might survive this gamble.

Down by the harbor, the crew swarmed between the ship *Mathilde* and the shore, while a number of children ran errands. Anna sighted Nikolas and another boy carrying a trunk, followed by an older woman with thick grey hair tied back in a careless fashion. When Nikolas and his companion handed the trunk over to one of the sailors, Nikolas turned and saw Anna. He waved and grinned.

"Are you coming with us?" Anna asked.

At once the laughter vanished from his face. "No. I'm never going to Vyros. Never again."

"But you were there—"

"I made a mistake," Nikolas said flatly.

The other boy laid a hand on Nikolas's shoulder and murmured something in Kybris. Nikolas leaned his forehead against his companion a moment. "It was a mistake," he said softly. "You know that, Theo."

"I know," Theo said. "Come on. Captain wants to weigh anchor before the tide runs out, and we have more to do."

A shout came from the direction of the cliffs. Both boys immediately darted away, Nikolas sending a brief apologetic smile to Anna.

"I wonder what that meant?" Anna said, half to herself.

Then she spotted Eleni Farakos off to one side. Eleni was staring after her son, for a moment appearing as nothing more than a worried mother, intent upon her child. But then her attention veered to Anna and Maté, her eyes narrowed in a gaze of unnerving intensity.

* * * *

A day and night later, Anna stood on the sands of Vyros once more. The *Mathilde* under Hahn's command was rapidly disappearing around the bend of the coast. The sun hung low above the horizon, a blurred red disc against the morning sky. Rags and scraps of clouds raced overhead, but the air felt close and charged, and the crew unloading the boats muttered to each other about the approaching storm.

There was a different kind of storm brewing, Anna thought. Several times during the brief passage, she'd noticed Koszenmarc studying her from a distance. If she had to put a name to his expression, it would have been…dissatisfied. Though she couldn't tell if that disappointment was aimed at her, or their expedition. She'd wanted to ask Maté if he had noticed anything amiss, but she could never find a moment that was truly private.

"Elise!"

Daria Ioannou and Andreas Koszenmarc stood off to one side, near the edge of the jungle. Maté was there as well, his hands clasped behind his back in what Anna knew to be his soldier's resting stance. Next to him stood the same older woman she had seen with Nikolas back at the island stronghold—a short wisp of a woman, whose grey hair was barely contained by a ribbon. Her dark face was lined and weathered, as though she spent all her days under the sun. Though she was dressed in the same loose-fitting shirt and trousers as the others, Anna had the immediate impression that she was not a sailor.

"I want you to make a thorough sweep," Koszenmarc was telling Maté. "We're fairly certain it was Druss and her crew who ambushed Sarrész, but we want any evidence you can find, no matter how insignificant you think it."

"As you say, Captain." Maté's face had taken on that bland expression that said yes, he knew how to conduct a search, thank you and dammit, but he also knew better than to contradict a commander.

Koszenmarc must have heard a part of that unspoken reply, because his mouth quirked in a wry smile. "Naturally, I leave the details to you, Kovács. I'll pass the word to the perimeter guard not to interfere unless necessary."

A not-so-very-subtle hint, which Maté took with a sour smile, but he dutifully saluted Koszenmarc and set off to carry out his part of the investigation. Koszenmarc watched him a moment, then turned back to Anna. All the humor dropped away from his face and he regarded her with a carefully blank expression.

"So, *Elise Fischer*, now for your part. I'll give you the same promise I did Kovács—no interference unless you make it necessary. In your case, however, I want Thea here to observe whatever magic you use."

Thea smiled at Anna. "Hello, Elise. My name is Thea Antonious. We've met, though I doubt you remember me."

Ah, yes. Koszenmarc's mage who had tended her after the kidnapping. The *first* kidnapping.

"Oh, but I do," she said softly. "Thank you for taking care of my headache."

And spelling the ropes against magic. And telling this gods-be-damned Koszenmarc to take precautions.

Thea's lips tucked into a smile, as though she'd heard those unspoken thoughts. "You're very welcome."

Koszenmarc stared at them both, then shook his head and stalked off toward the men who were dragging the boats over the sands.

Thea appeared amused. "He's overcomplicated the matter, as usual. I simply wanted to observe how you scried the past."

"And," Daria added, "while Thea watches you, I shall watch over her."

"You have no need to glare, my love," Thea murmured. To Anna, she said, "You look much improved from when I first saw you."

Anna pretended a smile. However friendly Thea appeared, it would not do to underestimate her.

She turned away to scan the shore. Rains had smoothed out the sands, unfortunately, and the pirates' landing had churned them up again. A glance back toward the trees showed the point where the goat track broke the expanse of greenery. Sarrész had run directly toward the ocean, a man driven by terror. He had stopped once to look over his shoulder. She remembered the evidence from her last exploration. Then he had sprinted hard for the seas, only to disappear before he reached them.

Her attention wholly upon the shore and that past day, she lost sight of Thea Antonious and the rest of Koszenmarc's people. She went straight to the goat track, dimly recorded the sight of Maté within the forest, picking over the track itself and the surrounding area. She turned back toward the blindingly bright shore. Straight ahead, yes. She walked halfway to the waterline and murmured a prayer to the gods.

Ei rûf ane gôtter. Komen mir de strôm. Lâzen mir älliu sihen. Lâzen mir älliu hoeren.

It was as though a hand had reached out and stilled the world around her. Then, the crash and gurgle from the surf doubled, just as before. The same birds wheeled past. She saw herself standing a few feet away—she had misjudged the path of his flight after all—and the ghostly figure of Sarrész pelting madly toward the water.

Faster and faster he ran. Blurred. Blinked.

Was gone.

The fault, the gap in memory and sight, was not hers, but in the vision. Her own eyes were dry and burning with the effort. She blinked at last, but Sarrész did not reappear.

Show me, she demanded. *Show me where and when and how. Show me who.*

Wisps of the magical current drifted around her, so faint she thought she imagined them, except for the unmistakable tang, like new grass crushed underfoot, like the tang of pine trees in the hills north of Duenne.

She let these thoughts drop away until she had left behind any sense of the physical world, and her magical self drifted with the current. The current shuddered and swirled, stronger than before, but with no trace of her quarry. No trace of that otherworldly signature.

Show me, she demanded again.

The answer, at first, was so faint she thought she imagined it. Just a hint of that signature. When she focused upon it, however, she realized the signature was far stronger than it had any right to be. Nine, ten days old, but still discernable. It occurred to her that Maszny would recognize its importance.

He knew about Sarrész. He knew about the temple.

But he had not guessed how Druss had lured Sarrész to this lonely shore.

She fell to her knees in the water. The current rushed past her, the sands streaming like time. Daria caught her by one arm and pulled her upright. "What in the names of all the gods are you doing?"

Anna needed a moment to shift from *then* to *now.* "Examining the evidence." Her throat was parched. Her tongue felt thick and clumsy in her mouth.

"*What* evidence?"

"His..." How to explain?

"She is tracking him, just as Kovács tracks the footprints in the forest." That was Thea. "Let her go, Daria."

Anna wrenched herself free and stumbled forward into the surf. There, there it was. The traces of magic much stronger than before, as though the magic spell that enveloped Sarrész had saturated the waters, like dye running in all directions.

A voice was calling to her—not with anything so plain as words. No, this voice spoke in deep chords that reverberated through her bones. Anna heard the faraway murmur of voices, felt warmth and wet envelop her, a curse, then hands gripping her arms, but even those glimpses of the physical world faded as the chords bore her upward, and her body dropped away just as the dried husk drops away from the seed. A small part of herself cried out a warning about this dangerous magic, which she had never attempted before, but it was difficult to attend when all around the music sang in that otherworldly chorus and her senses drowned in strange scents and textures and flavors, as though her body struggled to interpret what it could not.

Who are you?

Words. Plain words. The voice unknown. The language unrecognizable, but even so Anna understood.

I'm looking for a man, *she answered.* His name is Aldo Sarrész.

No words this time, but the unmistakable sense of confusion. She fell back to imagining Sarrész's face, as she remembered it from the sketches Brun showed her and the few times she'd glimpsed the man himself. One image in particular had imprinted itself upon her mind—a man of middle years, with full lips quirked into a smile so disarming, she found it difficult to believe what Brun had told her about him. That he had carelessly and thoroughly seduced a priest in the employ of the Emperor's chief mages, had persuaded him to produce a priceless, magical jewel, had poisoned him before stealing away into the night.

Yes, him, *the voice said.* I can show you. Come with me.

Anna blinked. Her surroundings had changed. She stood on the edge of a precipice, while overhead bright pinpoints of light streamed. Behind her lay the world she knew, with sunlight and sands and the endless ocean surrounding Eddalyon. Ahead was a void, its tides and currents that of magic and not the salt seas. Anderswar, in the old language of the Empire, the void between worlds, where the souls of the dead made their passage from one life to the next.

And there, so faint she thought she imagined it, was a trace of Aldo Sarrész's magical signature, intertwined with another she recognized. Not-Sarrész. Elusive and graceful, like sunlight winging through a velvet darkness.

The same signature as now surrounded her.

Look, *said the voice.*

Now her vision reversed itself. The magical void lay behind her. She knelt upon the edge of the ordinary world and saw the dark blue of oceans, adorned by the glitter of islands. Not just any alien world, not just any islands. She recognized the pattern and number as though she gazed upon the maps in her father's library, or those in Koszenmarc's island stronghold. Eddalyon, arcing north to south over the southern seas like a string of pearls. And there, a dozen luminous footprints, running in a straight line from one world to the next.

Yes. Sarrész. He had come this way.

You came almost too late, *the voice said.* I set a fragment of myself here, to watch and to guard. But even I cannot withstand time's erosion.

Anna turned to see an eddy of darkness, as though the voice acquired substance enough to create its own shadow.

Who are you? *she said.*

She thought she heard the voice reply, Ishya.

CHAPTER 10

Anna dropped back into the ordinary world, into a driving rain and high swells. She was in the *Mathilde*'s launch, lying on her back, a folded square of tarp under her head. Dark clouds raced overhead, driven by high winds across a murky sky. When the boat plunged into a trough between waves, water broke over the prow, and for a terrible moment, Anna was certain she would drown. In a panic, she struggled to sit up.

A pair of strong hands lifted her clear of the water. It was Koszenmarc, his hair plastered over his skull, his face barely visible in the uncertain light. "Row harder!" he shouted to the crew. "Paulos, Karl, start bailing!" Then to Anna, "Stop fighting me. You'll overset us."

He paused only long enough to make certain she was sitting, then took up his paddle and joined in the rowing. Anna wanted to ask what had happened while she had lost herself to magic's thrall, but her stomach heaved up against her ribs. She raced through the invocation to magic—just in time. When the boat jerked over the next swell, she grabbed the side of the boat.

"Steady," Koszenmarc said. "Nearly there."

The boat rode over the next gigantic swell and came up beside the *Mathilde*. The launch swung around and pitched to one side as Koszenmarc stood and seized a rope ladder. "Send down a rig," he shouted, as several of the crew scrambled up and aboard the ship. "Hurry!"

A mass of ropes connected to a square of canvas came tumbling over the side. Koszenmarc untangled them and bundled Anna into the chair. "Hold steady," he said. "The enemy's in sight, but they haven't caught us yet."

The fog of magic cleared, and she gripped the chair's ropes in sudden terror. "Maszny?"

"Never mind who." Koszenmarc whistled sharply, and the chair jerked upward.

Old Hahn waited by the railing and hauled Anna over the side. In the storm's strange, flickering light, his face looked older and grimmer than ever. Then his gaze jerked up and he stared intently at some point in the distance. Anna turned to see the ocean veiled in foam, the horizon little more than smudges of black and grey. And there, driving toward them, the pale red sails of another ship. Then a second and a third materialized from the gloom.

Daria seized her by the arm. "Get below," she roared. "Now!"

She spun Anna around toward the nearest hatch. Anna scrambled down the ladder as fast as she could, past the region occupied by the officers, down to the deck where the sailors slung their hammocks, where she landed in a wobbly heap.

From far overhead came the echo of many feet pounding over the deck. The ship gave a twitch, like a nervous horse, before it went racing forward, the waves hissing on either side. Anna's stomach lurched against her ribs, and she clamped her lips together.

Once, twice more, the ship jerked. Once, twice more, Anna swallowed hard. Dimly she became aware that the berth was empty of any sailors. The faint grey light from above had vanished with the last crack of thunder. The darkness in the berth was thick and heavy, as if day had been dipped into night. Panic washed over her, and she cried out a summons to the magic current.

Ei rûf ane gôtter. Ei rûf ane strôm. Komen mir de leiht...

A pale white globe coalesced in the air. Anna cupped her hands around the light and brought it close, breathing in the sharp, strong scent of magic. Whatever came next, capture or death or the unimaginable, at least she had a light in the darkness.

A clattering—someone hurrying down the ladder—roused her. "Anna. Elise?"

"Maté!" Anna gave a cry of relief. She had not known how much she feared that Koszenmarc had left him behind for Maszny's soldiers. "Where have you been?"

Maté swung off the ladder, only to stumble and collapse onto the deck. In a moment, Anna knelt beside him, her magical light hovering above them. Dark wet blotches stained his shirt.

"You idiot," she whispered fiercely. "What happened? Did you think you could take on the world by yourself?"

He gave a breathless laugh. "Hardly. Here, help me. Let's see the damage. The left arm."

Anna slung his arm around her shoulders and helped him onto a coil of ropes. He immediately collapsed, breathing in gulps. Oh, she was no surgeon, but surely that wasn't a good sign. Her hands shaking, she undid the ties of his shirt and tugged his left arm free. Then she summoned her magical light to hover over them while she examined the wound. Something had left a deep furrow on his upper arm. It bled freely, which was good. She thought. Maybe. But his eyes were too bright, his skin felt hot to her touch, and if that weren't convincing enough, he was slick with a fever sweat.

"Not good, not bad," she murmured. "Tell me what happened."

"Arrow," he breathed. "I stopped to help carry a few wounded below."

"They didn't bother to send *you* to the surgeon?"

"They did. Wanted to find you first," he said, as easily as though they'd merely lost sight of one another in the marketplace. Then in a softer voice, he said, "Our cat was nearly trapped by an even bigger cat."

"Maszny?" she whispered.

"No, Isana Druss."

Thunder cracked the air. Anna flinched, then stumbled as the ship lurched to one side. Her grip upon magic faltered and the light vanished. She was about to recall it when Thea's voice distinctly said, "No, no. We can't have that. We're running dark, my friends. Captain's orders."

A thump sounded next to Anna as the other woman landed in the hold. Then there came a second, softer thump, and the faintest clink of glass against glass. Thea set a shaded lantern on a nearby shelf and directed its narrow beam onto Maté's face. "Daria sent you below for good reason," she said. "Never mind how easy a wound festers. Druss and her people are using poison on their arrows."

Anna choked back a cry of horror. "But that's—"

"That is Isana Druss," Thea said. "What did you think? That we're playing a harmless game of hide-and-seek?"

"Of course not! Can you save him?"

There was the barest hesitation before Thea replied. "Yes. But we don't have much longer before the answer changes to no. Let me get to work."

Thea washed Maté's wound with a clean rag and a sharp-smelling liquid that made Maté swear and try to wrench himself free of her grip. "None of that," she said calmly. "You should know better, my pretty soldier boy."

Maté gasped out a laugh. "I should. Sensible, though. Hah. Never claimed I was."

"Then you are at least honest, if foolish. Now hold still and do not fight me."

She hummed a low, wavering tune. No words, but Anna thought she recognized the same rise and fall of the invocation she used to summon the magical current. *Ei rûf ane gôtter*, she thought. *Ei rûf ane strôm...* The air shuddered and turned unnaturally cold for the space of a heartbeat. Then Maté gave a gasp, and the heat seemed to evaporate, as though the fever were running out free like a tide. Anna brushed a hand over his face. The sweat was lifting away, and his skin felt cool to the touch.

"All he needs is sleep," Thea said. "Help me get him into the nearest hammock. Then I can give him a proper dose."

Even without the dose, Maté was nearly asleep, but together they shifted him from the coil of rope into a hammock. "Your turn, my young friend," Thea said to Anna. "Sit, please." She pointed to a trunk.

She redirected the lantern's beam to Anna's face. With a light touch, she examined each eye in turn, then counted Anna's pulse. The air drew tight around them and a sharp green scent invaded the berth. Warmth spread through Anna's veins, and within moments she no longer felt hollowed out inside.

"That was a dangerous trick," Thea murmured. "Cutting the bond between flesh and spirit. Even if you did know what you were doing. Which I doubt. However, you seem to have escaped any lasting harm. Even so, I want you to take a dose as well. It will help you sleep, and you'll need your strength once the captain decides to question you."

"I would like to question her now."

Koszenmarc crouched on the ladder, just a few steps above them. His eyes glittered in the lamplight, and he held himself still and tense, as though he might spring upon them any moment.

"It's not like you to leave the deck at such a time," Thea said in a mild voice. "Or have we given our enemy the slip?"

"We have. Now I want to ask our new companion how our enemy discovered us so easily."

Anna closed her eyes. Oh. Yes. That explained so much.

"Do you have an explanation?" he asked, finally.

He thinks me a gods-be-damned mouse. Perhaps I am, but this mouse will bite.

"I do not," she said crisply. "My friend, however, took an arrow serving you, Captain. And I did exactly as you asked and more. If you cannot bring yourself to trust me, even now, hand me over to Commander Maszny and have done with it. But if you wish to learn what I've discovered, I suggest you let me deliver my report to you and your officers. Then we can have a reasonable discussion about what we do next."

"My ship is not a council of equals," Koszenmarc snapped back.

"Neither am I your bonded slave." Her voice shook with all the rage and terror from the past few days. "But oh, you have made me into one, my *lord*. You took me prisoner, you chained me with threats, and now you beat me with accusations. I want nothing more than my freedom and my reward, Lord Koszenmarc. Let me earn it."

Shadows masked his face, but Anna heard his indrawn breath. She was all too aware how the lamp shone directly on her face, exposing every shift in her own expression. She willed herself to keep her gaze fixed on him, to show as little emotion as he undoubtedly did. But she knew she failed.

"Very well, I shall," he said at last. He vanished up the ladder.

Anna released a breath she had not realized she was holding.

Thea laid a hand on her shoulder. "You'll do. You'll do very well."

* * * *

Four days later, with the sun slanting toward the horizon, the *Mathilde* came home at last. The seas were empty in all directions, the water the color of blue silk, and the ship skimmed along at an easy pace. Anna stood by the rail with Maté, newly released from the sick bay. For the first time, she had a chance to see the whole of Koszenmarc's island domain. Asulos was its name, as Daria told her in passing.

Three islands broke the surface of the ocean. The largest was a massive rock, two hundred feet high, with cliffs plunging in a straight line from peak to waves. That would be the main stronghold, with its many grottos and caves. The other two were hardly more than dark smudges, rising a few dozen feet above the waves. As the ship tacked around toward the harbor entrance, however, Anna could see that one island was at least a mile long, with broad grassy fields edged by a thicket of trees and a stream that emptied into the sea. Goats and sheep and several horses grazed in the fields, tended by children. The second was a bare, flat expanse of sand and stone, where a dozen figures moved about. Anna realized they were members of Koszenmarc's company, drilling with weapons.

"Like a lord and his manor," Maté said softly.

"I had the same thought," Anna replied, just as quietly.

Daria shouted out orders to haul sail and tack, tack, may the gods damn this useless crew for all their lives. *Mathilde* swung around the main island and with a sigh the sails fell slack as the ship glided into the harbor.

The anchor hit and yanked the ship to a stop. Both boats went over the side, followed by ropes and ladders. As Anna descended to shore, she heard snatches of conversation between the crew and those below.

Six goddamned hours on shore. That Druss, like a shark hunting for blood. A near thing before the storm hit full and hard. Don't see what good any of it did.

Koszenmarc was the last to disembark. As if summoned by magic, Eleni appeared. "Captain. We've had a quiet few days."

"That, I like to hear. We have not, alas. Pass the word for all my officers. We have a report to hear and plans to make."

* * * *

Once more they were in that airy chamber high above the seas. The windows were shuttered today, the great lamp overhead burning bright, the echoes and whispers from below more pronounced.

"So," Koszenmarc said. "Let us have our sensible discussion, with all my officers present, as Elise insists. What makes you believe Sarrész lives?" he asked Anna. "What is this clue you discovered?"

He spoke softly, but there was no mistaking the command, however politely he phrased it. Anna had spent most of the hours on the journey back considering how to describe that strange magical presence and the vision it had shown her.

"I saw Lord Sarrész, the same as before," she said. "He ran directly from the forest toward the ocean and vanished. This time, however, I tracked the man from our world into Anderswar. And *this* time, I found traces of his passage."

Koszenmarc nodded. "What kind of traces?"

This was the most difficult part to describe. "Footprints, you might call them," she said, "except they were nothing so ordinary. Their shape and direction corresponded exactly to those we found on the shore. It was as though he made that leap, still running from his enemies, then made a second leap from Anderswar back into the ordinary world. And while I had only one clear glimpse, I swear those prints led directly back to Eddalyon."

"Is that possible?" Eleni asked.

"I've read any number of accounts that say it is," Thea said slowly. "But not likely for this particular man, unless we've been misled. You spoke about a bought spell before. Is that what he used?"

"That was the only explanation," Anna said. "Or so I believed. Now..."
She paused, uncertain how to describe that otherworldly presence. "I
believe another agency was present."

"Another mage?" Daria asked.

"Another agency," Anna repeated. "I can't tell you more because I don't
know myself." How to explain that eerie chorus? Already the memory of
that voice, that moment when she perched on the edge of the void between
lives, was fading. "Whatever or whoever came to Sarrész's aid," she said
slowly, "they plucked him from that gods-be-damned shore and away from
Druss's ambush. And then, they set him down, still running, somewhere
else among these islands."

A long moment of silence followed.

Koszenmarc leaned back from the table. "There are twelve chief islands
in Eddalyon. A hundred or more smaller ones, with only enough sand and
fresh water for a fishing village here, or a temporary port there. Those
are the islands the mapmakers know. There might be a thousand more
scattered over the southern seas."

"In other words, you've set us an impossible task," Eleni said.

At the same time, Maté said, "We never did explore those ruins."

"Too dangerous," Eleni replied at once. "Besides, knowing Druss, she
and her people have undoubtedly pillaged that temple for every clue it
held. Or are you merely being *hopeful* again?"

He shrugged. "It's my nature."

Eleni snorted. But Koszenmarc was shaking his head. "Eleni is right.
We can't risk going ashore on Vyros. Besides, I don't like how Druss
happened upon us. It was too convenient."

Anna gave an involuntary shiver. She had not forgotten that tense
moment when Koszenmarc accused her of betrayal. *He was right. I will
betray him—but not to Isana Druss.*

Her glance crossed Koszenmarc's. He too was remembering that moment,
because he gave a brief shake of the head. And Eleni was watching them
both with an odd expression.

To her relief, Hahn spoke next. "I wouldn't be so surprised about Druss,"
he said. "After all, she's hunting Sarrész herself. Most likely she came back
to see if the fool reappeared exactly where he vanished."

"Still too dangerous." Koszenmarc rested his face in his hands for several
moments, then abruptly stood and walked over to his desk to stare at the
largest map on the wall. "He could be anywhere, anywhere at all." Without
looking around, he said, "Are you certain about what you saw, Elise? You

were in the void between worlds, after all. How do you know those islands belonged to Eddalyon? And not an entirely different world altogether?" She wanted to answer back as sharply as he'd spoken, but she heard the note of anxiety in his voice. "Yes, I am certain."

He continued to stare at the map in silence. Then, "We would be years visiting every island. So. We make a two-pronged attack. Joszua, Daria, I want you both to play spy for me. Each of you take a ship and a small crew. Listen to the gossip in the ports. Vyros and Idonia, obviously, but you might have some luck with Kyra or Yskopi. Ask questions, but discreetly. I can't believe a stranger could appear suddenly from the air and no one has heard of it."

It's possible, Anna thought. *If the magical void spat him out weeks later, on an island far beyond the edges of the Empire.* But she didn't want to mention that.

The same thought must have occurred to Thea as well, judging from her grave expression. The others seemed equally uncertain. Old Hahn was frowning. Daria Ioannou played with her knife, slowly turning it over from hand to hand, her gaze turned inward, as though she contemplated their impossible task. Even Joszua had lost his cheerful air.

Koszenmarc gave up studying the map and returned to the table. "We are not a council of equals, as I've said, but this isn't one of our usual missions. I want to hear what you think, every one of you. Do you disagree with my plan? Do you have other suggestions?"

Hahn shook his head. Joszua gave a wry smile and murmured, "As if I ever had a better suggestion."

Eleni frowned, but she said nothing.

After a moment's hesitation, Maté said, "You said a two-pronged attack. What is the second one?"

"Magic," Koszenmarc said. "Elise, I want you to teach Thea the spells you used to examine the past. Thea..." He hesitated. "This is the most dangerous task of all. I want you and Elise to map a more exact trajectory for Sarrész's flight into the islands."

Thea drew a sharp breath. *"That* means walking Anderswar itself."

Anderswar, the void between worlds, between lives. Anna had to suppress a shiver. She'd nearly lost herself the last time, as Thea had pointed out.

To be fair, Koszenmarc seemed to understand the danger. "I know. Do not...don't take any unnecessary risks."

"Only the necessary ones," Thea murmured. "But, no. You're right. We've reached the tipping point in our search. A few weeks or months later, and Druss will find the man before we do." To Anna she said, "We shall both have to hone our magic before we make the attempt."

She spoke matter-of-factly, but Anna had not forgotten her comment from before. *A dangerous trick,* Thea had called Anna's own leap into the void. *But what choice do we have?*

Unless they knew where Sarrész had landed in the islands, theirs would be a long and sifting search. Like tracing sunlight through water.

CHAPTER 11

Two days later, Joszua set off with the *Konstanze*, while Daria took command of the *Mathilde*. Both ships had been painted fresh with new colors to make them less recognizable, and both carried a handpicked crew who could fight as well as sail the ship. Over the next few weeks, the ones who remained behind drilled with weapons twice a day, while their captain led them through maneuvers in case of invaders.

A matter of common sense, Maté had said to Anna during one of their few encounters. *He's a thorough man, our Lord Koszenmarc.*

Koszenmarc, Anna thought with bitterness, was too damned thorough. She ought to have realized that the moment he rescued her from Commander Maszny. Somehow, he had learned about her arrest. Somehow, he had anticipated the commander's decision to take two separate routes to the garrison. Somehow...

Her stomach twisted into a knot. Anna didn't want to think about Maszny, or what Lord Brun would say about her pact with Koszenmarc. Nothing good. That much she knew.

"Stop," Thea said. "You're trying too hard." She leaned close and clasped Anna's arm. "You don't need to sacrifice yourself for a thief and his goods, no matter how lovely the prize."

They both sat cross-legged on the floor of the surgeon's quarters. A shallow basin with a heap of incense occupied the space between them. The incense had burnt to ashes an hour or more ago, but its scent still hung in the air, like an echo of the current itself.

"I was almost there," Anna whispered.

"You were not," Thea said crisply.

Anna wanted to argue, but she could not. Her goal was to achieve that balance between the magical and the mundane—to achieve and *hold* the balance for longer than a moment—and no matter how much she wished to debate the point, she had not done so. Her head throbbed, and her skin felt aflame with undirected magic. From a distance came the sussuration of waves over sand and stone. Normally she found this a soothing counterpoint to Thea's voice as she led Anna through their magical exercises, but today, the cave felt close, and she sensed a charged quality to the air, as though a storm hovered over the islands called Asulos.

"I just need a few moments," she said.

"Perhaps more than a few," Thea murmured.

"But…"

"But nothing, my young friend." The other woman laid a hand upon Anna's head and hummed softly. There were no words to this invocation, but the air stirred with magic's clean, clear scent. The tension that gripped Anna's skull eased and she drew a long breath. "Good," Thea said. "Now, no more arguments. You're a talented young woman, my friend, but you *are* young, and your teachers—whoever they were—drove you far too hard. You are much like a bud forced to bloom."

She'd said those same words before, when she insisted that Anna first practice what she called the rudiments of magic. Finding the balance point between the magical and the mundane, learning to exist in that moment for longer than a breath, following the patterns of the magical current instead of bending them to her human purpose. Anna wanted to argue that her father *had* taught her the rudiments, and much more, but she knew what Thea meant. The tutors Lord Brun had hired had pushed her over and over, insisting that she memorize those cursed spells. Spells for battle. Spells for assassination.

And for a very good reason. Anna needed to find the jewel and quickly.

"Thank you," she said. "I feel much better now and—"

"And I said no more magic today." Thea stood and held out a hand. "A nice brisk walk in the ocean air will clear our heads. I heard Joszua and the *Konstanze* returned just a few hours ago. If we wander by, we might hear some gossip."

The *Konstanze* stood at anchor in the inner harbor, with a sizable crew at work repairing damage from a storm. Anna and Thea threaded their way between the sailors and had reached the harbor's narrow entry when the *Mathilde* came drifting between the cliffs, with Daria and her second-in-command at the rail.

Daria waved to Thea. "My love! I am so glad you didn't go into a decline in my absence."

Thea waved back, her eyes alight with humor. "Will you have a day or two before you set off again?"

"I shan't know until I report to our captain." Daria tossed off a kiss to her hand, then turned back to confer with Felix as the ship glided past.

Thea gazed after her beloved a moment longer with narrowed eyes. Over the past three weeks, Daria and Joszua had each returned twice from their search for Aldo Sarrész. *No news* was the official word, but each time, they'd spent half a day in private conversation with Koszenmarc. And each time, Anna had overheard the tense whispered conversations in the night between Thea and Daria as she lay in her own small chamber next to theirs.

What if I was wrong, and he died in the void? No, she had seen those footprints running, leaping from the void back into Eddalyon. But time passed differently in the place called Anderswar. For all she knew, the man could still be falling, falling from one world to the next.

She and Thea continued around the island, walking along the narrow band of rock and sand. A band of dark blue clouds blurred the horizon— another sign of the coming storm. Across the way, the senior members of Koszenmarc's company were drilling with swords and staffs on the smaller of the neighboring islands, and the crack of wood against wooden blade echoed over the water. Anna recognized Maté's silhouette as he parried, then with a sudden burst of strikes, drove his opponent back.

"Your friend makes his partner work for every hit," Thea said. "He must have been a soldier or a guard. Not that I'm asking," she added hastily.

"I'm not sure he'd mind if you did ask," Anna replied. "Though I can't promise he'd answer *truthfully.*"

Thea laughed and shook her head. "That much I had guessed already. He reminds me of Daria. And myself, a bit."

It was the closest any of Koszenmarc's people had come to talking about their personal histories.

I'm lucky they don't, or they might ask me questions I can't answer.

They came to the far side of the island, which faced east over the open sea. Here Thea paused and lifted her face to the breeze. Her hair, which was loosely tied back with a ribbon, rose into a silvery halo. The clear morning light picked out the lines etched in her face, and she seemed far older than Anna's previous impression of the woman. A mage and a surgeon, a gifted teacher. What had brought her into Koszenmarc's company?

Bu that stirred up too many questions about her own motives.

The wind blew fresher and stronger. Anna closed her eyes and breathed in the salt air. For a moment, she had the same sensation of kneeling on that otherworldly cliff, with all of Eddalyon spread below her. In between the worlds, in between magic and air, one moment and the next...

Eyes still closed, she whispered a tentative invocation to magic. A whiff of pine tang colored the salt-scented air. Her skin prickled, and she sensed a gap in the fabric of the world. She held her breath, felt the balance tipping first one direction then back...

...then, oh, yes, the moment of balance. Here, magic waited. Here, anything was possible.

Anna released her breath, and with it, her hold on the magic current. This time, the power trickled away like raindrops, and even when it had entirely left her she did not feel that sickening lurch she had thought the necessary price of magic.

"You had it," Thea said softly.

"I... Yes, I did."

It seemed such a small thing. Nothing like the spells to summon cold fire, or draw down destruction upon the enemy. But as Anna automatically erased her signature, a trace of that balance remained behind.

"Do you always do that?" Thea asked. "Wipe away your magic?"

Anna shrugged. "My teachers insisted. A matter of discipline, they said."

A precaution, so mages could not track her, but that was part of her own secret history.

"A useful habit," said another voice.

Anna jumped and immediately wanted to curse. Koszenmarc stood a few feet away, a curious expression on his face. How long had he been watching?

"Thea," he said. "Go to your quarters. Daria has news for you."

Thea spared them both only a keen glance before she left. Anna hesitated, not certain if she ought to follow, but Koszenmarc gestured for her to stay. "I have news for you as well. Come, walk with me."

He indicated the shore leading toward the far point of the island, which angled toward the north. *North and Valentain,* Anna thought, but she said nothing as they made their way through the rising surf. For a dozen yards or so, the shore disappeared entirely beneath the waves, only to reappear as a wide expanse of sand, while the cliffs that surrounded the rest of the island tumbled down to a rolling slope thick with brush.

When they reached the point itself, Koszenmarc stopped, hands in his pockets, his gaze toward the north. Though he and his company had been careful never to mention exactly where Asulos lay, Anna could guess.

East of Vyros and the main cluster of islands, though how far, she wasn't certain. Several hundred miles south of the mainland. Within the known charts, but close to the edge, where few traveled. From the distance came the echo of swords clashing against swords. The senior drill had ended, she could tell, because she heard Eleni calling out instructions in a slower, much more patient voice. Two hours at least had passed since the *Mathilde* had made port. Longer still since Joszua and *Konstanze* had arrived.

"Joszua has news about our friend Sarrész," he said.

"Where?" Anna said quickly. "And is he alive?"

"Idonia, to answer your first question. Possibly, to answer your second. According to Joszua's friends, a man very much like our quarry was sighted four days ago in a tavern, in the port city of Kasteli, gambling for ship's passage back to the mainland. He lost that gamble, and no one has heard from him since. But I have an idea. We shall leave for Idonia with the evening tide. I want you to scour the past with your magic, and I want Thea to observe."

It was at once a command and a request. Anna paused, not certain how to respond. "I should pack my gear," she said at last.

He held up a hand. "In a moment. I have more news that touches upon you."

The noise from the drill had died away. Only the growl of the surf and the occasional bleat from the goats and sheep across the water intruded upon the stillness. *Cat and mouse,* Anna told herself. That lovely calm she'd felt when she achieved the magical balance had vanished.

Koszenmarc did not appear to notice her uneasiness. "Joszua is a most valuable spy," he went on. "He has a number of contacts on Vyros and Idonia. His family. Several friends who do a brisk trade with Vyros and other islands. They brought him word that your friend Raab not only escaped, he seems to have vanished entirely."

He is not my friend. But her heart gave a leap at the thought of Raab free and able to get word to Lord Brun.

"That's a fortunate thing," she said carefully. "We wouldn't want Commander Maszny to question him. Otherwise he might learn about Sarrész and our plans. Our clients would dislike that very much."

"Possibly," Koszenmarc murmured. "Maszny did question your maids. They knew nothing of course, other than the Lady Vrou's men hired them shortly before you departed the mainland. He concluded the maids were innocent dupes and gave them each a sum of money and the price of their passage home."

Now she was truly grateful for the news.

"I'm glad," she said.

He glanced at her, again with that keen and curious glance. "You are."

They had not spoken since he accused her of luring Isana Druss to trap them all on Vyros, and she wasn't sure what to make of that statement, or why he had told her about the maids. She waited, expecting him to say more, but he made no other comment. They turned back toward the inner harbor where they parted, he to his sanctuary at the island's peak, and she to pack for the voyage.

* * * *

Once more, Eleni Farakos remained behind. So too Daria Ioannou and Maté. Anna told herself the latter was a reasonable decision—they had no need for a skilled hunter and a landsman—but when she heard the news, she couldn't help but wonder if Koszenmarc deliberately kept them apart.

If I asked, would he answer? she thought. *If he answered, would I like that answer?*

She had no time for wondering or guessing. A few hours later, she was aboard with the rest of the crew, and the evening tide saw the *Konstanze* away from Asulos. Koszenmarc had plotted a course arcing north around Vyros, through the open seas between the islands and the mainland. The wind held true, and within three days the lookout had sighted land.

Anna and Thea heard the commotion above decks and broke off their morning session of magic. Koszenmarc was already on deck with Old Hahn by his side. As Anna followed Thea to a spot by the rail, out of the crew's way, Hahn called out orders to the crew aloft. The sails came down and the steersman tacked to port, then they were beating against the wind toward an island that seemed to fill the horizon, dark and massive and rising up to a series of mountains that overlooked a wide harbor.

Idonia. The heart of the old kingdom. Their destination was the port city of Kasteli, where Eddalyon's kings and queens once ruled. The ruins of the old palace were visible on the heights above the city—a sweep of jagged walls, breached here and there, and one lone tower rising against the dark green of the mountainside, a warning left by the conquerors from the mainland.

They dropped anchor in midharbor, and Joszua climbed down the side ropes into a waiting harbor boat, which would take him dockside to handle the port fees. "We'll take in supplies for the ship and for back home," Hahn said to Anna. "Makes it more likely why we're here, in case anyone cares."

Anna could imagine any number of people caring about the *Konstanze*'s presence, but perhaps the crowd of boats and ships in the harbor made a better camouflage than paint or patterns. The *Konstanze*'s launch made yet another of that crowd. The crew guided their launch to an open slip on the west end of the harbor, where they made fast. Koszenmarc gave orders to wait for the supplies, then return directly to the ship. He motioned for Anna and Thea to follow him.

The district immediately around the harbor was a warren of streets lined by shipping offices and warehouses constructed of unadorned stone. Beyond lay neighborhoods with wine shops and taverns, and a few houses. Koszenmarc led them to a stone building with a tiled roof and a sign in Kybris that read simply Agathé. Next to the entrance, a slate listed half a dozen dishes and their prices. The place had a quiet, prosperous look, not a place where one gambled recklessly.

"Thea explained something of the magic you use to track our friend," he said quietly. "Here is the tavern he supposedly visited. Memorize what it looks like, remember the path we take from here. We'll go somewhere quiet and safe for the magic itself."

Anna glanced to either side, taking in the street and what buildings bordered the tavern. Then she stepped to the Agathé's entrance and pretended to study the menu. She noted the large open room inside, the wooden counter running the length of one side, the several rows of tables with benches, where a dozen men and women ate and drank tea or wine. Most definitely not a place for gambling, but possibly a venue a man like Sarrész would visit.

Once she had memorized every detail, she stepped back to Koszenmarc's side. "When did Joszua say our friend was here?"

"Four days before we set sail. Is that too long ago?"

Seven days past. Yes, it was possible she could sort through the events. She nodded. "I can do this."

"Good. Let's go to our quiet place."

Their path took them up a dozen flights of steps, through the center of the port city, with its mixture of ancient and new buildings, then into a district that Anna would swear dated back to the foundation of the old Eddalyon kingdom. Here the stone buildings had strange figures and faces carved into the portals, and the cool damp air had a whiff of the jungle. Nearly all the signs were written in the Kybris script, but she also saw the occasional placard in Veraenen.

At last they arrived at their destination, a temple that surrounded three sides of a small courtyard. Koszenmarc mounted the half dozen steps to the temple entrance and tossed a few denariie into the offering bowl beside the entrance.

Anna paused a moment. The stones, the magic, the strange quiet reminded her strongly of the bare ruins atop the mountain on Vyros. This was their quiet place? But Thea had already followed Koszenmarc, and she had to hurry to catch up with her companions.

The entry hall was a large square, with lanterns hung from the ceiling. Statues occupied all four corners. Lir, in her aspects of maiden, mother, and crone. Blind Toc, a bandage over his eyes to symbolize his sacrifice that gave the world the sun and moon. Magic pooled here, like shadows drifting between the tiled walls.

Koszenmarc led them around Toc's massive figure and into a series of ever-narrower passageways until they reached a small room. Dark blue tiles, veined with silver, covered the floor and ceiling. Frescoes decorated the walls, depicting Lir and Toc from various legends. Toc, sacrificing his eyes to make the sun and the moon for his sister. Lir, grieving over Toc's body, her tears transformed into stars. Lir and Toc in their season of love, giving birth to all creation. Sections were faded and flaked, with the stone underneath showing through, but someone had recently applied new paint with a delicate hand.

"We're in a sanctuary of sorts," Thea said. "The stories say the old priests built their temples from stones imbued with spells of silence, so that anyone might pray to the gods without fear of being overheard. The old kings and queens of Eddalyon were no less given to spying than our own Imperial masters," she added dryly.

"*The rot and poison of power*," Koszenmarc murmured. He shook his head, as though dispelling unwanted memories. "Elise, you and Thea shall have as many hours as you need. The important thing is to know when Aldo Sarrész visited that tavern, and where he went afterwards. I'll stand watch here, and there will be others keeping watch on our perimeter."

More precautions, more layers of *if this, then that.*

They took their places on the floor, legs crossed and facing each other, just as they had every morning on Asulos, or aboard the *Konstanze*. Thea leaned forward and clasped Anna's hands in hers. Her palms were warm, her skin papery thin.

"You shall be the leader," she said. "I'm here to watch over you, to witness whatever you discover."

Trust me, said that solemn expression.

I believe I can.

Anna drew a deep slow breath and closed her eyes.

Ei rûf ane gôtter...

The magic current curled into life around her. Anna felt a flutter of anticipation beneath her ribs as the sharp scent of magic filled her senses, so strong she could taste it. After so many weeks of practice, she knew the pattern she sought, just as Maté knew the shape and scent of a trail he followed.

Wenden, wenden zuo Idonia...

Gradually, the temple room receded. Her mind emptied of all thoughts. Her pulse beat slow and steady in counterpoint with Thea's.

Thea. Thea was her anchor. Thea was her guardian. But then even Thea's presence ebbed and faded, until Anna drifted alone through the magic current, with only the faintest thread connecting her to the ordinary world. A snip, and her soul would fly free into Anderswar.

She drew back from that temptation with an effort that nearly undid her balance. *Gently, gently,* said a familiar voice. Her father's. Her first tutor. But also a woman's voice. *A featherweight is all you require.*

Just so. With the lightest touch she could manage, Anna called up her memories of Kasteli's streets, the path she had walked a few moments or hours before. Her soul lifted from her body and drifted out the temple doors, into the plaza outside, then through the salt-laden air and along that remembered path, until she came to that stone building with the sign reading Agathé.

Here. Here was her anchor. And now.

For a moment, she did nothing except exist in the balance of now. It took another effort to detach herself from today, to unwind the hours and unreel the past. She saw...a stream of people in the streets. Children running backwards. A string of carts that flickered in and out of view. She saw herself, a small, dark figure clothed in drab clothes, with Koszenmarc at her side and Thea a few steps behind.

The sun arced from early morning to night, then through the days before. As the moments flickered past, she caught a glimpse of magic, a letter sealed, a candle lit, an elderly man reciting prayers to Lir and Toc, so that the current swirled around him. But none of these carried Aldo Sarrész's signature. None was that magical presence that had snatched him from Vyros's sands and death by Druss's people.

She was so focused upon the inn and Aldo Sarrész she forgot to keep track of the passing hours. The moon of the past had waxed and waned before she suddenly remembered. With the greatest effort, she slowed the time unwinding, slowed and stopped it, so that she hovered there, months before the man had ever landed in these islands.

Nothing, nothing. He is not here. He never was.

From a distance, she felt a tug from her body. How many hours had passed in the present, while Thea and Koszenmarc watched over her? She ought to return before her soul forgot the way back to her body and she wandered through the past forever.

No. He came to this island, if not to this tavern. I know it.

Perhaps the harbor itself held the clue. Perhaps he had landed there and traveled a different direction.

Anna's soul spun toward the harbor, even as she heard Thea calling her name. But she was already flying along the streets and down the many steps, while time reversed once again. Ahead lay the ocean glittering under the sun, the ships like scattered pearls that winked into and out of sight as she came closer to the now of her life. A month ago, a week ago. Still no sign of Sarrész as she ran toward the present.

And then...

Below her the stream of people checked and parted. A company of soldiers, a hundred at least, both mounted and on foot, pressed through the crowds. With a shock, Anna recognized their leader.

Maszny.

A part of her registered that she no longer saw the past, that Maszny and his soldiers were marching and riding the same streets she and Thea and Koszenmarc had traveled this morning. She felt another, stronger tug from her body that plucked her from the panic that had frozen her. She fled as fast as her spirit could fly. Onward past the tavern, up the flights of stairs that climbed Idonia's nearest mountain. A mile or so, and she overtook a mass of men and women, a rough and dangerous crowd with knives and clubs and swords. They too were hurrying toward the temple...

Anna blinked and gulped for air. A pair of strong arms held her steady; two hands cupped her cheeks. Her chest ached and she could not see more than indistinct shadows. Then a woman's face moved into view. Thea, making a swift examination by touch and magic. And it was Koszenmarc who held her in his arms.

"You forgot to breathe," Thea said dryly. "No wonder you tumbled out of the current like that."

Anna had to swallow hard before she could speak. "Soldiers!" she gasped.

Koszenmarc's hold tightened, and she flinched at sudden, unwanted memories. He immediately loosened his grip. "*What* did you say?"

"Maszny, by the harbor. Maszny and soldiers." She swallowed again. Koszenmarc held a leather flask to her lips. Cool, sweet water. Anna drank and drank until the flask ran dry and she could finally speak coherently.

"I saw nothing of Sarrész by that tavern," she said. "I thought to check the harbor district. But he wasn't there, either. Not now, not at any time. That's when I saw a company of soldiers with Maszny at their head."

Koszenmarc went so still Anna thought *he* had stopped breathing. "How interesting," he said softly. "How far away were they?"

"And how far into the past were you?" Thea said.

"Close to the harbor," Anna said, "and not more than an hour or two. But that's not all. I saw…men and women, all of them armed, hurrying toward the temple. A mile, maybe less, from here. It could be a coincidence, but—"

"But it's not. We should collect our watchers and be off."

He stood and drew his sword. Thea held out her hand to Anna.

Anna needed a moment and a whisper of magic before she could scramble to her feet. She nodded briskly to Koszenmarc. He smiled and nodded in return. Captain to crew, ally to ally.

The idea of Koszenmarc as an ally stopped her for a moment. Then Thea was urging them out of their temporary sanctuary and through a series of corridors. They exited through a door at the rear of the temple, which opened onto a narrow alleyway. The alley was deserted, except for a few dogs lying in the sun and Joszua standing guard.

"Captain," he said. "Have we found our man, then?"

Koszenmarc scanned the lane and his eyes narrowed. "Alas, no. We've a different set of problems. Maszny is heading in our direction with a company of soldiers. And there's another set of someones hunting us as well. Where did you put the rest of the perimeter watch?"

Joszua went grey. "It was so quiet, I sent them back to the ship. I'm sorry—"

Koszenmarc flicked his hand impatiently. "We don't have time for excuses. Let's get back to the *Konstanze*."

He led them away from the temple and Kasteli's broad avenues into a maze of winding lanes. Several times, he halted at an intersection, only to double back and turn into a covered passageway that Anna had missed before. She had lost all sense of direction, and so had Thea. Joszua knew the city well, according to Koszenmarc, but even he seemed puzzled by their route.

After what seemed like hours, they reached the city walls and a clear view of the harbor. Koszenmarc sheathed his sword and signaled for Joszua to do the same. Anna leaned against the nearest wall. It was quiet here, quiet and shaded, the air dense with scents from the jungle above them.

"Ah, interesting," Thea said. "The *Konstanze* is not where we left her."

Anna immediately came alert. Joszua did as well. Only Koszenmarc seemed unperturbed.

"That is according to orders," he said. "Now for the second part of our plan."

Oh, really? Anna thought. *And how many other lovely plans have you kept secret for today?*

But she kept her curses and objections quiet as Koszenmarc set off at a slower pace. She recognized the ploy. They were just a group of friends strolling along and chatting about inconsequentials. At least, Koszenmarc and Thea chatted. Anna could not stop thinking about Maszny and his soldiers. Joszua was silent as well. No doubt he was dreading a lecture from Koszenmarc.

At last they came to the shore, at the far end of the wharves. A wide launch was tied to the last post between the docks. An old man and woman were drinking from bottles and playing cards on an overturned bait tub. Ropes, rags, more tubs overflowing with bait, and an open box of gear were scattered about.

Koszenmarc dropped into the boat. "Máur. Katerina. Who's winning?"

Máur spat a viscous wad into the water. "She is, dammit."

"I always do," Katerina said. Then to Koszenmarc, "We got trouble, Captain?"

"What do you think?" he said. "Thea, Elise, get under cover. Joszua, make yourself look disreputable."

One by one, Anna, Thea, and Koszenmarc dropped into the boat and hunkered down in the bottom. Máur and Joszua spread a tarpaulin over them and tucked in the edges. Katerina untied the rope to cast off. Together, the three of them maneuvered the launch away from the docks.

Anna closed her eyes and forced herself to breathe steadily. Her nose was pressed against what had to be one of the bait buckets, and she was acutely aware that a very thin plank was all that separated her from the water streaming past the launch. Once or twice, another sailor hailed them. Each time, Anna held her breath and tucked her magic tight inside lest Maszny had watchers and spies who could detect her. But no one shouted a warning, no one called for them to halt.

She could tell the moment they left the harbor behind. The swells grew stronger, the launch climbed higher, then plunged into the next trough. Now all three crew were pulling strongly with their oars. Anna bit her lip against the rising tide of nausea and counted the passing moments.

At long last, a whistle echoed over the water from far away. Three rising notes, repeated a second time.

"All clear," Katerina said softly.

Joszua and Máur threw off the tarpaulin. Anna sat up, blinking. They had sailed clear around the island, to a lonely rocky point. Twilight had fallen and a cool breeze washed over them. Overhead, the first stars were winking in the violet sky. Not far away, a small cutter was drawing close. The *Daemon*, which Anna thought they had left behind at Koszenmarc's stronghold.

The launch pulled up beside the cutter. Rope ladders came down, and Koszenmarc swarmed up, followed by Thea. Joszua offered his hand to Anna, who gratefully accepted. When she landed on deck—unsteadily—she found Koszenmarc deep in conversation with Eleni Farakos.

"Hahn is waiting for us farther out," Eleni was saying.

"Any trouble?"

"No more than we expected."

Koszenmarc smiled, but it was a tense, unhappy smile. "Good enough. Let us head out to sea, then we'll have a conference. I have news to report, and so does Elise."

* * * *

Once they had rejoined the *Konstanze* and set course for home, Koszenmarc passed the word for Anna and his senior officers to meet in his cabin. This time, there were no flasks of coffee or ale, no jokes. Old Hahn wore a grim expression. Joszua glanced around anxiously at everyone but his captain. Eleni, who had come over from the *Daemon,* wore a contained expression that could be anger, worry, or something in between.

"So," Koszenmarc said. "That was far more exciting than I wished."

Only Eleni didn't appear astonished. "You expected trouble."

Koszenmarc gave a shrug. "Of course I did. However, the kind and quality did surprise me." He glanced over to Anna. "Tell them what you discovered about Aldo Sarrész."

Oh, yes. That. Anna took a deep breath. "Nothing at all."

"Nothing?" Joszua said. "But—"

"I searched the past around that tavern," she said. "Every moment, every day, for the past month at least. I even searched the harbor district, in case we had the wrong tavern, or the wrong days. I found no trace of Sarrész's presence, or his magical signature, or any trace of that other agency."

"Are you certain?" Hahn said. "How can you know you didn't miss a moment or three? What if his magic faded?"

But Thea was shaking her head. "His, maybe. That other one? No. From what I saw myself on Vyros, that other signature was much, much stronger. It would never fade in seven short days."

"Unless Sarrész is alone now," Eleni said. "Or he's worked no magic since. Is that possible?"

"It is," Anna said slowly. "But the magic itself means nothing. I am convinced our Lord Sarrész never set foot upon Idonia. He certainly never visited that tavern."

Everyone sat in uncomfortable silence at her words. The implications were obvious. Sarrész might have survived his brief journey through the void. He might have landed safely somewhere in Eddalyon. But where?

"We shall discuss what to do about Sarrész later," Koszenmarc said. "Tell us what else you discovered, Elise. What you saw at the very last."

By the harbor, he meant. "I saw Maszny," she said. "He had landed at Kasteli with a company of soldiers." Now she recalled more details that had escaped her at the time. "They had at least one mage, besides Maszny himself, and they took the same route we did, as though they knew exactly where to find us."

That caused an uneasy stir through the officers. Koszenmarc, however, simply nodded. "What about the others you saw?"

That offhand mention caused a second, stronger stir among the officers. Anna had to take a moment to recall exactly what she had witnessed in those last scrambled moments before her soul dropped back into her body.

"I saw at least two dozen men and women," she said. "All of them carrying weapons. They looked...rough and dangerous."

Eleni gave a soft exclamation, but Koszenmarc waved her to silence. "Go on. Give us all the details you can remember."

Anna closed her eyes and concentrated on that brief glimpse. The slap of their bare feet as they jogged through the lane. The glitter of sunlight on metal. The chain wrapped around one man's thick waist. The vivid pattern of red ink on one woman's arm. She recited as much as she could remember.

"What was the pattern?" Koszenmarc said.

Again she had to think. "A thick band, at least a finger's width, drawn in dark red ink. Not solid. Speckled or spotted, I can't be sure. But I do remember she wore a sleeveless shirt, and the band showed midway between her wrist and elbow, like a rope or—"

"A serpent," Eleni said. "So Isana Druss was there. Hunting you, just as you said."

"But *how* did she know where to find us?" Thea said. "And *when* to find us?"

"And how did Maszny know?" Hahn said.

"Perhaps he was hunting Druss, not us," Joszua said.

Koszenmarc shook his head. "That might explain why he brought so many soldiers, but it doesn't explain Druss at all. I think…" He blew out a breath, leaving the sentence unfinished. "We shall have to make new plans. And take better precautions."

He pressed his hands together and closed his eyes. None of his officers spoke. Anna had the impression they were braced for possible squalls. It was only by Koszenmarc's foresight, after all, that ship and crew and captain had not been taken by either Druss or Maszny. And that was the most baffling piece of the puzzle. Druss might have sighted them from afar and recognized the ships, but how had Maszny known about their expedition? Either coincidence could be just that, but together…

At last Koszenmarc opened his eyes with a sigh. "Do you have more to report?" he asked Anna. His voice was soft and colorless. Angry, then, but no explosions.

She shook her head. He acknowledged that with a nod, then laid both hands on the table. "That will be all, then. I want everyone, including you, Hahn, to take a watch below. Iris can take the evening watch, and Felix the next. I'm to be called if they sight any sails. Elise, stay a moment. I want to ask you a few questions."

Anna had stood with the rest, but she sank back onto the bench. Koszenmarc's officers filed out of the cabin with no more than a casual salute to their captain, though Joszua exchanged a worried glance with her.

Once they were alone, Koszenmarc smiled ruefully. "You look anxious. No, I think we've learned to trust one another. And I am grateful to you. Druss or Maszny would have taken us by surprise, except for your warning. Then there is the matter of what you discovered with your magic."

"Except I found nothing," she said carefully.

"Not exactly. You determined that nothing was to be found. That alone is an interesting point. Are you hungry?"

She started at the unexpected question. "I—What?"

That provoked a smile, however fleeting. "I am—hungry, that is—and I thought you might be as well, after all that magic. I also have a few questions to ask, away from the others. Let me send for dinner so we can discuss things more comfortably."

Things. Anna's skin prickled with apprehension.

He went to the door and spoke briefly with someone outside. Moments later two ship's boys arrived with a basket of flatbread, cheese, and a jug of wine. Shortly after, a girl hurried in with a platter of grilled fish and wine cups.

Koszenmarc poured wine for Anna, then himself. "Thea tells me you overtaxed yourself today, but this is a discussion that cannot wait. We can eat while we talk."

He gestured to the dishes between them. Anna helped herself to a serving of bread and cheese, watching with quick glances as Koszenmarc did the same. His face had all the marks of exhaustion and more than a little anxiety. *It's not just the jewel that worries him.*

For several moments, she had a reprieve as they ate. Koszenmarc finished off a serving of the fish and drank a cup of wine, then refilled his plate with bread and cheese before he spoke again.

"I mentioned that Joszua brought me news from Vyros," he said. "There's more than what I told you before. The details seemed irrelevant, but that was before today." His expression had turned thoughtful, as though he were still sorting through the implications of that news. Or, Anna thought, he wanted to choose how many of those details to reveal. He had mentioned trust, but she knew theirs was a limited and temporary trust.

He went on, "I had ordered Joszua to investigate the aftermath of your arrest. Along with what I told you before, he learned there were several robberies in the city. Swift, professional robberies, each costing the victim a substantial sum of money. One of the victims was murdered when they discovered the thief in the act."

Anna thought she understood the drift of this news, but she waited in silence.

Koszenmarc smiled faintly, as though he could read her thoughts. "That alone is nothing unusual. But the robberies stopped after six days. Not long after that, a mage connected with certain city gangs vanished. My question is this... Might there be a link between your friend Raab and what happened today?"

Her mouth went dry. "I would not call him my friend. A useful associate would be more accurate."

"So I thought. Do you trust him?"

She managed a careless shrug. "For certain matters, yes."

Koszenmarc tore off a piece of bread and rolled it between his fingers. Without meeting her gaze, he said, "I had wondered. He was not part of our agreement, after all. It's possible he wishes to rescue you and Maté. Or he wishes to rescue the stolen goods himself for your client back in Duenne."

"That is possible," she said reluctantly. "Truth be told, my client would... dislike our agreement. He wished us to accomplish our task discreetly and quickly, neither of which has happened. And even if your client agrees to negotiate with mine, I suspect he will demand a very high price."

"I suspect you are correct," Koszenmarc said. "One risk of our trade is that our clients are not always reasonable."

There was nothing she could say to that, so she simply smiled.

Koszenmarc smiled back. "At least your other companion is a friend. Eleni believes you were both bonded servants. Likely to the same master, she said."

Anna froze. Ah, so, this friendly dinner was simply another, gentler form of questioning. She would have to tread carefully—and find the means to speak privately with Maté again to make sure their stories agreed. "We were, once. We've remained friends, as you can see."

He abandoned the bread, now reduced to a heap of crumbs, and took a sip of wine. "You were lucky to earn your freedom together. Your old master must have been in a generous mood. Is he the one who had you trained in magic?"

She hesitated, uncertain where he was leading this conversation. "I began my studies with my father. When he died, I sold my bond and my new master allowed me to continue. He wanted a mage in his service, you see."

"He must have thought highly of you."

He only thought to make use of me.

Immediately, her appetite vanished and she set her fork down.

"What's wrong?" Koszenmarc asked.

"Nothing." Her belly shivered, and she was certain that her voice did too. She drew a long breath to steady herself. "Other than a very tiring and frightening day."

He lifted his eyebrows, but when she didn't say more, he murmured, "My apologies for touching upon unpleasant memories." He refilled their wine cups, then took a drink. "Quite a few of my company took service for much the same reasons. Eleni did. When she was twelve, she sold herself to a rich man on Vyros so her brothers and sisters would not starve."

Anna needed several moments to realize what he'd said. *It seemed a good idea,* Maté had said. *Yes, I know how that is,* Eleni had replied. Only now did those words carry a deeper and darker meaning. "She won back her bond, then?" she said.

"No." His gaze flicked up to hers, then back to his plate. "She ran away with her son. I haven't asked her why, but I can guess. You see why I don't give her any missions on Vyros or the other large islands."

So much left unspoken, but Anna thought she could guess those reasons. "What about Nikolas?"

He had the grace to look embarrassed. "That was a mistake. I wanted to send one of the boys or girls after you, to make certain you were safely delivered on Vyros. Nikolas insisted he would not be in any danger, if he landed well away from the city. He was wrong. The shore patrol nearly caught him. Eleni was...not pleased."

It was a mistake, Nikolas had said to his friend Theo.

"Why are you telling me this?" she asked.

He shrugged. "No reason."

When he spoke next, it was to make an observation about her magical studies with Thea. Anna gave a suitable reply, and gradually the conversation drifted away from the personal to more general topics. History. The Emperor, his heirs, and his Court, about which Koszenmarc seemed remarkably well informed, despite his long absence.

Under any other circumstances, Anna might have enjoyed their conversation, but she had told this man too many lies. It would be too easy to let slip a remark that contradicted the story she had given Koszenmarc about her supposed client in Duenne. Or worse, that might lead him to suspect who that client was. The thought of what Brun might do if that happened...

With a start, she realized Koszenmarc had asked her a question.

"I'm sorry," she said. "What did you say?"

He smiled. "Nothing important. I'm afraid I've been chattering. Perhaps I should follow my own orders about taking a watch below. As you said, we've had a long and exhausting day. We should both turn in."

Anna stood, grateful for the reprieve. Koszenmarc raised his cup as she left the cabin. But later, as she lay in her hammock, unable to sleep, she wondered if she had revealed anything that would in time betray her.

CHAPTER 12

Nine days later, Anna Zhdanov sat opposite Thea Antonious with the scent of incense rising up from the copper bowl between them. It was midmorning of an early autumn day, and though the seasons in Eddalyon were nothing like those in Duenne, there was a marked difference in the quality of the sunlight, and the far more frequent storms left a lingering trace of electricity in the air.

Anna sighed and attempted to pin her thoughts on the balance point. Thea had given her a more difficult task—to translate herself to the edge of the magical void, to the moment where her soul could take flight, and then to hover there for the space of three breaths. Once she had mastered that, she could make the leap into Anderswar and, perhaps, discover the exact trajectory of Sarrész's path when he reentered the ordinary world.

She breathed in, held the air inside her lungs, then released it slowly as she whispered the words in Erythandran to summon the magical current.

...Komen mir de kreft, komen mir de strôm...

Her skin rippled. The dark red-and-black patterns against her eyelids turned to unrelieved blackness. The air felt thicker, more alive, and she felt a curious lightness within. Another breath and her soul would lift from her body...

Her throat squeezed shut in sudden panic, and the current vanished.

Damn, damn, damn.

Anna pressed the heels of her hands against her forehead. Six attempts today. Six failures. At this rate, they would never find Sarrész. Off to one side, Daria Ioannou sighed and muttered a few curses of her own.

"Daria, my love," Thea said. "Why don't you take a walk?"

Daria lay on her back, arms flung out to either side, taking up most of the floor in Thea's chambers. She was the very picture of exasperation. If Anna had not been so frustrated herself, she might have been amused. "I took a walk," Daria said in a plaintive voice. "Twice, no, three times today. What I want is a ship, a ship and a crew, as bloodthirsty as possible, but our beloved captain…"

She trailed off with a hiss.

No need to explain that hiss. When the *Konstanze* returned from Idonia, Koszenmarc had declared a state of siege. No more secret missions to seek out Aldo Sarrész. No more visits to port cities to take on victuals and other supplies. The company would forage on neighboring islands for greenstuff and lumber, he said. As for rope and iron and other such items, they would make do until the crisis had passed.

If it ever does, Anna thought. Koszenmarc had sent Joszua with the cutter back to Idonia, to visit his family in secret and learn whatever he could about Druss's and Maszny's actions. Joszua had returned, pale and shaken, with the news that Maszny had issued a warrant for Koszenmarc's arrest.

Anna blew out a breath and dismissed all thoughts of Koszenmarc. Her task was the balance point between worlds. And for all his sudden fanatical precautions, at least the man had not forbidden these magical attempts.

Perhaps he knows it's our only chance.

She closed her eyes and concentrated on that balance point, all it represented to her, to the company. Everything, was her first thought. She laughed, a light and breathless laugh, which brought her back from the edge of despair. It was possible. She knew it was. She only had to pin her thoughts and will upon that moment, just as Thea had taught her.

Before she could utter the first syllable of the magical summons, Thea touched her wrist lightly. "No."

Anna blinked. "What? I was about to—"

Thea glared at her. "You were about to launch yourself into the magical void. No thought. No planning. Just…leaping into nothing without any thought. Gods-damned stupid child," she went on, with more heat than Anna expected. "I have no wish to lose you, simply because you overreached yourself."

"But Thea—"

"But nothing. Stop. We'll try again tomorrow, after you've had some proper rest."

Anna pressed her lips together. She could not explain how urgent the matter was. If she could cross into the void, she could track Sarrész's path from Vyros and back into Eddalyon. She could recover the jewel and win her freedom.

It's already too late. He told you autumn.

No. He'll understand.

He won't. You know him well enough, Anna Zhdanov. He'll take the jewel and take you back into bondage. He might even pretend regret as an afterthought. It won't make any difference.

"You have that look again," Thea said softly. "Stubborn and irrational."

"Like you, my love," Daria said.

"Perhaps," Thea said. "We're all a bit on edge these days." Her gaze narrowed. "Elise, would you please do me a favor? Take that basket over by the wall, the one I packed this morning, and find a quiet spot outside. I need you to sort through the medicines, the way I taught you. Daria and I need to have a talk."

It was an obvious ploy to send Anna away, and the reason didn't matter. At the same time, Thea was right—until Koszenmarc lifted the siege, the company depended on whatever supplies they possessed. With a sigh, Anna slung the basket over her shoulder and exited the room, leaving the other two women to their private conversation.

Thea's chambers were a twist and a turn from the inner harbor, now crowded with sailors at work. The cutter *Daemon* had been hauled onto the sand to repair a leak in her hull. Both *Konstanze* and *Mathilde* had been emptied entirely with a view to examine all their stores and, for the *Mathilde* in particular, to improve her handling.

Several of the company on the shore glanced in her direction. It was not a friendly glance. Anna resisted the urge to glare back at them and continued on her way, rounding the point of the island, until she came to the low, flat shore on the western side. The sands here were wet and grey and scattered with broken shells. Across a short expanse of water lay the other two islands in Koszenmarc's domain. Both were empty—yet another outcome of that ill-fated visit to Idonia. No more drills. No more goats and sheep grazing in the open air. Everyone and everything had been gathered into Asulos's main sanctuary.

A fringe of clouds blurred the far horizon and the wind was freshening, blowing in directly from the west. There would be rain before sunset. Anna breathed in the scents of salt and mud and the coming storm and felt her own unsettled nerves grow quieter. She had not conquered the world and all its magic today. As Thea said, they would make a fresh attempt tomorrow and soon, soon—

She turned away from the open sea and continued her circuit to the far side of the island. Here the seas rolled on without interruption to the horizon. Here a small passageway cut into the island, one of dozens that honeycombed the rock. A few large boulders shielded its entrance from the sea, with more that could be leveraged to block the entrance entirely in case of attack, as she had learned from Daria.

It was almost as though Koszenmarc had expected an invasion long before he had kidnapped her from Maszny. Who was he, damn him, this man who understood warfare on land and sea? Perhaps later, once she had regained her freedom, she might look into his past.

She settled onto the sands and picked a jar at random from the basket. *Morinda (Leaves)* read the label, followed by a notation in Thea's hand. Harvested six months ago, apparently, from a trusted supplier in the central islands. Bought two weeks later by Thea herself.

Five months ago, I left Lord Brun's household to find a thief.

A task she'd failed to accomplish.

Her stomach gave an uncomfortable lurch at how badly she'd failed.

She ordered her unruly organ to behave and set the jar onto the packed sands. Ought she sort the medicines by date first, and then examine their potency? Thea had not said. Still considering how to approach her task, she picked up another jar. *Saltbush (Sap),* read the label. Acquired two months ago, from the markets of Iglazi.

Two months ago, she had set sail for Eddalyon, along with Raab and Maté. According to Koszenmarc, Raab had since disappeared. As for Maté, he might as well have vanished. Even with the entire company crowded into the heart of Asulos, Anna had not spoken to her friend since her return from Idonia.

It was no accident. That much she knew. Everything—their quarters, their chores, even the hours they took meals—had been arranged to ensure they had no chance to speak privately. Abruptly she shoved the two jars back into the basket and stood. It didn't matter where she spent the next hour, as long as Thea had her privacy and Anna checked over the medicines. She slung the basket over her shoulder and ducked into the passageway.

By now she knew every route along the lower levels, knew which branch to take at which intersection, which stairs led to other halls or passages, and which deliberately ended in a blank wall. She turned left and left a second time, past the next intersection to a wide set of steps that brought her into a wider tunnel where a dozen members of the company were playing a noisy game of dice.

The moment Anna appeared, the game stopped, the players went silent. She dropped her gaze and passed by, trying to ignore how the back of her neck prickled. It wasn't until she had rounded the next bend that their conversation resumed, and only in whispers.

It doesn't matter, she told herself. *We only need to find the jewel, then they'll be happy enough again. And Maté and I will be gone.*

She came at last to the great gathering hall and stopped as a wave of noise washed over her.

Once, she had accompanied her father to a lecture hall at Duenne's University, on the day a famous professor was to give a speech. The din from a hundred men and women and children echoing off the high stone walls reminded her of the din the students made as they argued over the best seats. If the voices here were punctuated by the bleating of goats, or the clash of sword against sword, well, the resemblance still held.

Across the way, she spotted Maté on one of the raised steps that circled the hall. He had a leather apron draped over his lap, and a neat stack of weapons off to one side. One of the company's dogs lounged next to him, tongue hanging out in the heat. Anna picked her way between the knots of men and women, many of them bent close in whispered conversation. There were more pointed stares and sudden silences. Anna ignored them, though once again her neck prickled with the weight of so much attention.

Maté glanced up at her approach. His expression was nearly impossible to read, but when he didn't tell her to leave, she took a seat next to him and began to sort through her basket. After a glance around the hall, her friend shrugged and resumed polishing a blade. In the center of the hall, Eleni led a group of the older children in a drill with wooden swords. She had sent one expressive glance toward them before she turned her attention back to her students.

"I missed you," Anna said softly.

"He's made sure of that," Maté replied, just as quietly.

No need to say Koszenmarc's name. She wondered if Thea had not expected Anna to seek out her old friend.

Or perhaps she gave me the opportunity.

"He might not trust us, even now," she murmured.

"Oh? I've heard—" He broke off and turned his attention to a spot of rust. "What I heard wasn't fair or true, but it was ugly."

She'd heard ugly rumors before, in Lord Brun's household. They still stung. "I've done nothing but look for that thrice-bedamned Sarrész."

"I *know.* I said it wasn't fair or true. What troubles me is that anyone thought so." Then, in a low voice, he said, "Half the hands believe you and

I betrayed the captain to Druss. The other half disagrees. They believe the traitor is one of their own. Neither one is a comfortable thought."

"Comfortable," she muttered. "Only you would use such a word."

"Oh. Well. I've lived through mutiny before."

Anna caught her breath. "Do you believe...?"

"I don't know. Maybe. I only know our captain must mend the trust between his officers and his company. An unhappy ship means the enemy has already won."

He left off speaking to concentrate on his work. Anna took the hint. She picked a jar at random from the basket and read its label. *Fennel, Essence Of.* Harvested the previous month by Thea herself. Thea had had some success with growing fennel in pots, but she could not raise nearly enough for the company's needs, and so every bit counted.

Anna wrapped her hands around the jar and centered her thoughts on its contents. A few breaths brought a whiff of magic to the air, cool and clean and with the scent of crushed grass. Next to her, Maté paused in scouring the blade, as if he had sensed magic's presence, and a few others close by glanced in her direction. Anna closed her eyes, savoring the current. No panic, no perception that her soul had loosed its grip on her body. Just a small, ordinary kind of magic, one that she had become adept at over the past month.

Komen mir de strôm. Zeigen mir de kreft.

Her thoughts gradually detached themselves from her surroundings. She was aware only of the smooth polished surface, the weight resting in her hands, the faintest indication of moisture drawn from the air that might indicate an approaching storm. All that in a passing moment. Now her awareness sank into the contents themselves. The oil distilled from the fennel seeds with hot water and smelling sweet. She caught a fleeting image of sunlight and green leaves, a scent like that of magic, still strong and potent.

Without releasing her hold upon the magic, Anna set the jar off to her right and selected the next. *Pepper, Root Of, Decoction.* Acquired three months ago. An antidote against poison, a valuable medicine, given Druss's liking for poisoned arrows. Pepper root was more fragile than fennel, and when she swiftly examined its potency, she wasn't surprised to find it somewhat faded. She wavered a moment, then set the jar next to the first.

The next three were easy to classify. Two jars of willow bark, and one of ginger, all old and empty. Anna placed those to her left. Once she had sorted them all, she would repack the basket with the contents divided. Then she and Thea would draw up an inventory of their supplies, with notes on which herbs and decoctions to discard, and which Thea thought could be revived with magic.

But Anna didn't want to think about the coming weeks, when jar by jar, their medicines faded beyond recall, or dwindled to nothing, all because there was a traitor amongst the company. Instead, she worked through her task, while at her side, Maté cleaned and polished weapons.

Meanwhile, the drill practice for the children had come to an end. Eleni bent close to one of the youngest children, showing her a better grip on the hilt. Nikolas, Theo, and a girl had gathered off to one side, discussing the session in highly technical terms, while the senior members of the company took their places in the center of the hall.

Maté set his work aside. "Time for my twice-daily beating."

Anna snorted. "No one beats you. Though perhaps they should."

"Oh, there are a few…"

He shrugged himself into a leather vest, then settled a helmet on his head. The company used wooden blades for their drill practice, but Koszenmarc insisted they wear proper gear. There had been too many injuries of late, and a wooden blade was just as dangerous as steel, depending on where the blow landed.

Maté bent down to pick up his leather guards. One of the younger men, named Berit, happened to be passing by. He bumped against Maté, who stumbled. Before Maté could catch himself, someone else hooked a foot around his leg and sent him sprawling. In the space of a moment, a dozen more men and women crowded around Maté.

Half the hands believe you and I betrayed the captain…

Anna thrust her basket to one side and launched herself to her feet.

A woman whose name escaped her grabbed Anna by the hair. "Don't make any trouble, girl. Or you'll be next."

Anna glared at her. *Two gods-be-damned words, and I could roast you with fire.*

But just as she drew a breath to speak, everyone retreated several steps, leaving Maté and a giant of a sailor named Karl facing each other. Maté's helmet had vanished. He had a bruise on one cheek and a cut over his left eye. Karl too had several bruises and his mouth was bloodied.

"What in the name of all the gods is going on?"

The crowd parted immediately. Eleni, sword in hand, stalked toward the two men. "You," she said to Karl. "What do you think you're doing?"

"I wanted a fight," Karl growled. "A gods-be-damned fight with this fucking traitor. You know what they say."

"I know exactly what they say," Eleni said sharply. "But if it's a fight you want, then you shall have one."

With a roar, Karl lunged toward Maté. In one quick motion, Eleni jabbed the hilt of her sword into his ribs. Karl dropped to his knees, and she grabbed a fistful of his hair and bent his head back. "Not you," she said in a soft, cool voice. "Me."

She released his hair and shoved him away. Then she swung around to face Maté. All the cold rage had leaked away from his expression and he stared at her with a strange and wondering look. "A fight," he said. "You against me."

She nodded. "It seems a good idea."

At that he smiled faintly. "Ah. Yes, I believe I understand. I shall need a weapon, then. Wooden blades?"

Eleni shook her head. "Steel. Winner draws first blood. Choose the best blade you can find, Kovács. You shall need it."

Everyone withdrew to clear a space for them. Someone—Daria—shouldered her way through the crowd with several sheathed swords, which she offered to Maté. He inspected each one, still with that faint smile. Joszua appeared next with a vest and helmet for Eleni. The silence in the hall was as thick as a fog rolling in from the sea.

Maté chose his sword. Eleni donned a leather vest and helmet. Both took their places in first stance, as if for a drill. Eleni touched her blade to his. There was a soft ping of metal against metal that echoed throughout the breathless hall.

"Begin," she said.

Their first exchange was a quick rattle of blows—strike and parry, parry and strike. Maté's expression was unreadable, Eleni's equally so, but underneath that seeming indifference, Anna detected an unmistakable air of excitement from both.

A second and third exchange took place, even faster than before, if that was possible. Once or twice, Maté nearly penetrated Eleni's defense, but though he had the advantage in height and reach, she was faster and nimbler. She danced away from his blade, deflected the next blow, then slid her blade underneath his. Maté had to retreat quickly to avoid the point.

A fight to first blood only, Eleni had said. But Anna knew how easily a sword could slice through a critical vein.

Now Maté pressed his attack, and Eleni gave way before him. The crowd murmured but no one attempted to interfere. Sometime in the past several moments, Nikolas and Theo had appeared at Anna's side, and they gripped each other's hands. Gods. There could be no good end to this fight.

Another quick exchange of blows and the fight reversed itself. Eleni drove Maté back and back around the same circle, their blades moving so fast the metal had turned to a blur. Eleni's eyes were bright—no trace of that mask now—and Maté was grinning. It was a conversation without any words, and Anna held her breath, not entirely sure what it meant.

Still giving way, Maté reached the edge of the circle. He beat off Eleni's next attack and sidestepped to gain room. In that moment of his distraction, Eleni slipped past his defense and her blade furrowed his arm.

Both froze. Then Eleni jerked her sword back.

Maté dropped to his knees. Very carefully he laid his sword at her feet. Blood soaked through his shirtsleeve and trickled down his arm.

"My lady," he said. "Victory is yours."

Eleni tucked her sword under one arm and held out both hands. Maté clasped them and stood, wincing. A roar broke out from the crowd—a happy roar—followed by the company surging toward the pair. Nikolas and Theo had already vanished. Anna started to leave as well, but checked herself at the sight of Karl off to one side, with Joszua talking to him earnestly.

Karl glanced up. His gaze met hers and he glared.

Anna flinched back.

It's not over, not nearly, she thought. The swordfight might have pricked the bubble of rage for today, but it had not solved anything.

She dropped to her knees and fumbled for the jars around her basket. The commotion had knocked the basket over, but to her relief, only one jar had broken, a vial of foxglove. The rest she would have to reexamine and re-sort later. Well, it wasn't as though she had no time. She had nothing but time until Maszny left off hunting for Koszenmarc.

The commotion in the hall had died away. Maté and Eleni had both vanished from sight. That swordfight had not been planned—she was certain of that—but the way they had stared at each other in those last moments...

She retreated around the hall and back through the passageway, to another intersection that led her to the inner harbor and Thea's chambers. The other woman was leafing through one of her many books of essays. At Anna's entrance, she glanced up. Her gaze immediately sharpened, and she shut the book. "What is it? What happened?"

Anna suppressed the urge to swear. "Am I that easy to read?"

Thea smiled at her. "If I were a softhearted woman, I would say, of course not. But I'm not. What happened?"

Anna related everything, including that last unsettling glimpse of Karl as Joszua attempted to calm the man. Thea's lips thinned into a straight line.

"I'd heard the rumors," she said. "I hadn't realized how close we were to disaster. We shall have to attempt crossing into Anderswar soon, but I don't like it. You aren't ready, and neither am I."

So. Thea had been practicing as well. Anna felt an unreasonable sense of relief and exasperation. Relief that she had a companion in this madness. Exasperation that Thea had mentioned nothing to her.

She turned away from Thea to unpack her basket. If only she could recall exactly what she had seen in Anderswar. She knew exactly what she did remember—a blurred figure leaping from the edge of the magical void. She could almost imagine the direction of that long, long leap, but she wasn't certain. Her memory of that glimpse had faded with time, just as these herbs and powders had faded over time. If only Thea could restore her memory as easily and reliably as she could the potency of her medicines...

She paused, her hands resting on the jars. "Thea. You know how to restore herbs, am I right? What about memories?"

Thea observed her with narrowed eyes. "What do you mean?"

"I mean." And here Anna had to draw a shaky breath. "I mean could you restore the potency of my memories? One particular memory. Of what I saw in Anderswar."

Thea was silent for so long that Anna nearly repeated her question, but the other woman finally said, "I can. But it's dangerous."

"How dangerous?"

"It's a question of influence," Thea said slowly. "And trust. If you attempt the spell on yourself, you might recall a false memory, or you might alter a genuine one through the influence of your own wishes. The trust, now, that's even more dangerous. You see, whoever works that spell upon you can ask you whatever they please and you will answer. You will need to trust them absolutely before you submit to it. Do you?"

So many questions wrapped up in that one. And yet, that Thea had warned her meant so much more.

She nodded. "I do. Come with me."

* * * *

Six guards occupied the ledge outside Koszenmarc's sanctuary atop Asulos. Anna recognized them. These were his most trusted guards, men and women who had served their captain the longest. So, she thought. He was not entirely oblivious to the potential for mutiny.

Further changes were evident inside the sanctuary itself. Koszenmarc had cleared away all the books and scrolls from his desk and stowed them neatly away in their shelves. The largest of his maps lay spread over the table in the middle of the chamber, with notes pinned to half a dozen of the islands. Koszenmarc himself sat bent over the table. His face was drawn, his eyes rimmed red.

"You have a suggestion?" he said. His voice sounded rough with exhaustion.

Anna exchanged a glance with Thea, who wore a carefully bland expression. "I do. That is, we do. Thea and I believe we can discover where Aldo Sarrész landed in Eddalyon."

Koszenmarc's response was a shrug. "He might be dead, our lord and thief, and the goods he stole at the bottom of the sea."

Anna had braced herself for any number of replies from this man. A challenge. A renegotiation of their terms. But not this weary indifference. Was this the same man who carried her off on that mad ride through Iglazi's streets and across its mountainside?

"He might be dead," she said carefully. "But we shall never know unless I make the attempt."

And if I don't, your company shall rend itself to pieces while you hide from the Emperor's dogs.

"You must understand," Thea said. "The magic is dangerous. Not the kind of danger where a soul drowns in magic or loses itself in Anderswar. I mean that Elise must trust me completely, because once she submits to that magic, you and I might question her about anything and she will answer truthfully."

"Ah." He gave a faint smile. "I understand. Yes." His gaze swung to Anna's. "I promised you once I would do you no harm. I promise that again. Our only questions shall involve Lord Sarrész and his whereabouts, nothing else. Are you willing?"

He spoke softly, but she did not miss the urgency behind those words. "I am," she said. "I trust you, my lord. You and Thea both."

Koszenmarc regarded her with a bright and curious gaze. "Do you, now? How very unexpected. I wonder..." But just as he seemed about to say more, he seemed to recall himself with a shake of the head. "Never mind that," he said. "Let us make this attempt."

* * * *

Koszenmarc ordered away all the guards and lookouts. He wanted no one present who might be tempted to break Anna's trust, or to influence what she remembered under Thea's magic. "Memory is a delicate matter of what is writ upon our minds," Thea told them. "Desire, anger, mistrust, all the passions color what we think is the truth, and when the memory itself is faint, the least suggestion can alter what you recall."

So. No other witnesses. The shutters opened to admit the freshening wind, to clear away the scent of old memories, but also, as Anna noted, to drown the whispering from the many vents around the chamber. Koszenmarc moved the table and benches to one side to provide a clear space. Anna and Thea settled cross-legged upon the worn stones of the floor.

Thea took Anna's hands in hers. "We bind the current together, you and I. I shall start off with the summons. You shall reply with whatever phrase you believe follows. It should be like the call and response in Lir's temples, or the ones you learned from your tutors."

Anna thought she understood. She nodded. "I'm ready."

Once more, the scent of incense filled the air. Once more, Anna held Thea's hands lightly within hers. Once more, they would call upon the current together.

Ei rûf ane gôtter, Thea said.

Ei rûf ane zauberei unde strôm, Anna replied.

Ane Lir unde Toc. Ane bluot unde vleisch, ane sinne unde sele unde verstant.

With each exchange, the scent of magic grew stronger, and the current that brushed Anna's face changed in quality, from the ordinary and familiar ocean breeze to one that spoke of a world outside all worlds.

Gently, gently, said Thea's voice inside her mind.

As soft as a feather, as light as a soul, Anna answered.

Thea's voice rippled with amusement. *As if a soul were anything but the greatest weight of them all. Come, child. Take me into your mind, if you will.*

Anna hesitated only a moment before she reached out for Thea. She felt a momentary shock, as though they were two clouds and lightning had arced between them. Her breath shivered inside her chest. Thea went still.

Your name is Anna. I won't tell him. But you see why I asked if you trusted me.

I understand. My name doesn't matter.

Anna could hear the laughter in Thea's voice. *The philosophers would disagree. Are you ready to show me your memories?*

I am.

She sank deep and deeper into the magical current, suspended between moment and moment, between the now on Asulos and the days unwinding to the past. Thea's presence had withdrawn. No, she was following close behind Anna, both of them leaving ghost prints in time. Back to the morning she woke in the grotto. Her desperate impulse to make a pact with Koszenmarc. Her relief that Maté lived. Memories as vivid as the moment she lived them.

Vyros, Thea said. Her voice echoed between the magic and the ordinary world. *Remember what you saw on Vyros.*

Anna's memory shifted abruptly. Suddenly she stood on the sands of that lonely inlet. A patchwork of images flooded her mind. The brilliant sands. Terns and gulls wheeling overhead. The dark green shadows of the forest beyond. And more than images, the strange spicy scent that she had come to associate with Eddalyon. The texture of the sands imprinted upon her knees and hands as she knelt to trace that otherworldly signature. Thea's voice, rough and low, as she ordered Daria to let her go.

Remember the void. Remember Anderswar.

Another twitch, and she knelt upon the edge of that magical void between worlds and lives. Once again that eerie chorus rose up around her. Once more the ordinary world lay before her, and she could make out those twelve footprints that marked a man running in terror from one world to the next.

Soft and slow, my child. Soft and slow. Find the moment and the balance. Look. Look and remember.

It was as though time hung motionless. Anna pinned her attention upon the footprints. She traced their direction, and as she recalled what she had missed before, she sighted a blurred figure as it plunged from the void, as though a finger had drawn Sarrész's path in her mind.

Soft and slow, slow and soft, Thea said, but Anna didn't need the reminder. She hung there, in the eternal balance of magic, entirely focused on the image before her.

Three irregular squiggles against an indigo sea. Two of them little more than an interruption to the rolling waves. The third a sturdy barrier, but even that was a tiny blip in the vastness of the southern ocean.

Anna bit down on her lips and willed herself to remember more. She drew back from those three small islands, drew back until her vision encompassed them and the next collection of sand and reef, back farther still until she had fixed in her mind the distances between Idonia and Vyros, between these islands and what she now called Sarrész's islands.

Now, she said. *Now I remember. Thea, bring me back, please.*

Thea must have heard, because time gave an unnatural shudder. For a moment, Anna felt herself suspended between two moments, two worlds. The magical void where she crouched, facing outward to the ordinary world. And the ordinary world itself, where she sat upon the stone floor of Koszenmarc's chambers.

But then, the past and its magic vanished, and she collapsed into the world. A pair of arms surrounded her, warm and strong and steady. For a moment, she thought herself back in the temple on Idonia.

She drew a long breath. Heard an answering one from Thea, felt the quick rise and fall of Koszenmarc's chest against her back.

"I saw..." Her throat was clogged. She coughed and tried again. "I saw... everything. I saw where Sarrész fell."

She pulled away from Koszenmarc and tried to stand, but her legs folded. Koszenmarc caught her before she fell.

"You are doing much better," Thea said. "But that was still a chancy bit of magic. You should rest a bit. Have a cup of tea."

"No." Her lips still didn't work properly, and she had to grip Koszenmarc's arm to keep from falling. She coughed and tried again. "I need. To show what I saw. Before I forget."

"As you wish." Koszenmarc slung her arm over his neck, then circled his arm around her waist. Anna was grateful for the support, but by the time they reached his desk, she was able to stand by herself.

"Bring me the map," she ordered in a rasping voice.

Koszenmarc fetched the map from the table and spread it over the desk. Anna stared at it, her vision still blurred from magic. The map was a man-made thing, the ocean depths and current rendered in neat ink lines, showing a world properly ordered and predictable, when the gods themselves knew that worlds and lives and the universe had no order except the pull from life to life again.

She drew a picture in her mind of those islands, a cluster of reefs and sand bars making a great circle around them. She drew back from that image to the wider one that showed a vast expanse of open seas. Farther back and she saw the familiar shape of Vyros and those smaller islands that surrounded it.

Now she transferred her attention to the map. *East,* she thought. East and somewhat south, but as she traced her finger along the direction she remembered, she came to the edge of the chart.

"Your map doesn't show the islands I saw."

"How much does it show? Can you make a better chart?"

She was afraid to promise too much. "I'm no mapmaker. I can't promise to be exact."

"It's more than we had before. Make a copy of what you saw, as best as you can. I'll have writing materials sent to your quarters." Then, after an infinitesimal pause, he said, "Burn any copies you discard. And tell no one."

He didn't mention Maté by name, but he didn't need to. Even a trusted friend might be suspect, and keeping this secret from Maté would only prove his innocence.

"I understand," she said. "You can trust me."

"I know. I have."

His gaze swung up and caught hers. All the bleakness, all the weariness had vanished, and she thought she saw a much younger Lord Koszenmarc, before his days as a pirate, before his days in Duenne's Court.

Koszenmarc seemed just as unnerved as she was. Then he gave himself a shake. "Prepare for a long voyage. Bring herbs and spells and books, whatever you need. We sail within two days."

CHAPTER 13

By the time Anna descended from Koszenmarc's airy chambers to her own small grotto near the sea, she found the mood of the company entirely changed. Koszenmarc had passed the word for all his officers, senior and junior. He had not given a reason, but he hadn't needed to. Those on watch outside his sanctuary, the same ones who had regarded her coldly the day before, now smiled at her with satisfaction. Daria, hurrying up the ladder, gave her a cheeky wink.

It was the relief of action—any action—that lightened the crew's mood. She felt it herself. But if they didn't find Sarrész...

She tried not to think about that as she hurried back to her quarters. A pot of freshly brewed tea awaited her there, along with the promised writing kit and a generous supply of paper. There was even an overturned crate to serve as her desk. Anna settled herself on the ground and took up a pen.

What if I fail? What if I forget?

She closed her eyes and drew a steadying breath. Found the balance point. And now the memories Thea had revived flooded back into her brain. No, she would never forget. She drew a sheet of paper to the center of her makeshift desk, dipped her pen in the ink and tapped away the excess. She had just drawn the first few tentative lines when someone spoke her name.

"Anna."

Anna jumped, overturning her desk. Her teacup bounced over the stones, splattering tea over the walls and floor. *Damn, damn, damn.*

Maté stood in the doorway, grinning at her confusion. Of course. Who else would call her by her true name? If she'd had a moment to think, she would have realized it right away.

"You." She gathered up the teacup and pens. "I should smack you for scaring me like that. Oh, yes, except someone already has."

He dismissed her comment with a wave of his hand. "I've heard the news. You found Lord Sarrész."

She hesitated, not certain how much she was allowed to say. "Not exactly. I...remembered what I saw before."

He'd noticed that small pause before she spoke. "And you cannot say more. Captain's orders, no doubt. Does he know about the jewel?"

Anna pressed a hand against her forehead. *One crisis at a time*, she told herself. But Maté was right. Once Koszenmarc discovered that Sarrész's *stolen goods* were in fact not just a jewel, but the same one the goddess Lir had given to humankind, all his promises would vanish.

"No, I've not told him," she said. "I'll tell him once I must. If I must."

"Lies make everything harder," he said quietly.

He spoke as though he'd spent the past few hours considering all the lies she and he had told these past few weeks. And because they were such old friends, she asked, "What about Eleni? Have you told her anything?"

He shook his head. "No, those secrets aren't mine alone, as you very well know. But, Anna..." His voice caught momentarily. "Anna, I cannot lie to her today, and ask for her trust tomorrow."

And Eleni Farakos did not offer trust lightly.

"I wish our blessed Emperor had never set eyes upon that jewel," Anna said in a low voice. "I wish that miserable Sârrész had never stolen it, and I most especially wish our Lord Brun had never decided to meddle in Duenne's thrice-damned Court."

Maté laughed softly. "Oh no, that wouldn't do at all. Without our thief and the jewel, you'd still be in Duenne without any hope of buying back your bond. Don't worry about me, Anna. Draw your chart, and I'll figure out what happens after we hunt down Lord Sarrész."

He left her to her task. After staring at the ink-splattered sheet in front of her, Anna crumpled the sheet of paper and set it aside. She took a fresh one and dipped her pen in ink. Find the balance point, she told herself. Everything else would follow from there.

* * * *

Two hours later, she burned all her discarded attempts and tucked the final copies into her sash before she climbed back up the rope ladder to Koszenmarc's chambers. This time, there was no delay before the guard announced her, and she walked in with more confidence than she felt.

"The map you require." She laid out five sheets of paper on his desk. Koszenmarc's mouth quirked in a smile as he surveyed her work. "Very nice. And quick, considering all this." He indicated the several different versions of her chart. "Why did you make so many drawings?"

"Because I wanted to show the islands in as much detail as I could recall, but I also wanted to show the larger picture, with the known islands for a reference point. You *did* say these were off any known charts." Then, as he continued to examine her work closely, she added, "They are not as exact as I would like."

"And you love to be precise," he murmured. "No, these are very good. We can circle Idonia and complete our water along the way, not to mention taking advantage of the current. From there…"

He had clearly forgotten about her, about anything outside the problem of Sarrész and where to find him. Anna was fairly certain she could withdraw and he wouldn't notice. But she had one important favor to ask of him, now, while he was so pleased with her work.

She cleared her throat. Koszenmarc glanced up.

"I have a request," she said. "I know your ship is not a council of equals, but I wondered if you would consider including Maté as part of this mission. I understand why you kept us apart, but I believe he would prove useful in case we need to—"

He held up a hand. "You don't need to convince me. I agree. Besides"— his mouth quirked in a smile—"you aren't the first to make this request."

Oh. Eleni, of course. Well, then.

She ducked her head to hide her embarrassment. "Thank you."

He regarded her with a faint frown. "You're welcome. I had not expected— Well, never mind what I expected. Please tell Thea I need to speak with her. We've a great deal to accomplish before we set off."

He bent over the maps again, already tracing out their route, and hardly seemed to notice when Anna exited the room.

CHAPTER 14

Two days of hard work for the entire company followed, from senior officers down to the youngest of the ships' boys and girls. Anna had thought all three ships well stocked and in prime condition, but she soon realized how wrong she was. Greenstuff gathered from the nearest islands, sails and sheets and spars inspected, the *Konstanze*'s hold emptied and restocked with fresh supplies. A fresh coat of paint, of different colors and a different pattern. Every blade inspected and scoured clean.

What held true for the ships and for their weapons, also held true for Thea and Anna's supply of medicine. They were awake from dawn until midnight, sorting through their powders and herbs and infusions, throwing out any that had entirely lost their potency, enhancing any that had promise. Thea kept a strict log of their decisions, so they knew what to replenish later, and sent Joszua off in the *Daemon* to collect various herbs from nearby islands that might do as a substitute.

Meanwhile, Koszenmarc spent hours in conference with his officers to determine who would accompany the ship and who would stay behind.

A few sweet hours of sleep broken by the dawn bells, and to work once more.

The morning of their departure was even more exhausting and chaotic, if that were possible. Anna and Thea working quickly, snatching up this or that forgotten item, while Daria shouted for everyone to board the ship, *now, now, now.* Anna shoved one last roll of bandages in her satchel and immediately jerked back her hand, dripping blood. A surgical blade had found its way into her bag. She stopped only long enough to bind the wound with a rag. There was time enough aboard ship to tend to it, she told Thea.

Aboard the ship at last. The crew hauled up the boats and tied them. Eleni rapped out orders. Men and women swarmed up the masts and rigging. Another series of commands and sails rose up from their lines to billow out, turning the pyramid of ropes into one of bright white cloth. A faint humming filled the air. They were in motion, the island shrinking on the horizon.

CHAPTER 15

Anna leaned against the railing, face lifted to the breeze. Over the past two weeks, the steady rise and fall of the *Konstanze* had become as familiar to her as the pattern of their days. The change from watch to watch, the daily sessions with Thea to practice their magic, the kind and quantity of each meal that marked the passage through the week. It was as though they had dropped away from the true world and now skimmed over an endless blue disc.

"Wishing on a drowned star?" Koszenmarc said.

Anna jumped and bit back a laugh. "You surprised me."

"Good. Terrible thing for a pirate, to be predictable."

"I would never accuse you of *that*," she murmured.

His mouth twisted into a wry grin. "And I can always trust you to be honest."

She could not think how to reply to that. They had talked very little over the past two weeks, and only about their mission. From time to time, he asked if she'd caught any glimpse or hint of that strange magical signature. From time to time, she asked about their progress. Koszenmarc had brought up the possibility of taking bearings with magic, just as a captain might take bearings from the stars and sun. But nothing more about Anna's past, nor anything beyond the moment they overtook Sarrész.

Today, he lingered by the rail, his eyes narrowed against the glare from the ocean swells. "I don't like the look of that weather," he said, indicating the blurred horizon to the south. Mist, or clouds, Anna couldn't tell which. It was as though a thumb had smeared the sky and sea together. The wind had kicked up in the past few moments, and she thought she could smell rain. She said so.

He nodded. "The glass tells me we'll have a storm before nightfall." Then, "Do you know, you've not been seasick once since we set sail." She sent a sideways glance in his direction. "So kind of you to notice." "Oh, I pay attention to all my people."

His tone was amused, which irritated her, but he was right. She had not needed to summon the magic current even once to ease her stomach. Thea had mentioned a possible connection between that and her newfound skills with the balance point. Anna was not entirely convinced, however. "Most likely, I've finally become accustomed to the sea," she said.

"Most likely," he agreed. "Do you— That is, would you care to stay in the islands after this? Pleasant weather. Far away from the Empire. Mind, you don't need to hire with a pirate company. Any number of merchant ships would gladly hire you as a surgeon, or a navigator. Or, if you didn't mind the pirates, you could join my company. Thea would be happy for your assistance."

It was the closest he had come to asking her plans for after. After they tracked down Sarrész. After he discovered the truth about the *stolen goods.* She stirred uneasily. "No. Thank you, but no. I'm happier in the north. By the way, when should I try to take those magical bearings?"

Koszenmarc shot a quick glance in her direction, but he replied in a neutral voice. "Tomorrow will do. We're close to the edge of my charts—all the charts except yours. Do you see those tall rocks over to the north?"

Anna squinted against the sun. Far ahead, she could just make out a cluster of bare rocks rising up from the sea, surrounded by a dance of mist and breaking waves. "I see them. What are they?"

"The Imperial mapmakers named them Desolation. I've heard a number of other names the islanders use, none of them fit to repeat. But they mark the edge of the Empire, and the edge of the known islands. Aldo Sarrész's islands lie a day or two north and east of them, depending on the wind and weather. We'll record the hour we pass Desolation, then—"

"Sails!" cried the lookout. "Sails two points to the south!"

Koszenmarc whipped out his glass and swore. Three pale red dots had emerged from the bank of clouds to the west. Oh gods. Those were Druss's ships, sails taut against the wind. *They were following us.*

Following and gaining fast.

Eleni Farakos appeared on deck, shouting orders. The entire watch scrambled aloft, and in moments more sails rose up their lines. The ship jerked forward, then leaned hard to starboard just as a cloud of light and smoke exploded from the largest of Druss's ships. Within a moment, the cold clean scent of magic rolled over the *Konstanze.*

Before the significance of that magic could register, a volley of liquid fire arced toward the *Konstanze*, a bright burst of white-hot flames that sucked all moisture from the air. Anna caught the scent of a bought spell, sharp and green but missing the intensity of magic summoned in the instant. The fire missed the *Konstanze* by a hundred yards. A second volley followed a moment later, much closer. "Tack to larboard," Koszenmarc shouted. "Faster, faster, you miserable slugs! Stand by to raise the shields!" He swung around to Anna. "You. Go below at once."

Koszenmarc's order plucked Anna from her daze. She scrambled toward the nearest hatch. Behind her, sparks and smoke and flames exploded through the air. A man screamed. Anna tumbled down the hatch, grabbing for the ladder, and landed two levels down in the cargo hold, her arms nearly wrenched from her body.

She lay there, bruised and breathless, huddled between the water casks and spare sails. From far overhead came the pounding of feet as sailors raced to obey orders. The ship shuddered to a stop, then plunged forward, the song of the lines rising higher and higher. More shouts, then another explosion, and this time the ship rocked far to one side and she smelled the scent of burning flesh. Her stomach lurched against her ribs and she had to swallow hard.

Go back, she told herself. *Never mind what the captain ordered. You learned those cursed battle spells.* But it was incredibly hard to stand and follow through.

She did, at last. She grabbed hold of the ladder's rails and hauled herself up to the next deck. Here, the stink of smoke and charred flesh was even stronger, but she gathered her courage and set her next foot upon the ladder.

"There you are."

Thea beckoned to her. "I need your magic," she said. "Come with me." When Anna hesitated, she said gently, "You won't be much help above decks, not with you flinching at every attack. Come with me to the sick bay where you might do some good."

Thea's sick bay was a small corner toward the back of the ship's berth, with a curtain to mark it off from the sailors' hammocks. In the middle were two large chests, pushed together. One of the hands, a young man named Berit, lay on his back. He squirmed away from Thea's touch, making small mewing noises.

"I thought her poison bad enough," Thea said. "But now she's bought some gods-be-damned magic fire. Just give us a few moments," she said quietly to Berit. "I'll have you resting easy, my friend."

She took Anna's hand and placed it over Berit's forehead. "One hand here, the other at his wrist. You know the balance point. Hold him there while I do the rest."

Thea hummed softly. The air, so still and thick, awoke to the magic. Anna felt a tickle of warmth against her palms. She looked down. A mistake. The great ugly burn covered half of Berit's face and throat, the skin bubbled and black. She choked.

"Close your eyes," Thea said. "Find the balance."

Anna swallowed and did as Thea commanded. Thea continued to hum, and the stink of burnt flesh receded. A fresh sharp scent filled the sick bay, and the tickle of warmth grew stronger—not the stifling heat of belowdecks, but a warmth that reminded Anna of holding snow-chilled hands before a strong fire. She breathed in the scent of magic and let her thoughts drop away from the sight of that terrible wound, into the rhythm of Thea's humming. The current flowed into her, round and about and back through Berit, growing stronger with each moment.

"There," Thea said. "He'll do for a bit. Now for the next patient."

Two more had arrived while they worked over Berit. One sat on a chest, slumped over and cradling her left arm in her lap. "Broken," Thea said after a quick examination. "You can wait," she told the woman, inserting a knotted rag into her mouth. "Chew this to help with the pain."

"Ginger infusion," she said to Anna. "Brewed strong."

The other was an older man with a broken-off arrow buried in his shoulder. "Barbed and poisoned," Thea said in a low voice. "I'll make a potion, but I need you to hold him steady."

Together they extracted the arrow, then while Anna held him in the balance point, Thea brewed the necessary potion to draw out the poison. Once they had made him comfortable, Thea splinted the woman's broken arm, then checked on Berit. More wounded came below. Another poison-arrow wound. A woman with a massive splinter embedded between her ribs.

A lull followed, during which Thea brewed a pot of fennel tea and ordered Anna to lay out more clean bandages. Their splinter wound rested easily, as did the woman with the broken arm, but Thea shook her head over the sailors hit by the poisoned arrows.

Meanwhile, Anna could tell by the deep hum that the *Konstanze* continued its mad flight across the seas, which felt rougher than before. There was a storm coming up, said one sailor, who came below to check on his companions. One of Druss's ships had fallen off. Its foremast had cracked under too much sail and nearly caused them to founder in the high seas. But the other two kept at them like dogs after a rabbit.

Vicious dogs, Anna thought as she worked. Under Thea's direction, she learned how to wrap bandages and extract splinters. Again and again, she helped to direct the magic current to deaden a patient's agony while Thea worked over them.

"Well done," Thea murmured to Anna. "You've helped me save more than one tonight."

Reports came down with every wounded sailor. From Joszua, Anna learned they had almost been pinned between the enemy and an island, but the captain had taken advantage of how *Konstanze* steered closer to the wind and slipped between the two remaining ships. Now they were sailing east toward the open sea and hoping for nightfall. Between the new moon and the rising storm, they might be able to lose Druss and circle back west.

"Another one," called out Old Hahn, as he carried a limp body into the cabin.

Nikolas. Anna went cold at the sight of the boy's grey face. As Hahn maneuvered his burden through the doorway, Nikolas's head flopped over. His leg hung twisted at an unnatural angle.

Thea cleared off the trunk and ordered Hahn to lay the boy there. "What happened?" she asked as she examined him.

"Chains," Hahn said shortly. "Two of them at once. Caught the boy and flung him against the mast, while t'other…. Well, you can see what happened."

Thea nodded. "Head's got a lump." She probed gently. The skull gave way under her fingertips. Suddenly queasy, Anna had to turn away.

"We'll splint the leg and hope it heals straight," Thea said. "Elise, look in my chest for a vial of blue liquid. Mix one part with five of water, then soak a rag in the mixture and lay it over the boy's mouth. Better pinch your nose while you do it."

The vial held a fiery blue liquid that burned with magic's scent. Anna carefully measured out its contents and mixed it with water as Thea had directed, then laid the rag over Nikolas's mouth. The boy's nostrils flared, but his eyes remained closed and his skin felt clammy to her touch.

Eleni appeared at the door. Without speaking, she glided into the cabin and knelt by Nikolas's side. She brushed the hair from her son's face, laid a hand on his cheek, her lips moving silently in some prayer or wish or curse, Anna could not tell which, then swiftly departed.

Thea touched Anna's shoulder. "Come. We have work to do."

CHAPTER 16

The storm struck at sunset. The ship lurched and froze in place for a heart-stopping moment, then jerked to one side. Thea had been measuring a dose of fennel infusion for Maté's sprained fingers. The potion splattered. Lightning flashed. A heartbeat later, thunder crashed around them and the ship pitched into darkness. Anna scrambled to the floor, gathering up scattered instruments, while Thea saw to their patients. Maté wound a bandage around his fingers. "Captain needs me," he said and vanished above decks.

"Damnable idiot," Thea muttered. "If only I could dose them with common sense as well as herbs."

More lightning blazed, illuminating the sick bay with a strange flickering glow from the hatches above. Every flash and crackle was followed by a roll of thunder, each one faster than the one before. Anna and Thea righted their potions and implements. Thea relit their shaded lanterns with a spark of magic. Several inches of water covered the floor, and more leaked through the planks.

We are going to die. The thought made Anna furious. She did not deserve to die. Neither did Maté or the rest of Koszenmarc's crew, not for a gods-be-damned Emperor and his jewel.

"You're afraid," Thea said.

"Of course I'm afraid! Aren't you? We might all drown tonight. Or worse."

"And so? Everyone dies. Everyone lives again. It's the one promise Blind Toc made that I believe. Sit and let me brew you a cup of tea."

Thea brewed tea over a tiny brazier, then added a few drops from another of her mysterious vials. Once Anna had finished a cup, she recovered her sense of proportion. Yes, she was afraid, but panic would do neither of them any good. She set herself to tending the patients in their sick bay, following Thea's orders to change bandages, or to administer fresh doses. Over the next hour, the trickle of patients slowed, then stopped altogether. Thea used the lull to set her medicine chest in order. To Anna, she gave the task of boiling their needles and surgical blades.

A dozen patients treated and sent back to duty. Berit would live, with the blessing, Thea said, but another sailor, a young woman, bled to death even as Hahn laid her on the operating table, and a third was close to death by poison. Eight more sailors remained in the sick bay, bandaged and dosed and lying uneasily in their hammocks, but most of these were uncomplicated cases, according to Thea. Nikolas lay in an uneasy doze. His color had improved, but his breathing remained uneven. "I'll operate tomorrow," Thea said.

At long last, no more patients came below, and the roll of the ship eased. Anna and Thea ate their long-neglected dinner of cold meat and flatbread. Thea brewed another pot of tea and stirred in a spoonful of herbs from her medicine chest.

"Take a watch to sleep," she said, once they had drunk their fill. "I'll bunk down here. I've done that often enough. If I need you, I'll send word."

It was quiet belowdecks, with only a snuffling here and there, and the whisper from the ship's wake as it parted the waters. A soft, clean-scented breeze filtered down through the open hatches. But there were no hammocks free, and no spare room in the corners, where more of the crew had made nests of blankets. Koszenmarc must have ordered all the watches below except the bare minimum of crew to steer and sail the ship.

Anna climbed up on deck, to a world almost forgotten these past ten hours. Clouds stippled the sky, limned with the starlight and the fading brilliance of the moon. She heard rather than saw a few hands moving about the deck. All was quiet, except for the hushing of the seas as the ship skimmed along, sails taut with a steady wind. Off to one side, Koszenmarc stood with a glass to his eye, staring into the darkness.

Anna made her way to the railing next to him. He acknowledged her presence with a nod, then continued to scan the seas. She drank in the breeze, letting it wash away the remembered stink of burnt flesh and blood and vomit. Slowly, her muscles unknotted.

"Are we free of her?" she asked after a while.

"We were. That changed a few moments ago. Here."

He handed her the glass. At first, she saw nothing but a murky, surging darkness. Then Koszenmarc stepped close behind her, and with a light touch guided the glass to the right.

A pale red speck sprang into view.

She started back. "Druss. How—"

"She's a clever captain, especially when she's on the hunt. We lost her for a time, but she's guessed every one of my maneuvers. It's strange. Almost as if—" He broke off and took the glass back from Anna. "How goes it below?"

Horrible, she thought. But she was able to give a competent report.

"Three dead. Eight more under watch. Thea says all but two are uncomplicated, but I don't know what that means. Nikolas is one of them," she added.

He sighed. "So I heard."

He resumed watching the sea and Druss's ships. Anna told herself to go below or find a place on deck where she could sleep, but she could not bring herself to abandon deck, not while that pale red speck grew larger and larger. What if Druss overtook them? No storm. Fewer hands, and many of those exhausted.

"What can we do?" she murmured.

She had spoken more to herself than the man at her side, but he answered her nevertheless. "We sail directly before the wind, with as much sail as she'll bear. Once the moon sets and I'm certain we've outrun her, we'll circle around to the south. That she won't expect."

"Do you know where we are?" she asked.

And what about Aldo Sarrész?

"Beyond all the charts," he said, "including yours. As soon as we reach a quiet moment tomorrow, I'll take bearings."

The officer of the watch—Joszua—called out to him, and Koszenmarc left the railing to confer with him. Anna let her head drop into both her hands. She no longer wished to find Sarrész or the jewel. She only wanted a quiet refuge where she could make an independent life for herself.

One room for me, a second for my books, a door with a lock...

She drew a deep breath to unlock the ache in her chest. It was then she detected a familiar scent. The clean, cold scent of magic. A whiff of the current that hovered in the air. A signature she knew as well as her own.

"He's here," she said suddenly. Then louder, "Captain! Andreas! I've found him!"

Before she could launch herself over the side, Koszenmarc caught her around the waist. "What is it?" he demanded. "You found *him?*"

Anna wanted to smack him. "You gods-be-damned idiot, of course I mean *him*. Let me go."

Instead of letting her go, Koszenmarc barked a string of commands. Chaos broke out on the deck, as Felix and Joszua ran to do his bidding. The watch below went aloft with only a word, with Eleni on deck soon thereafter.

"Elise and I need to leave the ship," he told Eleni. "You take command, with Hahn as your second. Make a boat ready. We'll need water and stores, enough for several days. The moment we've parted from the *Konstanze*, raise more sails—as much as she will bear—and light half a dozen lamps. You know the trick. Be a firebug and lure her away, then douse the lamps one by one and circle around."

Eleni ran to carry out her orders. Now Koszenmarc loosed his hold on Anna. "We go to find our man," he told her. "You and I. Get whatever you need for two, three days. Ask Thea what medicines to bring."

Right. No telling what state they would find Sarrész in. "Aye, Captain," she said. "Orders received."

That won her a brilliant smile. Her heart lifted at that smile, and she hurried below.

Joszua met her outside the cabin she shared with Thea. "Thea's compliments," he said, as he handed over a heavily laden bag. "She told me exactly what to pack. Clothing, soaps, bandages, whatever medicine she could spare."

Anna slung the bag over her shoulder. "Thank you, Joszua. I—" And it came to her that if their expedition did not go well, or if Druss saw through Koszenmarc's trick with the lamps, she might never see this young man, or anyone else on the ship, again. She clasped him briefly by the arm, caught his startled look, then scrambled back topside.

Within those few moments, everything had changed. The moon was just visible above the horizon and sinking fast. All lamps had been extinguished, even the shaded lanterns, and the ship was running dark. Eleni Farakos gave the word, the sails were furled, and the *Konstanze* glided on in silence.

The song of the rigging died as the ship slowed. The only sounds were the creak and groan of the boards, the thump of her pulse. Now the crew lowered the *Konstanze*'s smallest boat over the side. Koszenmarc swung down the ladder and dropped a bag into the boat. He took Anna's from her and made the leap.

Anna hesitated. The seas were running high, and the boat made an invisible target in the great darkness below.

"Jump," Koszenmarc called out. "I'll catch you. I promise."

With a prayer to the gods, she leapt in the direction of his voice. Koszenmarc caught her in his arms before she tumbled over the side. She had only one moment of terror, convinced their small boat would drown beneath the ship, but Koszenmarc had already cast off the ropes to the ship and was pulling strongly on the oars.

Slowly, slowly, the distance between ship and boat widened. Eleni's voice called out orders to make sail. One bright lantern sparked into life high above in the upper crosstrees. At the same time, the ship began a slow and steady turn. Ten, twenty breaths later, a second light bloomed in one of the portholes. Anna found she was holding her breath, while Koszenmarc continued to row and the waves broke over the boat's prow.

Soon Anna could no longer make out the ship itself, just two bright specks that rose and fell with the seas. A third appeared, just like the firebugs she remembered chasing through the streets of Duenne as a child. Only here the firebugs were meant to lure Druss away from Anna and Koszenmarc.

A fourth light appeared, at what had to be the waterline of the ship. Druss must surely have spotted the *Konstanze* by now. Would she suspect the ruse?

Koszenmarc paused rowing. He was breathing heavily. "Time...to take...bearings." He gulped down a breath and spoke more easily. "It would be a terrible thing if we missed the island and went sailing off into the emptiness."

He spoke lightly, without a hint of anxiety—as if he trusted her magic to pinpoint an island, at night, in the middle of uncharted seas.

"Aye, my lord captain," she said. "One nearly invisible island, just as you wish."

She had the satisfaction of hearing his stifled laugh.

But there was the question of that invisible island. Anna hunkered down in the boat, her knees lodged against the cross planks. Her clothes weighted down, damp and cold. The seas were running crossways, with high, sharp crests that argued with each other. Anna closed her eyes and tried to forget the seas, Isana Druss, and the miles between them and any shore. Magic was for every moment, Thea had said. In the quiet of your chamber, in the midst of grief and war. *Well, this will be a test, won't it?*

The rise and fall of the boat as it rode the swells was like the rise and fall of her chest as she breathed. There, there was the moment between trough and crest. There was the moment between breath in and breath out. The moment when waves rose on either side of the boat, and another when she hovered above the ordinary world.

Ei rûf ane gôtter. Komen mir de strôm.

A fresh scent, like a storm-cleansed breeze, like the orchids of Eddalyon, like the taste of pines from her homeland, rolled through the air.

...the wind, a magical wind, strong and irresistible, lifted her from the boat, and she hung suspended between worlds. There was the Konstanze *with its lanterns, flying before a strong wind. There, not far behind, was a larger ship with red sails. Even as she watched, one lantern aboard* Konstanze *winked out, then another. It was hard to turn away from the chase, but Anna forced herself to scan the seas, which were like a luminous expanse of silk. She saw Vyros, Idonia, the string of islands arcing south and east. Now her sight sharpened. She saw the small isles, the cluster of rocks named Desolation.*

...and there, there was the boat with her and Koszenmarc. Beyond that, two small islands with a reef arcing around and sand bars farther out. She drew a deep breath. Yes, there was Aldo Sarrész's signature, faint but unmistakable. And there, much stronger, the signature of that otherworldly presence...

Anna released her hold upon magic and dropped back into the ordinary world. A world where she was drenched in salt water and afraid. But a sense of that magical vision lingered, and before it could fade entirely, she reached over to Koszenmarc and laid a hand on his arm. "Do you see?" she whispered.

"I do," he whispered back. "Half a mile, no more."

The stars faded to nothing. The dark waters swelled and sank. Anna wished she could grip that image of magic as hard as she gripped the side of the boat. It was only the promise of those two magical signatures, growing stronger and stronger as Koszenmarc plied the oars, that kept her from true panic. She found herself wishing for a lamp, or even a candle, to light the way.

But they did not dare risk a light, even one as weak as a candle, and so they were both unprepared when the boat rammed into the sands.

Anna fell into the bottom of the boat, amid the bags and gear. Koszenmarc tumbled backwards. He lost his grip on the oars only a moment, then drove one home and held tight as the surf tried to drag the boat back into the deep.

"Not bad without a compass or a watch or anchor," he said.

Anna picked herself up from the bottom of the boat. "Better than sailing into the emptiness." She felt far more cheerful than she had any right to be. Perhaps it was the exhilaration of escape, or the giddiness of a very long night.

Koszenmarc had already disembarked and was holding the boat steady. "I quite agree. Here, help me drag her clear of the surf."

Together they hauled the boat away from the tide lines, into a thicket of coarse grass. Anna sank onto her knees and breathed in the air, thick with salt and mud and the faintest whiff of green. Magic? Wildflowers? She tried to recall what plants grew in Eddalyon's more remote islands.

Koszenmarc extracted a lantern from their bags and struck a flint to the wick. A spark leapt through the dark, and suddenly the shore was illuminated with a pale white light. Koszenmarc closed the lantern's shade so that only a tight beam poured over the sands.

They had landed upon a narrow verge of sand and pebbles, between the rising surf and a brush-covered ridge. A line of seaweed marked the high tide, a foot or less below the ridge itself. Anna glanced over her shoulder at the blank expanse of sea. "Do we make camp here?" she said doubtfully.

"Too exposed," Koszenmarc said. "We'll cross that ridge and see what we find."

Anna struggled to her feet and slung her bag over her shoulder. Together they climbed the steep ridge and crossed into the grassy ravine beyond. Here a shallow stream ran along the bottom, with deeper pools where mud and brush blocked the flow. On the far side, the ground climbed steeply to another ridge crowned by a scattering of boulders and low trees.

"The ground's damp," Koszenmarc said. "But it could be worse. We'll have fresh water, dry tinder, and that ridge to block us from the shore. Let me see what lies beyond. Wait here."

"But—"

He was gone before she could utter a word. Anna sank into a crouch, gripping the straps of her bag. Her stomach felt empty, even though she was certain she had eaten aboard the *Konstanze*. Or had she? She remembered a hastily eaten meal, but not when that had happened.

To her relief, Koszenmarc returned far sooner than she expected.

"No good," he said. "We've got mud here, but over that ridge we've got mud and lumps and a field full of rocks. We'll make camp here."

Anna could only nod her head in agreement. The wind had picked up, and she shivered in her wet clothes. "What about Sarrész?"

"Our blessed thief can wait until tomorrow. I'd rather face him and all the problems he brings us in daylight. Come, I know you're weary, but we ought to fetch our things from the boat."

It took them three trips to transfer their bags and the provisions from the boat to their campsite. By this time, the wind had died off. The night air was cool, however, and Anna was glad to wrap herself in as many blankets as she could find.

"We can risk a fire," Koszenmarc said. "You rest and keep warm. I'll collect firewood."

He soon gathered a pile of kindling, which he expertly layered with dried seaweed, then set ablaze with his tinderbox. Once he was satisfied the fire would burn steadily, he set two pots of water to boil, then another, larger pot to warm next to the fire. But when he offered Anna a piece of flatbread, wrapped around cold mutton, she shook her head. "I'm not very hungry."

"You are," he said. "You just forgot. Captain's orders."

Reluctantly, she accepted the sandwich. To her surprise, her appetite woke with the first bite. She finished off one, and Koszenmarc handed her a second. He ate three sandwiches himself, then pulled out a leather flask from his belt.

"A toast," he said, "to finding our thief."

He offered the flask to Anna. It was red wine, warm and flavored with the tang of leather.

"We haven't found him yet," she said. "Nor the...whatever goods he stole."

He shrugged. "We will tomorrow. Trust your captain."

The water was boiling by now. Koszenmarc added tea leaves and set it aside to brew. "It's been a long hot day and a long cool night. We'll take a wash, then change into dry clothes."

He tucked the wine flask into his belt and poured them both a cup of water. Warm dry clothes. Well, they didn't have those, but they had clothes dry enough and warmed by the fire. Anna changed her damp shirt and trousers for ones from her bag.

By then, the tea had brewed. Anna had thought she could not keep her eyes open a moment longer, but an odd wakefulness overtook her. It was the strangeness of the hour, she thought. The solid, unmoving land instead of the roll of the ocean. The absence of the crew. The silence around them, broken only by the nearby surf.

And this man, sitting across the fire from her, his dark face limned by firelight.

On impulse, she said, "How did you come here? To Eddalyon, I mean."

"By accident."

His voice was sharp, his expression suddenly remote.

Anna flinched. "I'm sorry. I didn't mean to pry."

Koszenmarc blew out a breath. "No, I'm the one who should apologize. The answer's true enough, though. My father sent me to Court when I was seventeen. I'm the second son, you see. The one intended to represent the family's interests to the Emperor and his Council. I did well enough,

I suppose, but every day was a misery. I hated the lies, the flattery, the scheming of faction against faction. One day, I...left."

He paused for such a long while, Anna thought he had finished his answer, but then he gave a laugh. "Oh, I left. Left it all behind with a note to my father that I could not taint myself in politics, even for the best of causes." He laughed again, this time soft and bitter. "Gods, how arrogant of me. My father, of course, refused to support me. I took to wandering then. I headed east to Morauvín, to a city called Melnek, simply because it lay in the opposite direction from Valentain. I traveled down the coast until I came to Fortezzien, where I walked on board a ship bound for Vyros. By then, I'd spent all my money, which left me with few choices, and none of them good."

And there it was—that hint of anger. Even so, she had the strongest impression that she might ask him anything and he would answer.

"Is that why you became a pirate?" she said softly.

He took a long sip of tea. "It wasn't anything so deliberate. I found a place on a smuggler's ship. It was ugly and dirty, but it supplied me with reliable wages and the means to learn a sailor's trade. I served long enough to escape one miserable ship for a second and a third, until...until chance gave me a better turn at last. What about you? How did you come here?"

She had thought she wanted to hear his secrets. Now she regretted the question. "An accident," she whispered. "Several of them."

"You ran away from your bond master."

He made it a statement, not a question.

"I— Yes, I did." A lie, but not entirely so.

"But you weren't always bonded. You said your father was a scholar."

Choosing her words carefully, she said, "Yes, my father was a scholar—a freedman and a son of a freedman. When he died, he left behind debts, and besides, I had nowhere to go."

"And no money. I understand."

It was on her lips to admit the truth—that she had come to Eddalyon for the money to set herself free. But one admission would lead to a dozen more, and she had no desire to spend the evening explaining herself. The secrets were not just hers alone. Maté's safety depended on her discretion.

When she did not reply, Koszenmarc sighed. "We had best wash ourselves while the water is hot. There's soap in my bag. I'll bank the fire."

Anna found the soap and rubbed it into a lather with a clean rag. She scrubbed her scalp, face, and under her shirt, then tipped the bucket over her head to rinse. Koszenmarc had banked the fire and begun to wash himself. Except for the glow from the fire's embers, it was entirely dark.

In spite of that, Anna could follow his movements as easily as if she had summoned a magical light.

She wrung out her hair and worked at the knots with her fingers.

"Let me help."

He rummaged through his pack. A moment later, he crouched behind her and lifted up the mass of her tangled hair.

Many, many times, he must have combed a woman's hair, she thought. He started with the ends, inserting the comb into the knots and gently working them free. Inch by inch, he combed her hair smooth, from her scalp to the ends.

A memory long forgotten drifted up. *My mother did this for me years ago.*

But these were not a mother's hands. No, they and this moment were something altogether different. Her pulse beat faster.

Andreas paused, and laid a hand on her shoulder. "Elise?"

She half turned. He laid the comb aside. Kissed her softly on the lips. *Oh yes, oh yes.*

She leaned into the kiss. Drank in the scent of his body. Pressed against his bare chest and felt his pulse beat against hers.

Oh. My. Yes.

He was nothing like Lord Brun.

A shock of memory washed over her, and she flinched.

"What is wrong?" Andreas whispered.

"Nothing," she said. "But I—"

"But, no. You don't need to explain yourself to me."

He drew back. She wished she could see his face, was glad he could not see hers.

"Good night," he said softly.

Good night.

Heart strands disentangled. Cut one by one.

Anna crawled over to her blanket. All too aware of Andreas lying a few feet away, she twisted her hair into a loose plait, then lay down. Overhead, the stars wheeled, bright pinpoints against a black infinity. Anna kept her eyes upon them, counting, counting, counting, as she tried to drown her own desires.

CHAPTER 17

She dreamed of home, of the many iterations of home throughout her lives. Aboard the ship with her sister and her beloved, hurtling westward toward new lands. In a tent stitched of rough hides, with skies traced by the northern lights. In Duenne and the small parlor where her father had lectured her about logic and history and magic.

Anna's eyes blinked open to sunlight, bright, relentless sunlight that spilled over the crest of the ravine. *Midmorning,* she thought groggily. She heard a stamping nearby. Koszenmarc, no doubt. Up and cheerful, with no thought about what had happened between them.

She rubbed the grit from her eyes and blinked.

A hairy face interposed itself between her and the sky. A hairy face with broad lips and two stubby horns and pale slitted eyes. A...goat?

The goat bleated noisily and lipped at her nose. Anna batted the creature away and scrambled to her feet.

"We have some new friends, it seems."

Koszenmarc was perched on a boulder on the opposite bank of the ravine, looking faintly harassed. Small wonder. Half a dozen black-and-brown goats swarmed around below, eyeing his boots as though they were a delicacy. Another dozen jostled and butted heads, stopping only to chew whatever they found lying about the campsite. Her shirt and trousers showed signs of their attention. So did Andreas's.

Andreas gestured upward, to a young boy crouched at the edge of the ravine. The boy wore patched trousers of an indeterminate color, rolled up to his knees. He had the thick springy hair, bound in long braids, and the bony features of an islander, but what caught her attention was the great ugly scar that covered half of one cheek. Anna had seen scars like that among the company. Daria once told her that slave owners marked their property with tattoos, some of them wrought with magic in case the slave attempted to escape. Those who were desperate enough cut the tattoos out with knives.

The boy grinned at her. Or possibly the goats who nibbled at her blanket.

"His name is Mihali," Andreas said. "He says he brought his goats to graze. He thinks we can't be slave catchers, or if we are, we're very stupid ones, which is why he didn't stab us in our sleep."

"He's a runaway?" Anna said.

He nodded. "And he's not alone. There's a village at the other end of the island. I've asked him to introduce us to his family, and perhaps we might speak with the stranger his father and uncle rescued from the sea."

Sarrész. We were right. I was right.

The boy gave a derisive snort. "I never promised any of that. Not yet."

"No, you didn't," Andreas admitted. "We were discussing that point when you woke up," he told Anna. "Mihali isn't entirely convinced he should help us."

A rapid conversation broke out between Andreas and the boy, mostly in Kybris. Anna could only make out half the words, but she recognized a negotiation when she heard one. Andreas wanted Mihali to be their guide. The boy objected. *He* trusted them, if only because no slave catcher would be so daft as Andreas and Anna, but his mother and aunts were not so easy to convince. They might murder his new friends before Mihali could explain. Besides, he added, the goats needed to graze.

"The herd can graze on the journey back," Andreas told him. "And we shall convince your mother and your aunts otherwise."

He jumped down from the boulder, scattering the goats, and went to the pile of bags, now somewhat chewed and tattered. From his bag, he extracted a tinderbox and two large knives. "These useful items, which you surely recognize. Also..." He brought out a handful of copper denariie. "Money."

Still the boy seemed reluctant. "You must not tell *anyone* about us."

"I swear," Andreas said. "I will tell no one."

The boy glanced at Anna. "And her?"

Anna laid a hand over her heart. "I won't betray you. I swear it."

Mihali eyed her suspiciously, but eventually he held out a hand. "Good enough. Give me the money and we can be off."

"Half the money," Andreas countered. "The rest I hand over to your mother."

Mihali grumbled but finally agreed. While he rounded up his goats, Anna and Andreas hurried through breaking camp and packing what few items were not already in their bags. Andreas ordered the boy to carry the supply of provisions back to their boat, and to report back if he saw any ships on the horizon. To Anna's surprise, Mihali accepted those orders as naturally as if he'd always served the man.

It's how he gives those orders, Anna thought. *A captain to his crew.*

But that wasn't entirely fair. Koszenmarc knew how to inspire loyalty— one only had to see how everyone, Eleni and Hahn and even that miserable Karl, worked to please him. She had done the same herself.

Like last night.

Abruptly she stood and swung the bag over her shoulder. A pang shot through her skull at the sudden movement, and she stumbled. Koszenmarc caught her by the elbow. She wanted to shrug him away, but between the restless night, the forgotten meals, and now the sun beating down from overhead, she wasn't certain she could do without his support.

"You look ill," he said quietly.

"I miss my breakfast," she said, carefully. "And I could do with a nap."

"Ah." His smile was faint and brief. "I understand that. Mihali tells me it's an hour at least to his village, but we can make a few stops along the way."

The island, it turned out, was far larger than Anna had guessed from her brief remembered glimpse from far above. Beyond their ravine stretched a rolling grassland, crisscrossed by streams and more ravines, and rising steadily upward toward a line of hills to the north. As Koszenmarc had promised, they broke their journey twice for a cold meal and a pot of tea while the goats grazed, though each time Mihali complained bitterly at the delay.

By the time they reached those northern hills, the sun had crossed over the meridian. No more stops, Mihali insisted. No, he didn't wish another coin. He merely thought it wiser if they did not dawdle. He led them east, around the shoulder of the tallest hill, into a pass surrounded by rocky cliffs. Very quickly, the pass narrowed, until the cliffs nearly met overhead, with only a ribbon of sky visible. Other rifts and passages branched off to either side, but Mihali never paused to consider which direction to take.

Anna had lost all sense of time and direction when a long warbling whistle floated down from above, like that of a dove. At once, Mihali stopped and held his fingers to his lips. Then he gave an answering whistle, thin and sharp. Once, twice, three times. There was a pause, then came a repeat of the first whistle. Mihali gave a satisfied nod and continued, the goats streaming behind.

"What was that?" Anna murmured.

"Lookout," Andreas replied softly. "These are clever runaways."

The narrow passage took several abrupt twists, like a snake doubling back upon itself. Then, so suddenly it took Anna by surprise, the pass opened into a sunlit valley. Mihali's goats swarmed ahead, bleating, but Mihali himself paused after a few steps. Koszenmarc followed cautiously, then motioned for Anna to join him.

It is a refuge, she thought. *A pocket of freedom.*

Hills ringed the valley, which was barely a mile long, with a narrow stream running through the middle. Fields of hay alternated with green, leafy crops that had to be yams. Farther down stood a cluster of houses, next to thorny enclosures with chickens and swine. And not far off came the roar of the surf breaking against an unseen shore.

Five women stood in the fields with spears in their hands. Two more with babies in slings hung further back, but they too were armed. All of them stared at Anna and Andreas. None of them looked welcoming.

The oldest of the women shifted her attention to the boy. "Mihali. Your sister gave the signal for friends. How are these people friends?"

Mihali licked his lips. "They aren't slave catchers. I know it."

She snorted. "Stupid boy. That doesn't make them friends. Go. Take your goats back into the hills. As for you," she said to Koszenmarc. "I see you have any number of fine weapons. Perhaps you might kill us, but I doubt it."

"I don't want to kill," Andreas said. "I've come to make a trade."

She regarded him with wide, bright eyes. Her hair was twisted back into a tight braid, her face cut in sharp lines. Like Mihali, she bore a scar on her left cheek. So did all the other women. "Mihali, I said go."

Mihali hesitated, but when his mother flipped a hand in his direction, he swung his stick around, driving the goats back into the narrow pass. Again, the woman nodded. "Very good. You didn't kill my son before he could take his idiot self away from here. That speaks well. What kind of trade do you want?"

"Money," he replied.

She gave a bark of laughter. "As if we cared about money."

Andreas hissed in frustration. Before he could speak, Anna laid a hand on his arm.

"Medicine," she said. "We have medicine to help with fever, with poisoning. We also have weapons."

The woman eyed her carefully. "And what do you want in return?"

"To talk to a stranger you pulled from the ocean," Anna said. "Nothing more. Mihali says—"

"We found no one," the woman said harshly. "Take your gods-be-damned bribes and go. Go before I decide I ought to kill you. You might have a pretty sword," she said to Andreas, "and you might stink of magic," she said to Anna, "but we aren't helpless."

Anna drew a sharp breath. How had the woman known about her magic? But Andreas went on as though the woman had not interrupted. "This stranger is a friend of a friend," he said. "We want to help."

He took out the coins, knives, and the tinderbox, and set them on the ground in front of him. To that, Anna added three precious vials of medicine. The woman stared at their offering for a very long moment. Anna recognized that expression. Weighing the risk to herself, to her companions, against the value of medicine and tools on this lonely island.

Finally, she said, "If you harm this man, I will kill you myself." Andreas nodded. "Fair enough. Where is he?"

She pointed toward a house at the edge of the village. "That one. Lija took him in when no one else wanted to."

Anna and Andreas picked their way through the fields, down toward the house the woman had indicated. All the women continued to watch them, their spears held ready. Anna's neck prickled with the weight of their silence.

Lija's house stood at the very end. It had its own garden, neatly tended, and several lines strung between the house and the forest, with washing hung out to dry. There was no door, only a wide opening with flowers around the frame.

As they ducked inside, a woman called out, "Who are you?"

Lija knelt on the ground next to a man who lay sprawled on a bundle of fresh hay, a pot of water and a collection of rags at her side. In spite of the bundles of dried herbs hung from the ceiling and the fresh breeze sifting through the windows, Anna caught the unmistakable scent of a wound gone bad.

Koszenmarc must have recognized that scent as well, because he nodded at Lija briskly. "We made a trade with your friends outside," he said. "We only want to talk with Lord Sarrész."

"There is no lord here, just my man. He's taken sick."

"Very well. We still want to talk with him. Mihali's mother said we might."

Lija stared at him and Anna. Then she slid out the door—to argue with Mihali's mother, no doubt. But Anna's whole attention was now fixed on the figure that lay on the floor.

Lord Aldo Sarrész. Her quarry of so many months. He lay there, naked except for a pair of water-stained boots and a loincloth. His eyes were closed and sunk like dark pits in a grey, gaunt face. Pale stubble covered his jaw, and his hair had been chopped short. He looked nothing like the soft and elegant man she'd glimpsed in Brun's household.

Sarrész stared up at them. "Who are you?" he whispered. "And don't try to pass off that miserable excuse about being a friend. I have no friends."

"Let us say we have several acquaintances in common," Andreas replied. "I spent several years at Court, as did you. I also know you killed a man and stole the Emperor's jewel. For the murder alone, you ought to face a trial. Let me have the jewel, however, and I will leave you here in peace."

Sarrész cursed. His voice was weak, but his vocabulary inventive. "Leave me here to die, you mean. Gods-be-damned jewel. It dropped me into the ocean a mile away from these islands. Thank the gods I can swim. Thank the gods Lija's cousin was out with the boat that day. I'd be fine except for that fucking fish. Bit me hard right as they were about to haul me into the boat."

He waved a hand at his left leg. Anna immediately knelt to examine it. Sarrész cursed and tried to kick her. "Stop interfering," she demanded. "Unless you want to die a miserable death."

"Does it matter?" he whispered.

She glared at him. "Of course it does. I've chased you through half the western Empire, you miserable creature. I won't let you die until I find the jewel you stole."

"Wish I'd never set eyes on that damned thing," he muttered.

A sentiment she could agree with.

She set to work to examine his injuries. Ribs bruised, body covered with half-healed scrapes. The right leg badly bruised. The left one, however, had a row of angry red punctures, the flesh torn and worried. Pus oozed from the wounds, and the surrounding flesh was puffy and red.

Anna rummaged through her bag. Joszua had packed for her, but just as he'd assured her, Thea had added all the necessary items. Bandages. Powders. Vials of potions, like the ones she had used to trade with the women. Her hand closed around a small flat object wrapped in a bloodstained cloth. She stopped, disturbed by the unexpected sting of magic. A magical device? She hadn't noticed such a thing among Thea's stores.

No time for that now. She set the bloody rag off to one side. More rummaging turned up a vial of that eerie blue liquid. *To be used in case of dire need,* said the label, marked in Thea's neat script. Anna seized Sarrész's nose between her fingers and dribbled a few drops over his lips. "Breathe," she ordered.

Sarrész sucked in a breath, gasped and shuddered. His face flushed with a brighter color and the terrible grey cast to his skin vanished. That would keep him alive while she worked. She laid both hands on his chest and called upon the magic.

Ei rûf ane gôtter. Komen mir de strôm.

Thea's training and that night of terror belowdecks had done some good. She directed the flood of magic from her body into his. Sarrész stiffened, then relaxed with a soft sigh as Anna coaxed the current to sink deeper and deeper. The magic coursed through her and into Sarrész, warming his blood like the sun. She could read how fast the pain leached away by how his breathing slowed and his muscles gradually relaxed.

Sarrész released a slow breath. "Oh, that is better. Much better."

Andreas leaned close to her. "Any sign?"

"No. None at all."

She leaned back and covered her eyes with both hands. Perhaps the signature was simply a remnant of a spell he had purchased back on the mainland. No, that wasn't right. And yet, she was too exhausted to pick apart the mystery.

Koszenmarc had taken up the rag bundle she had tossed to one side. He untangled the rags and extracted a thin metal disc, with curious engravings on both sides. Frowning, he slipped the disc into his pocket. "Where is it then?"

"I have no idea."

"What have you done to him?" Lija shoved her way past Koszenmarc and Anna and dropped to her knees beside Sarrész. With light, quick touches, she ran her hands over the man, as though to reassure herself. Sarrész captured her hands and kissed them.

"You see, we haven't murdered him," Anna said dryly.

The other woman glared at her.

Well, yes. If I were a runaway slave, I'd hate strangers too.

Andreas cleared his throat. "Back to our negotiations. Now that you're no longer dying, my lord Sarrész, let's discuss the jewel you stole from the Emperor."

Sarrész eyed them both suspiciously. "Who sent you here? The Emperor? Or was it that traitor Brun?"

Traitor?

Cold washed over Anna, in spite of the heat and closeness in the hut. "What do you know about Lord Brun?"

"Too much," Sarrész said in a low and bitter voice. "I know he offered me a fortune to steal that bauble. Ten thousand denariie for the jewel, a hundred thousand if the princess liked him well enough..."

"You're lying," Anna said automatically.

Sarrész's gaze flickered up to Anna. "I remember you. Back in Duenne, in Brun's house. You're one of his people. You might want to watch out for yourself."

"I'm not— What do you mean?"

He laughed, then coughed. "I mean he lied to me. He told me his precious spell would send that priest to sleep. *Death* was where it sent that feckless lad. Soon as I saw that, I thought, *Self, you'll be next. He wants no one alive who knows his plans, that one.* So I took off to Eddalyon. Thought I might sell the jewel and start a new life."

Anna rocked back on her heels. *No, no,* she told herself. But oh, all the clues now shifted into place. The reason for this pointless secrecy. For her pretense as Lady Iljana. The true reason for Raab. Brun had paid Sarrész to steal the jewel. He wanted to present the jewel to the Emperor to gain favor, possibly win the hand of the princess. But he also wanted to make sure that no one could betray his plot.

She stumbled to her feet and ran from the house. The women in the fields paused to stare at her. She hardly noticed them. All she knew was that she had to get away, from Sarrész, from Koszenmarc. From her own gods-be-damned self.

"Anna! Anna Zhdanov. Please."

Anna stopped and doubled over, suddenly bereft of air. A long-forgotten memory reappeared, sharp and unwelcome. The day after Brun had claimed her for his bed. She'd tried to run away, but the guards had caught her before she could escape the grounds and marched her back into the house, where she'd spent a night in the cellar as punishment.

She sucked in a long breath, then another. All was silent, except for the distant rumble of the ocean, the rustle of leaves upon leaves from the nearby jungle. Slowly, she turned around. Andreas stood a few feet away, his hands held loosely at his sides, as though to convince her he wasn't a danger.

"You know who I am," she said.

He hesitated. "Not everything. Your name. Lord Brun's. That you and Kovács were searching for the same jewel I was."

Yes. He had confronted Sarrész immediately with the jewel and its theft. She had missed that before, in her relief at finally coming face-to-face with the man she had hunted for so many months. What else had Andreas Koszenmarc failed to mention? What other lies had he told her?

"How long? Did Thea—?"

"Thea said nothing. I heard you, that first morning, when you talked to Maté. On the island, when I left you both together."

She remembered that morning. She'd thought herself so clever to check for listening spells, but now she recalled those fluttering spiderwebs, the scent of old ashes carried by breezes from deep within the hillside. And in Koszenmarc's chambers, atop the island, the whispering from the vents inside the cave. Of course, there had been no signs of magic. None were necessary, if he could overhear her conversations through such ordinary means.

"You pretended to believe me," Anna said. "Why?"

He looked as uncomfortable as she felt. "The truth is, I didn't want to put you on your guard. I hoped that if I pretended to believe you, I might overhear more of your plans. Then, when I learned that I could trust you, I hoped you would trust me enough to tell me yourself."

The cramp in her stomach eased a fraction. "And if I had? What then? Whatever Lord Brun intended, he meant to turn the jewel over to the Emperor."

"Anna, we can talk about this later, but I promise you—"

A shout interrupted him. "Raiders!"

Anna and Koszenmarc both jerked around. A young woman stood on a ridge to the north. "Raiders!" she called out again. "Rounding the point!"

All the women in the field dropped their baskets and snatched up their spears. Everyone scattered in different directions into the southern hills, the young woman who had acted as lookout not far behind. Mihali's mother paused long enough to fix Andreas with an angry stare. "Yours? Goddamn you for a lying bastard." Then she shouted, "Lija! Raiders!" before she too vanished into the hills.

Anna started to follow, but Andreas was heading back toward the village. "Did you hear?" she cried out. "We must go."

"We can't leave Sarrész behind," he called over his shoulder.

For a moment, she considered abandoning him. Only for a moment. He was right, damn it. If slavers took Sarrész, they might wring the truth out of the man and take the jewel for themselves. Swearing under her breath, she hurried after Koszenmarc. "He likely lost that jewel in the ocean," she muttered. "Not that I would be surprised. It's just like him to..."

Her voice died at the sight of two dozen men and women cresting the hills. All of them armed with short swords and knives and clubs. Her first thought was to run, to lose herself in the maze that burrowed through the hills, but a second wave of strangers had already cut off their escape. Anna pressed close to Koszenmarc's side as the circle shrank, with them in the center. All those flat bright eyes staring at her. She could see death in her reflected image.

A woman shouldered her way to the front. She was short—not even reaching Anna's shoulders—but stocky and muscled. She wore dark blue trousers in the Eddalyon style and a sleeveless shirt, which exposed a tattoo running around her arm. Pale scars crisscrossed her dark face.

"Isana Druss," Koszenmarc said softly.

"So I guessed," Anna murmured.

Druss stopped a few feet away. "Hello, my friend. How happy to see you once more."

Her voice was rough, her accent that of the southern provinces on the mainland, but softened by years in the islands.

"If you are that happy, perhaps you should offer us a reward," Koszenmarc said.

"Hardly. But if you cooperate, I might grant you a quick clean death."

She glanced pointedly at his sword. He shrugged and dropped the weapon on the ground, followed by the knife from his belt. Druss nodded in satisfaction. "Karim. Yasin. Go fetch Sarrész. Which hovel is his?" she asked Koszenmarc.

He hesitated, then pointed toward the house at the opposite end from Lija's. Druss smirked. "Karim, you start at one end. Yasin, take the other. Lies," she said to Koszenmarc, "are paid back in kind."

Anna had not let go of Koszenmarc's hand, and now she gripped it tighter as Karim strode toward the opposite end of the village, while Yasin made for Lija's hut. A few moments later, a noise broke out from that direction. A woman's voice, rising in panic. A man protesting, first in Veraenen, then in Kybris. Then a thin, sharp shriek, suddenly cut off.

Yasin hauled Sarrész from the hut and dumped him in front of Druss. Sarrész groaned and spat dirt from his mouth. Blood from a scalp wound trickled down his face. Druss bent over him with a dagger in her hand. She touched the point to his throat.

"You have something I wish," she said. "Something you agreed to sell me weeks ago. Where is it?"

Sarrész licked his lips. "Back on Vyros."

Druss pressed the knifepoint a fraction closer. "Where, precisely?"

He was sweating and shivering. "By those ruins. Outside the walls. You won't find the spot without me, though. I bought a couple of spells back on the mainland. I used one to hide the jewel. Another one to get away from your people." He gulped down a breath. "You need me alive, though, to unlock its magic."

He was making up the entire story, Anna thought. It was like him, to spin out lies upon lies, until he could find another opportunity to escape.

Isana Druss stared hard at him, as if she too doubted his explanation. "How convenient for you," she said softly. "However, you are in luck today, because I have no wish to dig up an entire mountaintop. You will come with us to Vyros. You will show us exactly where you buried that jewel. And if you have lied, you will regret it very much."

Her gaze shifted to Anna. "As for you. You are also very lucky. I shall want you to examine the jewel with your magic. You will teach me how to use it."

After which, Anna's usefulness would vanish, along with her life. *Unless I can use the jewel to win my freedom.*

It would not do to seem too agreeable, however. Anna frowned, as though considering Druss's commands.

A mistake. With two quick strides, Druss closed the distance and grabbed Anna by the chin. "Speak, girl. Tell me you aren't going to make any trouble."

Her dagger winked in the sun, very close to Anna's eye. The older woman's hand was hard and callused, her sun-darkened face crisscrossed by whitened scars. There was a strange light in Druss's eyes, an unsettling air of excitement.

"No trouble," Anna whispered. "Unless…"

Druss's dark, round eyes glinted. "Kill the other one."

"No!" Anna cried out.

A cool blade pressed against her cheek. Off in the distance, the damned goats were bleating. "It matters what happens to your captain," Druss observed. "Excellent. But let me make absolutely clear the cost of any lie, any trouble."

She released Anna and swiveled around. At her signal, one of the two sailors took hold of Koszenmarc's arms and jerked him down to his knees. With a kick, he forced Koszenmarc's legs apart. Druss leaned down and seized Koszenmarc's groin.

She gave a hard twist. Koszenmarc bucked and gave a harsh cry.

"It hurts," Druss said quietly. "So it should."

She jerked her hand upward again. Koszenmarc squealed and collapsed. His face had turned grey, and he was gasping for breath. Druss stepped back with a smile. "Do you understand?" she said to Anna.

"I…I understand. I promise. No trouble. No lies."

"Good." Druss tucked her dagger into her belt. "Then let us set sail for Vyros."

CHAPTER 18

At Druss's signal, Anna found herself thrown face down onto the ground. She spat out a mouthful of dirt and tried to squirm free, but one man pinned her with an enormous hand, while another ran a rope from her wrists to her ankles. They hauled her to her feet and one of them hooked his arm around her waist. "Sweet," he said. "Maybe Druss will give you to us for a bit."

Anna snapped at him. He laughed, avoiding her teeth easily.

"Best be careful of that'un," his companion said. "She bites."

"Maybe I like that."

"Maybe," the other said. "But she bites with magic." He unwound the scarf from his head and gagged Anna. "There. Now she can't talk or bite."

"Right enough." The pirate slid a hand under Anna's shirt and squeezed her breast. "Pity we don't have a few moments now. But once our captain is done with you..."

Koszenmarc slammed his head back against one of his captors. The man howled and clutched at his face. A second man grabbed Koszenmarc's arms and flung him to the ground. Koszenmarc tried to roll away, but first one, then another of the pirates kicked him. Before they could land more than a couple of blows, Druss shoved her way through the crowd, beating the men away with the flat of her sword. "Damned fuckwits," she barked. "I told you I want him alive."

"But he tried to—"

"Never mind him. He's trussed up good and tight, or did you forget?" She leaned over Koszenmarc, who lay in a heap on the ground. Druss scowled and nudged him with her boot. He stirred and gave a faint groan. "Lucky bastard," she said. "You and him both. Now take these three aboard ship, and no more stupid games."

Sarrész was carried off first in a makeshift litter. He lay still with his eyes closed, his lips moving in what seemed to be a prayer. Anna didn't have time to utter a prayer herself. The tallest of her captors swung her over his shoulder and set off with the rest of the crew. Anna's last sight of Andreas Koszenmarc was his limp body slung between four of the pirates as they half carried, half dragged him along.

Beyond the village, on the northern shore, two boats had been hauled onto the rocks. Anna's captor dropped her in the nearest one. Her stomach lurched in time with the boat as it launched to the swells. She'd run out of curses, she had run out of terror altogether. Druss would torture Sarrész until he confessed what he'd done with the jewel. He had likely lied about everything. Druss would slit his throat, then hers, then Andreas Koszenmarc's. Her only consolation was that her next life could hardly be more miserable than this one.

The boats drew alongside the ship, and she was hauled up in a sling and dumped onto the deck. Two of the hands grabbed her and swung her onto her feet before dragging her toward an open hatch. Down she went, handled like a sack of flour, and just as carelessly. More thumps and bruises. Down another ladder into a dark, cavernous hold, with only a faint shaft of light leaking down from above. They dropped her onto a heap of ropes and left.

The hatch closed, shutting out the light. Anna strained against her bonds, trying to work her wrists free. A rat scrabbled over her face. Anna yelped and whipped her head back and forth until the rat vanished into the dark. She shrank into a tight ball, breathing hard through her gag. The ship's planking groaned, and water trickled over the ropes. There were more rats, not far away. She heard the scratch of their claws, the short sharp squeal as a fight broke out. She was in the cable tier, or a lower storage hold. What had they done with Sarrész? Or Andreas Koszenmarc?

From far above came the echo of running feet. A woman shouted out orders, and within moments the ship gave a sudden leap. To Vyros, Druss had said. How many days was that? If she could believe her own charts, a week, but she had the distinct impression that Koszenmarc had misled them all, including her, with his constant change of course.

She rolled onto her back. A few faint lines painted in sunlight showed far above—gaps between the planks, just above the water line. A hard blow would mean water rising in the hold. Unless Druss remembered to send someone to see to her prisoners, Anna might drown just as easily as die from a pirate's knife.

She closed her eyes and focused on the ropes that bound her wrists. She only needed to unravel the knots. But when she summoned the magical current, an answering magic, thick and cold, oozed from the ropes. The magic was like a visitation from the far north, so cold it burned her flesh. Anna lost her hold on the current.

Damn them. Damn them through all their lives.

The ropes were spelled against magic. That meant Druss had prepared for Anna's magic long before she and Koszenmarc had set off on this last expedition. There were clues here, but she didn't have strength to examine them.

She was not certain how long she lay there, damp and aching and hungry, her thoughts circling around uselessly. Once, she thought she saw a lantern off to one side, a brief flash of light that glanced over the hold, but none of the crew descended into the hold itself. She fell into an uneasy doze, woke, and dozed again a while longer, only to wake when a rat scrambled over her. Anna flung herself backwards, startling more rats.

Hours had passed. The hold was completely dark. The only sounds were the hiss of water streaming past as the ship rode through the seas, the high-pitched thrum from the lines far above, and the constant creak and groan of the planks.

And in the distance, the harsh, wet rasp of something—no, someone breathing. Another prisoner? Could that possibly be Andreas?

She braced her feet against the rope coils and shoved herself in the direction of that noisy breathing. Once beyond the ropes, she had to wriggle and squirm to make any progress. More rats scuttled past. She gathered herself into a knot and pushed. Her head bumped into an unexpected obstacle. Warm. Breathing. *Alive.*

Whoever it was lay on their side, facing away from her. She worked her way around until they lay face-to-face. She tentatively brushed her cheek against the other's and felt the rough stubble of a beard. His clothes were sticky with blood, and his every breath made that faint gurgling sound. *Andreas.* He was alive, but he would die unless she could somehow summon the current, in spite of her gag, in spite of any other traps Druss had laid for them.

Don't worry about Druss. Find the current.

Anna closed her eyes and focused on the point between. It was harder, summoning the magic by thought alone. She called up the memory of Thea sitting opposite her, with the sweet scent of incense filling the air, the *hush, hush* of surf from the nearby harbor, the bells in the distance, ringing the change of watch.

Choose an object, Thea told her. *Anything at all. Good. Now close your eyes, picture it in your mind, and breathe. Magic is impossible, life is impossible, unless you learn how to breathe, slowly and deliberately.*

She pictured the tapestry in her father's parlor. Lir, the goddess, alone but smiling, as if she could anticipate her brother-god's rebirth, though all around her lay winter and death.

Ei rûf ane gôtter. Komen mir de strôm. Komen mir de zaubernis.

She breathed in, the taste of salt and blood upon her tongue, willing the current to flow into Andreas's body. Memories of Thea's singsong chants guided her, urging the magic as it pulsed in time with her heartbeat. On and on she went, reciting all the spells she knew, by thought alone, even with doubts whispering after her that thought alone was not enough...

Andreas coughed. "Anna? Is that you?"

She tried to answer, but the gag muffled her words.

Andreas shook in silent laughter. "Ah. It must be you. Silenced. You frightened them, I think, with your magic. Hold still."

He bit into the cloth beside her mouth and tugged. His lips were warm and soft, his cheeks rough with a days-old beard. Anna went still, hardly able to breathe. It was the closeness of the air, she told herself. The rats. The terror of facing Druss that sent her pulse racing. Not Andreas's mouth so close to hers.

She shivered. Andreas stopped at once. "Did I hurt you?"

"No," she mumbled through her gag.

Andreas bit into the cloth again. With some experimentation, Anna discovered she could help by twisting in one direction as he pulled in another. Slowly, they worked the cloth loose, until Anna could spit the gag from her mouth. She licked her dry lips.

"Better?" he said.

"Yes. Thank you." Her voice came out as a croak.

"Thank you," he said. "Don't think I haven't noticed how you saved me with your magic."

His cheek brushed against hers, and she could feel his smile. "I wish," he murmured, "we had my wine flask. But now even a handful of clean, cold water would be welcome."

Against her will, she felt laughter bubbling up within.

"What is it?" he asked.

"Oh, nothing," she whispered. "Just if I were wishing...I'd wish for so much more."

"Ah, you should be a pirate. We petition the gods for small things. The hard ones we grab ourselves." Abruptly he pressed his lips to her ear and whispered, "I hear someone. Pretend to be asleep."

A lantern, much brighter than before, cut through the darkness of the hold. And this time, whoever came to check on the prisoners climbed all the way down the ladder and landed with a thump. Andreas immediately went limp. Anna ducked her head into his shoulder. If anyone noticed she no longer had a gag...

After a few stumbles and curses, the footsteps paused. A boot prodded Anna's ribs. She groaned. When he prodded her a second time, she muttered a curse and wriggled closer against Koszenmarc before she pretended to fall back asleep.

"Damned idiots," a man muttered. "If you weren't both tied up like hogs, you'd be rutting in the muck, I don't doubt." He stomped back up the ladder. "They're alive," he called up. "But they don't look so good. Should I fetch them water and bread? No? Well, if that's what the captain says..."

Anna waited, breathless, until she heard the man mount the ladder. "We were lucky," she whispered.

"For now," Andreas said. "Do you know how many days we've been on the ship?"

"I don't know. Why?"

"I'm thinking we can't trust Druss," he said.

She gave a huff of laughter. "Did you ever?"

"Of course not. But once we've landed on Vyros, we have less than a day before she decides Sarrész isn't worth keeping alive, jewel or no jewel. Could your magic be persuaded to unravel these ropes?"

Her laughter gave way to a growl. "I tried. The ropes are spelled against magic. It's almost as if they knew what to expect from us."

"And exactly where to find us. Very odd, that is."

He lapsed into silence. Anna rested her head against his chest, taking what comfort she could from the steady beat of his heart. They were alive, she told herself. Starved and thirsty, but alive. They would survive. They had to.

Andreas stirred. "I have an idea," he said. "About the ropes."

"What kind of idea?"

"A very desperate one. Roll over, please. "

Anna maneuvered herself onto her side. "Didn't they take your knife?"

"They did. But I still have my teeth."

His breath came in short grunts as he worked himself closer. Briefly he rested his head against her back. Then came more scuffling noises, more grunts, and not a few curses. Without warning, his lips met the flesh of her wrists and Anna jumped.

"Sorry," he muttered. "I promise not to bite hard."

She had bitten him once, as hard as she could.

"Why not?" she breathed. "It would only be fair."

Andreas gave a wheezing laugh. "So it would. Nevertheless."

He set to work chewing at her ropes. His progress was slow. Every few moments he stopped and made spitting noises. And the ropes were thick, the knots tight. If only they had Mihali's goats, Anna thought bitterly. Goats could chew these gods-be-damned ropes into pieces in less than a moment. But all they had were rats and slime. Rats might chew fast enough, but only if—

"Andreas," she whispered.

"Mmm," came his reply.

"Stop ruining your teeth. I have an idea."

His head turned. He made another spitting noise. "Oh, excellent. What is it?"

"Rats," she said.

A pause followed. "Explain, please."

"Rats," she repeated. "They chew everything. Like goats."

"What about goats?"

"Never mind the goats. Rats have teeth. Sharp ones. They chew and chew, just like goats. What if we could convince them to chew through *our* ropes? Roll over. And stop laughing."

He was still laughing as he twisted around. A weak and rasping laugh, but one that cheered her unreasonably. Anna waited until his back bumped into hers, then fumbled at his shirtsleeves. Her hands were numb from the tight bonds, but she managed to catch hold of the cuffs and tugged.

"What are you doing?" he demanded.

"The ropes are spelled, but your clothes aren't."

"You want me to take my clothes off?"

A brief, vivid picture of him naked invaded her thoughts. "Don't distract me."

She tugged at Andreas's shirtsleeves, pulling them over his wrists. It took more effort to wedge the cloth underneath the ropes. Now she pressed her wrists against his and turned her focus inward to the magic. It came more easily each time, and she hardly needed to speak the words out loud.

Ei rûf ane gôtter. Ei rûf ane strôm. Komen mir de zouber unde kreft...

Blood pulsed just beneath her skin. She called to it, called for Andreas's blood to answer. It was a trick of the magic, to slip open the skin and allow the blood to flow free. Warmth trickled over her hands and soaked into the cloth. Was it enough?

She was so intent upon her task that she nearly missed the first whispery scratching above and around them. Before it registered what she heard, a mob of hairy creatures swarmed over her. Rats, dozens upon dozens of them, poured over her face and arms and body, over Andreas. They nipped and slashed at them both. She had summoned too much magic—

Anna's bonds snapped. She rolled away from the rats and tried to scramble to her feet, in spite of the ropes around her ankles. She stumbled and dropped to her knees, cursing.

"Keep away!" Andreas called out. He tried to say more, but the rats overwhelmed him. He thrashed about, a garbled cry bursting from his throat.

"Andreas!"

Andreas flung himself upright, beating off the rats. He tore off his bloody shirt and hurled it away, and the rats swarmed after it. Anna sped the beasts along with a hurried, whispered spell; sparks of light and fire illuminated the furry horde, a sight that brought Anna's gorge into her throat. She swallowed, tried to forget the sensation of their claws on her face.

"Andreas?"

Andreas had slumped over, breathing hard. "I'm all right. Mostly. Just some scratches and bites. You can have Thea slather me with her ointments later. What about you?"

Her wrists were raw and bleeding. Scratches on her face and arms oozed fresh blood. Oh, but she was alive and free—almost free. With a little effort, she untied the ropes around her ankles. "I'll do," she said. "Though Thea will want to slather me as well. Now what?"

"We can't do much until they land and Druss takes most of her crew away."

No sooner had he spoken than the ship gave a lurch. Overhead a commotion broke out, audible even this far below the open decks. Anna and Andreas both went still. The commotion went on for a bell or longer, then the ship fell silent once more.

"That was not a small thing the gods gave us," Anna whispered. "But I'll not argue."

"Neither will I." Andreas lurched to his feet and stumbled away into the darkness. She heard him cursing, then a loud crash as he fell against something.

"What are you doing?"

"Looking for water. No use storming the castle if we're too thirsty to fight. And if we are very lucky... And so we are. Anna, come here."

Anna crept toward the sound of his voice. Her hands encountered his, and he pulled her to her feet. "Here," he said, "is our deliverance."

He guided her hand over an enormous wooden barrel—one of the ship's water casks. Koszenmarc knocked on the side and muttered a curse. "Empty, but there are more."

He made his way down the row, rapping on each one. At the third one, he stopped. "Thank the gods, we're in luck. Now if I can just get this plug out."

There was a popping noise. Suddenly water gushed over Anna's feet. "What—"

"Hurry," he said. "Before it runs dry."

He scooped up water and splashed it over his face. They took turns drinking handful after handful of that blessedly fresh, cool water. *Water,* Anna thought. *The loveliest creation of the gods.*

Andreas dropped to the deck and pulled her down next to him. The tap was above their heads, pouring over them like a waterfall. "Water," he said. He was grinning.

"Water," she said, wiping away the water streaming from her hair into her eyes.

"It's wonderful," he agreed. "And do you know what else we have?"

He fumbled at his sash. Then he handed her a leather flask, the same wine flask they'd drunk from at least a lifetime ago.

"How did they miss it?" she said.

He shrugged. "I don't know. Too busy kicking me, perhaps."

They both drank, then leaned back against the cask. Koszenmarc pulled Anna close, so she lay tucked into the crook of his arm. Water dripped over them from the opened cask, like raindrops falling from leaves in a forest.

"Water," Anna said. "And wine. The gods were listening."

Abruptly the giddiness vanished. Tears burned in her eyes. She swiped them away.

"What's wrong?" Andreas asked.

"The gods," she said. "If they were listening, why did they let Druss murder Lija?"

He leaned against her and rested his cheek against hers. "I don't know. What I think—if that matters—is that the gods don't meddle unless they can't avoid it. Instead they steer us, poor, ignorant, blind humans, to where and when and how we can do our best."

"What if we don't? Do our best, I mean."

"Then they steer us again and again, throughout our lives, like stubborn goats, driven to pasture. We goats sometimes take six or ten or a hundred lives before we stop chewing on garbage and listen."

"Goats," Anna said. "We are like them, aren't we?" She hesitated a long moment. "I'm sorry I lied to you."

He buried his nose in her hair. "I'm sorry I lied to you."

Lies make everything harder, Maté had said.

In a low voice, she said, "I never knew Brun had hired Sarrész. I swear it. But I knew about his plans for the princess."

No reply to that abrupt declaration.

"I told myself it meant nothing," she went on, in spite of that unnerving silence. "I convinced myself he would return the jewel, but even if the Emperor rewarded him, nothing else would happen. I didn't even tell Maté at first. I—" Her voice caught. "I knew the truth, but I didn't want to admit it, even to myself."

He sighed. "What did you plan to do with the money?"

Once, she'd had a simple answer to that simple question. To buy two rooms, one for her bed and one for her books. Two rooms with locks and keys, so that no one could enter but herself. But if she were being honest, she wanted far more. She wanted to make her own way in the world. To discover the borders of herself, without any reference to another human being. But all those answers were the same, she realized.

"To be free," she whispered.

"I believe I understand that." He leaned back against the cask. "I'm sorry too. I can't explain everything now, because certain secrets are not mine alone."

"I understand," she said.

He tilted his head to meet her gaze. "Do you? Anna—"

Andreas leaned close and kissed the corner of her mouth. Anna gave a soft exhalation of surprise, but when Andreas paused, she offered her own soft kiss in return. A nibble. A nip. Like small rats or tiny goats. The thought of tiny goats kissing made her giddy, and she laughed. That must have been the right reaction, because Andreas pressed another kiss on her lips. All thought of what was right or true or safe vanished from her thoughts. Anna hooked a hand around his neck and pulled him close for what seemed a lifetime and longer. When at last she drew back to catch her breath, he nearly toppled forward chasing after her mouth.

Andreas's laugh was a ripple of sunlight in this dark hold. "You," he said. "I'm so glad—"

Then they were locked in each other's arms, kissing and touching, her hands running over his chest and arms and back, his tangling in her wet hair. A pause. A breath. Another kiss. They were both breathing fast.

The ship gave a sudden jerk, sending them sprawling onto the deck. "What is it?" Anna said. "A storm? A—"

A second crash rocked the ship. From overhead came the thunder of feet.

"I believe," Andreas said, "that the *Konstanze* has found us."

CHAPTER 19

Andreas rolled onto his knees. "Come, quick. We'll add to the confusion."

"What do you mean? Andreas—"

He held out a hand. "If I make my guess correctly, Druss's people are all above decks, dealing with my crew. You and I can make a quick search for weapons. Swords, daggers, even a blunt staff will do. We can attack from behind and make trouble. Anything to make it easier for Eleni to take the ship."

He spoke rapidly, as though the plan were unfolding before his eyes and he was simply reading the text. Perhaps that was always how it was with him. Plans, woven within plans, drawn up as quickly and easily as he breathed.

"Afraid?" he asked.

She ought to be. And yet her pulse thrummed with anticipation.

"I'm ready," she said. "Let us join the battle."

They made their way cautiously and silently across the hold to the ladder. Koszenmarc listened intently, then nodded. "Quiet enough, but I'll scout ahead first. Wait for my signal. But first—"

He drew her into a tight embrace and kissed her. She smelled the wine on his breath, tasted the salt from his skin, a taste like the ocean and the islands.

"For luck," he whispered.

"Because we might die?"

"No, because we might live."

Laughter fluttered against her ribs. Anna pulled him into a second kiss, hard and fast. Andreas was grinning, and so was she, as he swung around onto the ladder and swarmed up the rungs. A pause while he eased the hatch open. A longer and more anxious interval while he disappeared from sight. Anna counted the moments, one for every beat of her heart. What if Druss had left a watch below? What if they had swiftly and silently knifed Koszenmarc? What if they waited for her to grow impatient and follow, before they did the same to her? She had just enough time to review all the spells she knew when at last his voice floated down from above. "All clear. Come with me."

Always, she thought as she climbed the ladder.

The hammock berth was empty and shadowed, except where one open hatch admitted a spill of sunlight. Now Anna clearly heard the tramping of feet over the deck, the ring of sword against sword, and was that Karl's roar that echoed from above?

Andreas touched her wrist, then pointed toward the port side of the hold. "Start from the hull," he said softly. "Work toward the middle. I'll do the same from the opposite side. Quick and quiet is the word. We don't want Druss's people to hear what we're up to. And remember, it's a weapon if you can bash someone over the head with it."

She stifled a laugh. Andreas grinned and made his way across the hold to begin his own search. Anna did the same. It was slow work, and tedious. Druss's crew had stashed their bags in careless heaps. The bags themselves were stuffed with the usual assortment of clothes, most of them worn and patched, but others clearly meant for shore leave. No swords, however. No convenient stash of weapons, unless you counted a few chipped and blunted daggers set aside for sharpening. Anna blew out a breath in exasperation. Even a broken stave would be useful.

She had just reached a collection of sea chests, which seemed promising, when Andreas caught up a heavy wooden pin. "Yes! A bit of luck at last. Anna—"

He had no time to complete that sentence. Two men dropped down through the upper hatch. For one brief moment, everyone froze. Then one man whipped out a knife from his belt and lunged for Andreas. The other, an enormous, thickset man, hefted an axe in one hand as he stalked toward Anna.

"You," he said in a rasping voice. "You, I get first."

He charged, the axe raised high. Anna's mind went blank with terror. But the weeks and weeks of training with her tutors, then with Thea, took over.

Light exploded between her and her attacker. He stumbled, blinded and cursing. Anna fell to her hands and knees and scuttled to one side, half-blinded herself, but when she tried to dodge past the man, he dropped the axe and grabbed her by both arms.

"Gotcha," he said.

"Not yet," she breathed.

She pressed her hands against his chest and summoned the magic current, just as she had when she tried to bloody herself and Andreas to lure the rats, only this time, she didn't hold back.

Ei rûf ane gôtter. Ane Lir unde Toc. Komen mir de bluot. Komen mir älliu *de bluot.*

The man's neck swelled, and his face twisted in a strange agony. He gave a strangled gasp. His heart heaved against his ribs, sudden and hard. Then his neck burst open, and gouts of blood poured from his body.

A mighty crash, of ship against ship, sent her tumbling over the deck, locked in an embrace with the dead man. His fingers dug into her arms, frozen in death. Anna tried to break free but could not. They rolled over and over, arms and legs entangled, from one side of the hold to the other. When they fetched up at the opposite side, Anna found herself pressed up against his chest.

His skin was already cold. His eyes, veiled in blood, seemed to stare at her from the distance of a thousand lives. Anna swallowed hard, and with a mighty effort she wrenched herself free and scrambled to her feet, staring around wildly for Andreas.

Andreas had circled around until he'd put a row of hammocks between himself and the other man. Once or twice, the other man lunged forward, but Andreas fended off the attack. This could not go on much longer. How long before more of Druss's crew appeared?

Her attacker had dropped the axe to grab her. Anna located it quickly amidst the chaos on the floor. "Andreas!" she called out.

Both men shifted their attention to her. Anna sent the axe spinning over the floor toward Andreas. Without a pause, Andreas flung the wooden pin hard at his opponent and snatched up the axe. The pin only distracted the other man a moment, but Andreas used that moment to close the gap between them.

The blade struck the man with an audible thunk. The man dropped into a bloody heap.

Anna gripped the nearest hammock. She was sticky with blood. Her legs felt like water, and a roaring in her head drowned out Andreas's voice. Dimly she was aware of a renewed commotion from above. She was trying to tell Andreas that she could not fight anyone, not anymore, but he was pulling her to her feet and pointing toward the hatch.

"Ours," she heard him say. "Look, Anna."

A high excited voice broke through. "Captain! It is you!"

A girl swung down from the ladder. She was tall and wiry, her hair tied in braids that flew around her face. She gripped a sheathed sword in one hand, and she was grinning with excitement.

"Fighting's over," she announced. "We took prisoners. Eleni sent me below to find you and give you a sword." She laughed. "As though you needed finding or a sword."

"I'll take that sword gladly," he said. "Now get back and report that your captain is grateful for this rescue. Elise and I will follow in a moment."

The girl tossed him the sword and scrambled back up the ladder. Koszenmarc fastened the sheath to his belt, then handed Anna the wine flask. "Drink. It helps with the shakes after a hard fight. We'll get you cleaned up above decks."

Her hands shook too much to hold the flask. Koszenmarc held it to her lips until she'd swallowed twice. The wine washed away the bitter taste in her mouth. Her trembling died away, but she still felt hollow inside.

He laid a hand on her shoulder. "You did well. You did what you had to."

Her stomach heaved, but she held it under control. She could still feel the bitter cold of death on her skin. "I know. I still hated it."

"So do I," he said softly. "Let's go on deck."

Above, a river of blood reflected the noonday sun. Koszenmarc's crew was hard at work, hauling up buckets of water. Saltwater sluiced the decks, sending the blood running over the deck and over the side. One of the men poured a bucket of water over Anna's head to wash away the worst of the gore that clung to her. More of the crew were at work wrapping the bodies of the dead in sailcloth. The *Konstanze* remained close, and parties of sailors were crossing back and forth. Less than a mile away lay Vyros. Anna could tell at once this wasn't the same inlet where she and Maté had first tracked down Sarrész. The shore here was a thin grey band of broken rocks, almost invisible between the high cliffs and the sea.

Andreas had already vanished into the chaos. Anna gripped the railing with both hands and breathed in a deep lungful of fresh air. The scent of blood hung in the air, mixed with salt tang and the stink of her own body from days locked in the hold.

"Elise! Godsdamn you and bless all the gods!"

Anna spun around to see Maté striding across the deck. An impossible weight lifted from her heart. "Maté!"

He paused only a moment, taking in her bloody clothes, then caught her in a breathless hug. "Elise, I worried— Are you—?"

"He knows," she whispered. "Andreas, I mean. He knows about Brun. About us and who we are."

Maté's eyes widened. "And?"

"It's fine," she answered hurriedly. "He understands."

His gaze sharpened. "*Fine* is not how I would phrase it. *What* does he understand? There must be more. Tell me——"

"I can't. Not yet."

He pressed his lips together, and he regarded her with a strange expression. "But you will. Soon?"

"As soon as I can."

A sharp whistle interrupted them. "Make the prize ready," Eleni called out. "We aren't in safe harbor yet." Her gaze caught on Anna's. "You," she said. "Go across to *Konstanze*. Thea wants you in sick bay. Now."

It was like that first hectic arrival, when Andreas Koszenmarc had dropped her into a horde of strangers. Someone had strung ropes between the ships. Anna managed to clamber across without dropping into the water. One of the crew caught her by the arms, then held her steady until she found her bearings. As soon as she could, she scrambled down the nearest hatch.

The *Konstanze*'s sick bay was nearly empty, except for two patients. One of them was Berit, asleep in one hammock. The second was Nikolas Farakos, wrapped up in bandages and fretting over some dose Thea insisted on giving him.

"Elise!"

Nikolas tried to fling himself upright. Thea pressed both hands against his chest. "Stop it," she said. "Unless you want to rattle the dice with Blind Toc. Gods-be-damned fool," she muttered. "Even if I should be thankful you're strong enough to cause trouble."

Nikolas grumbled but didn't attempt more. His face was pale, his eyes not entirely focused. Anna wanted to gather him into her arms, if for no other reason than that he lived.

Oh, but Thea. Thea's face was drawn with fresh lines, and her eyes were shadowed with dark smudges, faint against her dusk-brown face. But before she could do more than frown, Thea folded Anna into a tight hug.

"You," she said softly. "You lived and our captain too."

Anna hugged her back and for a long moment, neither of them spoke.

"We made a search of the island," Thea said at last. "We found that village. One of the children overheard Druss's orders so we knew where to find you. Cheeky boy. He demanded six gold denariie before he would say anything. Eleni gave him fifty."

Mihali. He lived. Good.

"We found Sarrész," Anna said in a low voice. "And lost him. And... and the captain knows my name."

Thea drew back and studied Anna's face with a searching gaze. "You told him? No, don't say anything. We'll talk about this later, and elsewhere," she added with a brief glance in Nikolas's direction. "For now, we need you fed and tended to."

Thea pointed to a trunk off to one side. Anna obediently sat and drank the potion Thea measured out for her. The potion tasted like the jungles, green and dense, with a hint of sunlight. Or perhaps she was giddier than she first thought. A sudden warmth spread through her body, as if the potion had lit a fire within her.

"You must teach me how to make this," Anna said with a gasping breath.

"Later," Thea said. "Now for all the rest that ails you."

She went to work, methodically cleaning and bandaging Anna's bites and bruises, many of which Anna had not noticed. Before she was done, one of the ship's boys arrived with a tray of soup and biscuits, and a pitcher of fresh water.

"Captain wants you both in his cabin the next bell," he said. "Sommat about Druss and making plans."

"Surely he did not say exactly that?" Thea murmured.

The boy flushed dark. "No, he didn't, but I heard—"

"Never mind what you heard," Thea said. "Go, fetch Theo from whatever mischief he's plotting. I want someone to watch over my patient while I'm with the captain. A bell isn't nearly long enough," she muttered to Anna, when the boy left. "But he's right. We can't let Druss get away from us."

She bullied Anna into finishing the soup, which she thickened by crumbling in a few biscuits. When Nikolas complained that he was hungry too, Thea sighed and gave him the rest of the biscuits. "Tell Theo to bring you porridge," she told him.

He grumbled, but the promise of Theo's visit had clearly cheered him up.

"He's angry because he missed the fighting today," Thea told Anna. "As if he hadn't had a bellyful of danger just a few days ago."

"He could have had my share and gladly," Anna said. The memory of that man dying before her eyes flooded back, and her throat closed. She felt Thea's hand press against her cheek. Just for a moment, then Thea was handing her another mug of water. This one tasted of herbs and the faintest tang of magic's green.

"That should give you back your strength," Thea said. "You've been working strong magic again, haven't you? Likely you'll need to work more before we're done with Druss and that gods-be-damned Sarrész."

Before the next bell sounded, Anna had scrubbed herself down with soap and cold water, then dressed in clean clothes from the ship's stores. Theo arrived soon after that with a basket stuffed with sweet rolls, and what had to be the latest gossip.

When Anna and Thea came to the captain's cabin, they found Daria and Eleni already seated with Koszenmarc at a long table underneath the cabin's broad windows. Koszenmarc had taken a few moments to wash and change into fresh clothes, but he seemed even more drawn and weary than before. None of the junior officers were present, nor was Hahn, but as Anna and Thea crowded around the table with the others, Hahn came running into the cabin.

"So," Andreas said, once everyone had taken a seat. "Report on what happened after Anna Zhdanov and I left the ship."

Hahn sent a sharp look at Andreas, then Anna. Eleni blinked at Anna's name, but answered. "It was strange," she said. "Very strange. Druss gave chase right away, and we played hide and seek for oh, five, six bells. I nearly thought she would catch us, and I was ready to order the lights doused, when she disappeared."

"How so?" Koszenmarc said.

"Just what I said. I thought she meant to trick us, just as we meant to trick her. I waited another two bells before I doused our lights, then sailed on north and east. It was a very long night."

A night filled with doubts and second guesses. No wonder Thea and all the others looked so drawn.

"We kept a lookout the whole time," Hahn added. "No sign of pursuit, by Druss or anyone else. It was as though she had given *us* the slip. So at dawn, Eleni gave the orders to round about. It took us a few passes, what with the hurry the night before, and we didn't have exact bearings, so we didn't raise the islands until the afternoon." He paused and licked his lips. "That's when we saw Druss's ship. She was headed away from the island."

A prickle of apprehension ran down Anna's back. Druss had arrowed back to those isolated islands as if she knew exactly where to find them.

"The traitor," she whispered.

Koszenmarc nodded. "Even Druss, clever as she is, could not have guessed our plans so exactly. She had help, and a bit of dangerous magic. Tell me what you think of this, Thea."

He pulled a metal disc from his shirt—the same one Anna had discovered amongst her medical supplies—and handed it over to Thea.

Thea hissed the moment the object touched her skin. She dropped it onto the table and stared at it, eyes narrowed to slits. The medallion lay there, a small disc of gold, with words etched deep into the surface in a strange angular script. Blood had caked in the grooves of those words and there was a smear of blood over the surface.

"A finding spell," Thea said in a flat voice. "A very expensive one, keyed to a single person, and triggered by their blood. I've seen the likes of this before, but only amongst the very wealthy. They use it as a kind of insurance against kidnapping. If you search Druss's cabin, you will no doubt find the map paired with this device."

"Who did this?" Eleni said.

"You already know," Andreas replied. "You tried to tell me, didn't you?"

She shook her head. Her expression was deeply unhappy, as though she wished she'd been wrong. "I did, but I had no proof."

"Now we do. Hahn, pass the word for Joszua. Make ready for trouble."

A stir went through those around the table as Hahn left to fulfill those orders. Thea looked even older, the creases in her face more marked than before. Daria laid her hand over her beloved's, but she seemed distracted, as though she could not quite take in what had happened. Only Eleni appeared unmoved, but by now, Anna had learned not to trust her first impressions with Eleni Farakos.

A very short time later, Joszua arrived with Hahn close behind. "You wanted me, Captain?"

"I do. I have a few questions. Stand over there, please." Andreas indicated a point at the opposite end of the table.

Joszua hesitated a moment before he obeyed. He must have guessed something, because his skin was damp with sweat. "What's wrong?"

Koszenmarc regarded him with a strange expression. "What could be wrong, Joszua? Druss took Sarrész, but we can take him back. Not easily and not without payment in blood, but we can. I do have one question. Why did you betray us?"

Joszua's eyes went wide. "What? I never—"

"You did," Andreas replied. "You're the one who came back with that convenient rumor about Sarrész on Idonia. You sent my perimeter guard away from the temple. You insisted on packing Anna's bag before we left the ship—the bag where we discovered this bit of magical treachery."

He pointed to the medallion. Joszua shuddered and glanced around wildly. For a moment, Anna thought he would try to flee, but perhaps he understood he could not escape, not with Hahn guarding the door, not with Daria playing with her knife so openly.

"She killed my father," he whispered.

Andreas nodded, as though that were expected. "Go on."

"She took my family hostage," Joszua went on. "It was after you brought Elise and that man Kovács to Asulos. She said she would murder everyone, even my sister's children, if I refused. I...I waited too long. She killed Anastasia in front of my eyes. That's when I told her about Idonia." He was speaking quickly, the words tumbling out. "But I'm no traitor. I never wanted to betray you. So I sent word to Maszny through a friend. Told him where and when to find Druss and her people. He was to arrest Druss before she could overtake you."

"You failed," Andreas said.

Joszua swallowed hard and nodded.

"How many died?"

"Two more." That came out as barely a whisper. "My mother. My youngest brother."

"That is when you agreed to take the medallion."

"I did not *agree*," Joszua burst out. "She said if I refused, all my sisters and brothers and cousins, everyone who claimed blood ties with me, they would die. So yes, I took that gods-be-damned medallion. But I waited, as long as I could. I never betrayed Asulos—"

Andreas stopped him with a gesture. "You did enough. My next question is, what shall I do with you?"

Joszua dropped to his knees. He was weeping. "Please. Let me make amends."

"Too late for that. We've dead of our own because of you. I won't execute you, but I want you gone. Now. Give him a boat," Andreas said to Hahn. "One of Druss's, though you might want to check if it's seaworthy. Stock the boat with water and biscuits, nothing more. He can find his own way from now on."

Hahn gave a signal. Five of the largest and ugliest members of the crew flooded into the captain's cabin and hurried Joszua away. Joszua made no trouble. He looked stunned, as if he could not quite take in what had happened.

The rest of the officers appeared shaken as well. Koszenmarc pressed both hands against his eyes. There was no joy in this discovery, Anna thought, nor any mercy in sparing his life. Joszua's death would not restore their companions.

At last, Koszenmarc lowered his hands with a sigh. "Next task," he said. "What do we know about Druss's plans. Daria?"

Daria needed a moment before she could collect herself. "Druss left five hours ago. She took Sarrész and a dozen of her crew, her best and nastiest warriors, the ones who can fight on land and ship. According to our prisoners, she expects to return by tomorrow evening, either with the jewel, or with Sarrész's blood on her hands."

"What do you believe?" Andreas asked Anna. "Was Sarrész lying to Druss when he said he buried the jewel?"

"I don't know." Frustration leaked out in her voice. "He hid the jewel, obviously. But I cannot believe he walked away from a treasure worth so much gold. Even if he meant to return later."

He nodded. "My thoughts as well. Which means we must find the man before Druss discovers that lie and murders him. You say Druss took a dozen with her?" he asked Daria.

Daria shrugged. "If we can believe our prisoners."

"Eh, a dozen is a sensible number," he said, "and Druss is sensible when it comes to such things. If she is twelve, we shall be twenty. Daria, you take charge of our prize. Eleni, you have command of *Konstanze*. Hahn, I want you as my second-in-command—"

Eleni held up a hand. "One suggestion. Take me as your second and leave Hahn aboard ship."

Koszenmarc regarded her with a wary expression. "Why? You can't risk the slave catchers."

She met his gaze with one equally cautious. "No, I can't. But unless I'm wrong, you might wish to send a message for reinforcements to a certain man, in a certain city on Vyros. I'd rather face Druss than…than what might happen if I were in command of the *Konstanze* when she sailed into Iglazi's harbor."

His wariness gave way to…surprise? Dismay? Anna couldn't tell. "Ah," he breathed. "This is a day for uncovering secrets. Very well. Hahn, you take command of the *Konstanze*. Eleni shall be my second on this mission. Let us say twenty of the crew, unless you have further suggestions, Eleni?"

"None that matter," she replied with a cool voice.

Anna had the distinct impression she—and all the rest of the company—had interrupted a long-delayed conversation between the two of them. Koszenmarc seemed aware of that, because his mouth twisted into a sour smile. "So, so. I see I've been overmatched. Very well. Here are the people I want…"

He went on to name twenty men and women, including Maté. All of them were senior members of the weapons drill. With few exceptions, all had served Koszenmarc four years or more. "Thea, I cannot spare you from the ship. Make up a bag with supplies for Anna. Eleni, pass the word to our people to make ready for a long trek. We'll want gear, weapons, and provisions for two days. No, make that three, in case matters prove less straightforward."

Hahn snorted. "They always do."

Koszenmarc's smile was like a bright flash of sunlight, but clearly not a happy one. "The one lesson my father taught me well. So." He laid both hands flat on the table. "We are done here. Eleni, make ready for our mission. Daria, see to the state of the prize. Hahn, Eleni was right. I shall need to speak with you about a certain message before I leave the ship."

Eleni and the other officers left at once to carry out their orders. Anna rose to her feet to follow, but hesitated. Koszenmarc had spoken so confidently, as if they did not face a dangerous trek over the mountainside, with a hard and bloody fight at the end. As if the jewel they both sought was simply an ordinary object, not the Emperor's rare and powerful weapon.

Something of her uneasiness must have shown on her face because Andreas smiled. "You look worried. Don't be. We shall find Druss, and that miserable Sarrész, and by tomorrow, we'll have that jewel."

"What about your client?" she said softly.

"That is the least of my concerns. Trust me, my client shall be well satisfied. Don't be worried—"

"But I *am* worried. I cannot do otherwise. Especially after what we've learned—"

"Anna," Koszenmarc said softly. "Never mind what came before. I know what Brun intended for you and Kovács. I swear that once we are done with this matter, you need not go back to him—"

"How?" she cried. "We cannot steal the Emperor's jewel and expect anything but death, or a life spent in hiding."

Koszenmarc opened and shut his mouth, as if he struggled to find an answer to dispute the indisputable. Anna waited a moment, then shook her head. "I best go."

He made no gesture to stop her. She hurried from the cabin to prepare for what came next.

CHAPTER 20

Within the hour, the crew had landed on shore and stowed the launch and the other boat among the trees. The youngest two of their expedition—Wim and Iris—cooked a hot meal of porridge and grilled sausage, while the others divided and repacked their gear and supplies for the trek up the mountain. Off in the distance, the *Konstanze* and Druss's ship were almost invisible black specks on the horizon.

"No grog, no rum, until we've won the battle," Andreas told everyone. "We're hunting a shark, and we need all our wits about us."

Karl grunted his agreement. A whisper ran through the rest of the crew. They were all on the edge of anticipation. They knew the risk and the possibility of a grand reward. Anna's throat closed at the thought of facing Druss once more, but she ate doggedly, knowing it was necessary.

"Anna." Maté crouched at her side. "A word with you, please?"

He wore that same remote expression he had the day he rescued her from Koszenmarc in Iglazi's streets. She set her plate aside and followed him to the edge of the forest. Eleni shot them a sharp glance, which Maté answered with a shrug.

A few yards into the shadows, away from the others, he said, "What *happened*?"

It was clear what he meant.

"Nothing," she said, a bit too quickly.

He snorted. "Liar. What happened between you and the captain?"

She hesitated. But this was Maté, her best and oldest friend. "We...we landed on that island. We made our camp, and a damp, uncomfortable camp it was. Rocks and sand and fleas. You can't imagine—" She broke off. She was babbling to no purpose. "We talked," she said quietly. "He kissed me."

Maté drew a sharp breath. "That gods-be-damned bastard." He checked himself and stared at her with a curious expression. "Unless you wanted him to kiss you."

"No," she said at once. "Yes. I'm not sure. Later, I did. But Maté, there's more." This part was difficult to tell. "When we found Sarrész, he told me Lord Brun *paid* him to steal the jewel. He claimed it was Brun who arranged for that priest to die. Sarrész ran because he believes Brun doesn't want any witnesses—including us."

"That...explains a great deal," Maté said softly. "So. What do we do now?"

"I don't know. That's what I wanted to ask you."

"Ah." He laughed softly. "Because of Eleni."

"Because of her and—"

"—and you aren't certain what Andreas Koszenmarc himself intends."

"I didn't say that."

"You didn't need to. If he meant to turn the jewel over to the Emperor's people, he would have announced it to his company. A reward is a reward, after all. Instead he—"

"Zhdanov. Kovács."

It was Eleni, summoning them to their business. Maté stuffed the last bite of sausage into his pocket and headed off. Anna watched the glance they exchanged. Did she detect a wariness in Eleni's expression?

The crew struck their temporary camp and buried the ashes of their fire. By now the sun was slanting toward the horizon. Druss had set off at least six hours before them. Their goal, Andreas told them, was to reach the temple ruins by the third bell of the evening watch.

The trail was narrow, edged by stones and packed with dirt. Mountain freshets cut across their path, and from time to time they came across a shelter of rough-cut logs—more evidence of smugglers—but Andreas didn't call a halt until they reached a clearing on the mountainside, halfway between the shore and the summit. The sun had set hours ago, and the skies had turned to the darkest blue as twilight advanced toward night. Below them, the ocean spread out in a dark expanse, the surf marked by glittering lines.

Andreas ordered a cold meal shared out—rolls stuffed with smoked pork, cold porridge, and tea left over from their earlier meal. Anna's appetite had vanished hours ago, but she ate her share and drained her water flask as ordered.

After the meal, Andreas hung a shaded lantern from a branch and spread a map over the ground. "We are here," he said, indicating a point along the dotted line that was the trail they followed. "And here are the temple ruins." The temple ruins lay close to the summit, on a broad flat expanse dug into the side of the mountain. Anna could recall how it looked beneath the midday sun, an empty square of stone that vibrated with magic. She suppressed a shudder at the memory and concentrated on Andreas's next words.

"Druss will have a perimeter watch set," he said. "So, we split into three parties here. Felix, you take command of five. Go downhill and around the temple until you are directly beneath it. Druss won't expect any visitors, so she'll have a campfire lit. The better to question her prisoner," he added.

That provoked some uneasy laughter.

Andreas grinned. "Just so. Once you reach your goal, Felix, give the signal. Whistle three times. What kind of bird was it that you told me about?" he asked Katerina.

"Nightjar," she replied. "Such a nice innocent bird. I can do that."

"Good. Then you go with Felix."

Karl muttered under his breath. "Gods-damned fucking birds."

"Would you rather announce yourself to our friends?" Andreas said. "No, I thought not. Then a nightjar it is. Eleni, you take another five uphill from the temple. Give me your own signal. What will it be?"

"The same," she said. "It's the best choice. One bird calling to another."

He nodded. "Good enough. Felix, when you hear a monkey's screech, shoot a flight of arrows toward the temple. Make as much noise as you can and draw the outer perimeter away. Eleni, your task is to get Sarrész away from Druss—as quickly as you can, before she slits his throat. My people will secure the camp. Once we do, I'll give a shout. That is when you," he indicated Felix, "will turn back and engage the enemy. At least that's the plan."

"What about me?" Anna asked. "What is my part in this madness?"

Now Koszenmarc hesitated. "This will be a messy, bloody fight in the dark. I want you out of Druss's way until later, when we question Sarrész about the jewel."

"A truth spell?" she said doubtfully.

"I was thinking the man would be grateful for his rescue," he said dryly. "No, I mean to offer him a substantial reward in exchange for his cooperation. But Druss will not be gentle with him. We'll need your medicine and your magic to keep him alive, and once we persuade him to hand over the jewel, you are the only one who can determine if he's given us the genuine thing. The man could be on the verge of death and still be telling lies."

Others laughed, but Anna bit her lip. A glance at Maté showed that he was frowning.

Maté's words came back to her, more unsettling than before. *If he meant to turn the jewel over to the Emperor's people, he would have announced it to his company.*

Later, Anna told herself. *Later I will ask him questions. And he will answer. And if he doesn't, I will have a different kind of answer, won't I?*

Everyone refilled their water flasks, then the company set out again, single file. Their progress slowed as the trail bent up and up again and the footing turned uncertain, despite the quarter moon above, a bright sliver just visible through the thick trees.

One or two bells later, a warning passed down the line. Anna halted and drained her water flask. The moon had set, the stars themselves were little more than faint pinpricks against the sky. Koszenmarc walked down the line, speaking a quiet word to each member. Felix and his people split off to the left, along an almost invisible track that wound down the hillside to make a long, long circle around the ruins. Eleni and her party headed up the slope to take their position on the opposite side.

"Anna." He had come to her at last. "You're angry with me."

She wasn't angry, precisely. It was Maté and his questions that had awakened doubt in her. "I don't want to be an afterthought," she said at last.

His fingertips grazed her cheek, a brief electric touch. "Ah, no. You are anything but. We cannot succeed without you. *I* cannot succeed without you."

He spoke with a strange intensity that unsettled her more than anything else these past few weeks. But she knew that this was not the moment for questions and answers. She touched her fingers to his lips, felt him smile. Then he was making his way back to the front of the line.

Their party continued along the trail another half mile or so. Once more they stopped, and everyone drew their weapons. Koszenmarc led Anna off the trail, down the hillside, to a thicket of saplings and thorn bushes. "Stay here until I come for you," he whispered. "If all goes wrong…"

"If all goes wrong, I shall murder Druss myself," Anna whispered.

Andreas laughed softly. "I believe you."

His lips brushed hers and he was gone.

Anna huddled down in her hiding place, her bag between her feet, her cloak at once thick and insufficient against the damp autumn night. Faint starlight cast a patchwork of pale silver far above, but here the ground lay in darkness so thick she could almost taste it on her tongue. The rich scent of damp earth, of orchids dying on the vine, all of this overlaid by a musky thread from some wild creature. One of Koszenmarc's monkeys, no doubt. As for Koszenmarc himself, she could just make out the faint rustle that marked his passage back to the trail.

More silence. Her heart beating too fast, too hard. She held her breath as long as she could, sucked in a lungful of air, and tried again. Again. How long, dammit, before Felix gave his signal?

A thin, high cry broke the night. Anna flinched. Another cry sounded, ending in a sob. Her imagination invented a hundred terrible explanations. The rational part of her brain informed her that the cry came from a distance. Sarrész. Druss had lost her patience.

A heartbeat after that realization came a piercing warble, almost the echo of Sarrész's cry. Once, twice. Three times. An agonizing silence followed, and Anna had time enough to wonder if what she heard was Felix's or Eleni's signal. Then came a repeat of that same warbling, this time from far above.

A screech, like that of a startled monkey, answered the second warble. Anna could not hear the arrows themselves, but she imagined a flight loosed toward the enemy. A strangled yell, the crash of broken branches, as if a hundred soldiers stirred up the forest—

The attack had begun.

Loud curses broke through the night. Druss, her voice unmistakable, shouted orders to her people. The noise of battle echoed over the hillside, much louder than she had expected. Where was Maté in all the confusion? Koszenmarc had assigned him to Felix's party. Anna had already guessed he didn't want Eleni or Maté distracted from their duties. Stupid man. As if a soldier like Maté, or a warrior like Eleni, would allow themselves to be distracted.

A crash sounded in the forest, a few feet away from her. In a panic, Anna burst from her hiding spot. Her foot caught in a tree root and she went tumbling down the hillside. One bump, another sharp drop, then she landed atop a blanket of dead leaves and...

...the ground gave way beneath her.

Anna reached out wildly. Her fingers closed around loose dirt and crumbling leaves. She had just one moment to curse her bad luck, then she was falling, falling through dust and dark.

She landed abruptly in a heap. For a long moment, she could not breathe, could not think. Then her lungs sucked in a painful breath. Dust clogged her throat. She choked, drew another wheezing breath, then coughed out the dust and bits of leaves. Anna gathered enough spit to wet her mouth and swallowed. Slowly her scattered thoughts collected.

A pile of dirt and leaves had broken her fall. Above, the opening was scarcely visible against the night. Below...the air was thick and close. She staggered to her feet, one hand pressed against her aching ribs. Someone, some damned fool, had dug a hole in the ground, in the middle of the mountainside. Anna reached out, expecting to find the edge of the hole, but her hand met nothing but air. She shuffled a tentative step forward. Her boots scuffed against stone—no, stone *tiles*, cut and laid.

Then it struck her.

This was not a hole. It was a tunnel.

The secret passageway.

Anna gulped down a laugh. The innkeeper at Iglazi had not lied after all. There *was* an underground passageway, as romantic and impossible as you could imagine. She pressed a fist against her mouth, trying to stifle her giggles. A part of her understood she was panicked and desperate. Another part knew she had to keep quiet.

With an effort, she swallowed her laughter. She could not summon a magical light—the enemy might be searching for her aboveground—so she dropped into a crouch and felt around until she located the pile of dirt where she had landed and found her bag. She slung it over her shoulder and gripped the strap with trembling hands.

More cautious exploration brought her to the tunnel's wall. It was lined with brick, with buttresses at regular intervals. Anna slid down to the ground and leaned against one, hugging her bag close. What next?

From a distance came the echo of voices.

Anna's heart leapt against her chest. Yes, they were coming in her direction. Druss's people? Andreas Koszenmarc's? She couldn't take any risks. She eased herself onto her hands and knees and crept around the buttress. Just in time, because light rippled over the tunnel walls. Anna huddled as far as possible into the corner. If these were Druss's people...

It was then she heard a voice, a very familiar voice, cursing in the mainland dialect.

"Gods damn you," Raab said. "Gods damn you until the end of our lives. You're not worth the trouble."

"Then let me go." Aldo Sarrész was whimpering. "I've nothing you want."

"Except your life, you worthless slug. No, if Lord Brun wants you, Lord Brun shall have you. Now walk, dammit, or I'll drag you down the mountainside by your hair."

A noisy struggle followed. The torchlight swung up and down. Then Anna heard a loud clatter and the light ebbed to a dull glow. Raab swore, then delivered an audible blow. Sarrész gave a muffled cry, but he obviously was resisting, because Anna heard a scuffling, then the sound of a heavy weight being dragged over stones.

"You," Raab breathed heavily. "You will pay for every gods-be-damned step. But I won't leave without you."

"You won't leave at all," said another voice.

Oh gods. Anna recognized Druss's voice. She pressed both hands over her mouth to keep from whimpering in panic. Oh gods. No, this plan had not survived even the first few moments. Not Andreas's. And apparently not Raab's.

"Captain Druss," Raab said. "We had an agreement."

"Which you betrayed."

"No. The circumstances have changed—"

"Then we renegotiate the terms."

Anna heard the whisper of a sword pulled from its sheath, a second drawn just as quickly, the crash of metal against metal that vibrated through the air. Someone gave a wail, Sarrész, she thought, then came the back-and-forth of footsteps, the rattle of a faster exchange. The noise of their battle echoed up and down the tunnel, and Anna could not tell which direction the fight had taken them. So it took her by surprise when she heard a grunt, like that of a punch delivered strong and fast, then a heavy weight hitting the ground.

Oh. Oh gods. She knew the sound of death when she heard it. Only... whose?

The gods were not delivering timely answers that day. She heard a cough, a series of thuds she could not decipher, then a soft and wordless plea from Sarrész.

If he dies, we lose everything.

Anna set her bag to one side and rose to her feet. She had one moment, no more. She seized her focus, found the balance point within a breath or two, and stepped out from her hiding place. A word, all she needed was a word...

Light bloomed in her hand. Druss stood not three feet away. Raab lay at her feet in a pool of blood, his eyes wide open in the stare of death, his sword still clutched in one hand. An irregular shadow lay against the opposite wall. Sarrész, whether alive or dead, she could not tell.

Druss's eyes glittered in the magical light. "You," she said softly. "I told you that you would regret making any trouble."

She raised her sword and slid a dagger into her other hand.

A shout rang down the length of the tunnel. "Druss!"

Andreas.

Druss did nothing more than glance in his direction, but it was long enough for Anna. With a word, she called up the magical current in an explosion of light.

Druss staggered back, blinded and swearing to all the gods. Andreas had not even paused. He closed the distance. One strike, and he slashed Druss's left arm, sending her dagger skittering over the stones. Druss staggered back and raised her sword high. Not soon enough. With one smooth motion, Andreas drove his blade through her belly.

Druss bent over double, staring at the blade in her stomach, her mouth rounded in an O. Her hand jerked open. Her sword fell to the ground. Very slowly she sank to her knees, then toppled over.

CHAPTER 21

Like a breath leaking out, Anna's magical light faded to grey. She immediately summoned the current again. There was a hiss, then a pop, as if lightning arced across the closed space of the tunnel, then light flared, casting splashes of brilliant gold all around. Anna cupped the magic in her palm, lifted her hand high.

The secret tunnel was far broader and higher than she had guessed. Its brick-lined walls reached up ten feet at least. The floor was paved in flat stones that glittered. Centuries of dust had caught in the grooves, but the stones themselves were unbroken, unworn, as if they'd been laid yesterday. Now that she was no longer terrified, she felt the whisper of magic all around.

A dozen feet away, Andreas Koszenmarc stood over the body of Isana Druss. Blood ran from a cut over his left eye, and even in the uncertain illumination she could see the bruises on his face. He shifted on his feet—unsteadily, she thought. Then his gaze swung up to hers. "Did she—?"

The poisoned blade, he meant.

"No, you stopped her in time. What about you?"

He made a dismissive gesture. "A few knocks. Ah, no, you don't."

Aldo Sarrész had lurched to his feet and was stumbling away. Andreas gave chase and tackled the man to the ground. Sarrész fought back, harder than Anna had expected, until Andreas grabbed him by the hair and yanked his head back. He slid a knife from a wrist sheath and pressed its point against Sarrész's throat.

"Cooperate," he said. "You'll be a much happier fellow."

He shook Sarrész like a dog shaking a rabbit, then let go. Sarrész's head hit the stone pavement with an audible crack. He lay disconcertingly still.

"You didn't kill him, I hope," Anna said uneasily.

Andreas blew out a breath that might have been laughter, or exhaustion. "Tempting, but no. Here, help me make sure he cannot escape again."

He pressed one knee against Sarrész's back, then cut wide strips from the man's own shirt with his knife. Braided together, the strips made durable bonds, which Anna used to hobble Sarrész's ankles, while Andreas tied his arms behind his back.

Once he was satisfied, Koszenmarc hauled Sarrész to his feet. "Stop pretending. We know you're awake. March, or I'll drag you back up those stairs myself."

Sarrész whined under his breath about a world filled with enemies, but when Koszenmarc prodded him, he shuffled along in the direction Koszenmarc indicated. Anna caught up her bag again and followed with her magical light cupped in one hand.

Not far beyond where Anna had fallen through, the tunnel angled toward their left and began to slope upward. Koszenmarc moved slowly and stiffly, and Anna thought she could feel every bruise from her tumble down the mountainside. Sarrész had not ceased his complaints, but he kept them to a murmur.

Two more bends brought them to a winding stairwell cut into the earth. Like the rest of the temple, the stones here vibrated with magic. Koszenmarc knelt and untied the hobbles from Sarrész's ankles. "Up you go," he said.

Sarrész gazed up the stairs, as if contemplating one last excuse to delay the inevitable, but when Koszenmarc prodded him with the hilt of his dagger, he sighed and started to climb. Koszenmarc followed close behind, and Anna after him.

Unlike the tunnel, the staircase was narrow, scarcely wide enough for a single person, and it coiled tightly around a stone pillar carved with prayers in letters and a language that resembled Kybris, but seemed far more ancient. This was no smuggler's work, Anna thought. An escape route?

The stairs ended at a wide tile, which lay askew over the exit, leaving a narrow opening. Anna extinguished her magical light. One by one they squeezed through the narrow opening. Sarrész immediately fell into a heap. Anna staggered. Andreas caught her by the arm and held her steady. He had his sword drawn.

They were in a far corner of the square, near a statue of Lir, recognizable only by a pattern of stars along the hem of her gown and what could be her brother Toc's sword at her feet. Beyond was the familiar square, empty under the starlit skies. The fighting had ended. Not far away, Koszenmarc's crew had taken over Druss's campsite outside the ruins—building a generous fire, setting up tents, and clearing away the bodies of the enemy.

A shout went up from one of the crew on watch. Then Eleni was striding toward them. "Captain! I thought—" She caught herself, then glanced from Anna to Sarrész and back. "You found our prisoner."

Koszenmarc gave her a weary grin. "I didn't get myself killed, no. And yes, we have our man. What about up here?"

"Two of ours killed, Elias and Ajar. Five wounded. No sign of Druss—"

"She's dead. Have someone fetch her body—two bodies, actually. I'll show you where in a moment. Perimeter guard?"

"Already set. A few of Druss's people got away from us," she added.

He waved a hand. "I would be shocked if it were otherwise. Meanwhile, take charge of our new friend. Set a guard over him and make certain he doesn't cause trouble. Oh, and send out a patrol to see if there are any more underground passageways..." He paused and raked his hand through his hair. "Sorry. You know what to do."

Eleni hauled Sarrész to his feet. She ignored his complaints and bundled him over toward the camp. Anna started after them, but Andreas stopped her with a gesture. "We'll need to question him before the night is over. We don't want to give him time to invent new stories."

His face was masked by shadow, his voice oddly strained.

"I won't force the truth from him," Anna said.

"I don't want you to."

"Then what are you trying to say?"

"I'm not sure. Only...we *must* find that jewel."

His voice was low and quick. Urgent. She ought to understand. She had—once had—her own reasons for recovering the Emperor's jewel.

"I should see to our wounded," she said at last.

He released an audible sigh. "And I ought to make the rounds, if only to show everyone I'm alive."

One of the guards directed Anna to a shelter near the fire where five of Koszenmarc's crew lay. It was far better than she had feared. Two had only minor injuries—bruised ribs, a sprained wrist. One man had a broken arm, which Katerina was binding with a makeshift splint. Karl had a gash along his ribs.

Then she came to Felix.

Felix lay close to the fire, shivering under several blankets. His skin was grey and cold to the touch. Anna made a quick examination. No gut wounds. No broken bones. The only injury was a shallow cut on his cheek, which had already scabbed over. He was muttering to himself in a dialect of Veraenen she didn't recognize.

Poison, damn her.

She hurriedly measured out five drops of Thea's strongest potion into a mug, then filled the rest with water. With some coaxing, she managed to persuade Felix to swallow the dose. His face immediately flushed dark red, and he wheezed alarmingly. The next moment, his color subsided and he drew a long breath. His pulse was weaker than Anna liked, but at least he was breathing more easily, and he no longer had the look of the dead.

"Will he make it?" Eleni said quietly.

"I...don't know," Anna replied in a low voice.

Eleni exhaled sharply. "Damn that Druss. Well, we must do what we can and trust the gods for the rest. I'll have Katerina watch over him. She'll send for you if anything goes wrong. Right now the captain wants you for questioning our prisoner."

Sarrész had been deposited in a small tent on the other side of the camp. Andreas stood outside, hands clasped behind his back, waiting for her. He had the air of someone deeply frustrated.

"He's proving difficult," he said in answer to her questioning look.

"And this surprises you?" she asked.

He gave a short laugh. "Fair enough. I'm hoping you'll have more luck than I."

The tent was barely large enough to hold three people. A lantern hung from the tent poles overhead and cast a dim light over the dirt floor. Sarrész lay curled around himself at the far end, as though he expected another kick. The strips of cloth they had used to bind him had been replaced by sturdier bonds of rope, wrists and ankles both, though someone had shown him mercy and tied his hands in front.

At Anna's entrance, Sarrész jerked his head around and winced. His face had that pinched look she associated with deep and unremitting pain. It was hard to imagine him seducing all those men and women. Then he turned his head, and the light caught his features just right, drawing lines and shadows across that once-voluptuous face. Yes, she could see it. Just.

Our prisoner.

The exhilaration of victory faded.

"You need a healing," she said.

Sarrész grunted. "As if anyone cared."

"It doesn't matter if we care, we have questions to ask," Andreas said.

"Or you'll do what? Torture me? Druss did that already. Gods, don't any of you get tired of asking the same fool questions over and over?"

"No torture," Andreas said. "A bargain. Tell us where you hid the Emperor's jewel. We'll share the reward with you."

At that, Sarrész laughed, a wheezing, silent laugh. "And when I do, you hand me over to whatever bastard you work for. Then they kill me. I'm going to die, no matter what, so why should I do you any favors?"

"You won't die," Andreas said. "I need you for a witness."

He held a flask to Sarrész's mouth. The man eyed him suspiciously but took a sip. His eyes widened and he took another, longer swallow. When Andreas took back the flask, Sarrész gave a sigh and fell back on the blankets. Only now did Anna see the dark bruises on the man's face and throat, more on his chest, where his tattered shirt hung open—signs of a long and steady beating.

"Tell us about Brun," Andreas said.

"I told you already. He wanted that damned jewel. He offered me money. Same as Lord Brun and those others offered you."

"Not exactly like me. You say he murdered that young priest."

"Yes, yes. He wanted me dead too. So I ran."

"To Eddalyon, where you tried to sell the jewel to Druss."

Sarrész's answer came in a whisper. "Because I was tired of running. Tired of hiding from Brun. From Druss. The jewel's dangerous, you know, no matter how sweet she talks. Calls herself Ishya. Lovely as Lir and all the stars. But dangerous, damned dangerous."

"If you mean the Emperor's jewel, she is," Andreas agreed. "She's left a trail of dead from Duenne to Eddalyon, some of them friends of mine. Tell us where you hid the jewel, and we'll make certain you survive."

But Sarrész was having none of that. "You tell a pretty tale. What's the difference between you and Isana Druss?"

"None. I told you I need a witness."

Sarrész spat at him. "Fuck you and your promises. Kill me. I don't care. Dump my cursed body in the ocean and be done with me."

Andreas muttered a curse. Anna stared at Sarrész. He seemed indifferent to death. That was not in his character, not from any report, not from everything she had observed. He was planning yet another impossible escape. But how? He had almost drowned when the jewel dropped him in the middle of the ocean—

"You hid your precious jewel very well," she said softly. "In your boots, am I right? And now you think Ishya will save your life again. Andreas, let's take a look at those boots."

"Good idea." Andreas bent down and seized Sarrész's feet. Sarrész kicked and tried to twist away but was hampered by the ropes. He subsided, panting angrily, as Koszenmarc tugged off the boots and handed one to Anna. The other he examined himself.

The uppers had once been very fine, constructed from expensive black leather, but now they were stained and buckled from saltwater. Anna thought she could read every mile of their long, long hunt in these boots. And the heels...she had first seen their shape on the sands of Vyros.

Thick. So thick they were unfashionable. She ought to have recognized that at once.

She ran her fingers over the notch at the back of the heel. Nothing. Not even a hint of a signature.

Ei rûf ane gôtter. Ane Lir unde Toc. Ei rûf ane jeweul.

A long and heavy silence, so long she felt her pulse beating like the waves upon the shore. She was on the point of speaking again when she felt a shift in the world, a sudden gap and a cold sensation, as though the void had opened to her touch.

Anna uncurled her fingers. A small dark jewel lay in the palm of her hand. When she turned toward Andreas, it winked with a blood-red light, so dark and vivid it was as though it had absorbed all the light from the torches and campfire. The next moment, she saw a depthless blue spark inside her palm, then a shadowy green. Her vision blurred. A white fire flared, and she thought she saw the jewel blur as well, its shape melting into something far different. A man. A woman. An alien creature that defied any classification of sex or gender.

Oh, oh, oh. This was no magical *object*. This was a living, thinking being. Surely Lir had not imprisoned one of her creations and turned it into a slave of humankind.

No, said a voice.

Her breath caught. She *knew* that voice. It had spoken to her weeks ago, on the edge of the magical void, as she searched for Aldo Sarrész.

Ishya?

She thought she heard a faint whisper from the jewel, from Ishya, even as its presence folded upon itself and vanished. Once more, she felt a blankness where she expected magic to reside.

"What is it?" Andreas said. "What did you see?"

Anna shook her head. She doubted she had the words to describe what she had heard. Felt. Sensed. With shaking hands, she tore a strip of cloth from her shirt, wrapped up the jewel, and tucked it into her breastband. Her whole body trembled, whether from that strange, unaccountable magic, or the long night, or simply the release from terror.

"Your...your client will be pleased," she managed to say.

But Andreas did not have the air of someone granted a great victory. His was almost a pensive expression as he studied her. "Never mind about my client," he said with a glance toward Sarrész. "Let us leave our friend here to the watch. I have a few things to discuss with you."

Outside the tent, he paused to pass along orders to the guard standing watch. Water and a meal for the prisoner, and a fresh set of clothes. He was to be allowed a chamber pot and reasonable privacy. However, at each change of watch, the new guard was to double-check Sarrész's bonds, and no one was to speak with the man.

"Will your client release him?" Anna said softly.

"Hardly. He is not a forgiving man. But his testimony is necessary, and that might be enough to save his life afterwards."

What kind of client demanded a witness? But Anna was too weary by now to insist on answers. They crossed the campsite in silence, to a much larger tent near the tumbledown walls of the ruins. Here Koszenmarc gave orders for a meal to be brought. He held the tent flap aside and motioned for Anna to enter.

Only after she was inside did she realize this was his own tent, illuminated by a lantern, and with a bedroll laid out and his gear stowed neatly off to one side. Anna settled herself in one corner. Koszenmarc unfolded one of the blankets, and when the meal arrived, he laid out the tin plates and dishes himself. "It might be midnight," he observed, "but we'll sleep more easily with full stomachs."

Their dinner consisted of cold rice and smoked beef, flatbread soaked in honey, and hot, strong tea. By the time Anna had consumed her share, her head no longer ached. Rain had begun to fall, pattering against the canvas ceiling. A fair distance away, she heard the chatter of guards, Eleni barking at them to keep a proper watch, and then Maté's low, soothing voice.

Andreas Koszenmarc poured more tea for them both. He took a sip, set the mug aside. "I need to tell you several things," he said quietly. "The most important is what we must do with this jewel. I..." He drew a long breath. "I was lying when I said my client would pay us money for its return."

Oh. Gods. Just what she had feared. Koszenmarc's client was a hostage nation, one that had surrendered because it had no choice, or one that feared the Emperor's endless hunger for new lands. They might have promised any number of intangible things. Including a title or holding for a dishonored son.

"Andreas..." She folded her hands together. "Andreas, I can't—"

He held up a hand. "Let me finish. My client did promise a reward, but it's not one that can be counted out in coin. This jewel doesn't belong to you. Or me. Or to that miserable excuse of a thief Aldo Sarrész. I'm not entirely certain it belongs to the Emperor—"

"It doesn't," she said emphatically. "Andreas, the jewel is not a *thing*. It's *alive*."

He stared at her, his expression horrified. "Oh. Is that what you couldn't describe? That's—" He broke off and rubbed his forehead. "Oh dear gods. Are you certain? No, don't answer. Of course you are. So, what should we do if we don't return the jewel to the Emperor?"

Of all the answers she'd imagined, this wasn't one of them.

"What are you saying?" she whispered.

"I'm saying we have only a few choices," he said. "Return the jewel to the Emperor and hope for a reward. Sell it to the highest bidder. There are any number of provinces who want to break free from the Empire. Or we could drop the jewel into the deep, but then you wouldn't have your money."

Anna had a brief, horrible image of the jewel, trapped forever in the depths of the ocean. Then the full import of his words struck, and she swallowed against the knot in her throat. "You think I might object."

"No, but—"

"But yes. You do believe that," she burst out. "You said as much just now. Not with words, oh no. But you did with your eyes, the way you stared at me, with the tone of your voice that said you believed I wanted money more than honor. Yes, I wanted the money, but I do have honor. As much as the world allows me."

Her voice cracked. What did it matter, what Andreas Koszenmarc thought? With an inarticulate curse, she sprang to her feet. Andreas was faster. He seized her by the arm, then immediately snatched his hand back.

"And what did you think of me?" he demanded. "That I was a greedy pirate, who wanted nothing more than a bucket of denariie? You know nothing about me, or why I might *need* the kind of reward an Emperor can give me."

His eyes were large and bright, like polished coins. He was so close she could smell the scent of his sweat, the spicy scent of Eddalyon itself, like nothing else she had ever known.

Anna tried to draw a breath and could not, not with him standing so close. She needed miles and years and another lifetime, at least, before the weight against her chest eased. If it ever did. "Andreas..."

"I am not Marcus Brun," he said quietly. "I can't prove it inside of a night. But I would be grateful if you let me try. Tomorrow. Or longer—"

Her pulse beat faster. A warmth kindled in her gut. It was wrong, she told herself. She ought to wait, to let this man prove himself....

Anna reached up to touch his cheek. "We don't need to wait until tomorrow."

CHAPTER 22

His first kiss was like the breeze, a faint caress against her lips. He gave a soft exhalation, as though surprised, before he kissed her again, and again, each one deliberate and unhurried.

The moments slowed, the moments sped past in a fluid stream, as though the magical current carried them through the night. Memory scattered into bits in its wake. Her tugging off his shirt, him loosening her sash, their clothes falling into a puddle on the floor. His warm hands encircling her breasts. His mouth upon hers. Her legs opening to take him inside because she could not wait any longer. A sharp cry, strangled at the last moment, as she remembered the hands standing watch around them.

"I love you," he whispered.

Her belly shivered at the words. "You can't mean that."

They lay entangled in each other's arms, skin against warm skin. The camp had quieted around their tent, though from time to time Anna heard the rustle of footsteps as the perimeter guard made their rounds.

"I can," he murmured. "I do."

Before she could ask if he was serious, he gathered her into an embrace and pressed his lips against her, an endless, all-consuming kiss that blanked the questions from her mind and sent ripples down the length of her body. It was wrong, she told herself. Wrong, impossible, and so very dangerous to let him inside her defenses. Yet she had. She would again.

She dug her fingers into his hair. "Stop," she whispered.

He stopped.

"Now lie still."

"I..."

"Hush. Lie still. I want... Let me show you what I want."

He made a soft noise of protest, just once. Nothing more.

CHAPTER 23

Anna woke at dawn, little more than a suggestion at this hour. The camp lay quiet amidst the even deeper hush of the surrounding jungle. Andreas slept beside her, his left arm draped over her stomach. Soon enough the world would awake. Hornbill would call to hornbill; other birds would sing to the rising day as the watches changed. Soon enough the company would break camp and head back to shore.

And then?

For so many weeks, she had pinned all her thoughts on recovering the Emperor's jewel. She had shied away from any thought or plans for what would come later.

Now later had arrived. And here she was, even more impossibly entangled with Andreas Koszenmarc.

As if he'd overheard his name, Andreas shifted in his sleep and exhaled softly. The pale grey light of dawn had grown brighter over the past few moments, and Anna could make out his face. The bruises, dark against his brown skin. The thin red slash running just below his hairline. The mouth now curved in a loose and satisfied smile.

...His lips running over her skin, like touches of flame. The moment when his mouth closed over her breast. That last engulfing kiss after he drew back from her body and gazed upon her with a bright wondering look, and they both collapsed into each other's arms and into sleep....

"We have no future," she wanted to say. "Never mind the jewel. You're a duke's son and a pirate. And I—"

But Anna no longer knew who or what she was. Once, she'd been a scholar's daughter. Once, Lord Brun's bonded servant, entrusted with matters of magic and useful in bed. Now? Now she was no longer certain.

For once, she wanted to find a place in the world that was hers alone, and not defined by another person.

The noise of a distant conversation interrupted her thoughts. Voices, exchanging sharp words. An argument between the guards? Surely not.

"Andreas! Captain! We need you!"

Andreas rolled over, instantly awake. He pulled on his trousers and flung himself out of the tent even before he'd finished tying the sash.

Druss, Anna thought. *Druss had allies we didn't know about. Or...*

A dozen other possibilities came to mind as she scrambled into her clothes and followed Andreas.

In the center of the campsite, Eleni and Andreas stood close in whispered conversation. Maté had taken up a resting stance a few feet away, his hands clasped behind his back. At Anna's appearance, his gaze shifted briefly to her, taking in her rumpled hair and any number of details that Anna suddenly wished were invisible, then flicked away.

"What is it?" she asked breathlessly. "What's wrong?"

Eleni exchanged a glance with Andreas.

"Sarrész," he said. The name came out sharp, like a curse. "That gods-be-damned thief—" He broke off and, with an obvious effort, continued in a more ordinary voice. "He's gone, escaped. We don't know when or how, but we shall find out." He turned to Maté. "Pass the word for the guards who stood watch."

Maté ran at once to obey.

"I meant to double the watch," Eleni said in a low voice. "I should've expected something like this. Especially after what you told me."

"Don't," Andreas said at once. "Don't blame yourself, Eleni. Blame me, if you like."

"But after Joszua—"

"No," he said. "Perhaps two guards might have stopped him. Perhaps not. But if you want to make a list of mistakes, start with mine. *I* was wrong about Joszua. I decided he could not betray us from aboard ship. I decided to bring twenty, not thirty, people on this expedition. But most important of all, I failed to make clear to everyone how cunning Sarrész is. Ask Anna here how many times he's escaped her and Kovács."

Eleni shook her head. It was clear she didn't accept Koszenmarc's words. Anna might have done the same, blamed herself no matter what Maté told her, if she hadn't spent the past five months chasing after the man.

Before the argument could continue, Maté approached with three men in tow—the guards who had taken turns at watch over the prisoner. Two were older men, scarred and weathered, pirates who had served decades, either with Koszenmarc or with other ships. The third was a much younger man, his open face creased by an anxious frown.

The three arranged themselves in a line before Koszenmarc, hands clasped behind their backs, legs wide, as if braced against possible squalls. Maté and Eleni took up a waiting stance to one side.

Koszenmarc walked slowly down the line, studying their faces. "So," he said. "Tell me. Did anyone, friend or enemy, approach the tent during your watch? The prisoner, was he asleep, awake? Did he speak to you?"

Their reports were nearly identical. Nearly.

No one approached the prisoner, the first man said. He would swear that no enemy could have passed the perimeter guard without notice. As for the prisoner, he had fallen asleep shortly after the captain had questioned the man.

The second had checked the prisoner at the start of his watch and found Sarrész awake. Sarrész claimed he'd eaten spoiled food, but aside from groaning, he hadn't spoken after that.

Koszenmarc turned to the youngest guard. "And what do you say, Wim?"

Wim flushed. "I inspected the prisoner's bonds at the start of my watch. The prisoner...he was sitting on his pot and cursed me when I insisted on inspecting his bonds." His voice choked. "He asked if I wanted to watch."

Eleni's lips moved in a silent curse. The other two guards shifted uneasily.

"And did you watch?" Koszenmarc asked.

"No! I mean, yes, I did my duty. Those ropes were whole and tight. I made certain of that. Except..." Wim's voice failed and he stared at Koszenmarc with obvious despair.

Eleni made an exasperated noise. Maté rolled his eyes skyward. Koszenmarc did not speak. He let the silence continue so long that Anna thought Wim might expire from terror.

"Sarrész lied to you," Anna said. "Am I right?"

Wim jerked his head away but did not deny it.

"He always lies," Anna said. "How exactly did he lie to you?"

"He...he said he was sick. He was on the chamber pot half my watch. I know because I emptied it." Wim licked his lips again. "Then he made such a noise. Said he was dying from the flux." Another nervous lick. "I went to fetch him a potion from Katerina. Everything was quiet when I got back. I didn't want to wake him up, so I left the medicine just inside the tent. I...I didn't go in myself."

Eleni shook her head in obvious disgust. "He broke the pot and used the pieces to cut his bonds. Then he sent Wim on a fool's errand and made his escape."

Andreas studied Wim a moment longer, then sighed. "He's an idiot, not a traitor, thank the gods. We'll dock him a week's pay and give him scut duty for a month. Eleni, take our fool away. Kovács, I want you to scout the area. See which direction Sarrész took. Don't wander too far. We might have a few of the enemy lurking nearby."

He dismissed the other two guards, who vanished at once to their duties. Eleni took hold of Wim by the arm and bundled him away, no doubt to deliver her own lecture. Maté followed, leaving Anna alone with Andreas. "We have the jewel," she murmured. "And once we know what to do—"

"But no matter what we do, we need Sarrész to prove the case against Hêr Brun."

That gave her pause. Yes, Sarrész's testimony would prove her own innocence, but how could they hand over Sarrész and not the jewel itself?

"Come," Andreas told her. "We'll have an early breakfast, then break camp. Once we're back aboard the *Konstanze* with the rest of my officers, we can discuss what comes next."

What comes next. That implied so many things.

Anna thrust those implications aside as she checked over her patients. Máur was awake and muttering how he was ready to march, thank you. The woman with the bruised ribs moved awkwardly, but she was already at work with the others to break camp. Karl would do until Thea had a chance to examine him.

Felix, though. His color had improved, but his pulse was too quick, and when he attempted to sit up, he collapsed back onto his pallet, sweating. "Godsdammit, I tell you I can march."

"Of course you can," Anna said. "But not today."

She held a brief consultation with Eleni Farakos.

"It's too dangerous," she said softly. "He'll overwork his heart if he tries to march with us."

"He can't stay here alone," Eleni replied. "I'll have two of ours keep him company. Katerina, and whoever else she thinks is best. Give them whatever medicine is needed."

While Eleni ordered gear and supplies set aside, Anna sorted through her pack for the medicines Felix might need. A second vial of Thea's blue potion, in case of emergencies. A jar of willow bark, a potent batch, according to its label. She added several other vials—everyday herbs and powders, useful for a variety of injuries or illnesses. For all the *ifs* and *maybes* Felix and his companions might encounter before reinforcements arrived.

Maté soon returned with his own report. Druss's people had scattered over the mountainside, he said, and were headed toward the nearest coast.

Sarrész's tracks headed in the opposite direction, over the northern flank and in the direction of Iglazi.

"He's had over two hours' head start," Maté added. "And while I'd like to believe our lordling is too soft to fight his way through the brush and over the mountain, I've learned not to underestimate him."

Eleni scowled at the news. Andreas simply shrugged. "We don't have enough people to go haring after him. We'll pass the word to the garrison. That should be good enough."

The crew broke camp, having buried their trash and packed their gear. Anna wrapped the jewel in a scrap of cloth, tied it fast with a cord, and looped the cord over her neck. Felix was already settled in the tent Katerina and the other crewmember had erected in a hollow on the mountainside.

The company laid out the bodies of the dead. The enemy numbered seventeen in all, with Druss at one end and Raab at the other. Raab had worn gold earrings, the metal etched with symbols much like the designs on the medallion Joszua had from Druss. Andreas Koszenmarc held the earrings loosely in one hand and stared down at the bodies of his enemies, his expression unreadable.

"Leave them to the gods," he muttered.

The two dead from Koszenmarc's company had been wrapped in their own blankets, then covered with a sheet of canvas weighted down with rocks. The company stood in a silent circle.

"Until tomorrow, my friends," Andreas said. "We promise to return for you, so that you might return to the sea."

Earlier, he had asked Anna if she knew any spells to keep away scavengers. Now she stepped forward and spoke the words.

Ei rûf ane gôtter. Ei rûf ane strôm unde kreft…

The air shimmered at her words, a bright and golden net of light. A vivid affirmation of Toc's sacrifice to create the moon and the sun, of Lir's promise that death would lead into life.

Anna dropped her hands, and the veil fell over the bodies of their companions.

* * * *

The march back to shore went slowly and cautiously, with frequent breaks so the wounded could rest, and the sun had crossed the meridian before the company reached the halfway point. Once more, Andreas called a halt, and Eleni ordered a meal of cold meat and dried fruit to be shared out.

Anna dropped to the ground and rubbed her ankles. Her feet ached, and she was grateful for the thin ocean breeze that filtered between the trees. When Maté offered to refill her water flask, she gladly agreed. He returned with the flask and crouched by her side. "Have you noticed?" he said.

"Noticed what?"

He nodded toward a break in the foliage. Anna shaded her eyes and pretended a casual interest in the view. The shore was just visible as a pale white ribbon between mountain and sea. She could make out one ship standing close to shore. The *Konstanze*? Beyond, the ocean glittered blue and silver under the sun and she had to squint before she noticed that three more ships were driving toward the shore, sails spread before a favorable wind.

She and Maté were not the only ones who had spotted those sails. Eleni stared hard toward the ocean. "Andreas, I don't like the look of things. We should—"

"We go forward," Koszenmarc said shortly.

The company stirred uneasily. For a moment, Anna thought they might refuse the order. Then Maté exchanged a quick look with Máur, who shrugged. The two took their positions for the march. After a moment, the rest followed their example.

Anna fell back toward the rear, where Maté marched. "Those ships," she whispered. "Whose are they?"

"I don't know," he said, just as quietly. "I recognized the *Konstanze* farther out, but the other three ships… They aren't any of ours. I don't like it."

Anna remembered those last moments aboard the *Konstanze*, with Andreas and Hahn in close conversation. "Perhaps he has allies we know nothing about."

"Perhaps." But Maté did not appear convinced.

The trail doubled back sharply, then dipped into a fold in the hillside. The ocean vanished from view, and trees arced overhead in a luminous green tunnel. Andreas signaled to Eleni, who passed orders along the line, and the company changed position so that they shifted from single file to a square two deep on either side.

Someone muttered a curse. Karl shifted his weapon in his hand and glanced from side to side. Eleni said nothing, but she too was clearly uneasy.

The first warning was a metallic whisper that seemed to come from all directions. Before Anna could register what that meant, the rattle of many blades echoed down from the ridges on either side.

Eleni had her own weapon in hand within a moment. Andreas reached for his sword. He checked himself and glanced upward to either side. Anna's breath deserted her when she followed his gaze. More than thirty men, all of them armed with swords, had appeared at the ridgetops on either side. Anna swung around, to see several dozen more behind the company. Then she heard the tramp of boots from ahead and knew they were surrounded.

Druss. She had plans in case she failed. She had allies—

A hand brushed against hers. Maté. He gave the smallest of nods toward the front of their party. She turned and saw Marcus Brun emerge from behind another squad of armed men, who blocked the trail to the shore.

Brun wore an impeccable costume, with a stiff, high collar, and a jacket thick with embroidery. His hair was swept back in what had to be the latest fashion of Duenne's Court. Only the sheen of sweat on his face indicated that he stood under the hot south-seas sun.

"Gods-be-damned bastard," Maté whispered. "I should have expected this."

Brun's gaze flicked toward Maté. His eyes narrowed, and Maté went still, all expression wiped from his face. Oh, yes. It would not do to underestimate their lord and master.

Brun nodded in Anna's direction. "That one," he said. "Bring her forward."

Two soldiers seized Anna by the arms and dragged her over to Brun. At his signal, they shoved her onto her knees and stepped back.

"Anna," he said. "Greetings. You've met battle, it seems."

She knelt there, hands splayed in the mud. Dimly, she heard the shifting of men and women behind her. What could they think to accomplish? She was dead, and so were they.

"Druss," she said. "It was Isana Druss."

Her voice came out thin and wavery. She swallowed and tried again. "Isana Druss was her name. She commands, commanded a fleet of pirates. Surely I mentioned her in my reports?"

Brun tilted his head, clearly amused, which unsettled her even more. "No, I don't recall you did," he said. "Raab, however, told me a great deal about her. I gather you or your pirate captain killed her, or you would not be alive. No, never mind about answering. Let us take as given that Druss is dead. Raab must be dead as well." He sighed. "I suppose that's for the best."

For the best? Raab had been Marcus Brun's dog, the man sent to ensure neither she nor Maté betrayed their master. And if she read the evidence of these past few days aright, Raab had escaped both Maszny and Andreas Koszenmarc, he had bribed a mage to transport him away from Vyros, and he had negotiated an alliance with Isana Druss, all so that Brun got what he wanted.

Sarrész's words came back to her with a suddenness that left her throat dry and tight. *He wants no witnesses, our Lord Brun. That's why I ran.*

But Brun's attention had shifted to Andreas Koszenmarc. "Raab mentioned another pirate captain in his reports. My Lord Koszenmarc, I remember you from your time at Court."

Koszenmarc returned Brun's gaze with one cool and remote. He said nothing.

Brun's mouth ticked up in a satisfied smile. "I cannot say I'm astonished to see you here, in Eddalyon, even before Raab told me about your part in this affair. Tell me, shall I send my condolences to your family? Or have they disowned you entirely?" When Andreas continued to offer no response, he gave a soft laugh. "No matter. Anna, my love, you have a final report to give me. Tell me about Lord Sarrész. Is he among the dead?"

Anna licked her lips. "I don't know."

Brun signaled to one of the mercenaries. The man slapped Anna, hard enough to make her head ring. "Answer our lord," he said. "What happened to the thief?"

Anna swallowed, tasted the blood in her mouth. "I'm telling the truth, my lord. He escaped during the night."

"With the jewel?" Brun said. "No. I know you. You'd never leave it behind. You will hand over the jewel. Kovács here can track Sarrész down. If either of you fails, the other will pay for your betrayal."

Maté glanced toward Eleni, who shook her head. Throughout the exchange, Andreas Koszenmarc had not stirred, had not even breathed, as far as Anna could tell.

Brun watched them all. Evidently, he was satisfied they'd make no trouble, because he nodded, then held out a hand. "Give me the jewel, Anna."

Anna hesitated.

"Come," he told her with seemingly infinite patience. "You are making this entire affair more difficult than necessary. Give me the jewel, and we shall discuss your reward." At her continued silence, he smiled. "I promise you, Anna. I shall not harm any of your friends."

Brun wore an air of nonchalance, as though he expected nothing but obedience from her, but she caught a hint of impatience behind that facade. He was not entirely certain of victory after all.

Still on her knees, she drew the jewel from her shirt and unwrapped the cloth.

It was a small, plain-looking thing, rough-cut and unpolished, scarcely larger than her thumb, and there was no sense of magic about it, as though the jewel had deliberately wrapped itself in anonymity, within and without.

Brun frowned, disappointed.

"This?" he said. "That looks rather plain. Are you certain?"

"I am," she said.

She dropped the jewel into his hand. He sucked in a breath. He might not be a magic-worker, but he'd clearly felt the spark of magic. For a moment, Anna wondered if Brun would give over his ambitions to marry the Imperial heir. He might want to aim higher, faster, to take the jewel and the Empire for himself....

Brun tucked the jewel into his shirt, then raised Anna to her feet. He was smiling.

"You see," he said softly. "It's better this way."

His hand brushed her neck in a caress. Still smiling, he turned to the soldier at his side. "Take the man Kovács prisoner. Kill the rest."

The soldier roared out an order. At once the mercenaries surged forward.

Anna's shock lasted only a moment—long enough to see Maté slip his sword from its sheath. To see Eleni and Andreas close with Brun's mercenaries. Andreas ran his blade through one man. Eleni surged forward to thrust and parry and thrust again. Wim charged into the crowd, only to meet a sword thrust to his belly. He dropped to his knees and doubled over. Another member of the crew stepped over him....

Brun seized Anna by the hair and yanked hard. Now the lessons Maté had insisted upon proved useful. Anna fell backwards to throw Brun off balance. The moment his grip loosened, she dropped to her knees, drew the knife from her boot, and slashed out at Brun's face.

One of the officers grabbed for her knife. Anna rolled away and found shelter behind a tree. More mercenaries had poured down from the ridge and from the path behind. Koszenmarc and his company were fighting back, but they were so few. They could not hope to win, not with so many against them.

"You gods-be-damned whore."

Brun grabbed her by the shoulder.

"I shall have you branded," he said in a growl. "I'll burn your bond to ashes and sell you in the common market. Slave is what they'll call you. Good for a fuck and nothing else."

Anna was trembling, but she met his gaze directly. "Time," she said softly, "to prove my lessons well-taught."

Ei rûf ane gôtter. Ei rûf ane strôm. Komen mir de îs alsô swert.

The void between worlds split open. The current poured through, like a storm unleashed by the gods, a winter storm so bitterly cold that Anna gasped for breath. Her vision blurred, she could see nothing except vague shadows moving about her.

Anna lunged forward and grabbed Brun's shirt. Her hands closed over the jewel in his pocket. She felt it shift and alter in her hand, changing from an amorphous stream of power into a solid mass, with the shape and heft of a sword hilt. She took a step back and gripped it tight. Her lips pulled back into a grin, and she drove forward.

Brun recoiled. Too late. The magic plunged through his flesh like a knife through fog. He gave one harsh gasp. His throat rattled, as though to stop the air from escaping from his chest. Then his body went stiff and he toppled over.

Shadows rushed toward her—Brun's hired soldiers. Anna flung her hands upward. The magical current surged over them, like the tallest of ocean waves, drowning them in cold. They fell, all of them, stiff and grey. She spun around. The enemy on the ridgetops broke and ran, but the cold swept over them as well. Anna had one glimpse of them tumbling to the ground before her strength gave way and she fell to her knees.

The current swirled around her, still cold, still buzzing with electricity. Dimly she realized she was shivering. Small wonder. Snow covered the ground in drifts. More snow continued to fall, though not the blizzard of just a few moments ago.

And there, on the ground, a bright speck of color against the white, lay the jewel.

Anna scooped the jewel into both hands. It hummed, that deep and wordless hum that spoke of a world beyond her ken. Gradually the ache in her gut eased, but she knew she could never forget the moment when she had plunged the magical current through Brun's heart.

"Anna."

Andreas Koszenmarc reached down and took her hands. Snow covered his skin, melting under the sun. "We lived, Anna. We grabbed hard—*you* did—and we lived."

"We did." Her voice came out cracked and raw.

He raised her to her feet. Quiet had settled over the clearing, broken only by the rill of snow and ice melting, the water dripping from branches, trickling over rock and stone and running down the mountainside. A dozen or more bodies lay scattered about. She recognized death by now. That absolute stillness. The mouth opened in one last gasp. The eyes staring into forever.

Not all the enemy were dead. Some were scoured by frost and ice, blinded but clearly alive. Others attempted to regain their feet, but their movements were slow and clumsy, and Koszenmarc's people had them in hand.

Just a few feet away lay Marcus Brun.

She was shivering, and not from the snow.

"I killed him," she said. "I meant to do that."

"If you hadn't, you'd be dead."

She nodded. Her. Maté. Koszenmarc. Everyone else in the company. Brun would have murdered them all.

"I hate what I did," she whispered.

"You'd be colder than these bodies if you didn't. Come," he said. "We must make shore. Hahn will worry otherwise."

Oh, yes. Hahn and those mysterious ships. By now, the company had begun the work of identifying the living and the dead. Koszenmarc was explaining to Eleni about the necessity for witnesses, though Anna could tell his explanation didn't satisfy the other woman.

Maté limped over to Brun and stared down at the body, his expression unreadable. Then he glanced around to Anna and smiled, but that smile unsettled her even more.

"He's dead enough," he said. "And thank the gods for that. But we're not yet done with him. Not anywhere close to done."

"What do you mean?" Anna said.

"Don't know. Not yet. We'll find out in a few hours, won't we?"

It took half a bell or longer before Andreas and Eleni could sort out the aftermath of the battle. Anna's deadly spell had killed all but a dozen of Brun's mercenaries. The few survivors were frostbitten and blinded, unable to stand, much less fight. Even so, Koszenmarc ordered two of his people to remain behind to stand guard over them, until reinforcements could be sent from the ship.

Five of the company had died. By the grace of Lir and Toc, only three had been singed by Anna's magic. Several more had taken slash wounds, but they were able to march. Anna did her best to treat everyone's injuries until they reached the *Konstanze* and Thea's greater skill.

The final march to the sea took another hour. At Koszenmarc's orders, they made frequent stops while Maté scouted ahead, slow and silent, in case Brun had left more of his mercenaries to guard the rear. Twice he returned with news that the path ahead and all the surrounding area were empty. The third time, he insisted on speaking alone with Andreas and Eleni. The rest of the company waited, anxious or angry, while the three exchanged a whispered argument.

"We have no choice," Andreas said at last.

"Are you certain?" Maté replied. "You said—"

"He is right," Eleni said. "We can't run back to the hills, Maté. And...I believe I know what your plans are, Captain. Though," she added, "you should have told the rest of us sooner."

"I should have," Andreas said. "I'm sorry. Shall we get this over with?"

The remaining company was murmuring, but when Eleni gave the order to march, they set off on the last stretch without delay. Anna didn't need Maté's commentary to see that a large company had marched through here recently. The underbrush had been trampled, vines and saplings cut as though in passing, and the dirt and sand had been churned up by many, many boots.

Then her attention turned to the break in the trees ahead, the roar of surf, and the echo of numerous voices.

The company slowed, but when Eleni gave the signal, they gathered into a tighter formation and continued toward the shore.

Four ships crowded the small inlet. One had a battered look, the sails shredded and burned, as though it had survived a recent battle. The other three stood not much farther off, in a semicircle around it, as though they had pinned it to the shore and now wanted to make sure of their capture. One was the *Konstanze*. The other two flew Imperial pennants.

Oh. Anna thought she could see the shape of things now. Brun, landing here with his mercenary troops. Leaving only a skeleton guard behind, because of course he would have his victory and quickly too. Hahn, sent by Koszenmarc to Iglazi and the Imperial garrison. But what about his client? What about the jewel?

A dozen boats had landed with their squads of soldiers. Several more were underway. Maszny himself stood at the front of one, his hand on his sword hilt.

Maszny nodded at Koszenmarc. "I came as soon as your man reported to me. Just in time, apparently. We've taken a few prisoners, but they aren't cooperating. One of Druss's, I gather."

"Not exactly," Andreas said quietly.

Maszny eyed Andreas with faint suspicion. "How, not exactly?"

"Before I go on, do I have your word to honor your promise?"

"My promise depends on your success," Maszny said carefully. "Do you have the jewel or not?"

"I have it," Koszenmarc said.

"What about Lord Sarrész?"

"He escaped. Druss did not. Nor did Lord Brun."

At that, Maszny visibly started. He glanced from Koszenmarc to Anna and back. "I see."

"I doubt it," Andreas replied crisply. "To repeat my question, will you keep the promise you made six months ago? For everyone who is a member of my company?"

Maszny regarded him with narrowed eyes. "I gave my word on that."

"Then," Andreas drew a long breath, "if you will, we need help to recover our dead and wounded. And...you will find a number of other bodies along the way, and several witnesses who might be useful."

"Ah." Now Maszny smiled, though it was faint and edged. "You are a thorough man. Thank you. Now, to complete our bargain, please give me the jewel."

"No," Anna said. "You don't understand."

Maszny exchanged a glance with Koszenmarc. "We had an understanding."

"Ah, yes. Except—"

"No except this or that. You will hand over the jewel or you both will stand trial for treason."

Anna swallowed all her protests. She exchanged a glance with Andreas. All expression had vanished from his face and he was staring upward to the skies.

You, you are a coward, she thought. *And so am I.*

Reluctantly, Anna handed the jewel over to Dimarius Maszny. A spark of magic pricked her fingers, and she distinctly heard a faint, high-pitched note. She nearly drew her hand back, but it was too late. Maszny's fingers closed over the jewel. Immediately his eyes widened, and he gave a soft exclamation. His gaze snapped up to meet Anna's. For a moment she believed he would understand. She could almost hear the faint hum of Ishya's voice. Commanding. Pleading. Telling him how the myth of Lir's gift was but a lie. But the stiff, blank expression of an Imperial courtier dropped over his face, and he tucked the jewel into his shirt. "Thank you," he said to Koszenmarc. "Thank you as well, Mistress Zhdanov."

He signaled to the soldiers and they streamed forward, around Koszenmarc's people. Now Hahn appeared, looking older and more worn than Anna could remember. His gaze met Koszenmarc's and he opened his mouth to speak. Koszenmarc shook his head and set off for the shore without looking back.

CHAPTER 24

Koszenmarc remained silent on the trip back to the *Konstanze*. If any of his crew had thought to question him, their speech died in their throats. Anna thought she might demand a better explanation, but she was too weary from the past five days, and far too shocked by that last exchange with Maszny.

I should have argued harder. Andreas believed me, or I thought he did. Or perhaps he didn't understand.

Once, she glanced in his direction, but he kept his eyes closed until they came alongside the *Konstanze*, then swung himself up the first rope ladder and disappeared over the rail. Anna followed next, only to find he'd vanished into the crowd of sailors.

She went below to the sick bay, which was clean and empty, except for Nikolas, who slept in a hammock, and Thea, curled up in a swinging cot.

"Thea."

Thea rose in one fluid motion and hugged Anna in a tight embrace. "Dear gods. I am so glad to see you," she whispered. "Who—"

"—Druss is dead. We found the jewel. Sarrész escaped. Again. We met another set of enemies on the way back and—"

Her voice choked with tears.

"If only I had told you the truth about Lord Brun," she said. "We might have—"

"Anna, stop," Thea said. "*Might have* is the past. We'll mourn our brothers and sisters in due time. What else? I've only heard bits and pieces from Old Hahn. I'll hear more from Daria, no doubt. What about you?"

She had held up so well until then, but at Thea's words, Anna broke into weeping. "It's nothing, nothing at all," she insisted. "Only. I've lied to you. I've lied to everyone. And he lied to me."

"Ah." Thea did not ask whom Anna meant. "That man. He's lied to us all. We shall each have to ask for an accounting. Perhaps you should be first."

* * * *

She paused outside Andreas's cabin while the hour bells rang and the thunder of many bare feet echoed from the deck. The *Konstanze* was under sail. A few hours from now, they would dock at Iglazi. Maszny would surely take her away for questioning. Surely, he would keep her prisoner, or at least under watch, until the whole affair was sorted out. She didn't need to confront Koszenmarc, not now or ever. She could pretend to be exhausted and ill and grieving. All of that would be true. All of that would be a lie.

Anna drew in a breath, tried to find the center of calm within. How could she face this man without that sense of being centered? And yet, and yet...sometimes one had to stumble ahead even so. She knocked.

"Come in."

Andreas Koszenmarc waited for her by the wide curving glass of his cabin, his hands clasped behind his back. His expression was stiff and unhappy. When she closed the door behind her, he said at once, "Anna. I'm sorry."

She had once convinced herself she only needed to hear those words to make everything right. From her father, who had left her in debt and desperate. From Lord Brun, who had treated her as a useful implement in his quest for power. From this man, for any number of reasons. Now? She felt only a curious ache in her chest.

"We both lied," she said softly. "You know my reasons. What are yours?"

Andreas nodded. "Yes, I lied. I lied with words. I lied with silence. To you. To my company, to whom I owe a greater debt."

Anna remained silent, waiting.

After a moment, he continued. "So. I told you the truth about how I came to Eddalyon, and that I joined a smuggler's ship. But I lied when I said I had no idea they were smugglers. I knew. I didn't care. I needed the money and I needed a trade. It was my father's fault, I told myself.

"I'd been in the islands nearly two years when we were taken by an Imperial ship. The court sentenced us to hanging. I waited a week, expecting my father to rescue me. My death might mean nothing to him, but the manner of it would reflect on our house and our family. He didn't. Another week passed, and I had resigned myself to a swift and uncomfortable passage to my next life, when Maszny ordered me to his office. He spoke about my father's shame, if I were hanged for a smuggler. I cursed him and my father both. When Maszny said nothing, I continued to curse. He waited until I ran out of breath, then offered me a different choice."

"Pirates," Anna murmured. "Of a sort."

His gaze met hers, flicked away. "Exactly. But instead of looting villages and ships, I would kidnap troublemakers and deport them back to the Emperor's prisons. Also, there were families who would pay to get their errant sons and daughters back *before* they became troublemakers. My reward would be the ransom money plus a stipend from the commander. Far more than I deserved," he added.

It had also given a refuge to Eleni and her son, among others.

"What about me?" she said. "I'm no noble or runaway. You knew that before you kidnapped me."

Andreas smiled, unhappily. "But you were a troublemaker. Maszny had received reports from the Emperor's people about Lord Sarrész and the missing jewel. He suspected the man who called himself Lord Toth was the thief Sarrész, but Sarrész vanished before Maszny could arrest him. When you arrived on Iglazi with your questions, he thought you might be an accomplice."

"So he sent you to kidnap me?" That made no sense.

He shook his head. "No, I had my own reasons. I wanted to find the jewel myself. I—I needed the reward as badly as you did. Not just the money, but Maszny had promised me certificates of pardon for Eleni and everyone who served me. I grabbed hard, Anna. For me. For my company. I had no choice."

"No choice?" All her doubts from the past week rose up, strong and bitter. "Does that mean it was merely a tactic when you—"

"No."

His answer was short and sharp.

"No," he said again. "It was not."

Anna released a shaky breath. "How can I believe you? How can you believe *me*? We both lied. We both broke each other's trust."

She didn't wait for his answer. She was tired of plausible explanations, his or hers or anyone else's. She turned and left the cabin.

CHAPTER 25

Ten days had passed since Isana Druss had died. Eight days since the *Konstanze* had landed at Iglazi and Anna Zhdanov had fled the ship and its company for an anonymous inn far away from the harbor. Now she sat in Hêr Commander Maszny's office at his invitation, oh-so-carefully worded and delivered by a discreet messenger.

The commander's office was much as she remembered it from her first visit—an airy expanse of blue-tiled floor with windows overlooking the courtyard. A place shadowed and cool in spite of the afternoon heat, but edged with sunlight—much like Dimarius Maszny himself.

Everything else about this interview, however, was different.

No more lies, no more assumed personas. No more attempts at an intimate conversation. This time Anna sat in a carved wooden chair before Maszny's desk. The chair was a new addition to the room and clearly expensive, fashioned by a master craftsman. The dark fragrant wood had been polished to mirror-bright smoothness; its lines were perfection; its curves and hollows such that she felt as though someone had measured it to her body. Not an unusual acquisition for a wealthy nobleman, but not one she expected for a garrison commander, whatever his title. Nor one she expected him to offer to a renegade bondswoman he had recently charged with murder.

Except I am no longer bonded. He told me so.

That had been but the first topic of their conversation, the one that had lured her from hiding.

From outside came the muffled stamp, the clash of weapons, of many soldiers at drill. Within Maszny's office, all was hushed. Uniformed servants had delivered trays of exquisite delicacies, perfumed wines, cold tea, and hot coffee brewed in the Eddalyon style. Maszny had dismissed them and served Anna himself.

"Which do you prefer?" he asked, his hand hovering over the carafes. "Tea? Coffee?"

"Wine, please," Anna said.

His glance was brief, but expressive.

"Yes," she said, "I've changed."

"We all do," he said mildly. "You might say death is the last and most final change. Until we're born anew, that is. How do you find your new lodgings?"

"Very comfortable. Thank you."

He poured wine for them both and handed her a cup. She drank deeply and cradled the cup in her hands. Like her chair, the wine cup was a thing of loveliness, made of blown glass, a pale shimmering green, shaped to fit a woman's hand. When she turned her focus inward, her suspicions were confirmed. Yes, there was magic embedded in the cup that would mold its form to the bearer's hand. Very, very expensive.

"Do you find the wine to your taste?" Maszny said.

"I do," she answered. "Thank you."

He was becoming repetitious. In any other man, Anna would have suspected nervousness. She was nervous herself. She knew his stated reasons for this visit—to clarify those final few details concerning the Emperor's jewel and her own status in the Empire—but Anna had lived too long in Duenne to take anything as permanently settled unless by death. And as Maszny had pointed out, even death was a temporary state. So when he smiled at her, a warm and friendly smile, she felt a small shock of surprise.

Maszny choked back a laugh. "Oh gods. No, I won't subject you to another siege upon your honor. I thought we'd settled that, but I see you're not a trusting woman." His mouth tilted in an embarrassed smile. "Though I admit you've had little reason to trust me so far. I often wonder how different my life would be were I not an Imperial officer. I could invite a woman for tea, or wine, and not be suspected of conducting an interrogation."

Anna shook her head. "Do you lack in lovers, my lord?"

"Only the interesting ones."

Oh. That *had* been a pointed remark. "My sympathies," she murmured.

Her expression must have conveyed her irritation, because he flipped up a hand. "My apologies. My captains tell me I have a misplaced sense of whimsy. The truth is… These have been an interesting few months—more interesting than I like—but I'm glad of the outcome. The traitor Brun is dead. The jewel returned to the Empire. For your service, the Emperor grants you a full pardon, the freedom from your bond, and a reward of twenty thousand denariie."

She let her breath trickle out. He had stated all this the previous day in his message, but she'd found it difficult to believe.

"And Maté?" she asked.

Maté had tracked her down within the week. When they both received their formal summons, he had insisted on accompanying her to the garrison. Even now he was closeted with one of Maszny's subordinate officers.

"He's earned the Emperor's gratitude just as you have," Maszny said. "But let me phrase that in more definite terms. I, Hêr Prince Dimarius Maszny, Commander for the province of Eddalyon, do declare Anna Zhdanov and Maté Kovács free of their bonds to Hêr Lord Marcus Brun. I further declare you both innocent of the murder of the boy Giannis. All the monies the Empire confiscated from Lady Iljana will be returned to you or your designated agents by noon tomorrow, to be divided between you."

In a much different tone, he added, "There. Done. Is that pompous and official enough?"

Anna had to hide her smile by pretending a keen interest in her wine cup.

"What is so amusing?" Maszny asked. "Me? Or my stuffed uniform?"

"You," she said.

He laughed out loud—a free and easy laugh that transformed his face entirely. Perhaps that passing comment about a different life carried more than a few grains of truth. For the first time, she felt a twinge of sympathy for the man. Perhaps...

But no. She could not forget that moment when she was certain he heard Ishya plead for its freedom. She had handed over the jewel. He had chosen to hand it over to the Emperor.

We were both complicit. We will both pay for our choices that day.

But saying such a thing out loud would never do, even if the commander in question had recently displayed an actual sense of humor. Anna pretended to drink more of her wine, then set the cup aside and waved off Maszny when he went to refill her cup.

"I have a few questions," she said. "You mentioned that I might need to give evidence. How long must I remain here in Eddalyon?"

He regarded her with obvious curiosity. She regarded him back, with as much bravado as she dared.

Eventually he sighed and made a gesture of surrender. "You don't need to remain here any longer than you wish. You can give testimony to my clerk—tomorrow, if you like. And I shall give him the order for a note of hand, guaranteeing the money for your reward. Have you...have you decided where you wish to live?"

Anna smiled and shook her head. "The mainland, but where exactly, I haven't decided."

Maszny's eyes narrowed, as though he knew she was lying. But she had turned the problem over throughout most of the night. Duenne and its University could give her the refuge and the anonymity she needed. She could take a new name, become one of the hundreds of scribes or clerks employed there, and leave the islands behind entirely.

And I could buy a pair of rooms for myself. One for my books. One for my bed and a fireplace to cook my breakfast. And a lock on the door.

Maszny steepled his hands, fingertip to fingertip. "I believe I understand. And...if someday you feel it's possible, write to let me know how you are."

They drank another cup of wine, then Anna took her leave. A young private escorted her to the front gates and offered to summon a chair. Anna politely refused. She would wait for her friend, she said.

Outside the garrison, the streets were empty of pedestrians. The morning rains had passed, leaving the air cool and clean. She scanned the harbor automatically, noting the fleets of Imperial ships, a dozen or more freight boats, which plied their trade between the islands, and several that looked like ferryboats from the mainland. None with three masts and triangular sails, and the look of a very fast ship.

The gates swung open a second time. Maté stepped out beside her. He wore a very bland expression, but Anna didn't miss how he let out a long breath, as though in relief. She remembered how he'd never talked about his time in the army, and the few telling comments that had escaped him.

We both have wounds in our memories.

"Your interview didn't take very long," she said.

He shrugged. "Eh. There wasn't much to discuss. I have my bond canceled. You and I get whatever jewels or coin are left from your days as Lady Iljana. More's to come with that reward. And the commander made no objection to my staying here in Eddalyon."

Her throat tightened, briefly. Even before he'd told her that morning, she'd known he would remain in the islands. He had no ties to Duenne, nor family in that far-off northern province who remembered him. And he had made new ties here. Eleni Farakos. Her son Nikolas. Friends among Koszenmarc's company and crew. Even so...

"What about you?" Maté asked.

She gave an answering shrug. "Maszny said much the same to me. Though...I told him I meant to leave the islands. I didn't tell him where, but I want to go back to Duenne, just as I had planned before. Nothing has changed that."

"Nothing?"

She glanced up and away. "It's for the best, Maté."

Maté made no answer for a moment. He too scanned the harbor, his eyes narrowed against the bright afternoon sun. There were new creases beside his eyes, and at the corners of his mouth. Laugh lines. Worry lines. Eleni might give him more of both. It was something to think about, what a person wanted from their love.

"I heard a ship's leaving for the mainland in ten days," Maté said casually. "You might speak with the captain in the next day or two, if you want to secure a berth."

"Thank you," she said. "I will."

* * * *

Nine days later, Anna sat with Maté and Eleni in a small wineshop, near the gates where she and Andreas Koszenmarc had escaped from Maszny's guards. Maté had come upon the wineshop during his days of seeking out news of Lord Sarrész, and like all his other discoveries, it promised a delicious meal as well as good wine. The neighborhood was quiet, unlike the harbor district, and the air smelled of wet earth and moldering leaves.

Maté filled their wine cups. Anna lifted hers in a toast. "To all our tomorrows."

"And may they be good ones," Maté said.

They drained their cups. Maté set his down heavily on the table. "I'll miss you, Anna Zhdanov. I wish—"

Eleni laid a hand on his shoulder. "No. Wish all you like, but don't be sad. Who knows? They say true friends meet time and again across their lives."

She leaned against him, and they exchanged a brief, expressive look. Anna dropped her gaze to the tabletop. She would miss Maté. She would miss them all. Thea and Daria. Nikolas and Theo.

I meant to leave without any good-byes. I thought it would be easier.

But Maté had insisted on this farewell feast. His treat, he said, even before she brought the matter up. After all, her expenses would be greater than his for some time. "And besides," he'd added, "I want to."

Two serving girls arrived bearing platters of grilled fish, mounds of sweet potatoes, a tureen of cold, spicy soup, and pitchers of white wine. For a time, Anna and her friends left off talking for eating. It was a comfortable meal, not an elegant one, which made it all the more satisfying. Raindrops tapped against the windowpanes and on the roof, a constant soothing counterpoint to her own unsettled state of mind.

"You have everything you need for the ship?" Maté asked.

He had asked the same question the day before when he came to visit.

"Yes, yes," she said. "And I still have the names of your friends. I was even competent enough to pack my belongings without losing a single item or getting charged any overage fees."

Maté made a noise in his throat, either of exasperation or amusement, she couldn't tell which. Eleni's mouth quirked in a smile. "Maté likes to take care of people. I've noticed that myself."

She exchanged another glance with him, and Anna had the impression again of an entire conversation distilled into a moment. It was a mark of how much everything had changed since she and Raab and Maté had first arrived in these islands. She had always pictured Maté alone. Now she couldn't imagine him without Eleni.

Anna sighed. Maté gave her a questioning look. She shrugged and smiled. Eleni was right. Tonight was for friendship, for joy. She helped herself to another serving of fish. Maté refilled their wine cups, while Eleni called for fresh fruit and cheese.

More wine. The dishes cleared, and others brought. The rain hissed against the windows, much like waves hissing against the side of a ship. Eleni brought news of the company. The past three weeks had changed everyone's lives. Commander Maszny had issued letters of marque to *Konstanze, Mathilde,* and *Daemon*—public ones, this time—along with official pardons for the company, whatever their past. A dozen had decided to take their share and start a new life elsewhere in the islands. The rest had chosen to remain, Daria and Thea among them, though whether they remained on Asulos wasn't certain.

To no one's surprise, Eleni had been the first to offer her resignation. She and Maté had bought a small set of rooms in Iglazi. Maté intended to hire out as a tracker and guide for hunting expeditions. Eleni had taken service with a merchant fleet that sailed between Vyros and Idonia. Within a year, Nikolas would join her.

But throughout the hours, no one mentioned Andreas Koszenmarc.

The rains died away, the moon shone through a break in the clouds. The serving girls took away the last dishes, but at Maté's signal, they brought fresh pitchers of water and sweet rolls stuffed with pineapple and coconut. Anna could tell he wanted to delay the end of their feast. She did as well, she admitted to herself. But eventually, she set aside her cup and sighed.

"It is time," Eleni said gently.

"Time and past," Anna said. "And never time enough. I'm expected aboard the ship at sunrise."

Maté settled their account for the meal. He and Eleni accompanied Anna back to her inn, through streets wet from the rains and glittering in the moonlight. A final farewell outside the doors to the inn. A tight hug from Maté, who nearly did not let go. A clasp of the hands with Eleni. Then Anna was alone and climbing the stairs to the inn.

* * * *

She ordered a pot of tisane, brewed in the island fashion, to be delivered to her room. In truth, she had little to do except sleep. She had paid the innkeeper that afternoon. With her share of Lady Iljana's money and jewels, Anna had bought a store of plain clothes and other necessities. These were all packed in her single trunk, now locked and tied and ready for the carter. But some of Maté's caution had infected her, and Anna wanted to make one last review of her preparations.

She lit a lamp and sat at the small desk by the window. Once again, she checked over her papers—her bond of service stamped with the official seal declaring it dissolved, the even more official certificate of pardon, Maté's list of names and addresses for his friends in Duenne, and a letter of recommendation from Maszny himself, written in the elegant and flowery style of his first message to her. She smiled, remembering, then frowned, remembering the jewel.

Later, very much later, once she was certain of her new life, she would write her thanks to him. Then she would be truly done with Eddalyon.

She took out the small journal she had bought the day before, where she recorded her accounts. Two pages were filled with sums representing the monies she had received, the monies borrowed and paid, and the expenses she predicted for the coming months. Though she had checked them over twice, she did so again. So much for the ship's fare, to be paid on boarding. So much for meals on ship. So much for the boat transfer fees. So much for passage in a caravan from Hanídos to Duenne.

She set her journal aside and glanced out the window. The skies had cleared; the full moon hung low over the horizon. Here and there, white sails shimmered in the harbor. And high above, the stars gleamed bright and sharp in constellations that had become familiar to her.

I will miss them too. I wish—

A knock sounded at her door. Anna set her journal aside and admitted the sleepy-eyed kitchen boy. He set his tray on her desk, which she hastily cleared, then made a fuss over laying out the teapot and the cup on its saucer, along with two dishes of honey.

But when Anna tried to hand him a coin in thanks for his service, he held his hands behind his back. "No thanks needed, lady. Not for such a...a nothing."

He hurried out the door, leaving Anna wide-eyed.

She glanced suspiciously at the teapot and cup.

Oh.

A small square of paper, folded over several times, had been tucked inside the empty cup.

She touched a fingertip to one corner. A spark of magic stung her—a hint of magic's green scent—and the paper unfolded like a rose. Her pulse beating fast, she picked up the letter.

Anna, I am sorry. I wish you all the best in this life and all your lives to come. Andreas Koszenmarc.

For a moment, she couldn't comprehend what she read. It was impossible. Only Maté and Eleni knew her whereabouts. How had he—?

She hurried out of her room just in time to see the kitchen boy vanish into the stairwell.

Anna blew out a breath and retreated back into her room. She'd crumpled the letter in her fist without realizing it. Now she smoothed out the paper and reread the message. It was...not what she'd expected. He made no attempt to explain himself a second time. No plea for forgiveness. Simply, *I'm sorry. I wish you well.*

A message that didn't require any answer.

Then why do I want to send one?

She closed her eyes, briefly considered the consequences. Then reached inside for the balance point.

Ei rûf ane gôtter. Ane Lir unde Toc. Komen mir de strôm. Lâzen mir älliu sihen. Lâzen mir älliu der gëste sihen.

Time spun away. She watched the past moments in reverse—the kitchen boy taking up his tray and backing out the door. Another whisper to the gods and to magic, and she released her soul from her body to follow. Down the dimly lit stairs and through the servants' corridor, into the kitchen, and...

...out another leading into the alley.

Where the boy accepted the note and several gold denariie from Andreas Koszenmarc.

The bright lights spilling out from the open door illuminated his face, and Anna felt a small shock. His jaw was rough with stubble, his eyes were shadowed with exhaustion, and his face had a pinched look. Thea would have a word to say about that once he returned to Asulos.

Andreas turned away from the inn. Anna hesitated a moment. *This is madness,* she thought. Her father had taught her better about logic...

She marked his direction, then released her hold upon the magic current. Her soul rushed back into her body, so fast she almost collapsed, as she hadn't done in several months. But she couldn't wait. She had to find Andreas before he vanished into Iglazi's back alleys.

Anna ran down the stairs and out the inn. She heard a startled exclamation from the innkeeper, but she didn't stop to explain. Outside, the moon had dipped below the horizon and the streets were smothered in shadows. With a whisper of magic, she called up a magical light and hurried in the direction she'd last noted, hoping that Andreas had not taken a different route back to wherever he came from.

No sign of anyone at the next intersection. She gulped down a breath and forced herself to listen hard. Her ear caught the faint echo of footsteps off to her right. She darted down the street to the next intersection. There. In a lane winding down the mountainside, she saw a figure that she knew was him.

"Andreas!"

The figure halted a moment, then continued at a faster pace.

"Andreas, godsdamn you—"

She was about to summon up a magic blaze in pure frustration, when Andreas stopped and turned to face her.

Anna cupped her magical light in one hand and lifted it high. The alley was paved here and there with moss-covered bricks, the rest was packed dirt, turned into mud by the rain. Andreas raked his fingers through his wet hair. How long had he waited outside the inn?

"Thank you for the kind words," she said awkwardly.

He shrugged. Not an encouraging response.

She nearly turned around, but instinct said no, said to push ahead. Even so, she had to swallow several times before she could bring herself to speak.

"How did you find me?" she asked.

"Threats. Bribes. The usual." Immediately he flipped a hand outward. "I'm sorry. That was an awful joke. I was down by the docks this morning, seeing my gear aboard ship. I ran across a friend from the regular mainland route who said you were leaving Eddalyon tomorrow." He paused. "Perhaps I did bribe someone after all, but I swear I only meant to leave that message—"

"Wait. What did you say?"

"Ah." He paused and actually looked embarrassed. "Eleni didn't mention it to you?"

She glared at him, which was apparently answer enough, because he went on to explain.

"I've sold my ships," he said. "The *Konstanze* and—"

"I know the names of your ships, dammit. *Why* did you sell them?"

And where are you going, she thought, but could not bring herself to ask.

"Ah, right. I sold them to Daria and Hahn. They volunteered to take my place in serving the commander here. As for me…Well… Maszny had word two months back that the Emperor's survey ships discovered a new chain of islands to the east. The Emperor wants Maszny to command a new expedition to oversee construction of a garrison and a new trading outpost. And Maszny wants me to command a fleet dedicated to patrolling the waters around those islands. To guard against pirates and brigands."

"The edge of the Empire," she said softly.

"The new edge."

…the wind streaming past. The tang of saltwater in the air…

A position perfectly chosen for him, for his ambition and his abilities.

"I'm leaving Eddalyon within the week on the Imperial courier ship," Andreas continued. "Maszny will hand over the jewel to the Emperor, and he wants me in Duenne to attend the interview. After that, we'll work on provisioning the ships."

Her breath caught. Oh. Duenne.

At least their paths wouldn't cross again. And that was good, she told herself. She had money enough to recreate her life. Two rooms, a lock for the door. That mattered.

She released the light, so it floated high overhead, and reached out a hand. "I'm glad you sent me the letter," she said. "And I wish you all the best."

They shook hands—as two friends, two allies, two partners in danger. Anna found it hard to let go, and from his expression, so did Andreas Koszenmarc. Here, here was how she wanted to remember him. The rain-fresh breezes of this hour. The salt tang mixed with the spicy scent that was unmistakably of these islands.

"Anna…" Andreas's voice was rough and low. "Do you think…?"

Anna waited, her pulse beating fast. "Go on," she said, when he didn't continue.

"Do you think that you might—" With a sudden soft laugh, he gathered both her hands within his. "Anna, what if you joined the expedition yourself?"

That brought her heart to a sudden stop.

"What are you suggesting?" she whispered.

"Exactly what I said. Maszny would be glad to take you on. He wants more than just a crew of soldiers and sailors. He needs mages. Surgeons. Clerks." Andreas spoke faster now, as if to finish before she could argue. "You wouldn't need to see me at all, even after we land. It's a fleet of ten ships, after all. But if you wished—"

He drew a quick breath, as if to fortify himself, then gazed directly into her eyes. "Anna Zhdanov, I know you have no reason to trust me. But if the gods could grant me one favor, I'd ask for a chance to start over. To earn your trust and keep it safe, more precious than any jewel."

We ask the gods for small gifts, we pirates. We grasp the great ones ourselves.

Oh. And yet, could she believe him?

Jump, he'd told her. *I'll catch you. I promise.*

She reached up and touched his cheek. "Then, yes. My answer is yes."

THE END

ACKNOWLEDGMENTS:

I wrote the first notes for this novel many years ago, on an airplane bound for Hawaii. (Because, hey, a vacation on a lovely tropical island is a great inspiration for writing about adventures on the high seas.) It took me several years to finish this book, in between writing six other novels, working full-time, and moving house twice. But eventually, I did get to THE END with the help and encouragement of many friends.

A big shout out to Delia Sherman, Aliette de Bodard, Stephanie Burgis, Nerine Dorman, Sara Uckelman, and Hyeonjin Park for reading my drafts and cheering me along. I am forever grateful for all your wise and helpful comments and for keeping me focused on the story.

Many, many thanks to my eagle-eyed editor, Liz May, and to the team at Rebel Base Books for turning my manuscript into a book.

A round of applause to my awesome agent, Lane Heymont, for keeping things real.

Last, but never least, hugs and thank you to my husband and son for giving me the space and time and support to write.

Look for Anna and Andreas's continuing story in *The Empire's Edge*, available from Rebel Base Books.

About the Author

Claire O'Dell grew up in the suburbs of Washington, DC, in the years of the Vietnam War and the Watergate Scandal. She attended high school just a few miles from the house where Mary Surratt once lived and where John Wilkes Booth conspired for Lincoln to die. All this might explain why she spent so much time in the history and political science departments at college. Claire currently lives in Manchester, CT, with her family and two idiosyncratic cats.

Follow her on Twitter and Facebook @ClaireOdell99. Or visit www.claireodell.com.

Printed in the United States
by Baker & Taylor Publisher Services